# THE ROAD TO
# DUNE

# THE DUNE SERIES

## FRANK HERBERT'S DUNE NOVELS

*Dune*  
*Dune Messiah*  
*Children of Dune*  

*God Emperor of Dune*  
*Heretics of Dune*  
*Chapterhouse: Dune*  

## DUNE COLLECTION BY FRANK HERBERT, BRIAN HERBERT, AND KEVIN J. ANDERSON

### Dune Novels by
### Brian Herbert and Kevin J. Anderson

*Dune: House Atreides*  
*Dune: House Harkonnen*  
*Dune: House Corrino*  
*Dune: The Butlerian Jihad*  
*Dune: The Machine Crusade*  

*Dune: The Battle of Corrin*  
*Spice Planet* (in *The Road to Dune*)  
*Hunters of Dune* (forthcoming)  
*Sandworms of Dune* (forthcoming)  
*Paul of Dune* (forthcoming)  

### Dune Short Stories by
### Brian Herbert and Kevin J. Anderson

*A Whisper of Caladan Seas*  
*Hunting Harkonnens*  
*Whipping Mek*  
*The Faces of a Martyr*  

### Dune Films

*Dune*  
*Frank Herbert's Dune* (television miniseries)  
*Frank Herbert's Children of Dune* (television miniseries)  

### Biography by Brian Herbert

*Dreamer of Dune*

# THE ROAD TO
# DUNE

*Frank Herbert, Brian Herbert,*
*and*
*Kevin J. Anderson*

**TOR**®

A TOM DOHERTY ASSOCIATES BOOK

NEW YORK

THE ROAD TO DUNE

Copyright © 2005 by Herbert Properties, LLC

Copyright acknowledgments and permissions appear on page 491, which constitutes a continuation of this copyright page.

This book is printed on acid-free paper.

Edited by Patrick LoBrutto

A Tor Book
Published by Tom Doherty Associates, LLC
175 Fifth Avenue
New York, NY 10010

www.tor.com

Tor® is a registered trademark of Tom Doherty Associates, LLC.

Library of Congress Cataloging-in-Publication Data

Herbert, Brian.
The road to Dune / Frank Herbert, Brian Herbert, and Kevin J. Anderson.—1st ed.
p. cm.
"A Tom Doherty Associates book."
Contents: Spice planet, part I—Spice planet, part II—"They stopped the moving sands"—The letters of Dune—Unpublished scenes and chapters from Dune and Dune messiah—"Dune : a whisper of Caladan seas"—"Dune : hunting Harkonnens"—"Dune : whipping mek"—"Dune : the faces of a martyr."
ISBN 0-765-31295-6
EAN 978-0-765-31295-2
1. Dune (Imaginary place)—Literary collections. 2. Science fiction—Authorship. 3. Dune (Imaginary place). I. Herbert, Brian. II. Anderson, Kevin J., 1962– III. Title.

PS3558.E63A6 2005
813'.54—dc22

2005040583

First Edition: September 2005

Printed in the United States of America

0 9 8 7 6 5 4 3 2 1

## FOR BEVERLY HERBERT

There is no more moving tribute in all of literature than the three pages Frank Herbert wrote about Beverly Herbert in *Chapterhouse: Dune*, a novel that he completed at her side in Hawaii, while she was dying. Concerning his loving wife and best friend during more than thirty-seven years of marriage, he said, "Is it any wonder that I look back on our years together with a happiness transcending anything words can describe? Is it any wonder I do not want or need to forget one moment of it? Most others merely touched her life at the periphery. I shared it in the most intimate ways and everything she did strengthened me. It would not have been possible for me to do what necessity demanded of me during the final ten years of her life, strengthening her in return, had she not given of herself in the preceding years, holding back nothing. I consider that to be my great good fortune and most miraculous privilege."

His earlier dedication in *Children of Dune* spoke of other dimensions of this remarkable woman:

FOR BEV:
Out of the wonderful commitment of our love
and to share her beauty and her wisdom,
for she truly inspired this book.

Frank Herbert modeled Lady Jessica Atreides after Beverly Herbert, as well as many aspects of the Bene Gesserit Sisterhood. Beverly was his writing companion and his intellectual equal. She was Frank Herbert's universe, his inspiration, and—more than anyone else—his spiritual guide on the Road to Dune.

# CONTENTS

# Contents

# ACKNOWLEDGMENTS

WE ARE GRATEFUL to the people who contributed to this book, in particular to Frank Herbert, Beverly Herbert, Jan Herbert, Rebecca Moesta, Penny Merritt, Ron Merritt, Bruce Herbert, Bill Ransom, Howie Hansen, Tom Doherty, Pat LoBrutto, Sharon Perry, Robert Gottlieb, John Silbersack, Kate Scherler, Kimberly Whalen, Harlan Ellison, Anne McCaffrey, Paul Stevens, Eric Raab, Sterling E. Lanier, Lurton Blassingame, Lurton Blassingame, Jr., John W. Campbell, Jr., Catherine Sidor, Diane Jones, Louis Moesta, Carolyn Caughey, Damon Knight, Kate Wilhelm, and Eleanor Wood.

# FOREWORD

FRANK HERBERT HAD more fun with life than anyone I've known. He laughed more, joked more, and produced more than any writer I've ever met. With modest beginnings just across the Puyallup River from my own birthplace, and passionate about outdoor life, he judged people by their creativity, and by whether they met hardship with humor or with bile. Humor helped him to endure hardship and to enjoy his rise above it. Frank believed the suffering-in-the-garret stereotype was foisted onto writers by publishers so that they could get away with small advances. The only true currency that Frank recognized was time to create.

"Here it is, Ransom," he said. "First class buys you more time to write."

Never ostentatious, he lived as comfortably as he wanted but not as extravagantly as he could, always with close ties to the outdoors. Enjoyment A.D. ("After *Dune*") came from trying new writing adventures and from helping others succeed; Frank offered opportunities, not handouts, saying, "I'd rather give a man a hand up than step on his fingers." This echoes my favorite Dostoevsky line: "Feed men, then ask of them virtue."

Everything and everyone fell into two rough categories for Frank: It/he/she either contributed to his writing time or interfered with it. I've always had pretty much the same attitude. We knew of each other through our publication successes, but we noticed each other's successes because we both came from the Puyallup Valley, we both had fathers who were in law enforcement in the same district, and we'd had shirttail relatives marry. We moved to Port Townsend in the same week in the early seventies and discovered this when the local paper ran stories on each of us. I wanted to meet him, finally, but I wanted to be respectful of his writing time. Frank wrote a piece under a pseudonym for the *Helix*, my favorite underground newspaper in Seattle, just a few years earlier. I dropped Frank a postcard addressed to the pseudonym ("H. Bert Frank"), saying I wrote until noon but would love to meet for coffee sometime. The next afternoon at 12:10 he called: "Hello, Ransom. Herbert here. Is that coffee on?" It was, and thus began our fifteen-year routine of coffee or lunch nearly every day.

Frank believed poetry to be the finest distillation of the language, whether written in open or closed form. He read voraciously in contemporary poetry through literary and "little" magazines, and he wrote poetry as he worked through issues of life and of fiction. As a very young man, he discovered that he could make somewhat of a living from his nonfiction prose style, which was far more readable than most of the journalism of the time. His prose style, his eye for detail, and his ear for true vernacular coupled with that ever-persistent "What if?" question in his ear made for a natural transition to fiction. Success came to Frank in prose, but inspiration filled his notebooks and his fiction with poetry.

My first poetry collection, *Finding True North & Critter*, was nominated for the National Book Award the same year Frank's *Soul Catcher* was nominated in fiction. Perhaps if Frank and I had both been fiction writers off the bat, or both poets, our friendship may have developed differently. As it was, we refreshed and reenthused each other with our writing, and encouraged each other to risk something in our work, like crossing over into other genres, such as screenplays. The greatest risk of all, to friendship and to our writing reputations, came when we co-wrote *The Jesus Incident* and submitted it under both of our names. Frank pointed out that if the book were published we would each face specific criticisms for working together. People would say that Frank Herbert ran out of ideas, and that Bill Ransom was riding on the coat-tails of the Master. When these statements did, indeed, come up, we were better prepared psychologically for having predicted them in advance. Circumstances leading up to our collaboration were complex, but our personal agreement was simple: Nothing that either of us wanted would stand in the way of the friendship, and we shook hands. Nothing did, not even the publisher's preference that we release it just with Frank's name (the advance offer under this potential agreement was larger by a decimal point than what we received with both names on the cover). The power people also would accept a pseudonym, but they were adamant that a novel acknowledged to be by two authors would not fly with the reading public, and equally adamant about talk-ing only with Frank. In addition, they believed that my reputation in poetry circles would contribute nothing toward marketing the book; therefore, I should get 25% and Frank 75% of whatever we agreed on. Frank literally hung up the phone and bought a ticket to New York. The way he told the story upon his return with contract in hand, he simply repeated a mantra throughout his visit: "Half the work earns half the credit and half the pay." Frank took a 90% cut in pay and split the cover byline in order to work with me, only one example of the strength of his character and of his friendship.

The gamble paid off. We'd heard that *The New York Times Book Re-view* would cover it, and I was nervous. "Relax, Ransom," Frank said. "Even a *scathing* review in *The New York Times* sells ten thousand hard-backs the next day." John Leonard wrote a wonderful review, and we were launched. Now the publisher wanted two more books in the series, *The Lazarus Effect* and *The Ascension Factor*, with no further discussion about names on the cover. For two rustic, self-taught Puyallup Valley boys who ran traplines as kids, we did well because our focus always was on *The Story*. We had no ego conflicts while writing together, largely because Frank didn't have much ego as "Author." I learned from him that authors exist merely for the story's sake, not the other way around, and a good story had to do two things: inform and entertain. The informing part must be entertaining enough to let readers live the story without feeling like they're on the receiving end of a sermon. Writing entertainment without information, without some insight into what it is to be human, is a waste of good trees.

Frank believed that poetry was the apex of human language; he also believed that science fiction was the only genre whose subject matter attempted to define what it is to be human. We use contact with aliens or alien environments as impetus or backdrop for human interaction. Science fiction characters solve their own problems—neither magic spells nor gods come to their aid—and sometimes they have to build some intriguing gadgets to save their skins. Humans go to books to see how other humans solve human problems. Frank admired and championed human resolve and ingenuity in his life and in his work. He had a practical side about this, too: "Remember, Ransom," he said, "aliens don't buy books. Humans buy books."

Frank raised chickens, and he even did that first-class, with a two-story, solar-heated chicken house with automatic feeders that abutted the garden to enrich the compost. Beside the chicken mansion, but mercifully out of sight of the chickens, was a processing station complete with wood stove, steamer, and automatic plucking machine. Every activity of Frank's daily life was fair game for ingenuity and fun. He admired the very intellectual writers, like Pound, but had a particular soft spot for other blue-collar, self-taught writers who investigated human nature, such as Hemingway and Faulkner.

William Faulkner's work influenced Frank in many ways, not the least of which was creating a believable fictional universe built on a complex genealogy. Frank saw science fiction as a great opportunity to reach a very wide audience with "the big stuff." He was moved by Faulkner's 1950 Nobel Prize acceptance speech and he took it to heart in everything he wrote: ". . . the young man or woman writing today has forgotten the problems of the human heart in conflict with itself which alone can make good writing because only that is worth writing about, worth the agony and the sweat . . . the old verities and truths of the heart, the old universal truths lacking which any story is ephemeral and doomed—love and honor and pity and pride and compassion and sacrifice." Story itself provides the foundation for every human culture, and storytellers must respect this responsibility.

Frank had a guardian angel, someone who protected him and his writing time at all costs for almost four decades. Beverly Stuart Herbert honeymooned with him in a fire lookout, packed the kids up in a hearse to live in a village in Mexico while he wrote, and encouraged him to quit dead-end jobs to write what he loved, come what may. She had uncanny radar for detecting buffoons, hangers-on, con artists, and other fools, and Frank was pretty good at this, too. Not many got past Bev to test Frank. But Bev had the diplomacy and good graces to protect Frank while also protecting the dignity of those who would intrude on him. Later, over coffee and homemade pie, came the jokes.

Bev was the one who suggested that we collaborate on a novel. She was Frank's first reader and critic, and her opinion held serious water. Over our daily coffee sessions we'd been tossing a story back and forth just for fun. "You two should just write this story and get it out of your systems," she said. Each of us took on the project for very different reasons. I wanted to learn how to sustain a narrative for a novel's length, and Frank wanted to practice collaboration because he was interested in screenwriting, a notoriously collaborative medium. We both got what we wanted, and with his usual wit Frank referred to our process as ". . . a private act of collaboration between consenting adults."

Not all of our experiences together were celebratory. My writing work with Frank is bracketed by sadness for both of us. We began our

first collaboration when Bev was diagnosed with cancer and I was going through a divorce; we wrote *The Lazarus Effect* as Bev fought her
second round of illness (Frank wrote *The White Plague* at the same
time) and it was published shortly before her death. Our collaboration
on *The Ascension Factor* ended with Frank's death.

An unexpected benefit of our exercise in collaboration became Frank's
collaboration with his son Brian. Frank said that he had hoped that one
day one of his children might follow in Dad's writing footsteps, and Brian
began with some humorous science fiction. Father and son working together on *Man of Two Worlds* marked a breakthrough for Frank after the
long ordeal of Bev's final illness. Brian learned the fine art of collaboration at Frank's side, and Frank would be proud that the dual legacies of
the *Dune* universe and the Herbert writing gene survive him. Brian and
Kevin J. Anderson are having the kind of fun with writing that Frank and
I enjoyed, and they've added a new physical depth and enriched the
sociopolitical detail of the greater tapestry on which *Dune* was woven.

I was at about mid-point in writing the first draft of *The Ascension
Factor* when the morning radio announced that Frank had passed
away. Typically, he believed he would beat this challenge as he'd
beaten so many others. Also typically, he was typing a new short story
into a laptop when he died, a story that he'd told me might lead to another non-genre novel like *Soul Catcher*. In the crowding and confusion of those final lifesaving attempts, that laptop and his last story
were lost, like Einstein's final words were lost because the nurse at his
side didn't speak German.

I think of Frank every time I touch a keyboard, hoping I'm writing
up to his considerable standards. In the Old English, "poet" was
"shaper" or "maker." Frank Herbert was a Maker on a grand scale, the
most loyal friend a person could ask for—and a funny, savvy, first-class
guy. He continues to be missed.

—Bill Ransom

# PREFACE

ↁ

*A beginning is the time for taking the most delicate care that the balances are correct.*

— FROM FRANK HERBERT'S *Dune*

IT WAS LIKE finding a buried treasure chest.

Actually, they were cardboard boxes stuffed full of folders, manuscripts, correspondence, drawings, and loose notes. Some of the box corners were sagging, crumpled by the weight of their contents or partially crushed from languishing under a stack of heavy objects.

As Brian described in his Hugo-nominated biography *Dreamer of Dune*, Frank Herbert's wife, Beverly, was very ill in her last years and unable to keep up with the deluge of paper. For a long time before that, she had kept her prolific husband highly organized, using an ingenious filing system to keep track of old manuscripts, contracts, royalty reports, correspondence, reviews, and publicity.

In the boxes we found old manuscripts for Frank Herbert's various novels, along with unpublished or incomplete novels and short stories, and an intriguing folder full of unused story ideas. There were old movie scripts, travel itineraries, and legal documents from Frank Herbert's work on various films, including *The Hellstrom Chronicle*, *Threshold: The Blue Angels Experience*, *The Tillers*, David Lynch's *Dune*, and even Dino de Laurentiis's film *Flash Gordon*, on which Frank had worked in London as a script consultant. There were contracts and screenplays for numerous uncompleted film projects as well, including *Soul Catcher*, *The Santaroga Barrier*, and *The Green Brain*.

Salted among the various boxes full of materials for *Dune Messiah* and *God Emperor of Dune* (under its working title of *Sandworm of Dune*), we found other gems: drafts of chapters, ruminations about ecology, handwritten snippets of poetry, and lyrical descriptions of the desert and the Fremen. Some of these were scrawled on scraps of paper, bedside notepads, or in pocket-sized newspaper reporter notebooks. There were pages and pages of epigraphs that had never appeared in Frank's six Dune novels, along with historical summaries and fascinating descriptions of characters and settings. Once we started the laborious process of sifting through these thousands of pages, we felt like archaeologists who had discovered a verified map to the Holy Grail.

And this was just the material in the attic of Brian Herbert's garage.

It didn't include the two safe-deposit boxes of materials found more than a decade after Frank's death, as we described in the afterword to our first Dune prequel, *House Atreides*. In addition, Frank had bequeathed dozens of boxes of his drafts and working notes to a university archive, which the university generously opened to us. After spending time in the silent back rooms of academia, we uncovered further bounty. Kevin later returned for more days of photocopying and double-checking, while Brian tended to other Dune projects.

The wealth of newly discovered material was a Dune fan's dream come true. And make no mistake: *We are Dune fans.* We pored over hoards of wondrous and fascinating information, valuable not only for its historical significance but also for its pure entertainment value. This included an outline (along with scene and character notes) for *Spice Planet*, a completely different, never-before-seen version of *Dune*. We also found previously unpublished chapters and scenes from *Dune* and *Dune Messiah*, along with correspondence that shed light on the crucial development of the Dune universe—even a scrap of paper torn from a notepad on which Frank Herbert had written in pencil: "Damn the spice. Save the men!" This, the defining moment in the character of Duke Leto Atreides, might well have been written when Frank Herbert switched on his bedside lamp and jotted it down just before drifting off to sleep.

*The Road to Dune* features the true gems from this science-fiction treasure trove, including *Spice Planet*, which we wrote from Frank's outline. We are also including four of our original short stories: "A Whisper of Caladan Seas" (set during the events of *Dune*) and three connecting "chapters" surrounding our novels in the Butlerian Jihad saga: "Hunting Harkonnens," "Whipping Mek," and "The Faces of a Martyr."

Had Frank Herbert lived longer, he would have presented the world with many more stories set in his fantastic, unparalleled universe. Now, almost two decades after his untimely death, we are honored to share this classic legacy with millions of Frank Herbert's fans worldwide.

The spice must flow!

—Brian Herbert and Kevin J. Anderson

# THE ROAD TO
# DUNE

# SPICE PLANET

## The Alternate Dune Novel

By Brian Herbert and Kevin J. Anderson,
*from Frank Herbert's original outline*

# INTRODUCTION

FINDING SUCH A wealth of notes was just one step down the road, but the fresh material, ideas, clues, and explanations suddenly crystallized many things in the chronology of the Dune epic. It rekindled in us a kind of honeymoon excitement for the whole universe.

We photocopied boxes of this material and then sorted, labeled, and organized everything. The biggest challenge was to make sense of it all. As part of the preparation work before writing our first Dune prequel, we had compiled a detailed concordance and electronically scanned all the text from the original six novels so that we could better search the source material. Now, with highlighter pens, we marked important information in the stacks of notes, illuminating unused blocks of text and descriptions that we might want to incorporate into our novels, character backgrounds, and story ideas.

Scattered among the boxes, we found some sheets of paper marked with letters—Chapter B, Chapter N, et cetera—that were at first puzzling. These pages gave brief descriptions of dramatic scenes that dealt with sandworms, storms, and unexpected new spice-mining techniques. Some of the action took place in recognizable but skewed places, as if viewed through a fractured lens: Dune Planet or Duneworld instead of Dune, Catalan instead of Caladan, Carthage instead of Carthag, and the like. In *Spice Planet*, unlike *Dune*, the characters do not break the rhythm of their strides on the desert sand to prevent a sandworm from hearing them and attacking. Apparently, this had not yet occurred to Frank Herbert in the evolution of *Dune*.

The chapters of *Spice Planet* were populated by unfamiliar characters— Jesse Linkam, Valdemar Hoskanner, Ulla Bauers, William English, Esmar Tuek, and a concubine named Dorothy Mapes. These strangers were interacting with well-known characters such as Gurney Halleck, Dr. Yueh (Cullington Yueh instead of Wellington Yueh), Wanna Yueh, and a familiar-sounding planetary ecologist named Dr. Bryce Haynes. Although a minor character (a spice smuggler) had been named Esmar Tuek in the final published version of *Dune*, he was quite different in the newly discovered notes, a major player and clearly the original model for a well-loved figure, the warrior-Mentat Thufir Hawat. Dorothy Mapes filled a role similar to that of Lady Jessica. The nobleman Jesse Linkam himself was obviously the basis for Duke Leto Atreides, and Valdemar Hoskanner was the embryonic Baron Vladimir Harkonnen.

When we arranged all the chapters and read through the remarkable outline, we found that *Spice Planet* was a unique and worthy story in its own right, not just a precursor to *Dune*. Although the harsh desert is very similar to the one familiar to millions of fans, the tale itself is thematically different, focusing on decadence and drug addiction instead of ecology, finite resources, freedom, and religious fanaticism. In part of the short novel, the main character, Jesse Linkam, must survive in the desert with his son, Barri (an eight-year-old version of Paul Atreides, without his powers). This scene echoes the escape in *Dune* of Lady Jessica into the desert with her son Paul. *Spice Planet,* like *Dune,* is filled with political intrigues and a ruling class of self-indulgent noblemen, so there are plenty of parallels. Above all, this earlier concept gives us an insight into the complex mind of Frank Herbert.

Somewhere along the way, the author shelved his detailed outline for *Spice Planet.* Starting from scratch, with input from legendary editor John W. Campbell, Jr., he developed the concept into a much more vast and more important novel, yet one that he found nearly impossible to sell. It was rejected by more than twenty publishers before being picked up, finally, by Chilton Book Co., best known for publishing auto repair manuals.

Ironically, if Frank had written *Spice Planet* according to his original plan—a science-fiction adventure novel about the same length as most paperback books published at the time—he might have had a much easier task finding an editor and a publishing house.

Using Frank's outline, we have written the novel *Spice Planet* according to the original design, providing a window into the Dune that might have been.

# PART ONE

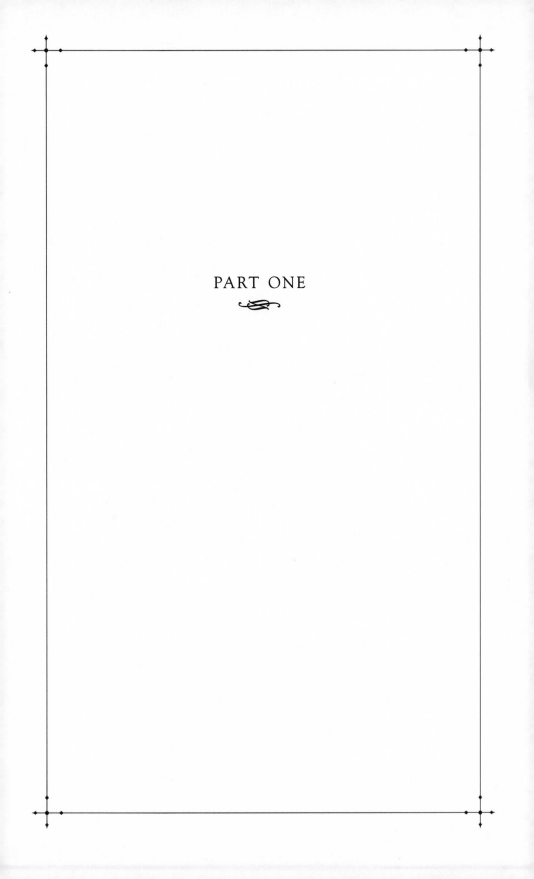

# I

*Duneworld is like the Empire and life itself: Regardless of what one sees on the surface, a clever investigator can uncover deeper and deeper layers of complexity.*

—DR. BRYCE HAYNES,
planetary ecologist assigned to study Duneworld

When the Imperial ship arrived at Catalan's main spaceport, the high rank and notoriety of the passenger told Jesse Linkam that the news must be important. The Emperor's representative directed his transmission to the House Linkam "protocol office," demanding to be met with full honors, and without delay.

Jesse politely acknowledged, not revealing who he was or that his household had no need for a formal protocol office. He preferred not to make an issue of his rank and enjoyed spending his free time among the working class. In fact, he had spent that very afternoon fishing on Catalan's vast and fertile sea, making a sweep for glimmerfish before an expected storm hammered the coast. When the message arrived, he'd been hauling in the sonic nets full of fish, laughing with the rough crewmen who struggled to get over their awe of the nobleman and accept him as one of their own.

Though he was the foremost aristocrat on Catalan, Jesse Linkam didn't mind getting his hands dirty. Tall and middle-aged, he was a quiet man with hidden strengths. The gray eyes measured, weighed, and counted everything. His classic features bore a rugged cast, thanks to a once-broken nose that gave his face the look of an offbeat metronome.

He was not soft and preoccupied with silly diversions like most of his noble peers on other worlds, who treated leadership like little more than a game of dress-up. Here on the "uncivilized" fringes of the Empire, too much real work needed to be done to bother with fashions and courtly intrigues. Jesse loved the fresh, salty air and considered sweaty clothes a better badge of honor than the finest whisper-lace from the Imperial capital world of Renaissance. How could anyone expect to rule a people well without knowing their daily toil, their joys and concerns?

However, because of his high station, Jesse was required by law to be at the beck and call of the Grand Emperor's envoy. Returning to his mansion, the Catalan nobleman changed his clothes and scrubbed the fish smell from his hands, while a doting servant spread a perfumed ointment on his chapped knuckles. As a last touch, Jesse pinned badges of office onto his own surcoat. He had no time for further grooming: Counselor Bauers would have to accept him as he was.

Out in front, he joined a hastily organized groundcar entourage already waiting to depart for the spaceport. "I hope this is important," Jesse muttered to his security chief.

"Important to you? Or to the Grand Emperor?" Esmar Tuek sat beside him in the lead vehicle as the motorcade moved with stately haste toward the landed ship. "How often does Emperor Wuda take notice of our little Catalan?" Since they were in private, Jesse allowed the old veteran to use familiar speech with him.

The question was a fair one, and Jesse hoped it would be answered soon enough. Banners fluttering, the groundcars approached the gaudy Imperial ship. The vessel's ramp was already extended, but no one had emerged, as if waiting for an official reception.

Jesse stepped out of the lead car. In the breeze, his dark hair whipped about like loose strands of sea kelp. He straightened his formal jacket and waited while the honor guard scrambled into position.

No doubt, the impromptu procession would only foster the impression of Catalan being a rude backwater world. On other worlds, noblemen drilled their soldiers in relentless parades and exhibitions. In stark contrast, though Jesse's volunteers would fight fiercely to defend their homes, they had little interest in twirling batons or marching in lockstep.

On the Imperial spacecraft's ramp, Counselor Ulla Bauers stepped out. His nose twitched as he sniffed the ocean-mist air, and his forehead wrinkled. The Grand Emperor's representative—a prissy and ferretlike man with a demeanor of foppish incompetence—wore a voluminous high-collared robe and dandy ornamentation that made his head seem too small.

Jesse knew not to underestimate this man, however. The Counselor's overemphasis on fashion and trappings might be a mere disguise; Bauers was rumored to be a swift and highly effective assassin. The fact that *he* had come here did not bode well.

With a flick of his fingers to one eyebrow, the traditional sign of allegiance to the Emperor, Jesse said, "Counselor Bauers, I welcome you to my humble Catalan. Won't you come and join us?"

The Imperial advisor descended halfway down the ramp with a smooth gait, as if his feet were on wheels. Bauers's piercing eyes swept the docks, the fishing boats, the weather-hardened shacks, the warehouses, and shops that ringed the harbor. He soaked up droplets of information like a dry sponge. "Hmm-ahh, yes . . . humble indeed, Nobleman Linkam."

The local guardsmen stiffened. Hearing an impolite grumble and a sharp, whispered rebuke from General Tuek, Jesse merely smiled. "We will gladly provide you with our most comfortable rooms, Counselor, and an invitation to this evening's banquet. My concubine is as skilled at managing our household kitchens as she is at organizing my business affairs."

"I have my own chef aboard this diplomatic craft." Bauers removed an ornately inlaid metal cylinder from one of his billowing sleeves and extended the messagestat like a scepter toward Jesse. "As for this evening, you would be better advised to spend your time packing. I return to Renaissance in the morning, and the Grand Emperor wishes you to accompany me. All the details are contained in this dispatch."

Feeling an icy dread, Jesse accepted the cylinder. Bowing slightly, he forced himself to say, "Thank you, Counselor. I will study it carefully."

"Be here at dawn, Nobleman." Turning with a swirl of his robes, Bauers marched back up the ramp. The dignitary had not even set foot on Catalan, as if afraid it might soil his shoes.

⤸⤷

A COLD RAIN stretched into the darkest hours of the night, while clouds masked the canvas of stars. Standing on an open balcony above the sea, Jesse watched raindrops sizzling against the electrostatic weather screen around him. Each sparkle was like a variable star, forming transient constellations just above his head.

For most of an hour, he had been brooding. He picked up the messagestat from where it rested on the balcony rail. When he pulled on each end of the cylinder, mirrors and lenses popped up, and words spooled out in Grand Emperor Wuda's voice: "His Imperial Majesty requests the immediate presence of Nobleman Jesse Linkam in the Central Palace to hear our decision in the matter of the spice-production dispute over Duneworld in the Arrakis system. As the complainant, and as a duly elected representative of the Nobles' Council, you are hereby notified that the defendant, Nobleman Hoskanner, has offered a compromise. If you refuse to appear, we shall dismiss your action, and no further arguments will be heard."

Jesse snapped the cylinder shut before the Grand Emperor's voice could reel off his tedious vocal signature, which included the customary list of titles and responsibilities.

Dorothy Mapes, his beloved concubine and business manager, came up behind him and touched his arm. After serving eleven years at Jesse's side, she knew how to interpret his moods. "Most nobles would be honored to receive a personal summons from the Grand Emperor. Shouldn't you give him the benefit of the doubt?"

Jesse turned to her with a quick frown. "It is couched in the best diplomatic language, but I fear this could be the end of us, my darling. Any offer from Valdemar Hoskanner comes with more than strings attached—a noose is more likely."

"Then be cautious. Nevertheless, you know you have to deal with Valdemar. You've been drawn into this dispute, and the other nobles are counting on you."

He gave her a wan, loving smile. She had short, dark hair interspersed with lighter peppery flecks. Set in an oval, attractive face, her large rusty brown eyes were the color of the polished myrtlewood found in the headlands. For a moment, he stared at the unusual diagem ring she wore on her right hand—his nobleman's pledge of love to her. Though a commoner, Dorothy was not at all common.

"For years, Dor, you've been my inspiration, my guiding light, and my closest advisor. You've turned our family's finances around, repairing most of the damage my father and brother did before their deaths. But I'm not so sure about Duneworld . . ." He shook his head.

The petite woman looked up at him. "See if this helps clarify your thinking." She placed a pinch of the spice melange on his lips. "From Duneworld. It's what this is all about."

He savored the cinnamon flavor, felt the pleasurable rush of the drug. It seemed everyone was using it these days. Shortly after the discovery of the substance on the inhospitable world, the Emperor's survey crews had installed forward bases and mapped the desert, laying the groundwork for exploitation of the spice. Since then, melange had become an extremely popular commodity.

In a commercial coup that left many suspecting bribery or blackmail, House Hoskanner had been granted a monopoly on Duneworld operations. Ever since, Hoskanner crews had worked the hostile dunes, harvesting and selling spice at huge profits, from which the Grand Emperor took an extravagant percentage. Imperial penal planets provided an army of sandminers as veritable slave labor.

At first the other noble families, preoccupied with court follies, didn't notice the preferential deal the Hoskanners received. Jesse was one of the few who had called attention to the imbalance, and finally, eyeing the wealth reaped by the wily Hoskanners, the other nobles agitated for a piece of the action. They shouted in the Imperial Assembly, issued charges, and finally appointed the no-nonsense Jesse Linkam as their spokesman to deliver a formal complaint.

"The nobles didn't select me because of my abilities, Dor, but because they hold nostalgic memories of my foolish father and Hugo, my inept brother." He glared at the messagestat cylinder, sorely tempted to fling it off the balcony into the waters that churned far below.

"Jesse, your father and brother may have been bad businessmen, but they did earn considerable goodwill with the other nobles."

He frowned. "By playing games at the Renaissance court."

"Take advantage of that, my love, and turn it to our own profit."

"Little enough profit will come of this."

After his older brother's pointless death in the bullring, Jesse had become the leader of House Linkam before his twentieth birthday. Soon afterward, his concubine discovered the muddled mess of Catalan's finances and industries.

After meeting with the Nobles' Council, Jesse soon learned that few of the modern nobles, having inherited their holdings, were good leaders or competent businessmen. Once vastly wealthy and powerful, but now sliding into decadence, many families groaned inexorably toward bankruptcy, most without even realizing it.

With extravagant festivals and poorly financed construction projects, Jesse's father and brother had brought House Linkam to the brink of ruin. But in recent years Dorothy's careful management and austerity measures, along with his own rallying of the people to increase productivity, had begun to turn the tide.

He gazed out into the rain-swept night, then sighed with resignation. "It always rains here. Our house is forever dank, no matter how many shields or heaters we install. This year the kelp harvest is down, and the fishermen have not caught enough for export." He paused. "Even so, this is my home and the home of my ancestors. I have no interest in other places, not even Duneworld."

Dorothy eased closer and slipped an arm around Jesse's waist. "I wish you could take Barri along. Every noble son should see Renaissance at least once."

"Not this time. Too dangerous." Jesse adored their eight-year-old boy, proud of the way Barri had matured under the careful tutelage of his mother as well as the old household doctor, Cullington Yueh. Barri was learning to be a good businessman and a good leader, too—traits that would serve him well in these days of fading Imperial grandeur. Everything Jesse did was for the future, for Barri and the advancement of House Linkam. Even his love for his concubine had to be second to that.

"I'll make this trip, Dor," Jesse said, "but I don't have a good feeling about it."

# 2

⤳

*Beware of compromises. They are more often weapons of attack than tools of peace.*

—GENERAL ESMAR TUEK,

strategy concepts

Ulla Bauers sat alone in the executive cabin of his diplomatic craft, thinking about the foolish nobleman he was transporting to Renaissance. Fishing! Jesse Linkam had been out on a boat performing the work of common laborers. What a complete waste of time.

The quarters aboard Bauers's spacecraft were crowded and austere, but he understood the reason. For such a long journey between star systems, fuel costs placed strict limitations on discretionary mass. Meals were nothing more than tablets of concentrated melange, another sign of the widespread importance of Duneworld's product; after more than a week in transit, the passengers and crew would begin eating great quantities of real food upon reaching their destination. Bauers was perpetually hungry when he traveled through space, and it didn't put him in the best of moods.

He heard his stomach growl. Taking another melange tablet, he savored the cinnamon flavor and felt the drug's soothing effects seep through him.

Spice made a person feel better and increased the efficiency of human metabolism, streamlining the intake of energy from food. From a practical standpoint, this meant that the bulky supplies normally needed for long space voyages could be reduced to a case or two, permitting cargo holds to be used for other things. Bauers had heard a theory that melange might even increase the human life span, though with only a few years of recorded use, no long-term studies had yet proven the claim.

While the diplomatic transport snipped shortcuts through the fabric of space, Counselor Bauers kept to his own cabin, making no attempt to socialize. Ironically, though he had great diplomatic skills, he didn't really much care for people.

⹌⹌

TWO LEVELS BELOW Bauers, Jesse sat in a passenger compartment with six hand-picked members of the Catalan home guard as his escort; he preferred spending time with his own men anyway.

He had chosen his best fighters, including General Tuek. A slender man with olive skin, the old veteran had stooped shoulders and a manner that demonstrated loyalty while at the same time rebuffing intimacy. His thinning gray hair was receding over a leathery tanned scalp. The bright red stains around his lips signified his successful battle against sapho addiction, and he wore the marks like a badge of honor.

The security chief had faithfully served both Jesse's father and brother, saving both of them from repeated assassination attempts, though not from their own recklessness. Sworn to serve any head of House Linkam without preference, in recent years Tuek had actually become Jesse's *friend*. In a rare unguarded moment, he'd once said that it was refreshing to see a man make important decisions based on sub-stance rather than a whim or a roll of the dice.

"We need to be ready for anything, Esmar," Jesse told him as they sat down to a game of strategy-stones in the cramped compartment. Meanwhile, the other five guardsmen blocked off the narrow corridor to practice rapier dueling and hand-to-hand combat, preparing to de-fend Nobleman Linkam against any attacks.

"I lie awake at night thinking of things to be concerned about, My Lord," Tuek said, as he began to beat Jesse in the first game. "My great-est hope is that Valdemar Hoskanner will slip up so I can find an ex-cuse to kill him while defending you. He needs to pay for the death of your father."

"Valdemar won't slip up, Esmar. We weren't summoned to Renais-sance by accident. You can bet your last credit that the Hoskanners have a clever plan in mind. I fear it's too subtle for us to see yet, far too subtle."

⟡

FROM THROUGHOUT THE star-spanning Empire, wealth flowed to the planet Renaissance, enabling the Grand Emperor to stage any gaudy extravagance he could imagine. And many generations of rulers had imagined a great deal of extravagance.

The Central Palace was a huge spherical construction inlaid with millions of crystalline panels. Armillary arcs curved along what would have been latitude and longitude lines on a celestial sphere, while lights spangled the outer wall, marking the astronomical locations of Emperor Inton Wuda's star systems. In the precise center of the sphere, the Emperor sat at the symbolic zero coordinate, thus presiding (figura-tively) at the center of the Known Universe.

As he went to meet the emperor, Jesse wore the formal cloak and pantaloons that Dorothy had selected from his rarely used wardrobe of courtly attire. His dark hair was oiled and perfumed with a cloyingly sweet scent that turned his stomach; lotions covered the calluses on his hands.

General Tuek inspected the five Catalan Guards, then made a show of removing even their ceremonial weapons before they entered the Imperial presence. Only Tuek and Jesse knew that his men still carried hidden weapons: sharp strangling wires concealed as strands of hair, self-stiffening sleeves that could be turned into cutting edges. Without doubt, the Hoskanners had taken similar precautions; the question was whether Valdemar would be so bold as to provoke a bloody attack right here in the throne room.

After a melodious fanfare, a bellowing crier announced the arrival of Nobleman Linkam, using the five primary languages of the Empire. Head high, Jesse marched toward the throne.

Suspended in a curved chair atop a high monolith, Grand Emperor Wuda was a plump, bald man with gelatinous skin. Though he was relatively young, a hedonistic life had made him age badly, and his body had already sagged into a fleshy dumpling. Even so, he controlled more wealth and power than any other human in the Known Universe.

Jesse stepped back as a second fanfare preceded the crier's multilingual introduction of Nobleman Hoskanner from Gediprime. Valdemar was strikingly tall, like a walking tree. He wore a black reflective-weave suit that shimmered like oily shadows around his lanky frame. Dark hair combed back from a prominent widow's peak surmounted a thick and heavy brow, on which was tattooed the sinuous shape of a horned cobra, the symbol of House Hoskanner. Valdemar's nose jutted from his face, and the lantern jaw seemed designed for extra power when he wished to clamp his teeth together. Keeping his gaze focused on the foot of the Grand Emperor's throne, Valdemar delivered a perfect, formal bow. Never once did he glance at the Linkam party.

Six Hoskanner bodyguards, the same number as Jesse was allowed, wore imposing studded uniforms. Their faces were blunt and blocky, almost subhuman, all of them also bearing the horned-cobra tattoo, but on their left cheeks. Tuek sneered at them, then turned back when the Grand Emperor summoned both noblemen. Dutifully, the pair marched along opposite paths toward the towering pedestal that held the high throne.

"Nobleman Jesse Linkam, you have filed a complaint on behalf of the Nobles' Council regarding the Hoskanner monopoly on spice production. We normally ask aristocratic families to settle their disputes without Imperial intervention. You have more straightforward means at your disposal—personal combat between champions, mutual arbitration, even kanly. None of these is deemed satisfactory?"

"No, Sire," both Jesse and Valdemar said in unison, as if they had choreographed their response.

The Grand Emperor's fleshy face descended into a scowl. He turned toward Jesse, his tiny eyes set deep within pale folds of fat. "Nobleman Hoskanner has offered a compromise, and I suggest that you accept it."

"I will entertain any proposal, so long as it is fair and just." Jesse glanced over at Valdemar, who avoided looking at him.

"House Hoskanner has met our spice requirements for eighteen years," the Emperor said. "We see no reason to change this profitable enterprise simply because other families indulge in a fit of pique. We must be convinced that any change is to our advantage.

"Nobleman Hoskanner is justifiably proud of his accomplishments. To prove a point, he is willing to surrender his monopoly on Duneworld for a period of two years. House Linkam—and Linkam alone—will assume control of spice harvesting. If, at the end of the probationary period, Linkam has produced more than Hoskanner did in the previous two-year period, we will award spice operations to his household, in perpetuity. You may then distribute contractual shares to the Nobles' Council as you deem fit."

"A contest, Majesty?"

The Grand Emperor did not like to be interrupted. "Nobleman Hoskanner has shown great generosity in making this offer, and he demonstrates an implicit confidence in his own abilities. If you can do better, then the monopoly is yours. Do you accept these terms as a reasonable resolution to your dispute?"

Jesse saw from the barely contained smile lurking on Valdemar's face that this was exactly what his rival wanted, but he could see no way out. "Am I to be allowed access to the Hoskanner production figures so we can determine at what levels we must produce?"

Hoskanner stepped forward. "Sire, my crews did not have a challenge or a target. We did our best and provided the required quota to the Imperial coffers. Providing Nobleman Linkam with an exact target would give him an unfair advantage."

"Agreed," the Grand Emperor said with a darting glance toward Valdemar. Jesse was convinced they had arranged this beforehand.

The Linkam patriarch did not give up easily, however. "But Hoskanner has had years to set up his infrastructure, train his crews, buy his equipment. My people would be starting from scratch. Before I go to Duneworld and begin the two years, I must be allowed an acceptable ramp-up time. Will House Hoskanner leave some of their specialized equipment for us to use?"

Valdemar scowled coolly, and his response sounded rehearsed. "House Linkam will already have the advantage of our experience, the data from eighteen years of working the sands. Our sandminers had to learn by trial and error and endure many setbacks. My engineers designed the spice-harvesting equipment and techniques, and it didn't always work well. In many ways, my opponent is already starting out with a more favorable position than we Hoskanners ever had." When his brow furrowed, the horned-cobra tattoo looked as if it were coiling, ready to strike.

With a bored gesture, Emperor Wuda said, "The disadvantages seem to balance the advantages."

"Sire, we must have some equipment to begin with!" Jesse insisted, then smiled. "Otherwise the spice operations will cease entirely until we have everything in place. It could take months. I doubt the Empire would want that." He waited.

"No, that would be unconscionable." The Grand Emperor sniffed. "Very well, House Hoskanner is hereby instructed to leave twelve spice harvesters and three carryalls on Duneworld. They will be considered a loan, to be repaid at the end of the challenge, regardless of the outcome."

Valdemar's features grew stormy, but he said nothing. Jesse pressed his advantage. "And may I also request an Imperial edict that neither Nobleman Hoskanner nor anyone connected to him may interfere with my operations? After all, House Linkam did nothing to hinder his in the past eighteen years."

The Grand Emperor's impatience bordered on outright annoyance. "We will not be drawn into the minutiae of your petty dispute, nor will we mediate a squabble that has already taken too much of our precious time. Additional rules and restrictions would only complicate the matter. At the conclusion of two years, House Linkam will compare its tally to that of House Hoskanner. As your sovereign, I must remain neutral, so long as the flow of spice is uninterrupted."

Jesse knew he would do no better. He bowed formally. "I accept the challenge, Sire." *No rules.*

The Grand Emperor folded his hands across his swollen belly and smiled. Jesse thought he could hear the steely jaws of a trap clamping shut around him.

# 3

*I have always considered the descriptive powers of poetry and song to be invincible. But how can one begin to capture the essence of Duneworld in mere words? A man must journey there and experience it for himself.*

—GURNEY HALLECK,
jongleur of House Linkam

A s an advance guard for the new Linkam operations, Esmar Tuek and a hundred Catalan men arrived on Duneworld.

The Hoskanners had packed up in a flurry and departed like tenants evicted in the night. They took most of their expensive spice-harvesting machinery and transport ships, leaving behind only twelve units, as ordered: but they were the most broken-down, poorly maintained equipment.

Esmar Tuek shook his head at the bad news. The Emperor had sent word that his concession was generous, so he must have set aside his own substantial stockpile of spice, more than enough to tide him over while leaving House Linkam to struggle against formidable odds to get their operations up and running. More than likely, the Hoskanners had bribed the Emperor with some of their own melange hoard, to influence his decision.

While a few ambitious independent sandminers continued spice-harvesting operations in the interim, Tuek's men set up a base of operations in the main city. Carthage was perched in a forbidding tangle of crags that rose high from the gulf of open sand, offering shelter from furious storms and other threats. Tuek would have preferred a more organized layout, but the rugged terrain allowed no discernible grid for constructing buildings, roads, and landing zones. Structures had to be erected in any open and level spot, no matter how small.

Most of the hired workers were forced to remain, unable to afford the exorbitant passage offworld. Support staff, cooks, water merchants, repairmen, sellers of sundries and desert garb remained in Carthage, ostensibly eking out a minimal living. Tuek suspected that many of them might be saboteurs, intentionally left behind to work against House Linkam.

The old veteran's first order of business was to secure a chief of spice operations, someone with experience as a sandminer but with no love for the Hoskanners. He wanted to choose a man well down in the ranks, believing that anyone high in the former hierarchy might feel loyalty to the previous masters, whereas a miner suddenly jumped in rank and responsibility—not to mention pay—would be inclined to offer his full allegiance to House Linkam.

Tuek and the Linkam family jongleur, Gurney Halleck, met with each of the men who applied for the job, as well as others who had learned not to call attention to themselves under the Hoskanners. A redheaded boulder of a man, Gurney had a sharp eye and a deadly blade, though his jovial demeanor kept his enemies continually off guard.

After interviewing more than forty candidates, Tuek decided on an ambitious spice-crew manager named William English. Even after the Hoskanners departed, English had taken charge of three spice crews and arranged for them to keep harvesting melange—and acquiring bonuses—during the change of government. In his favor, the manager came from a noble bloodline, his grandfather having been a Linkam ally before an economic downturn ruined House English. The left side of the man's face was rough and waxy, as if scoured by an industrial polisher. English had been caught out in a furious sandstorm, unable to find adequate shelter in the rocks. Most of his exposed left cheek had been worn away. The medical facilities in Carthage had been sufficient to save his life, but not to make him handsome again. He had no love for the Hoskanners.

Tuek was more interested in the unusual chevron tattoo over the potential foreman's right eyebrow, however. "What is that symbol? I've seen them in Carthage, often among the seasoned sandminers."

"Something to do with the Zensunni prison religion?" Gurney offered. "Were you brought here as a convict laborer?"

English's expression shifted into one of pride as he tapped the tattoo. "Most of us came here as prisoners, but this mark signifies that I am a freedman. I was convicted of a crime and sentenced to twenty years of hard labor in the penal caves on Eridanus V. Then the Grand Emperor and the Hoskanners offered amnesty to any prisoner who worked on Duneworld for a time equivalent to twenty-five percent of the original sentence. I had to work only five years of my original twenty."

Gurney grunted. "The Hoskanners needed a lot of manpower for their spice operations." Always eager to find new stories and material for the songs he loved to write, he asked, "What was your crime? Something to do with the unfortunate fall of your House?"

English's mood darkened. "My sentence has been commuted, the records expunged. Therefore, I committed no crime." He smiled wryly. "Isn't every person guilty of something anyway?"

Ever conscious of security, Esmar Tuek did not like the fact that most of his sandminers were convicts. How trustworthy could they be? However, he also knew that many of the best military fighters with whom he had served were those with shady pasts or guilty consciences.

In a conciliatory tone, he asked, "How long do you have left on Duneworld? I don't want a spice foreman who'll leave us in a few months' time."

"As I said, I am now a freedman. I have been here twelve years, seven past the end of my sentence."

Gurney exclaimed, "Then why haven't you left, man? I can't imagine anyone staying in this wretched place by choice."

"It is *not* by choice. When our time is finished, we are not allowed to leave unless we pay our own passage offplanet. Few except the most crafty and devious are able to acquire that kind of money. Thus, even freedmen stay here and work as virtual slaves. I've been saving for years and have only half of the credits I need." He grimaced. "Regrettably, I didn't notice the odious clause when I signed the contract."

"Sounds like a neat little scam," Tuek said.

English shrugged. "Scam or not, I wouldn't have survived the penal caves on Eridanus V, with the dripping acid and the tunnel collapses that maim and kill so many. And even if I did finish my sentence there, I would still have been a convicted felon when I emerged." He tapped the mark above his brow again. "Here, I am forever a freedman, not a criminal."

Suitably impressed, Tuek decided to give the man a chance, while keeping him under close scrutiny. "Mr. English, would you pilot an ornijet and take us on an inspection flight?"

"Nothing easier, General. I'll check the locations of the crews that went out today. Only a few of them could get their equipment going."

⁓⊗⁓

THE THREE MEN left the black mountain battlements and flew over the endless plains of buttery dunes. Gurney stared at the wasteland through the ornijet's tinted window. "'A desolation and a wilderness, a land wherein no man dwelleth, neither any son of man passth thereby,'" the jongleur offered from his vast repertoire of pertinent

48

quotes. He turned back to look at the blocky structures of Carthage nestled among the dark rocks. "As Isaiah said long ago on another world, 'He built towers in the desert.'"

Tuek peered disapprovingly at the dirty city the Hoskanners had built. "I wouldn't exactly call them towers."

As English guided the ornijet deeper into the desert, he opened the wings to full extension. They flapped slowly as the craft rattled and bounced in air turbulence. He wrestled with the controls. "Hold on, gentlemen. Could get worse, could get better."

"Ah, now that's covering your options!" Gurney said with a chuckle.

"Storm coming?" Tuek asked.

"Just thermals. Nothing to worry about." English touched the roughened, waxy skin on the left side of his face. "I can sense bad weather. My knowledge of Duneworld's storms is unfortunately intimate."

After he had stabilized the ornijet, English glanced at the old veteran. "I told you about my tattoo, General Tuek. Would you return the favor and explain those red stains on your lips? I have never seen anything like them."

Tuek touched the bright cranberry smears that forever marked his mouth. "I was once addicted to the sapho drug. It makes you euphoric, makes you lose your edge . . . and it ruins your life."

"Sapho makes those stains?"

"Sapho juice is colorless. These red stains mark that I have taken *the cure*—and survived."

"It was a true addiction?" English looked uncomfortable. "And you have beaten it?"

"Any addiction can be overcome if a person has strong enough will." At his sides, Tuek unconsciously clenched and unclenched his hands. He remembered the nightmarish agony, the days of longing for death. He was a veteran of many battles, but breaking his dependence on the drug had been one of his most difficult victories ever.

Once they had reached the appropriate area, English guided the ornijet toward a column of dust and sand that looked like exhaust from a chimney. "Spice operations."

"I can't wait to see the equipment they left for us," Tuek said, his tone sour. "Twelve harvesters and three carryalls to deliver them to the spice sands?"

"The numbers are right, but the machines are in lousy condition."

The old warrior scowled. "The Emperor insisted that the Hoskanners leave them for us, but I assume they will not be sufficient for us to exceed the previous production."

"We'll fall far short."

"Ho, that's a cheery thought," Gurney said. "'He who looks to the Lord with optimism secures the prize, while the pessimist also secures what he envisions: defeat.'"

The spice foreman shook his head. "It's not pessimism; it's the reality of mathematics, and this hellhole. Unless we find a way to dramatically increase spice production with the equipment we have, House Linkam won't stand a chance. In two years, the Hoskanners will return in force—and I'll be put to death." English looked strangely at his two passengers. "Nobleman Hoskanner does not look kindly on a man whose loyalties can be bought."

"Sweet affection!" It was Tuek's favorite saying. "Then why did you agree to the position, man?"

"Because you offered me an increase in pay. If I starve myself and earn maximum bonuses, there's a slim chance I can afford to buy passage off Duneworld before the Hoskanners return."

English tapped a control, and long, telescoping whiskers extended from the nose of the ornijet to pick up sensor readings from the surface below. "Where there's one vein of spice, there are likely to be others. These probes take readings to help us determine a good place to come back another time."

"What about all those little ships?" Gurney asked.

"Scouts spot good sand by surface markers, dune irregularities, and indications of worm activity."

"Worm activity?" Tuek asked.

Airborne lifters swooped down to the flurry of activity while smaller ships flew nearby in wide arcs. English gazed down at the operations. "Ah, looks like we're wrapping up for today. The crews can only hit each vein for an hour or so before we have to evacuate. See, that spice harvester is ready to be hauled to safety."

Below, while men sprinted to their main vehicles, a heavy carryall linked to a boxy hulk of machinery in a valley of dunes, then heaved it into the air.

"Hauled to safety? From what?" Tuek asked.

"Didn't the Hoskanners tell you anything about spice operations?"

"Nothing."

Below, only moments after the carryall lifted the spice harvester from the sand, an enormous writhing shape bucked through the dunes. A serpentine beast with a cavernous mouth launched itself toward the rising spice harvester, but the straining carryall climbed higher and higher, out of reach. With a crash of sand, the great worm thundered back to the dunes and thrashed around.

"Gods, what a monster!" Gurney said. "'And I saw the beast rise from the sea, with ten horns and seven heads.'"

"Harvesting vibrations summon a sandworm to defend its treasure— just like a mythical dragon," English explained. "Under the Hoskanners, I crewed on seven spice harvesters that were lost."

"Did everyone get away down there?" Tuek peered through the ornijet's window, searching the ransacked dunes for casualties.

English listened to the staccato reports. "Everyone checked in except for one scout flyer caught in a downdraft in the wake of a sand geyser."

"Sand geysers? Giant worms?" Gurney cried. "Does Duneworld breed strangeness?"

"In a dozen years, even I have yet to see all of its mysteries."

⟿

BEFORE RETURNING TO the mountains around Carthage, English landed at a small encampment where twenty workers in sealed bodysuits spread out, planting long flexible poles in the soft sand. The line of poles stuck out like quills from the back of a spiny beast.

The three men climbed out of the ornijet, breathing hot air through face filters. Around them on high dunes, Tuek saw a whirl of wind devils. Even active crews were spread across the sheltered valley, a great emptiness that was like a hungry mouth gulping every sound. Standing in the immense silence, he thought he could almost hear the desert breathing.

Gurney plodded through the soft sands to reach one of the flexible poles the crew had recently planted. He wobbled it like an antenna. "And what's this?"

"They are poling the sand to help determine the weather."

"Don't we have satellites in orbit? I was sure the Hoskanners left them."

"Those provide only a large-scale picture, and the terrain is a mosaic of microclimates. With fluctuating temperatures and tides of sand, the local weather is dangerously unpredictable. Each of these poles has a signal beeper. As they bend and twist in the wind, the transmissions help us chart storms. Blowing grains etch lines into the waxy surfaces of the poles. Some natives claim they can read the patterns." He shrugged. "I've never been able to see it myself, but their reports are as accurate as anything else we have."

One of the questing men on the far side of the basin plunged his pole into the sand and suddenly let out a loud yelp. He threw up his arms, wailing; his feet went out from under him as if a great mouth was trying to suck him down.

The alarmed spice foreman stood where he was, feet planted safely on the more stable dune, but Tuek and Gurney sprinted toward the man. By the time they neared the spot, the hapless worker had already

vanished beneath the powdery surface. Not even his fingers or a stirring of movement showed where he had been.

Gurney grabbed Tuek's shoulder and pulled him back. "Best stay far
away, General! Maybe it's another worm."

Tuek whirled to face William English, who walked grimly up to
them, picking his footsteps carefully. "Sweet affection! Couldn't you
do anything to help him?"

The desert man shook his head. "He was lost the moment he
stepped on the wrong spot. Sand whirlpools appear in unpredictable
places, sinkholes that spiral downward."

Hesitant to move, Tuek remained where he was for a minute, his jaw
muscles working like a tiny imitation of a worm. "Gods! What kind of
demon world is this?"

# 4

*Even in the most barren wasteland, a flower always grows. Recognize this, and learn to adapt to your surroundings.*

—DR. BRYCE HAYNES,
planetary ecologist assigned to study Duneworld

With her family balanced on the cusp of survival, Dorothy Mapes vowed that every moment on Duneworld and every action would count. "This is a serious planet that demands undivided attention," she observed, gazing out the oval porthole as the Linkam transport ship cruised over the sea of dunes toward a line of stark, black mountains.

Seated with Jesse on the starboard side of the transport, she saw his attention focused on a looming dust cloud that approached like an inexorable Catalan tide. Moments ago, he had said he was having second thoughts about this side excursion he had ordered the pilot to take after the cross-space journey, flying over the desert for a hundred kilometers instead of landing directly at Carthage. But he had wanted to see what the planet was like, showing his concubine and son where they were going to live for at least two years.

Now she hoped it wasn't a dangerous mistake.

"I think we can beat that storm," the pilot said. "I sure hope so, because we don't have enough fuel to go back into orbit."

Jesse did not say anything, and neither did Dorothy. He squeezed her hand in a private way that imparted reassurance, telling her that he wouldn't let anything happen to her, or to young Barri, who sat at another window, transfixed by the alien vistas outside. After more than a decade together, the nobleman and his concubine had ways of communicating through only a look or a touch. He ran a fingertip across her diagem promise ring.

Though Jesse was the patriarch of the Noble House, Dorothy Mapes took care of important business details and family matters. She had once compared herself to the wife of an Old Earth samurai, with her access to and control over a great deal. She understood full well that the spousal analogy was only her wishful thinking. Because of the Empire's strict and convoluted society, Jesse could never marry a commoner, no matter how deeply he cared for her and how essential she was to him.

Dorothy was the mother of his son, the male heir to House Linkam. Although she taught the boy important skills, she also pampered him—too much, according to Jesse. The nobleman wanted Barri to face enough adversity to make him strong. Under pressure, Dorothy would yield to Jesse's commands in this regard, or appear to do so; then, invariably, she would return to indulging the boy.

"Oh, I hope we get there soon." From across the aisle the kindly old family doctor fidgeted in his seat, while staring straight ahead and refusing to look out the window at the dizzying landscape sweeping past. Cullington Yueh had bristly gray hair and a salt-and-pepper mustache. "Oh, these bumps and vibrations are making me nauseated."

"Carthage dead ahead." The pilot's small voice squeaked over the speaker from the bridge. "Prepare for more turbulence as we approach the mountains."

"Wonderful." Yueh turned even paler.

Through the oval viewing window, Dorothy watched the city come into view, buildings and cleared areas interspersed among the dark crags. Such an ominous-looking place, expanded and fortified by the Hoskanners during their eighteen-year tenure. Narrow roads ran through gorges and valleys; blocky ledges held dwelling complexes and smaller habitation domes connected by paths and steep steps. Many of the largest buildings were linked by trams and tunnels to the rest of the fortress city. Though Carthage had no major spaceport, several airfields had been blasted into the rocks and then armorpaved, resulting in two main landing zones on opposite sides of the city—one larger than the other.

The pilot circled a flat area near the headquarters mansion. The russet-and-black structures of Carthage peeked around bulwarks of rock. Winds began to buffet the craft in advance of the storm, like a squadron sent in to soften up the enemy before a larger onslaught. The craft lurched and swayed, eliciting another round of miserable groans from Dr. Yueh.

With a resounding, rocking thump, the craft set down in a level region sealed by armorpave, surrounded by sharp cliffs. All around them, local ships and shuttles landed swiftly, eager to outrun the storm . . . they were like desert hawks rushing back to their nests in the high rocks. Particles of sand pelted the windows.

"We're home," Jesse said. "Duneworld looks like a nice, friendly place."

≈

DOROTHY HARDLY RECOGNIZED the two men who came forward as she and her party entered the central lobby of the receiving building. Dust swirled around their boots, bodysuits, and desert cloaks as they marched across the floor. But her sharp eyes identified the pair from the way they walked and interacted. Dorothy had learned the art of observing small details about people and reading their body languages: It was the only way to achieve success in a society that valued noble blood more than intelligence and wit.

With a flourish, Gurney Halleck swung open his cape, spraying the air with loose dirt. The jongleur's coarse face beamed impishly as soon as he saw Jesse. "About time you got here, laddie!" Beneath matted pale red hair, his forehead and stubby nose were grimy, but a patch around his mouth remained completely clean, where it had been protected by the mask.

Esmar Tuek kept his own cape closed, and his dark eyes peered over the top edge of the facial seal. "Sorry we didn't have time to clean up for you, My Lord, but we've been out in the desert. Those Hoskanner bastards left us with nothing but junk for spice-harvesting equipment! We need to get some decent machinery in here quickly. At a pretty price, I'm afraid. The Hoskanners have probably rigged the market."

"Our finances are stretched to the limit," Dorothy warned. "Anticipating problems, we've already ordered more equipment, what little we can afford."

"Looks like we need to order even more," Jesse said. "No matter how deep we have to dig into our coffers, we need the right tools for the job, or we can't do it at all." He smiled at her. "You'll find a way."

"Somehow, I always do." Countless times, Dorothy had set priorities for House Linkam, tightened the budget, even uncovered new sources of income. Now her mind spun as she considered the enormity of the problem.

Attendants surged forward to assist with unloading their luggage and belongings. Dr. Yueh, still wobbly, finally emerged. He took deep breaths of the dry air and made a face, as if smelling something unpleasant all around him.

The two dusty escorts led the newcomers toward the nearby mansion, along a steep path. Wind from the rising storm found its way through the sheltering crags and tugged at their hair and clothes. Jesse and Dorothy both ducked against the stinging breeze. Their son had run ahead, but she called him back. Reluctantly, the brown-haired boy waited for them to catch up.

"It's probably best for you to get a face full of grime the first day," Gurney said. "That's the way it is here on Duneworld, and we haven't figured out a way to clean the place up yet. The accursed sand and dust gets into everything. I've got the worst rash on my—" Glancing at Dorothy, he left his sentence uncompleted.

She took Barri by the hand as they continued walking. At a disapproving glance from Jesse, she released the boy to walk on his own, a few steps ahead.

"The main spice fields are fifteen hundred klicks from here," Tuek quickly filled the silence, "but Carthage is the nearest stable and defensible site for a large city and landing zones."

Gurney nudged Jesse and pointed ahead. "Feast your eyes on your new home, laddie."

Through a haze of blowing sand, Dorothy barely made out the old headquarters mansion in front of them, a rock-walled fortress that reflected the brutish architectural tastes of the Hoskanners. She thought again of their former home on the Catalan shores, the rustic yet welcoming wood furnishings, the rugs and fireplaces, the cheerful lights. In contrast, this place offered all the creature comforts of great hunks of stone and fused alloy beams.

*What have we gotten into?*

Immense statues of old Hoskanner family patriarchs lined the entry walk. "Those will have to come down," she said immediately.

"Old Valdemar won't like that at all if he comes back here," Gurney said, grinning more than scowling.

Jesse paused for a long time before he said, "If Valdemar comes back in two years, I will be beyond caring."

DOROTHY WOKE EARLY the next morning after a night of fitful sleep in a flinty-smelling bedchamber. Sitting up in bed to look at the harsh yellow sunlight bleeding through the shielded window, she noticed that Jesse was no longer beside her, though the sheets on his side of the bed were rumpled.

Detecting that she was awake, a tiny device like a fat bee buzzed in front of her face, and she blew a breath to activate the messager. Jesse's compressed voice said, "I'm on an inspection tour with Esmar and Gurney. You took so long to get to sleep, Dor, I didn't want to wake you."

She smiled at his consideration, but could not allow herself to rest, not on their first full day on Duneworld. Thousands of details demanded her attention for the household to run smoothly.

Barri was already up and bursting with energy. He had dark brown hair that remained unruly despite Dorothy's efforts to tame it. His nose was round and covered with a thin scatter of freckles easily disguised by the ever-present dust on Duneworld. His bright laughter came easily, especially when he amused himself by discovering interesting facets to even ordinary things.

The smart eight-year-old followed her throughout the morning, asking constant questions, poking into unlabeled boxes, exploring hallways and closed rooms. Dorothy issued instructions to the domestic staff she had brought from Catalan, as well as a handful of Hoskanner holdovers that General Tuek had screened with his usual care. Jesse might trust the old veteran's precautions, but Dorothy had quietly decided to make her own judgments about the staff. The consequences of an error in this regard were too high, the stakes too enormous.

She took a stone stairway down to the main kitchen. When she entered, the chef was discussing that evening's meal with two staff members. Piero Zonn had operated a gourmet restaurant on Catalan prior to joining the Linkam entourage; Jesse had brought him along to serve meals in the headquarters mansion, but the small, energetic man seemed at a loss as to how he would do his job properly. Dorothy wanted to reassure him, but she didn't know herself how many things they would have to sacrifice here.

The chef and his assistants fell silent when they saw her; she was a commoner like them, but they lived in different circles. Nearby, a Carthage-native maid paused while wiping dust from a decorative stone alcove, then resumed her work with renewed vigor. Dorothy felt very much out of place.

Later, as the two of them walked alone through a hall to the upper levels, Barri tugged at his mother's cool blouse. "What does Odokis mean?"

"Odokis?"

"The star we saw when we came into the system."

"That's Arrakis, dear. In ancient astronomy it meant 'the dancer' or 'the trotting camel.' It's the sun up in our sky now, on this planet."

"I'd rather be back on Catalan. I miss my friends."

"You'll make new friends here." In truth, though, Dorothy had noticed few children in Carthage, and the ones she had seen appeared to be street urchins. With a population of convict laborers and freedmen who could not afford passage home, Duneworld was not much of a place to raise a family.

With Jesse already throwing himself into the spice business, Dorothy spent the morning unpacking while Barri continued to explore. An exceedingly curious young man, he invariably pestered his mother when she was busiest or most agitated. But she found reservoirs of patience within herself, knowing that his curiosity was a sign of intelligence.

In the large master suite, she organized a few Linkam mementos, the bare minimum Jesse had permitted her to bring along, due to the weight restrictions on space cargo. The rest of their possessions had been left behind on Catalan. So much of her life remained back there, and not just *things*. Barri looked forlorn each time he realized that some toy or keepsake was far away, and possibly lost forever.

"It's good to start anew," she said aloud with a brave smile. While she studied inventory lists, the boy occupied himself by playing with something he had found on the floor in a corner of the large suite.

One of the articles she unpacked was a holophoto of Jesse's father. Placing it on the mantle of the bedroom fireplace, she activated it to show the heavyset Jabo Linkam in his gaudy faux-military uniform, the attire he had preferred to wear, though he had never served in any army. A sycophant at the Imperial court, the old fool had loved to dress in fancy costumes and throw extravagant balls that he could not afford. In the process, he'd nearly bankrupted House Linkam.

During one such banquet, a crazed chef had attempted to assassinate the father of Valdemar Hoskanner by slipping a powerful toxin into his dessert, a famous Catalanian layer cake. But the delicacy had been one of Jabo's favorite treats, and he had devoured the dish, not knowing it was poisoned, and it quickly killed him. Only a year later, emboldened by the death of his enemy, sure that House Linkam had been behind the poisoning attempt, young Valdemar had publicly challenged Jesse's brother, Hugo, to fight in a Hoskanner-sponsored bullfight. Hugo let himself be shamed into participating . . . and the bull killed him. Sheer stupidity. Thus the youngest Linkam had been left in charge of the Noble House.

As Dorothy studied Jabo's holophoto, she hoped her beloved Jesse never fell victim to the prideful ways of his star-crossed family.

Dr. Yueh stepped through the open doorway. "Oh, I'm feeling much better today, now that I've done some unpacking and started to get organized." He held up a long, wickedly sharp ceremonial knife in the form of a gilded and gem-encrusted scalpel. "I even found this old thing, from when I received my first medical credentials." He flashed a self-deprecating smile. "It probably wasn't worth the cost of shipping, even to this vain old man."

"I think we can indulge you in this instance, Cullington."

The old doctor rubbed his hands together briskly. "I'm about to have a late lunch. Care to join me? The nobleman hasn't returned yet, but I thought you might enjoy a break."

"Yes, of course. Barri, come with us to the dining hall." She was surprised at how quiet he had become while sitting cross-legged by a sealed window with his back to her. "What are you doing there?"

Still playing, he looked over his shoulder with a cherubic grin. His blue-green eyes sparkled with fascination. "I have a new friend after all, Mother. Look; it's like one of the tide pool crabs at home." He held up his hand to show a jagged-legged creature on his palm. The jet-black arachnid crawled up his bare arm, prowling. He giggled. "That tickles!"

Dr. Yueh's jaw dropped. "Oh, don't make any sudden moves!" The old doctor pushed Dorothy back and moved toward the boy. "It's an indigenous sand scorpion. The sting is deadly!"

With every muscle in her body, Dorothy wanted to leap to her son's aid, but didn't dare startle the creature.

Making a sudden move, Yueh slapped the scorpion from Barri's arm. The creature struck a settee near Dorothy, fell to the floor, and rolled into a black, defensive ball. She stepped on it hard, grinding with her heel. Though it was smashed and dead, she stomped on the sand scorpion again and again.

"That's all right," Yueh said soothingly as he pulled the boy away, but Barri struggled to get free, his eyes full of tears.

Drawing her son to her bosom, Dorothy said, "This is a dangerous place. You must not play with the creatures you find here. Even Dr. Yueh could not have saved you from a scorpion sting."

Barri glared at her for killing his new pet. "Cullington could have figured out an ant'dote."

The old doctor patted the boy on the head. "Let's not test my abilities, all right?"

# 5

*The living always stand on the shoulders of the dead. It is the nature of human advancement.*

—A SAYING OF OLD EARTH

J esse called a staff meeting on the top floor of the headquarters mansion. The plaz-windowed conference chamber was insulated against Duneworld's unrelenting sun. Through the plaz, he had a view in all directions: the desert, the crags, the spaceport landing zones, and the scattered buildings of Carthage.

Although the alloy-paneled room had been swept clean and scrubbed that day by household staff, a layer of gritty dust already covered the furniture and floor. Jesse smeared a finger across the table surface, looked at the mark. Such conditions would be his constant companion for some time.

Esmar Tuek and Gurney Halleck entered the room with the new spice foreman, William English. A houseman in a short brown cloak brought a steaming pot of spice coffee with four cups and then departed, closing the door behind him.

Before beginning, Jesse moved around the table and poured the rich, aromatic coffee for his companions, demonstrating that he was different from other noblemen. "I was greatly disturbed by what I saw during yesterday's inspection tour. The Hoskanners have prepared a nasty trap for us here."

"You've got that right, laddie," Gurney grumbled. "This might as well be a prison planet for House Linkam: We can't leave until we complete our sentence."

"Even then, going home doesn't seem to be an option," English said, his tone as bitter as spice-coffee dregs. "Not for most of us."

Jesse studied the scarred crew manager, whom Tuek had approved. In the days when House Linkam had fared better, English's grandfather had been on close terms with Jesse's. English seemed competent and dependable enough, but Jesse knew there were no certainties in life. Risks had to be taken. He had to rely on people.

*But people are prone to fallibility,* he thought, *and betrayal. They change with every breath they take.*

Nevertheless, he made up his mind. He looked around the table. "Even though most of the sandminers here are—or were—convict laborers, I do not consider them slaves. I've worked with the people on Catalan, watched them take pride in the most menial tasks if they had some reason to do so. I intend to give the people on Duneworld a *reason* to work hard. Our only chance of winning this challenge is if the populace is on our side. We can't do it without them."

"Very few workers are on Duneworld by choice, My Lord," English said. "The Hoskanners ground them under their heel, worked them to death, stole their hope as soon as they transferred here from prison planets."

"Then I will give them hope. For their benefit and for ours, I will show them that I am different from Valdemar Hoskanner." Jesse flashed a hard smile. "General Tuek, Mr. English, I want you to put out the word. Inform the sandminer crews that if House Linkam wins this challenge, I give my oath as a nobleman that every freedman shall have his passage offplanet. I'll pay for it myself if I have to."

"My Lord!" Tuek said. "House Linkam doesn't have the finances for that, nor can we afford to lose all of our most experienced crewmen!"

"Esmar, if we win the challenge, then we will have sufficient spice income to pay for it. We can begin training the senior convict laborers to take over for the freedmen, and perhaps we can entice some of the freedmen to stay."

English's eyes sparkled. "My comrades will be extremely glad to hear this news, My Lord."

Jesse drew a deep breath, knowing he had stepped off a precipice, and he only hoped he could survive the landing. Though Linkam family finances had improved under his stewardship, his family's credit standing remained low, thanks to the damages his father and brother had done. To fund this bold and risky venture, he had borrowed large sums from the Imperial bank and reluctantly accepted aid from a few politically allied Houses.

In scrambling for money, Jesse had been chagrined to discover that many of the noble families who had prodded him into contesting the Hoskanner monopoly now refused to support him when it counted most. He'd felt like an unprepared victim thrown into an arena while others cheered or jeered from the safety of their seats, casting wagers as to his fate. Jesse should have expected little else from most of them.

Despite all obstacles, though, he was determined to win the spice challenge. He had to get the workers on his side. Once he broke the Hoskanner monopoly, he would share the profits as he saw fit, rewarding his few supporters lavishly and leaving others in the financial deep freeze.

*This planet is a treasure chest,* he thought, *and I must find the key to open it.*

"I chose the course of dignity and honor, though it may have been a foolish one." Jesse slumped into his high-backed chair. "If only I knew more about how much the Hoskanners were producing here."

Tuek brought out a document, slapped it on the table, and slid it over to Jesse. "I do have a little something for you, My Lord."

Jesse recognized columns of spice-production figures. "Hoskanner numbers for the past two years? Where did you get this?"

"From an impeccable source." The old veteran looked at English.

The new spice foreman said, "I wasn't that significant when the Hoskanners were here, but documents did get passed around, to compare month-by-month results and motivate the spice foremen into competing with one another. They made copies for internal purposes and . . . lost track of some of them."

Tuek added, "William had to call in a lot of favors for this information, but it makes for interesting reading."

"Excellent," Jesse said. "Now we'll know where we stand."

"Or how far behind we are," Gurney suggested, with a smirk. "Look at the numbers, laddie."

Jesse whistled. "If these figures are right, the Hoskanners produced an incredible amount of melange! Has this much spice been distributed throughout the Empire? I had no idea its use was so widespread."

Tuek cautioned, "Could be a trick. Inflated amounts."

But Jesse shook his head. "If this was a trick, Valdemar would have under-reported to escape Imperial tariffs and lull us into a false sense of security."

Studying the document, Gurney said, "Sorry to state the obvious, laddie, but the Hoskanners had a whole fleet of spice-processing machinery. The twelve decrepit spice harvesters and three old carryalls they left us are not nearly adequate."

"The equipment spends more time in repair shops than in service," English said. "The Hoskanner scum took the most qualified crews with them, too, paid them a bonus for *not* helping us, including passage off-world." Though the scarred spice foreman glowered at the injustice,

Jesse suspected that English himself would have taken the offer, had the Hoskanners made it to him.

"Only eighty-one experienced freedmen stayed behind," Tuek said. "And our workers from Catalan need a lot of training. We've got a long way to go."

Jesse stood and began pacing. "I expected some of this. Immediately after accepting the challenge, I had Dorothy order six new spice harvesters and two more carryalls from the Ixian machine works, even paid for rush delivery." Jesse grimaced. "Last night, after the inspection tour, I sent for six more spice harvesters and another carryall."

"Can you afford it, My Lord?" Tuek asked.

"More than I can afford *not* to."

"That's twelve new harvesters and twelve old ones," Gurney said. "Still less equipment than the Hoskanners had."

"Then we'll just have to work harder and smarter than they did," Jesse said. "According to Dorothy, we've sold most of our valuable family heirlooms and mortgaged everything else. She says we're not stretching the budget—we're breaking it." He sighed. "But what choice do we have if we want to win? For the survival of House Linkam, we must win!"

English self-consciously rubbed the waxy scar tissue on his cheek. "The Hoskanners had a lot of trouble with the weather. Sand ate into the biggest spice harvesters and damaged the factory modules. The dust here is more corrosive and statically charged than anyone expected. Even with thirty harvesters, at least a quarter of them were down for repairs at any one time." He paused. "But there is a way to improve on that. I think." The room fell silent. Looking at Jesse, the spice foreman cleared his throat. "The Grand Emperor said this game has no rules, right?"

Jesse nodded. "It'd be nice to have that work to our advantage for a change."

"The Emperor's first inspection crews set up advance bases out in the desert, sealed structures that have been sitting there for years, filled with machinery and supplies. Some of my freedmen know where they are. Everything's in perfect working order, because they used live-rubber shielding over the structures."

"Never heard of it," Tuek said.

"A very expensive material. It's incredibly malleable, and could be fitted over the engine housings and other sensitive areas to keep sand out of the harvesters. There might not be enough live-rubber shielding for all the machines, but it'll definitely help. I've thought about it for years, but never got around to suggesting it to the Hoskanners. I was nobody to them, and they probably wouldn't have listened anyway." He smiled. "Besides, I rather enjoyed watching them struggle."

"Doesn't that property belong to the Emperor?" Tuek pointed out. "Technically?"

"No rules—the Emperor said it himself." Gurney was grinning.

"Duneworld has a way of making its own rules," English said.

Jesse made up his mind. "We raid the advance bases."

Deep in thought, he took a sip of spice coffee. As he gazed through the plaz toward the sands, he could feel the soothing effects of melange. "Collect all the data compiled by advance survey teams and as much intelligence as you can find about the spice operations of the Hoskanners. We'll need access to that information before we can rise above their mistakes and reach another level. Otherwise we won't know what we're doing."

Dorothy burst into the conference room, her face flushed. "We've just received an emergency transmission, My Lord! A carryall broke down and stranded one of the spice harvesters. They're calling for an emergency rescue before a worm comes."

"We have two other carryalls, don't we?" Jesse asked. "Send one quickly."

Now English looked distressed. "Sir, one carryall is in the repair depot, and the other is in a spice field near the equator. Much too far away. They'll never get there in time."

"What about all those men?" Jesse demanded. "Isn't there a full spice crew on that harvester?"

Dorothy's face darkened. "They shut down operations and dampened their noise and vibrations. But even if they lie low, they're sure a sandworm will come soon."

Jesse fairly lunged out of the room. "William, get me our fastest transport shuttles, anything that can carry crewmen. We'll save as many as we can. Gurney, Esmar—come with me! There's no time to lose."

# 6

*Nobility is not the same thing as bravery.*

—NOBLEMAN JESSE LINKAM,
private notes

For more than three decades General Esmar Tuek had served House Linkam, first as a member of the guard force, then working his way up to security chief. In earlier years he had tried to keep Jabo Linkam from accidentally killing himself, and the same with Linkam's eldest son, Hugo, but those noblemen had gone to great lengths to avoid using what little brains they had.

Now, at long last, Tuek had a chance to serve someone with a solid head on his shoulders. Jesse was a thoughtful man willing to perform honest work for what he wanted, much loved by his people back on Catalan. But was the young nobleman just as big a fool as his predecessors for letting himself be goaded into Valdemar Hoskanner's challenge? Perhaps it would still end badly.

Racing to rescue the stranded spice harvester, Gurney Halleck handled the controls of the transport ship with a kinesthetic accelerator connected to his fingertips. English stood behind him in the cockpit, struggling to hold his balance while guiding their course.

The roaring ship flew so low over the dunes that the noise of its passage rattled the sands. Looking back through the aft porthole, Tuek saw a monstrous worm surface just behind them, questing with its blind head.

The spice foreman had suggested a low and erratic flight pattern to confuse the creatures, and hopefully to prevent them from going after the disabled equipment. "They're unpredictable beasts," English said. "I wouldn't count on anything. There's never been a truly safe or effective means of harvesting melange."

Twenty years before, Donell Mornay, an inventor with the third Imperial expedition to this desolate planet, had developed the initial techniques for excavating spice, under contract from the young Grand Emperor Wuda. Mornay's early harvesters had been much smaller machines, and when most of them were devoured by worms, he conceived the flying carryalls to lift the mobile factories to safety and deposit them at other rich spice veins, a leapfrog process that always kept the harvesters one step ahead of the worms. When everything worked properly.

The Hoskanners improved the guerrilla mining technique with larger harvesters and more powerful carryalls. With any luck—and Tuek wasn't sure if House Linkam had any left—Jesse might further refine the techniques.

Finally, the fast transport reached the weathered spice harvester sitting in the orange-and-brown sand. The quiet machine looked like a frightened rabbit huddling motionless, hoping not to be noticed.

"A rich, rich vein," English said, his voice dismal. "A shame to just abandon it."

"We'll salvage what we can from the cargo holds—if there's time,"

Jesse said, watching tensely. "The crews made a good haul before they got into trouble. I've already called for help from the Carthage shipping yards. More carriers are on the way."

As the rescue transport arrived, a flurry of small ornijets rushed in from the west. Hovering overhead, five of them dipped vacuum tubes into the harvester's cargo hold, sucking up melange like hummingbirds sipping nectar.

Tuek dropped a rescue chute onto the sand beside the massive vehicle and switched on the mechanism's motor. "Put it in reverse," Jesse ordered. "I'm going down myself."

"My Lord, you don't need to do that. With all this increased activity, a worm will come soon. Bet on it!"

"I didn't ask your opinion, General." Hearing the rebuke in the nobleman's voice, Tuek did as he was told.

"Wormsign! Less than twenty minutes out!" English shouted, listening to a report from the ornijet scouts. "They have to hurry! Get salvage crews right now—off-load the spice! Save the melange!"

"Damn the spice!" Jesse called. "Save the men!"

He rode the stepped conveyor down to the sand. More than fifty sandminers had already boiled out of the harvester, seasoned freedmen and convicts still working off their sentences, along with new arrivals from Catalan. Jesse urged the men into the rescue chute. From above, Tuek barely heard their voices over the machinery sounds as he reset the conveyor.

Tuek saw a mound of sand coming toward the shut-down harvester. The old veteran set the conveyor to ascend as rapidly as possible. More and more men made it to safety.

Gurney said, "That machine's already scrap metal for the worms."

Desperate crewmen streamed out of the stranded harvester and ran across the sand toward the rescue chute. Dust-encrusted workers began to spill into the transport ship, spreading through the passenger compartment. English and Tuek guided them to the back, shouting for the men to cram together. "Faster! Worm's coming! Faster, damn you!"

Moments later, Jesse tumbled into the passenger compartment himself, staggering with an injured sandminer over his shoulder; the man's sleeve was torn and bloody, his arm bent at an unnatural angle. Tuek grabbed him, taking the weight from Jesse. "Here, My Lord. Let me help."

"Take him, Esmar! There's still more down there! More men!"

Wrestling the nobleman clear, Tuek looked back down the chute, where six frantic sandminers scrambled onto the rescue conveyor. Relieved of the injured man, Jesse turned, ready to climb back down and lend more assistance on the ground.

Then a giant mouth ringed with glittering crystal teeth broke through the sand and shot up toward the bottom of the chute. Tuek smelled a nauseatingly strong belch of cinnamon, and felt the heat of the monster's exhalations. Four men screamed as they tumbled into the maw.

The straining transport lurched into the air, and then the worm seized the end of the conveyor. English shouted from the cockpit, and Gurney lifted the ship higher, until the chute finally tore free. Suddenly loose, the aircraft recoiled up into the hot desert sky. Two remaining workers dangled from the torn end, trying desperately to hold on.

The blind worm sensed the clinging sandminers, and with a more vigorous lunge the beast bit off the rest of the chute, taking them with it.

Inside the passenger compartment, the terrified crewmen screamed. The transport craft spun and wavered unsteadily in the air, struggling to pull away.

"Higher!" English shouted.

Gurney responded, optimizing the kinetic controls. Staring down through the whistling gap, Tuek watched the worm turn its wrath on the abandoned spice harvester.

The rescued crew chief hunched on the deck, shaking dust out of his hair and bemoaning the disaster. "Must be twenty sandminers lost! Eight of them freedmen we rehired. All good men."

Jesse sat numb and exhausted, staring through the aft porthole. "I don't want to send more crews out until we can protect them. Let the Hoskanners burn in hell. I won't commit murder!" He shook his head. "I hope some of the new equipment arrives soon. We don't seem to have benefited much from paying extra for the rush delivery."

Tuek wanted to chide the nobleman for risking himself, but he would not do that in front of the men. Interestingly, because of Jesse's actions, the rescued crews looked at him with a strange, newfound respect.

Tuek also viewed the nobleman through fresh eyes. Perhaps Jesse *was* the sort of leader who could inspire men to overcome their fears, despite bad equipment and dangerous working conditions. The sand-miner crews needed that as much as they needed new machines.

Perhaps, despite the tremendous odds they faced, House Linkam would survive after all.

# 7

*Some people keep their secrets. Others build them from scratch.*

— DOROTHY MAPES,
reflections

Before allowing the Linkam family to set foot inside the Hoskanner mansion, General Tuek's men had scanned it for weapons, traps, electronic eavesdropping devices, and any number of hidden pitfalls. The veteran did find numerous traps, hidden explosives, tiny assassination devices disguised as "security systems," and poisoned food supplies. He even found two meek-looking household servants who, when strip-searched, displayed small horned-cobra tattoos on their backs signifying their ties to House Hoskanner. The security chief evicted them immediately and sent them to live with the convict laborers in Carthage.

Despite his indignation, Tuek seemed to think these hazards were not serious attempts by the Hoskanner nobleman—more a game to show his contempt for the Linkams. The security chief continued his search, trying to find something more subtle and insidious.

Though Tuek had combed the rooms and corridors to the best of his ability, Dorothy still sensed the old veteran had missed something.

With sharp eyes and attentive skills that, she believed, surpassed Tuek's, the petite woman studied the various chambers, the architectural layout, even the choices of furnishings, to better understand Jesse's nemesis. Valdemar Hoskanner had designed this building to flaunt his wealth, to demonstrate his power on Duneworld. He had left signs of his aggressive personality, and perhaps his weaknesses, everywhere.

Hoskanner supervisors and functionaries had shared communal residences with few amenities; their lives centered on work. No doubt they counted the days until they could be rotated home to Gediprime. Those buildings were now inhabited by the loyal staff members from Catalan.

Deeper in the town, the hardened freedmen had dwellings of their own, most of them squalid but private, while the newest convict laborers were assigned to prefab barracks. Duneworld's environment provided all the security necessary to keep the prisoners from escaping; neither convicts nor freedmen could go anywhere.

Every scrap of moisture was recycled and hoarded. But Valdemar himself, in open defiance of the desert, had built this huge headquarters mansion with cavernous rooms that needed to be sealed and cooled. To Dorothy, with her hard business mindset, the grandiosity seemed unnecessary and profligate. She would have to shut some of the wings and floors down in order to conserve.

As she looked around, Dorothy tried to get into the mindset of their nemesis. This imposing mansion suggested to her the sheer scale of spice exports, the incredible profits. Once she began to realize how high the stakes truly were, Dorothy knew that Valdemar Hoskanner would do anything to win. This had never been a fair contest, and the Hoskanners had never intended to offer an actual compromise. They wanted only to eliminate the annoyance of House Linkam through deception, and dispense with the objections of the Nobles' Council.

Dorothy intended to find some of the traps Valdemar had left behind herself, using her own sharp wits instead of Tuek's technology.

In the south wing, she noted with interest that a fourth-floor corridor seemed to go nowhere. A piece of the architecture did not fit. Having compared an aerial image of the headquarters mansion with on-site plans that Tuek's inspection team had drawn up, she realized now that the stone building's physical outline did not precisely match its interior layout. A small part of this wing was wrong.

To her sharp eye, the hall floor showed faint signs of regular passage. Why would that be so, if the corridor didn't lead anywhere? With nimble fingers, she touched the irregular contours of the wall, searching for anything unusual. Not surprised to discover that one of the stones felt hollow and seemed to be made of a material that did not match the other blocks, she figured out its movement and unlocked the clever mechanism.

With a gentle hiss, the hidden door unsealed and slid aside. Startlingly moist and mulchy air wafted toward her, so full of the smells of plants, leaves, roots, and compost that it struck her like a slap in the face. Alert for booby traps, Dorothy stepped inside.

Cleverly concealed mist nozzles sprayed moisture in the air, while automatic irrigation piping fed flower beds, hedges, potted fruit shrubs. Dorothy had no doubt that these were flora brought from Gediprime. She saw an explosion of colorful flowers—purple, yellow, orange— amid verdant ferns. One set of huge scarlet blooms turned toward her as she moved, as if sensing a human presence. A raft of capped mushrooms spread out, speckled with golden-brown spots and silvery flecks.

The smell of moisture in the air and the sight of misty droplets sent a wistful pang through her. Though she had only been on Duneworld for a few weeks, it seemed like years since she'd experienced an afternoon rain shower on Catalan. With delight, she realized she could bring Barri here whenever he grew lonely for his former home. It would be their special, private place.

But Dorothy understood that would make her as wasteful and excessive as Nobleman Hoskanner. Her practical mind ran through swift calculations, and she was appalled to estimate the expense this conservatory required.

When she thought of the people living in squalor in Carthage, she grew angry that Valdemar Hoskanner would have indulged himself so. These plants did not belong here. It was an insult to the freedmen who had worked themselves almost to death to complete their sentences, and who were now unable to afford passage offplanet.

Already mired in debt, with unexpected expenses and regularly occurring disasters, House Linkam had to pare their operating costs to the absolute minimum. They must adapt to this desert land, not expect Duneworld to change to suit their own needs.

She would have to speak to Jesse in private about this. Better not to let anyone know the precious garden even existed. The conservatory would have to be shut down immediately, to stop the hemorrhage of water.

INSIDE THE MAIN spaceport terminal, parsecs from his home on Catalan, Jesse leaned against the parapet of the landing-control tower and thought about loneliness. The night's first moon rose above the mountain-jagged horizon. He watched it through the blast shutters, looking into the haze of dust that had drifted in from the desert wilderness to the south. The moon shone brightly, and the rolling dunes beyond the cliffs gleamed like parched icing.

Already Gurney and his crews had gone out to the old Imperial stations to strip away valuable live-rubber shielding. William English had teams installing the shielding in the old harvesters, restoring them to greater efficiency. Jesse still needed a lot more equipment, but at least the machines he had should function better after this.

And word had spread about his offer to pay for passage offplanet to any freedmen, provided House Linkam won the challenge. Many of the sandminers were giddy at the prospect, even the convict laborers who saw this as a sign of hope. Some skeptical men—secret Hoskanner sympathizers?—grumbled that it was a trick, that the devious nobleman would tell any lie to win his bet, but the majority believed him. They *wanted* to believe. . . .

Though he had hoped for solitude, he heard soft footsteps, a gentle movement like wind through a stand of trees . . . but there were no trees on Duneworld. He turned to find Dorothy looking at him with an expression of concern on her oval face. He had told no one he would be out at the main spaceport, but she always seemed to know where to find him.

"It's late, Jesse. Why don't you come to bed?" Her voice carried a quiet invitation, as it always did, but she would let him decide whether or not they would make love. Often, troubled by the uncertain pressures of this dangerous new venture, he would spend an hour simply holding her before drifting off to sleep.

"My work is not yet finished for the day." He stared through the slats of the blast door. The bright moon seemed to beckon him.

She moved silently, touched his arm. "The day's work will never be done, Jesse. Nor tomorrow's. Don't think of it as an individual task to complete. Each day here is a continuing struggle, a marathon race that we must win."

"But if we succeed, Dor, it won't stop even then."

The possibility of winning seemed like a twisted hallucination brought on by the consumption of too much melange. The Hoskanners had been eighteen years establishing their facilities and operations, with no time limit or contest to drive them. Jesse's choices were death, bankruptcy . . . or victory. He was in over his head, much like that hapless sandminer Tuek and Gurney had seen sucked into a sand whirlpool.

Dorothy slipped her arm around his waist. She had always been more than just his lover; she was a sounding board, a trusted advisor whose words and objectivity he could always rely upon. "Would you rather stay here and talk?"

Jesse could not put words to his thoughts; articulating them would only make his troubles more raw. Instead he changed the subject. "There's so much we need to know about this world. I'm going to mount an expedition to the forward research base in the deep desert, where the Imperial planetary ecologist has been working for years. Maybe I can learn something I need to know."

"How far away is it?"

His face remained shadowed in the observation tower. "Almost sixteen hundred kilometers south, close to the equator. It's a research station and test oasis. That's where most of the deep-desert crews work."

"So far away. It'll be dangerous."

Jesse sighed. "Since accepting the Emperor's challenge, everything I do carries an element of danger. All I can do is forge toward our goal."

"Spoken like a true nobleman," Dorothy said with a wistful smile.

"And . . . I'm taking Barri with me. I want him to see the operations. He needs to learn our family business, and it's never too early to start. We'll be gone for at least a week."

Now she stiffened and drew away. "Not the first time you go out there, Jesse! He's only eight."

"One day he'll rule House Linkam. I'm not going to pamper him. You do that too much already."

"Most noble sons his age aren't half as advanced as Barri is."

"You know how I feel about most of those noble sons." He snorted. "Because of the position we're in, Barri has to be ready at all times, for any situation. My father was poisoned, my brother died in a foolish bullfight, and I've roused the ire of the Hoskanners. What are the odds I'll make it to my next birthday?"

"All the more reason you shouldn't risk Barri! I've seen the mortality statistics of the workers. Those men would be safer in a penal colony. How can you take our boy into the middle of that?"

Jesse took a deep breath. When Dorothy set her mind on something, it was like trying to pry open the jaws of a gazehound from its quarry. "I do it because I am the head of House Linkam, and he is my son. He goes where I say he goes." The iron tone of his voice cut off further protests, though he could tell she still had a lot more to say.

"As you command, My Lord." She would stew about it, running the discussion over and over in her head. Unwilling to accept his decision, and refusing to concede, she would be like ice to him—probably for days. "Stay here in the tower as long as you like. I will not wait up for you."

After Dorothy left, Jesse felt the great loneliness again. He feared that the next few days before the expedition departed would be even less pleasant than the storms of the deepest desert.

❧

COOLLY BUT DUTIFULLY supportive, Dorothy went to the secondary spaceport to bid her son farewell. Though she did her best to conceal her feelings, she could tell that the other members in the party sensed the wall between herself and Jesse.

While the men boarded the transport ship for the forward research base, Jesse stood on the ramp with a hand on Barri's shoulder. The grinning boy was clearly excited to be going on a grand desert adventure with his father. His blue-green eyes were alight above the face mask, and a tight hood held down his unruly brown hair.

Dorothy gave Jesse a chaste kiss, then embraced their son, holding him a moment too long. "Be safe," she said. Stepping back from the ramp, she lowered the gaze of her myrtle-brown eyes. Though General

Tuek had already completed his inspection, she had quietly double-checked their preparations and provisions, satisfying herself that the team had reduced risks to the extent possible.

"We'll be as safe as Duneworld allows us to be," Jesse said with a faint conciliatory note in his voice. Then he and Barri entered the craft and sealed the hatch.

Dorothy did not stay to watch the vessel lift off and disappear toward the sand-smeared desert horizon.

# 8

*The spice is a lens through which one can see the entire universe.*

—A SAYING OF THE FREEDMEN

Followed by two water-supply ships, Jesse's transport approached the forward research base near Duneworld's equator.

"Is that it?" Barri asked for the fourth time, as he looked past the pilot, through a front window. He'd mistaken practically every outcropping of rock for their destination, but when the base finally came into view, its appearance was unmistakable.

"That's it," Jesse said, putting a hand on the boy's shoulder.

The cheddar-colored wedge structure thrust up from the sand, surrounded by a low fortress wall of natural rock. Mottled tan domes circled the main building, everything aerodynamically curved so that storms could skim over the tops without causing damage. V-shaped rows of plantings fronted the settlement area like the ripples from a ship's prow forging through a sandy ocean.

Because the research outpost pursued Imperial-sponsored projects, most of the water burden was covered by a stipend from the Grand Emperor's private budget; even so, Jesse knew what an exorbitant cost this oasis drained from the planetary treasury.

William English worked his way back along the line of seats to sit beside Jesse. Outside, the bronze-orange sun settled toward the horizon. "We're lucky we weren't an hour later, or we'd have a bumpy ride. The rapid temperature change at sunset plays havoc with the weather."

"Will we see a storm?" Barri asked.

"Not tonight, boy," English said with a smile, tapping his scarred cheek. "I'd be able to feel one coming. I learned my lesson the hard way—so I can teach *you* not to take foolish chances."

"I won't," Barri said, his eyes wide.

In the lead, the water-supply ships landed at two of the outlying tan domes. Moisture silos? Kicking up blown sand, the transport shuttle came down on a hardened landing area. Barri bounded up from his seat, anxious to see the research base, but a stern General Tuek told his passengers to wait. He and his men emerged, staying alert for traps. Jesse and his son did not come out until the security chief had given his okay.

A brown-haired man with a sunburned face stepped up to greet them. He extended a dry, rough hand. "You must be Nobleman Linkam? I am Dr. Haynes, the planetary ecologist." His curtained blue eyes twinkled, as if he was amused to meet the new master of Duneworld. Did he expect the Linkams to be any different from the Hoskanners?

Though technically this man was an Imperial employee and not required to follow the instructions of any nobleman, Jesse hoped to secure him as a willing ally. "I understand that you're an expert on this planet, Dr. Haynes—more than any other person alive. We are eager to learn what you know."

"If *I* understand more than any man about Duneworld, then it is a poorly known planet indeed." He turned to Barri. "Is this your son?"

"He is the next Linkam nobleman in waiting."

"Some would say this world is not a fit place for children." The planetary ecologist frowned. "But those same people would claim that grown men don't belong here, either." He stepped aside to let the rest of the men exit the transport shuttle, and offered a familiar greeting to William English. The two men had obviously dealt with each other before.

Haynes led the visitors toward the main base building. "We will go out again after dark," he suggested. "On this planet, night is the most instructive time." The doors sealed behind them to keep precious wisps of humidity from leaking into the arid air. . . .

Hours later, guided by a small handlight, Jesse and Barri followed Dr. Haynes out into the rows of plantings. The softly cutting soprano smell of sage climbed a desert night lush with stars, and there came a stillness so unaltered that the moonlight itself could almost be heard flowing across sentinel saguaro and spiked paintbrush. Though Jesse still felt overwhelmed by his impossible task, he felt a special peace here, a barely defined reason why one might want to come to this world.

"All these plants have been imported, genetically modified to survive. As near as we can tell, no chlorophyll-based vegetation is native to the planet." Haynes walked among the rabbitbrush, trailing his fingers. A few night moths flitted in search of flowers. "With so little native moisture, even our most drought-resistant flora perishes without help."

"But why do this, then?" Jesse asked. "The only reason anyone would come here is for spice. Duneworld will never be a colony for anything else."

"I prefer to paint on a large canvas." Haynes stared wistfully into the night. "I believe it's possible to establish a permanent ecological cycle with humans in it as well as these hardy plants."

"No chlorophyll plants means nothing green," Barri said, proving he'd been paying attention. Jesse was proud of his son, impressed with the education Dorothy had provided him. He was even correctly pronouncing difficult words.

"Very perceptive, young Master," the planetary ecologist said.

"Is there other native vegetation then?" Jesse furrowed his brow. "Ah, there must be—otherwise there wouldn't be any air."

"Duneworld might look barren, but there's a rudimentary ecosystem within the sand itself: a form of plankton—we believe that's what the sandworms feed on—along with fleshy organisms we call sandtrout, which are like fish that burrow through the sands. Surveys have found native lichens surviving near the poles, as well as a type of moss and some wiry scrub. An additional source of atmospheric oxygen could be outgassing from volcanic vents. I believe there may be a large subterranean network beneath the sand."

"Underground? Can you use probes to map it out?"

Haynes shook his head. "Whenever we try to make a map, all we get is a jumble. The sand itself has magnetic ferrous granules, and the constant storms generate too much static electricity. Even the worms produce their own fields."

"Is it possible to mine under the dunes? How about drilling or using blowers?"

"Trust me, Nobleman, we have tried all these ideas. Subsurface shiftings always break the drills and pipes, and the shafts collapse. A standard stasis generator won't work, since static from the blowing sand burns out the equipment. And whenever we ground the generators, the pulse attracts and infuriates the worms. In twenty years, we've lost more than a hundred people in efforts to develop spice-harvesting technology. Grabbing and running is the only technique that has worked at all, and that's not terribly efficient."

Jesse gave him a confident smile. "Then perhaps, Dr. Haynes, I'll count on you to find something different that we *can* do."

The planetary ecologist led them along the rows of plantings. From the side of a dune, a vent gurgled and hissed, painted with a splash of yellow and orange.

"It stinks," Barri said.

"You know what that smell is," Jesse prodded the boy.

"Sulfur."

Haynes put his hand into the wisps of gas whistling from the fumarole. When he withdrew, his fingers were covered with yellowish powder. "Completely dry. No water content." He looked over at Jesse. "Out in the open, you'll see occasional eruptions, huge pillars of dust blasted into the sky like geysers. That strongly suggests an active world underneath the shifting dunes, trapped bubbles of superheated gas percolating explosively to the surface."

"Is that where spice comes from? Deep underground?" Barri asked.

Haynes shrugged. "Maybe. The melange from a fresh blow is particularly potent and easy to harvest. Unfortunately, the worms are also attracted by these eruptions, so our crews don't have much time."

"Infuriating guard dogs," Jesse said. "I wish we could get rid of them."

"None of our attempts have been successful. I wouldn't be surprised if it required an atomic blast to kill a great sandworm."

"We have atomics!" Barri piped up. "And all our ships run on reactor piles. General Tuek told me they can be converted if we get into a military engagement."

"We are not in a military engagement, Barri," Jesse pointed out.

"That is closer to the truth than you might think," Haynes said. "We make hit-and-run spice raids on a worm's territory, lightning attacks and rapid retreats."

He led his visitors past a stand of saguaros that stood in the shadows like the silhouettes of ghoulish men. When they reached the edge of the oasis, Haynes stopped them. "Stand there and face the desert. Open your mind and your senses—and just *listen.*"

As the three stood in silence, Jesse heard a long, slow exhalation, as from a living creature.

"Sandtides," Haynes said, "the dunes wafting slowly in one direction and another, tugged by the two moons. This peristaltic action makes the free-rolling sand move a thousand to fifteen hundred feet a year." Kneeling, he dug his fingers into the grains and closed his eyes. "The desert moves and breathes beneath you."

Barri hunkered down on the still-warm sand. "I miss the rain."

"Rain . . ." the planetary ecologist mused.

Jesse gave his son's shoulder a reassuring squeeze. He could not promise that either of them would ever see rain again.

# 9

*No other planet in the Empire warrants closer examination than this supposedly barren world. When peeled back, each layer reveals another just beneath it, teeming with energy.*

—DR. BRYCE HAYNES,
planetary ecologist assigned to study Duneworld

After the morning thermals had stabilized enough for ornijets to fly over the desert, Jesse, Barri, and Dr. Haynes went out to observe spice operations. Foreman English was already out on the sands, deploying a huge harvester in a new vein of melange that had been uncovered by shifting dunes during the night.

Dr. Haynes flew the small ornijet with ease. When another pilot transmitted a warning about a thermal sink, a patch of cold sand that created a pillar of dangerous turbulence, the ecologist adjusted course to avoid the anomaly. "Cold sands indicate ice caves deep beneath the surface," he said to Jesse. "The temperature gradient creates a hazard."

"Underground ice caves? How many more surprises does Duneworld hold?"

"More than anyone could tally, I'm afraid."

A plume of smoke and dust marked the ground operations. Jesse and Barri watched the giant mobile harvester lumber onto the dunes, gouging up great quantities of sand mixed with rust-colored spice. Scouts soared in widespread patrols to watch for any encroaching worms.

From the ground, English demanded a satellite weather report. "I don't like the looks of that line of dust on the eastern horizon."

Though the sky looked perfectly blue to Jesse, with only a bit of haze, he did not question the man's intuition. Maybe his scar was tingling.

"Weather satellites are clear. Nothing brewing."

"Check again."

A pause, then: "Still nothing on the sats, Mr. English."

"I'll get back to you."

When the diligent patrols did spot an approaching worm, the well-practiced workers rushed back to their vehicles and evacuated with an efficient system of managed chaos. The powerful carryall lifted the support equipment, spice harvester, and ground machinery just as the oncoming subterranean ripples reached the work site. Barri moved from window to window in the ornijet, hoping for a glimpse of the desert monster, but the worm never surfaced. Jesse saw it churn beneath the ground and then tunnel away.

Safe for the moment, the breathless crews reported how much spice they had excavated. It was a good haul. Jesse processed the numbers in his head: If only the crews could keep up that rate every second of every day for the next two years—without any mishaps—House Linkam might have a chance of beating the Hoskanners.

A moment later, William English's voice broke across the comm system. "We have a severe problem with the weather satellites!"

In the excitement of evacuating the harvester, Jesse had forgotten about the foreman's concern. "Nobleman Linkam here. What is it, English?"

"I just tapped our scout flyers, then took a run to the east myself. Twelve different sightings confirm it, sir—there's a Coriolis storm brewing in the vicinity, an anvil-shaped cloud covering the whole sky. I can't predict a detailed path by eyeballing it, but I'd say it's coming straight toward the base."

Jesse looked to the planetary ecologist for an explanation. Haynes picked up the transmitter. "If it's that big, William, how could the satellites not have seen it?"

"That's just it—they *couldn't* have missed it. But there's no mistake, and that storm is coming." A dark undertone of anger like a bloodstain seeped into his voice. "If we'd relied entirely on those satellites for a warning, we would've continued our operations until it was too late."

The answer flashed into Jesse's mind as clear as weapons fire on a silent night: *Hoskanner sabotage.* "Recall our crews and scouts to the forward base where we'll ride out the storm. Then somebody is going to get me answers. We need those satellites."

⤛⤜

INSIDE THE SHIELDED buildings, Jesse held a war council with Tuek, Haynes, and English. They sat at a long worktable, talking above the noise of furious winds outside.

Barri peered through an armored windowslit, trying to see past the murk. Like the men, he wore a sealable bodysuit with his face mask flapping loose. "Are we safe? Can the winds cut their way in here?"

"This shelter is protected enough, young Master," Dr. Haynes said. "Outside, though, that storm-driven sand can flay a man to his bones, and then etch the bones."

Getting down to business, Tuek spread documents on the table. "As near as I can determine, all the weather satellites were programmed to replace any readings of major weather disturbances with deceptively clear reports. Another goodbye gift from the Hoskanners."

Dr. Haynes looked at English with respect. "If you hadn't sensed the storm, William, we would've been wiped out." The scarred spice fore-man sat stiffly, as if trying to suppress his continuing uneasiness.

"It's still a disaster," Tuek said. "When we tried to delete the cor-rupted programming, we activated another trap, which shorted out the satellites. We're completely blind in the skies now." The veteran looked gray with disappointment. "I was searching for an outright as-sassination attempt, but this is much more insidious. Sweet affection, if only I'd foreseen it!"

Jesse simmered as he listened. "What'll it take to repair the satel-lites?"

English said, "The damage is too extensive. We need to replace them."

Jesse put his elbows on the table. "Options?"

English groaned. "Stop spice mining until we get new satellites."

"Unacceptable. That might take months."

Tuek suggested, "We could triple our scout flights to monitor the weather, do our best to predict dangers. But increased flights mean in-creased hazards as well. We'd lose flyers and pilots for sure."

Jesse looked around the table, hoping for more alternatives. "Else?"

English spread his hands flat. "How lucky do you feel, Nobleman? We could just continue spice mining and take our chances."

The planetary ecologist pursed his lips. "I may be able to modify a research satellite or two, enough to give us some weather data."

Everyone fell silent and looked at Jesse. "All right. Dr. Haynes, find out how much weather coverage we can put together. Minimize risks to our ships and crews—but we need to keep producing spice, no matter the setbacks." The sandstorm outside skimmed the dome roughly, like the abrasive caresses of Valdemar Hoskanner himself. Jesse looked at his security chief, lowered his voice. "Esmar, I don't know how we're going to pay for new satellites."

"Consult with your concubine, My Lord. But in my opinion, we do what we need to do. We have no choice."

"I'll tell Dorothy to increase our debt, as necessary, sell any holdings we have left on Catalan. But I want the network installed as soon as possible. Find out who can do it the fastest."

Jesse's instincts told him the Hoskanners were likely planning further grand gestures. The unexpected storm and the satellite sabotage emphasized the danger of even everyday activities on Duneworld. Right now, he felt an overwhelming need to be back with Dorothy, to talk with her, hold her. . . .

"As soon as this storm passes, I'm going back to Carthage. English, I'd like you to come with me so we can review our spice operations, combine resources, and make the most of what we have."

"It is not wise to rush a Coriolis storm, Nobleman," Dr. Haynes said. "They are unpredictable and dangerous."

Consumed with anger at Valdemar Hoskanner, Jesse felt his muscles tense like steel cables. "I can be unpredictable and dangerous, too."

BECAUSE ONLY THREE of them were returning to Carthage, they took one of the research base's ornijets instead of the larger transport shuttle. The dust-laden air was still fraught with capricious breezes, but the bulk of the storm had swung south.

English flew them north toward Carthage, more than fifteen hundred kilometers away. Below, the diamond-shaped oasis was already beginning to recover from the blowing sand, and within minutes all distinctive features were replaced by the monotony of nothingness. Ahead, a jagged line of black mountains jutted up like an atoll in the ocean of sand. From the cliff-walled pan he could see hundreds of blind canyons, cut not by water but by seismic action, ancient lava flows, and fierce desert winds. Over the next hour, even the intermittent backbones of rock developed a sameness to them.

The nobleman's thoughts drifted, and he mulled over possible solutions. Barri leaned his head on his father's shoulder and dozed.

As they cruised toward one barrier of mountains, English jerked the ornijet controls. "More storm readings ahead, sir." He glanced over his shoulder. "By the deity, it's a backstabber! The storm circled around!"

"Are we safe in the ornijet?"

"We should be able to fly over it."

Jesse saw a low-rolling tsunami of sand and powder crawling up and over the peaks like a slow-moving wave of milk. English kept working the controls, but his movements took on a more intense quality.

"Why aren't we going higher?" Jesse asked.

The wall of sand and dust grew larger, spreading to fill their field of view. The ornijet's wings flapped furiously, trying to gain altitude.

"The wings can only take us so high. I'm trying to kick in the jets to leapfrog us over the storm." English punched the controls again. "But the blasted craft isn't shifting modes—and without jets we can't make it!"

"Can we outrun the storm?"

"Not a chance. I may be able to bypass the switchover and tap into the jets directly. It might cause burnout in a hundred kilometers, but we might get away from the storm, where someone can rescue us." His face showed a relieved smile. "Ah, there's the bypass."

A small muffled explosion reverberated in their engines, a shot bomb detonating in the ornijet's rear components. "More sabotage!"

"Signal for help!"

The spice foreman fought with the controls to keep the aircraft from corkscrewing into the sand. "The bomb took out the comm, too. Must have been rigged that way."

"Just get us down, English." Wide awake now, Barri looked around in fear. Jesse grasped his son's arm, sealed the boy's bodysuit and his own, then put on their face masks.

The ornijet lost altitude, spiraling toward the dunes. Scanning ahead for shelter, English chose a small island of rocks, little more than a scramble of boulders poking up out of the dunes. Out of control, the craft thumped to the sand and spun around.

Before English could even shut off the engines, a towering wave of blown sand broke over them, utterly engulfing the ornijet and its occupants.

# 10

*Adaptation is an art form, and it is the single-most important aspect of being human.*

—EXCERPT FROM *THE SANDMINER'S MANUAL*

After the storm had washed past, leaving behind an endless ocean of pristine dunes, a slight movement stirred a pocket of sand. An indentation formed, then sank, and a small hand reached out while sand continued to stream into the buried ornijet's trapdoor opening.

Coughing, young Barri scrambled into the air as his father pushed him up and out of the uncovered hatch. Inside the dim cockpit, Jesse choked on a mouthful of dust. He quickly sealed his face mask in place. "We were lucky to survive the storm."

William English, his tattooed forehead bloody from a gash, stepped back until the sandfall dwindled to nothing. "A very small measure of luck, Nobleman." He looked up from the open control panel. "Our emergency locator beacon has been intentionally ruined. No one will be able to find us."

Jesse crouched inside the cramped cockpit, his voice muffled by the mask. "The Hoskanners are thorough. They know the value of redundancy." He looked intensely at the spice foreman, lowering his voice. "But I'm not willing to give up yet. The three of us are still alive. We'll just have to get out of this by ourselves."

Outside the crashed ornijet, Barri lifted his mask and shouted down to them, "I don't see anything up here—just a huge sandbox of dunes and dunes and dunes!" He brushed dust from his freckled nose. "At least the storm's gone."

"We'll be up there in a minute. Be careful where you wander! The sand can be dangerous."

English dug out a small first-aid kit and applied clotting salve and a gauze patch to his forehead. "Bear in mind, Nobleman, that surviving on Duneworld is a challenge even with the best equipment and technology. It's not a stroll through one of your rain forests on Catalan."

Jesse nodded. "We do have control over one thing, English: We can react to our situation with hope, or with despair. I prefer the former."

He climbed out of the buried ornijet to stand on a nearly pristine dune slope, with the exception of Barri's small footprints that trailed up to a high point on a newly sculpted hill, from which he had surveyed the landscape. Jesse felt very proud of his son. Other children, even many adults, might have panicked, but Barri seemed to have complete faith that they would get out of this trap.

"I hope you're geared up for a tough time, Barri. I need your strength."

"We'll be rescued, Father. General Tuek will know where to find us. He'll send out men."

The completely buried ornijet would be invisible to aerial searchers. Jesse considered spending a day or two digging it out, as a marker for rescuers to see. But that would take a lot of valuable energy, and the loose, settling sand and restless winds would probably erase each day's efforts.

English tossed a pack up onto the sand and climbed out of the buried ship to stand with the other two. The spice foreman squinted in the sunlight, then connected his face mask. "I know approximately where we are, at least a hundred kilometers from one of the old Imperial survey outposts."

"One of the stations Gurney just raided for live-rubber shielding?"

"Yes, and Dr. Haynes still uses them from time to time. Even if Halleck stripped the nearest station, there's still a solar generator I can use to send a signal. But it's going to be a long journey, even if the weather holds."

Jesse pressed his lips together. "You think that's our best chance?"

"The only one I can think of—other than waiting here and doing nothing." English shrugged. "I believe it's the best option."

"Then that's the one we'll choose. How soon can we set off?"

"Not until we're prepared." The spice foreman removed two handheld devices from his pack. "There's a paracompass in the survival kit, and I pried another from the ornijet's controls. We'll each take one. I've locked in the coordinates for the nearest survey outpost."

"So all we have to do is walk," Barri said. "A long ways."

English gave the boy a weary smile. "It'll be a trek like none of us has ever made before, young Master."

"I'm not afraid." Barri lifted his chin. "If that's what we've got to do, then I'm ready."

Jesse felt another swell of pride for the boy. "Barri's right. We'll do what we have to—even if it's impossible."

∽

ENGLISH INSISTED ON performing a second and third check of the crashed ornijet to make sure they scavenged every item of any possible use. Jesse left a scrawled note inside the buried cockpit with the coordinates they were trying to reach, just in case a search party found the wreck.

They had sufficient food to keep their metabolisms running—energy rations and packets of concentrated spice—but both Jesse and English knew that their water supplies wouldn't last for the number of days required to reach the outpost, even moving at their best pace in sealed bodysuits.

Before emerging from the cockpit for the last time, Barri peeled off several pieces of a reflective metal sheet. "Look, signal mirrors if somebody flies over us. They've got to see us, out here in the open desert."

"Excellent thinking, boy," English said.

It was late afternoon when the three began their long walk. Each step was plodding and difficult, and they sank in up to their ankles. Loose sand held them back, caressing their legs and encouraging them to stay, to stop walking, to sit down and welcome hot, desiccating death. . . .

"Will we see worms out here?" Barri seemed interested, but not fearful.

"Oh, they're out here, young Master. The mining vibrations of our spice harvesters attract them, but we're too small to get their attention, like pebbles tossed across the dunes."

"Even so," Jesse said, "keep your eyes peeled for rippling sand."

It was a balancing act to maintain a fast enough pace to cover distance before their supplies ran out without exhausting themselves to the point of collapse. Although they were weary by the time night fell, they rested only briefly before continuing their long journey in the cool darkness, when they would perspire less.

⤜⥈⥤

IN CARTHAGE, THE headquarters mansion was in turmoil. Static discharge from the dust had played havoc with comm systems across the planet, but General Tuek had transmitted a message as soon as the storm cleared. He'd been forced to shout his dire news twice before Dorothy could understand him.

"The search parties have found no sign of them?" She tried to be as strong and stony as one of the blocky statues the Hoskanners had left behind. "Has their whole flight path been checked?"

Static noises. A garbled response. She repeated herself, and Tuek answered, "Every flightworthy vehicle is combing the desert, but the Coriolis winds wiped out all signs."

Anger and accusations edged her voice. "How could you let them fly into a storm, General? You are responsible for the nobleman's safety!" *Even when he does foolish things . . . like his father and his brother.* Despair threatened to overwhelm her, like an inundation of sand burying her for eternity. *My son, my son!*

Tuek looked miserable himself, but frowned at her condemnation. "Madam, one doesn't prevent Nobleman Linkam from doing anything once he has a mind to do it. Sweet affection, if I had known, I'd have used a stunner myself and tied him up in one of the spice silos until he came to his senses."

"How about the observation satellites? Don't we have any with high enough resolution to scan for the ornijet's locator beacon?"

"Dr. Haynes has been working nonstop, but he's managed to get only four of the satellites working *at all,* and they're not worth much! We should already have picked up the beacon—unless it's not functioning."

"Can you scan for the hull metal? Debris?"

"Not with all the distorted fields." Tuek drew a deep breath, sounding impatient; apparently, he had already considered every suggestion she'd made. He acted as if she was stepping on his toes. Back on Catalan, he and Dorothy had both been powerful, often at odds but with clearly segregated duties. On Duneworld, though, business and defense overlapped heavily. "But we'll find him. I'm flying out on a scout patrol myself."

"Do you need extra men?"

"No, there aren't enough vehicles. I've shut down spice operations to devote all crews to the search. Please don't tell me how to do my job."

Dorothy bit her lip. Jesse would hate any slowdown in production, and so would the sandminers, who desperately wanted to earn their freedom. If only he had listened to her about the dangers of going to the forward base—and taking Barri with him.

The static was growing worse. "Just . . . send me regular reports!"

After signing off, she went to find Gurney Halleck. The jongleur would round up his own teams, commandeer any functional flyer, and send men to scour the desert. If stern old Tuek couldn't rescue her family, maybe Gurney could.

# 11

I have seen many worlds in the Known Universe: some beautiful, some bland, some so alien they defy description or understanding. Duneworld is the most enigmatic of the enigmatic.

—GURNEY HALLECK,
notes for an uncompleted ballad

Trudging across the cool, dark sands, the three figures followed the spine of a tall, snaking dune. Their moonlit footprints looked like the track of a centipede winding into the shadows. Barri took the lead, showing an energy and determination that went beyond the usual enthusiasm of an eight-year-old. Jesse drew strength from his son's tireless optimism.

Without warning, the boy stumbled into a pocket of loose powder, and his legs slid out from under him. He flailed for balance, but could find nothing solid to hold. Barri cried out, slipping down the steep slope of the dune. Dislodged sand washed like loose snow down into the basin. A few buried stones, some as large as a man's head, spat out of the dune's side, bouncing, tumbling.

Jesse ran toward him. "Barri!"

The young man had the presence of mind to jam his legs deep into the sand and thrust his arms into the flowing grains, and eventually stopped himself by digging in. Covered with sand, his face mask knocked loose, Barri looked up, coughing and choking, but managed to reassure his father. He actually grinned. "I'm all right!"

Sliding sand and stones continued to flow past him to the base of the dune, where the bouncing stones hit a hard white patch that broke apart and resonated. Compacted grains struck each other and triggered an acoustic shockwave like the heartbeat of a violently awakened giant. The thumping pulse boomed into the night.

Barri tried to scramble up the dune slope, feeling a mixture of fear and fascination. The pounding built upon itself, a thrumming vibration that rose to a crescendo.

"Drumsand!" English exclaimed. "Grains of a certain size and shape, acoustically packed . . . unstable equilibrium." The spice foreman was pale. "It's loud enough to draw a worm! Climb, lad; *climb!*"

Jesse scrambled to meet his son halfway, grabbed Barri by the arm, and pulled him up. "We have to get away from here."

Already gasping and exhausted, Barri could hardly stay on his feet. When they reached the dune crest, English gestured frantically. He bounded along, his feet stirring the sand. When the liquid dune slope began to drop them to a gully, the freedman cut sideways and skidded down the sands. "We have to get far from that drumsand!"

They slid into the gully, then slowed as they cut an ascending zigzag up to the peak of another dune ridge away from where Barri had first stumbled. From far behind, they heard a familiar hissing, stirring sound . . . the passage of something huge and serpentine.

"Stop!" English said in a harsh whisper. "Don't move. Don't make a sound."

The three froze and stared across the moon-silvered sands. They saw turmoil in the drumsand valley as a blunt head emerged like a sea serpent from the sandy depths. Sand grains showered from its massive body like diamond specks. When the worm plunged again, the reservoir of drumsand vibrated and thumped with a last few dying echoes until the creature destroyed the delicately balanced acoustic compaction.

English sank into a weary squat atop the dune ridge. Jesse and Barri sat beside him, holding their breath. The slower hissing sound of disturbed sand reminded Jesse of the whisper of waves on the far-away Catalan seas.

Finally, they got up and set off into the night again.

꧁꧂

TWO DAYS LATER in the heat of afternoon, the bedraggled trio stopped in the shadow of a rock outcropping. Concentrated spice had kept them alive and moving, but their carefully rationed water was now almost gone. Jesse and English both knew they would consume the last drops within another day. And according to the paracompasses, they were barely more than halfway to the automated outpost.

Leaning against the rocks, they kept their uncomfortable face masks in place to minimize moisture loss. While the spice foreman dozed, conserving energy, Jesse watched Barri, who was holding up like a champion. The boy never slackened his pace, did not moan or complain. Despite Dorothy's indulgent manner, Barri did not show signs of excessive coddling; he just needed to be given a chance to prove himself.

If his descendants were like this young man, Jesse held out hope for the future of House Linkam. With common sense and a strong foundation of moral integrity, Barri would grow up to be far superior to most of the Empire's spoiled and corrupt noble heirs. But only if the boy survived the next few days. . . .

Snooping among the rocks, Barri discovered a patch of gray-green lichen. He called his father over. "Something's alive here."

As Jesse approached, tiny furtive shapes began moving in the crevices. "They're . . . rodents!"

Barri reached in and found a nest, but could not catch the bouncing little forms. From a higher cranny, a little kangaroo rat poked out its narrow head, squeaking accusations and scolding the human intruders.

"How did they get out here? Do you think some of Dr. Haynes's specimens got loose?"

Jesse could think of no other explanation. "Maybe Dr. Haynes intentionally set them free. He said he wanted to establish an ecosystem on Duneworld."

Shoulder to shoulder, he and Barri watched the tiny kangaroo rats scurry about their business. Jesse took heart. "If they can survive here, Barri, so can we."

# 12

*Life is full of frayed ends. It is a terrible thing when you show anger to a loved one, never knowing that it might be the last time you are together.*

—DOROTHY MAPES,
*A Concubine's Life*

Jesse and Barri had been gone for too long. Much too long. Few things could have survived out in that desert for so many days.

With aching loneliness in her heart, Dorothy wondered if she would ever see her loved ones again. Though she was a sharp business manager and the financial watchdog of the Linkam holdings, she was also a mother, and a wife in everything but the title. Her stomach had wrenched itself into a tight knot.

As each unsuccessful patrol returned, she lost a fine thread of hope, a little bit of the precious connections she'd had with Jesse and Barri. The friction of her last night with the nobleman had left her full of regrets, guilt, and uncertainty. Should she have demanded that he bow to her wishes? Then Jesse and Barri might not be lost out in the infinite desert. Or should she have been more supportive, even if she disagreed with him?

If he ever came home, she knew Jesse would pretend that nothing had happened between them; but he wouldn't forget, and neither would she. The disagreement would hang like a curtain between them.

Intellectually, she understood why Jesse had wanted their son to understand hardship, to know how ordinary people lived and worked, to be tempered by real experience and difficult decisions instead of softened by pillows and pampering. But how could a mother not try to make her son as safe as possible? Barri had not yet reached his ninth birthday . . . and now he was lost out in the arid wasteland, probably dead.

When the boy had departed on the transport shuttle with his father, he had looked so dignified, so proud and manlike. She had never seen him look like that before.

God, how she hated this place!

Dorothy paced down the halls, trying to keep busy, looking for something to occupy her thoughts. If Jesse was gone, should she formally withdraw from the challenge on his behalf? He had designated her his legal proxy in business matters. Without Jesse, and Barri, there *was* no House Linkam, and the Nobles' Council would no doubt dissolve it, distribute the Linkam holdings, and absorb the administration into another family. She would go back to Catalan as a commoner again, alone except for her memories.

Ahead, she saw Cullington Yueh slowly climbing the main stairway, holding the stone railing. The gray-haired old gentleman reached the top short of breath. "Oh, Dorothy! I've been looking for you."

"Any word?" Her voice cracked with concern, though she tried to cover it with a dry cough. "Gurney should have been back hours ago."

"Not yet, but General Tuek says communications are fully restored, back online after the storm. He's quite interested in getting the spice operations going again. Some of the ships have been improved with live-rubber shielding, and they can fly farther and with less risk of malfunction. Oh, and Dr. Haynes has restored a few more satellites. Still, you know how problems can arise."

"Especially here. I hate those Hoskanners for leaving us with junk."

"No sign of the new spice harvesters or carryalls that you ordered from Ix, either." Yueh rubbed his gray mustache. "Aren't they overdue?"

"Yes, the first order is a week late." It struck her as odd that the kindly old family physician was interested in spice-harvesting equipment, but she appreciated his concern while Jesse was gone. *Gone.* Such a final sound to the word. Her heart sank, but she forced her thoughts into line. Jesse was counting on her to make sure House Linkam did not fall apart. "Something about production delays."

Gurney had attempted to follow up with an Ixian representative, but hadn't gotten a straight answer, and for the past several days all resources had been devoted to the search for the missing ornijet. She frowned. "You think the Hoskanners might have something to do with that?"

"Accidents happen," Yueh said. "And some accidents happen on purpose."

Sensing her misery, the old man massaged her shoulders and neck with his surgeon's fingers, working pressure points, but she could feel his hands shaking. "This used to make my wife Wanna relax."

"Your wife? I didn't know you were married, Cullington!"

"Oh, it was a long time ago. She died . . . something I couldn't cure. That's why I try my best to heal everyone else." He gave a bleak smile.

Yueh was a self-described "splint and pill man," earning his early medical experience on Grumman's World, a distant planet replete with odd swamp maladies and native fruits that oozed contact poisons. He had joined House Linkam years ago as their dedicated physician, claiming he wanted a peaceful, out-of-the way place like Catalan. Here on Duneworld, though, he seemed out of his depth.

Dorothy eased his hands away. "Thank you, Cullington. I feel much better."

His hazel eyes were filled with concern. "No, you're still worried. But I appreciate your saying so anyway." Then he ambled off on one of his many errands. Rarely did she see the doctor take a break.

Dorothy headed for the south wing. Encountering one of the maids, she requested a pot of strong spice tea and a large cup on a tray. Then, carrying the tray herself, Dorothy took a spiral staircase up to the fourth level. The melange would soothe her . . . and so would the conservatory.

She pressed the hollow stone on the dead-end wall. When the hidden door slid open with a hiss, she stepped inside and was assailed by the heavy odor of dead and decaying plants. Not a soothing place after all.

The secret conservatory had suffered for weeks, since she had shut off the irrigation system and diverted the water to vital uses. The speckled fungi had already collapsed into mush, while the once-verdant ferns had turned a sickly, yellowish brown. Formerly bright and colorful flowers were dried up now, with discolored petals scattered on the caked soil. Only a few plants still clung to life, though they had no hope of surviving.

Scuttling insects darted in and out among the dead plants, feeding off the remains. The decay had turned into a feast for the tiny scavengers, and they'd been reproducing madly. But that niche of life, like the rest of the enclosed ecosystem, would also end soon.

These plants were victims of an untenable situation, trapped in a place where they did not belong. *Like House Linkam*, she thought, *barely surviving on this barren world, hoping our lives will be returned to us.*

Feeling gloom wash through her, Dorothy placed the tray on a plaz table and brushed dirt and dead insects off a chair before sitting down. She poured the rich, aromatic tea into her cup, and steam escaped into the air. *Lost moisture.* As she lifted the cup to her lips, a rush of cinnamon tickled her nostrils.

Only she and Jesse knew this place existed, and only the two of them knew that the plants would soon all be dead. She could be completely alone here, undisturbed with her thoughts, though she doubted she would find any solutions. Dorothy finished the spice tea, and as melange seeped into her body, her mind's eye projected vivid images of watery, dreamlike Catalan. If only she and her family could be back there again. . . .

But mere wishes could not transport them home, could not erase the unfortunate events that had brought them here. Where were Jesse and Barri now? What if William English himself had remained secretly loyal to the Hoskanners? Had he dumped their lifeless bodies in the desert to shrivel like the plants around her?

Tears streamed down her cheeks. On this world, they called it "giving water to the dead."

# 13

In the desert, hope is as scarce as water. Both are a mirage.

—SANDMINER'S LAMENT

Even after the water ran out, they kept moving. They had to. English took the lead, frequently checking his paracompass, while Jesse and Barri plodded after him. There could be no turning back now. It was a hot afternoon, with the unrelenting sun in the western sky.

They approached a low-hanging, discolored haze, and Jesse realized they had stumbled upon a patch of fumaroles. Though they had little hope of finding water there, they traveled toward the hissing steam vents. If nothing else, the chemical steam would obscure some of the painful sunlight.

When the wind picked up, English looked around in concern. He touched the waxy scar on his cheek and met Jesse's gaze. "Weather's changing. I feel it."

"How soon until the storm gets here?" Jesse asked. Barri searched the horizon for the wall of dust heading their way.

"No telling," English answered. "They're capricious things. Could come right at us, no matter where we hide—or the weather front might turn aside and go somewhere else entirely."

Taking shelter in partial shade among the sulfur-painted rocks near the roar of a fumarole, they sat down to rest. Jesse opened the pack and withdrew his paracompass. "I need to know how far we have left to go." To his dismay, when he studied the coordinates, their destination seemed farther away than ever. The directional needle pointed at an extreme angle from where they'd been heading. "William, check your compass."

The spice foreman held his device next to Jesse's. After comparing, both men were astonished to see that the readings were entirely different. When English pushed the reset button, his needle spun until it landed at a new spot. Jesse did the same, and now the direction on his instrument pointed back the way they had come. The men looked at each other.

"More sabotage?" Jesse asked.

"No, I think it's magnetite in the dunes," English said, his voice thick with discouragement. "Static energy from the storm front or maybe from a sandworm. It scrambled the compasses."

Jesse reset his device again, and now the needle spun in wild circles.

English slumped in hopeless surrender. "We weren't going in the right direction! We have no way of knowing where the outpost is, and now we can't even find our way back to the ornijet. Our footprints would have been erased days ago."

Jesse was not willing to show fear in front of his son. They had been wandering in the desert, possibly going in circles. In the open expanse he could not begin to guess where anything might be—the Imperial outpost, the city of Carthage, the buried ornijet, or the forward base. They were utterly lost, and they had run out of water.

Reaching an edge of desperation, English staggered to the discolored sands near a fumarole. He stood there poised for a long moment, staring down as if in a daze. Jesse wondered if the man intended to plunge headfirst into the exhaling vapors.

"How can anything survive out here?" English finally said. "Every living thing needs water. Maybe we should have drunk the blood of those kangaroo mice."

"I tried to catch them," Barri said, his voice dry and raspy.

English bent closer to the crusty sands near the fumarole, as fiercely intent as a hunter. His voice dropped to a whisper. "But immense creatures live in the sands. There has to be water." The bedraggled spice foreman slowly extended his hands, toward shapes that writhed and squirmed in the warm sands around the steam vent.

He lunged, digging his hands through the powdery crust. Like a dog, he furiously scooped sand aside, burrowing, clawing, until he finally seized something. He struggled, cried out in triumph, and lurched backward, uprooting a shapeless blob that looked like a gigantic cell as long as his forearm. English tossed the thing onto the hard-packed sand, then dropped to his knees and flipped it over, trying to hold it down as it continued to flop.

Barri hurried forward, full of boyish curiosity, despite their ordeal. "What's that?"

"Sandtrout. Dr. Haynes told me they're often found near fumaroles." English looked up at them with reddish eyes. "All I care about is that it's alive, and there's some sort of liquid inside—blood, sap, protoplasm. Who knows?" He pressed his fingers into the pliable skin of the squirming thing, then drew a utility knife from his pack.

"Can we survive on it?" Jesse asked.

The spice foreman pulled his face mask aside and shrugged. "I've never heard of anyone eating a sandtrout. As far as I know, nobody's had to."

"What if it's poison?" Barri asked.

"Seems to me, young Master, that we're as good as dead anyway if we don't get some water soon." He tried to swallow, but could find no moisture in his dry throat. "I'm going to take a chance. One of us has to."

Jesse lowered his voice. "Thank you for not giving up, William."

With his fingers, English jabbed the sandtrout's leathery membrane, then broke through with the tip of the knife. Thick liquid oozed out like viscous saliva, and a potent aroma wafted up, a tang of harsh alkaline mixed with cinnamon so strong that it stung their eyes. "It smells like spice beer." English dipped his finger and touched it to his tongue. "Tastes like spice, too . . . extremely potent stuff. But different." Surrendering caution, desperately thirsty, he lowered his mouth to the still-squirming sandtrout. With his eyes closed, he took a long slurp of the slimy fluid.

Jesse had wanted English to take just a small taste, to wait and see if there might be adverse effects . . . but considering their complete lack of supplies, his warning would have meant nothing.

Barri moved forward, looking thirstily at the sandtrout and the slick fluid oozing from it.

Suddenly English sat ramrod straight and dropped the protoplasmic creature to the packed ground. "It burns! But it sparkles like a thousand tiny explosions in my mouth." He touched his sternum. "In my chest, moving its way down!" He drew a long, gasping breath and stretched his arms out to both sides, straining as if he meant to pull his own fingers out of their sockets.

"I can feel it all the way to my fingertips! Like land mines exploding energy to every one of my cells." He lunged to his feet and shuddered, then stared into a sky that was already growing restless from the oncoming storm. "This is the spice, the heart of Duneworld! I can feel the sandworms."

Jesse reached out to grab the man's arms. "William, take deep breaths. Control yourself. You're having an adverse—"

Eyes wild, the spice foreman turned in a slow circle. "I can sense everything beneath us, and all around. The spice, the worms, sand plankton, and . . . more. Wonders we have never seen or imagined. Ah!"

English struck Jesse, knocking him away, and dropped back to his knees. Like a madman, English grabbed the sandtrout carcass, plunged his face into the viscous moistness, slurped up more of the fluid, and began to laugh. When his eyes settled on Barri, he rushed over to the boy, yelling. "*I'm alive!* I can see the future and the past. But which is which?"

Jesse pushed him away, standing between the wild man and his son. "Stay away. William—"

"I can sail through the dunes, dive under them, tunnel deeper. Must protect the spice, the spores . . ."

He grabbed Jesse by the chest and leaned toward him, frantic. Blood leaked from his gums, staining his teeth. "Too much spice . . . but never enough spice. Must protect the spice! The sandworms. I *am* a sandworm!"

Hemorrhages blossomed in the whites of the scarred man's eyes. Within seconds, English began weeping blood. Still raving, he touched his eyes, looked at his scarlet-stained fingertips. "The spice! The spice! It has us all trapped. We'll never break free."

"Father, what's happening to him?" Barri cried. "We've got to help!"

"There's no way to do that," Jesse said. "He's had too much spice, an overdose."

English bolted into the steamy field of fumaroles. "Find the spice! Become one with the spice, one with the sandworms!" Screaming, he ran headlong—until the ground dropped from beneath him. The swirling mouth of a sand whirlpool.

"William!" Jesse rushed forward, but stopped himself, realizing the danger of the treacherous ground. "William!"

As the sand spun and sucked him down, English cried out with laughter and howled in delight. He seemed to *want* to be drawn underground—and the sand whirlpool obliged him.

Barri started toward the foreman, but Jesse held him back. English's upraised, slime-slick hands vanished, leaving only the faint stirrings of the top powdery layer.

"He's gone forever," Barri said.

Jesse sank down next to his son. "Now it's just the two of us."

After a long moment, Barri straightened his shoulders and clasped his father's hand. His voice was very small. "Just the two of us."

# 14

*He is one with the sand.*

—DUNEWORLD FUNERAL LITANY

Though she refused to accept defeat, Dorothy had performed her own calculations and projected the supplies that might have been aboard the ornijet, extrapolating how long anyone could have survived.

Search party after search party returned without success. In a desert as large as a planet, a human being was no more significant than a grain of sand. Like a voracious predator, the endless wasteland had swallowed Jesse, Barri, and English.

In the convict-worker barracks in Carthage and the freedmen section of town, Gurney Halleck had tried to encourage the men, to maintain their morale. She admired his efforts, the way he sang inspiring songs, but lately the verses he had repeated for her sounded increasingly tragic.

Freedmen sandminers, pulled from their work to continue the hopeless search, were beginning to grumble about lost bonuses. Dorothy couldn't blame them; for such men, bonuses were their only hope of earning passage off of Duneworld. The convict laborers did not want to be taken from the spice harvesters, either, fearing they would be sent back to even worse penal worlds such as Salusa or Eridanus V. And nobody looked forward to having the Hoskanners return. . . .

"Their ornijet could have crashed in the storm," General Tuek said, as he met with her in her office on the third level of the headquarters mansion. He stood with his hands on the back of a chair. "But it could just as easily have been sabotage. Anyone who knew the nobleman was out at the forward base could have laid a trap for him when he returned."

"Many people knew of the expedition, General." She stood near the window, with her arms folded across her chest. Something about this man always grated on her.

"You knew about it, madam. Any observer on the landing field could feel the friction between you and the nobleman as he left. What exactly was the nature of your disagreement?"

Red anger flashed through her eyes, burning through her grief and hopelessness. "Any personal discussions between Jesse and myself are exactly that—personal! How dare you even imply that I might have had something to do with their disappearance."

"It is my duty as security chief to suspect everyone, especially those who might benefit. You are the legal proxy for House Linkam. In my opinion, the nobleman has given a commoner altogether too much control over his finances and business."

Dorothy was so disoriented by the accusation that it took her a moment to grasp onto a thread of logic. "Leaving aside the fact that Barri is my own son—" She drew a breath, forced ice into her words. "If House Linkam is dissolved, then I would lose everything. I would be a fool to place Jesse's life at risk."

"You are no fool, madam. In fact, you would be smart enough to divert a great amount of Linkam wealth into secret accounts of your own." The veteran's red-stained lips were set in a grim line, showing no compassion.

She placed her hands on her hips so that she wouldn't try to throttle him. "That is quite enough, General—especially from a man who has implied he believes we should give up the search."

"I made no such suggestion." He stiffened defensively, stood at attention, with his arms at his sides. "I have served House Linkam for far longer than you have known Jesse, madam. I have already seen two noblemen die. If we abandon the search, then House Linkam dies and the Hoskanners have already won." His red-stained lips twitched. "However, if we cease all spice production, then that is also true. I merely implied that we should consider sending some of the teams back to work. Each day, we lose more ground against the Hoskanners."

Dorothy stared at him coolly, then asked herself the fundamental question: What would Jesse want her to do? Even in this terrible situation, he would expect her to hold on to hope longer than anyone else, but he also trusted her to manage the noble household, to be his proxy in business matters, and to keep his future safe for Barri. She knew exactly what Jesse's answer would be.

Speaking in a voice that allowed no disagreement, Dorothy said, "Continue the search, General, but assign a temporary spice foreman to oversee harvesting operations in the absence of William English. Get our crews out on the sands again, as soon as possible."

❧

AS THE STORM neared, Jesse settled his son against the shelter of the dune wall where the hard sands were crusted with chemical residue from underground volcanic vents.

Wearily, Jesse trudged to the top of the highest dune and saw a smothering curtain of dust billowing ominously toward them. The whistling wind picked up, flinging needle-sharp sand grains against his cheeks. His clogged face mask no longer worked well, and neither did Barri's. Both of them also had rips in their bodysuits, reducing the effectiveness of the conservation mechanisms. And they had no water left, not even a drop.

Jesse slid back down the slope and unpacked a reflective blanket. After testing the wind, he found the best place to sit in the lee of the dunes where they might ride out the oncoming storm. They huddled together with the blanket wrapped around them, listening to the sifting sand and dust. Jesse remembered all too well how English's face had been scarred by the abrasive winds, how other men had been scoured to skeletons. Their chances of surviving the night were vanishingly small.

Like a living thing, the wind swirled around the fumarole field, lashing the sulfurous vapors in all directions. A thickening layer of sand covered their blanket, muffling the fearsome sounds; intermittently, Jesse tried to shake it off so they wouldn't suffocate.

In the middle of the long night, the winds began to die down, and the storm noises grew distant. By morning, amazed to be alive, Jesse and Barri worked together to lift the sand-weighted blanket. After shaking off the sand and wiping powder from their eyes, they looked around. Only the edge of the storm had touched the fumarole field before it had swerved, leaving them unscathed.

Jesse hugged his son. "A miracle, my boy!" His throat was so dry he could barely speak, and his words emerged as a rough croak. "We survived one more day."

Barri's lips were parched and cracked, and his voice was no better than his father's. "Maybe we should just pick a direction and follow it."

Thirst burned like an ember in Jesse's mouth. "We'll keep going today and tomorrow . . . as long as it takes. Our chances aren't good, but if we give up, there's no hope at all."

The fumaroles coughed like a choking man clearing his throat. Gases continued to percolate out of the sand whirlpool that had swallowed the delirious William English.

After giving the boy strict instructions not to wander off, Jesse slogged through loose sand at the bottom of the depression, then climbed the other side of the towering rise. In the early light of day, perhaps he would see a landmark . . . or a fleet of rescue ships coming across the ocean of dunes.

When he reached the high ridge on top, Jesse shuffled ahead, his feet sinking in. Unexpectedly, his boot snagged on something buried beneath the surface. He tripped and fell forward.

Jesse rolled over, brushing himself off, wiping his face. He dug with his hands and extricated a bent white polymer rod. Loosened, the thin flexible staff sprang erect again: one of the many weather poles that sandminers had installed in the open desert to keep track of localized storms.

Casting his gaze right and left, Jesse moved off several paces until he found a second bent weather pole, which he freed. He wagged the whiplike rods, saw that they were unscathed even by being forced to the ground and buried under the sand. He drew a deep breath of flinty air, accepting the symbolism as an omen: *A survivor stays alive only by bending with the blows. Be flexible. Bend against the unstoppable force and then spring back when it has passed.*

Barri came running up. "Are you all right? What did you find?"

He turned to his son. "These are data-collection devices for the weather satellites. Help me clear them out."

Scooping sand, Jesse dug to the root of the pole. When he found its instrument package, he smiled for the first time in days. "And each one has a transmitter uplinked to the weather satellites! Dr. Haynes was tinkering with the satellite network. If he's got it functional again, and if we can modify these pulses . . ."

Barri understood. The two of them found six poles in a line. They removed each one from where it was embedded and took the devices back into the depression where they were protected from the winds. Jesse used a small multitool from his pack to dismantle the housings and access the tiny, hardened circuitry.

"If we get all six of these in phase, we can send a strong and regular pulse—not a complex code or a voice message, but if anyone is watching from the base, they should see the blip. . . ."

Most people might have given them up for dead already, but he doubted Dorothy would ever surrender hope.

By midday they had all the weather poles silently thrumming, sending out a modulated electronic signal, a repeating pattern that could not be missed. Gathering the blanket again to shelter them from the day's heat and to present a visible, reflective target, he held Barri. "Now it's only a matter of time. I hope."

# 15

*At the bleakest, blackest hour of night,*
*the dawn appears, washing away the darkness.*

—A SAYING OF THE DEEP DESERT

D orothy occupied herself with work. It was well past the dinner
hour, but she had told the servants not to prepare anything for
her to eat. The mansion seemed vast and empty, populated by echoes.
The Catalan workers were already asking persistent questions, many of
them believing that the nobleman and his son would never be found.

Jesse had made her the legal proxy for House Linkam, but had never
married her. Without him, she had no continuing status, and her decisions would no longer be binding. Once, in private, Jesse had told her,
"You are far more than a concubine to me, more even than a traditional wife. A noblewoman could never replace you in my heart. You
are the mother of my son, who is the heir to House Linkam. You are
the inspiration for my soul." No vapid daughter of a decadent blue-
blood family could take that away from her.

But that was no solace at all if Jesse and Barri were lost. Her soul ached for them, and despair welled up within her. It had been much too long.

In her distress, she did not at first hear the shouts from the main entry hall. "Dorothy Mapes! Where are you?" It was Gurney Halleck's voice, bellowing for her. "I have fantastic news!"

Her heart racing, Dorothy took two stairs at a time and bounded down to the closest landing. She came upon the startled jongleur so unexpectedly that he half drew the sonic dagger from on his hip. Recognizing the petite woman, he let the blade slide back into its sheath. "The satellites detected a signal out in the desert! It repeats without message content, but it's a clear pulse that shouldn't be there."

"It has to be Jesse!"

"It's certainly somebody," Gurney said. "But there were three people on the downed ornijet. No telling if everyone is still alive."

"Then what are we waiting for? Take me there—"

"There's nothing you can do right now. General Tuek has already dispatched a rescue craft. We should know more within the hour."

An irrepressible geyser of hope sprang up inside her, and Dorothy hugged the jongleur so furiously that he grew red in the face.

❧

A SQUADRON OF dusty rescue ships returned at sunset to the spaceport landing zone nearest to the headquarters mansion. A violent calamity of color spilled across the sky, then streamed away into darkness.

Dorothy could hardly contain herself as she waited with Gurney and Dr. Yueh. Excited, she watched one vessel after another as they set down, flapping their articulated wings and stabilizing their landing gear.

Finally, the last vessel touched down in a noisy rush of jets, creating a gritty cloud. When the air cleared, an entry hatch opened, and a rough-faced, red-eyed man appeared in the doorway. At first she didn't recognize him until she noted the familiar, though unsteady, way he moved. Details, beloved details! The gray eyes were familiar, but he looked so tired, so much older. Finally, the boy appeared behind him.

She ran forward. "I thought I'd never see you again!" Dorothy hugged them and kissed their dusty faces repeatedly.

With a chafed hand, Jesse wiped her cheeks, smearing her tear tracks into mud. "My darling, we're making a mess of you."

Old Dr. Yueh gave the two haggard survivors a quick once-over, checking their eyes, taking their pulses. "Good, good. Oh, I'll give you both full examinations later, after you clean up." He grinned. "It'll waste a lot of water just getting those layers of dirt off you."

"I don't care," Jesse said. "For once in this hellhole, I'm going to wallow in a bath."

"Me, too," Barri said. "I want to stay home forever."

Dorothy listened with sadness as they told her what had happened to William English. Such a tragedy. Still, as she looked at her family she shuddered with relief. Jesse had exposed their son to unimaginable danger against her clear wishes, but he had also saved himself and Barri from almost certain death. Dorothy was still angry with him, but if his own ordeal hadn't given him a healthy respect for the risks on Duneworld, nothing she could say would make a difference. The only way they could all survive this challenge was to stick together.

Arm in arm, they walked toward the headquarters mansion profiled against the abrupt desert sunset.

PART TWO

SECOND YEAR ON DUNEWORLD

# 16

*The only way to be truly safe is to view everyone as a potential enemy.*

—GENERAL ESMAR TUEK,
*Security Briefings*

Throughout their first year, Linkam operations suffered frequent equipment damage, the "accidental" destruction of supplies and tools, delayed deliveries of new harvesters and carryalls, and overt sabotage. Jesse had no doubt that Carthage was crawling with Hoskanner spies, despite the best efforts of his security chief to ferret them out.

To guard against potential attacks, another contingent of highly trained fighters from the Catalan home guard had arrived. General Tuek had redoubled his troops around the mansion, posting sentries and infiltrating new workers into the ranks of freedmen and convicts.

Despite their dedicated, backbreaking efforts, Linkam spice production remained pitifully low, barely a third of previous Hoskanner tallies, as they knew from the secret information William English had provided. To make matters worse, the sandminers were increasingly hostile and insubordinate, because reduced production meant fewer credits and dwindling hopes that they would ever leave Duneworld, despite Jesse's promises.

Awaiting the end of the challenge period on Gediprime, Valdemar must be laughing to himself. . . .

When a nearby storm brought enough dust to obscure visibility and prevent flights to the spice fields, Jesse quietly gathered his closest advisors in a small shielded conference room with no windows and only one narrow door. After Tuek had scanned for listening devices and covert spy imagers, he declared the room clean.

It was time for them to talk.

Jesse sat down and folded his hands on top of the table. His grim, gray eyes scanned the faces of Dorothy and Tuek sitting at opposite sides of the table, as well as Gurney Halleck, who had taken over as spice foreman after the tragic death of William English. Before Jesse could begin, Dr. Haynes hurried into the room, having just flown up from the forward research base, one step ahead of the storm. "I apologize for my lateness."

Since Jesse's ordeal in the desert, and his demonstrated resolve to survive, the planetary ecologist had become a surprising ally. Haynes made it clear that he respected Nobleman Linkam much more than he had the Hoskanners, though technically the Emperor's scientist was supposed to remain neutral.

Jesse, though, could not afford to allow mixed loyalties. He had to lay everything on the line. "If we are destined to lose, we will lose. But I will never give up and make it easy for them."

"The Hoskanners keep cutting our feet out from under us," Tuek said. "Sweet affection, what underhanded tricks! They know exactly how to hamstring our operations. However, with the new soldiers from Catalan, I can post extra guards on every operation. Round-the-clock surveillance of our most important equipment. I intend to eliminate sabotage completely."

"Even protecting our equipment won't be enough," Jesse said. "We simply don't have the production capacity to meet the goal."

Though she was normally quiet in these meetings, Dorothy pointed out, "For eighteen years the Hoskanners had unlimited resources and manpower. They could afford to replace expensive spice harvesters as fast as the worms and storms destroyed them." She shook her head sadly. "Even if half of our equipment orders hadn't been delayed or caught up in inexplicable bureaucracy, House Linkam still doesn't have the capital to keep up with that."

"We barely have half as many spice harvesters as we need," Jesse said. "One of the new-model units is due to be delivered from an alternative source on Richese, but it had to go through indirect channels."

"That harvester is a month late," Dorothy said, "but I'm assured we'll get it, just like those delayed Ixian deliveries. You can bet the Hoskanners had a hand in it. They just want to stall us, claiming we have 'credit problems.'"

"Curse the Emperor and his refusal to impose rules!" Gurney said. "If he wants the spice so badly, why doesn't he intervene?"

Jesse grimaced. "The nobles want it as well, but most of our 'friends' haven't come through as they promised."

Only three families, poor enough that they were willing to take a chance on a long shot, had offered to help with funding, but they could spare little; Jesse deeply appreciated their gestures, though the financing hadn't helped much. Four other nobles had taken advantage of the desperate Linkam situation, offering loans at crippling interest rates; Jesse feared he would have to accept their terms, unless he found some other way through the crisis.

And he still had another year left.

Dr. Haynes scratched his beard. "The scavenged live-rubber shielding has helped."

Jesse agreed. "Almost a year ago, we applied it to our harvesters— and that alone kept our machinery working much longer than expected. Thus, we were able to put more crews out in the desert, and bring back more melange. A step in the right direction, but not enough. Not nearly enough. We'll lose, unless something changes. For a year we've been following the techniques the Hoskanners used, but it's getting us nowhere. We need to think *bigger*."

Dorothy rested her chin in her hands, her brow furrowed in concentration. "We've already tried so many things, Jesse."

"But we haven't tried the *right* thing. There's got to be something else, an unexpected approach."

Over the months, following advice by the planetary ecologist or the suggestions of Gurney Halleck and Esmar Tuek, the Linkam operations had tried everything from explosives and energy bursts to poisons in the sands. Nothing worked. They had grounded static-shield generators to protect a boundary, but the fields drove the worms into a frenzy. They used pheromones, chemical signatures, various potent scents to deter the worms from the work perimeter, but the creatures did not respond; as near as Dr. Haynes could tell, the monsters were asexual.

Jesse steepled his fingertips. "The Hoskanner method of spice harvesting is not necessarily the most efficient technique. At a spice field, at least seventy percent of the time is involved in deploying harvesters and in evacuating the site. With blitzkrieg mining, we strike and then flee at the first sign of a worm. If we could only extend our time on the ground before a worm comes, every moment we keep digging would greatly increase our haul."

"Aye, we're like inept thieves robbing a treasure vault," Gurney said. "Give me five hours on a rich vein, and I'll provide a month's worth of melange! My sandminers would work themselves to death if they had an opportunity like that."

"We have found no way to kill the worms," Jesse said. "We've tried everything."

Tuek stared straight at the nobleman. "Not quite. We didn't try our atomics."

Dorothy bridled. "There could be serious political repercussions. Some of the powerful Houses are pushing for prohibitions against atomics."

Tuek contradicted her, "But there are no prohibitions yet—and we do have our own arsenal. As a worm approaches, we could launch a small-yield atomic warhead."

"I'd like to try that out," Gurney said. "Get revenge for some of the miners we've lost."

Dr. Haynes lurched to his feet and turned to Jesse, who had never seen such vehemence from the planetary ecologist. "Nobleman Linkam, you must not consider such a thing! Even if you killed the worm, you would contaminate the spice fields and gain nothing. Melange is extremely susceptible to radiation. Coriolis storms would disperse the fallout all over the planet."

"But there must be a way, Dr. Haynes," Jesse said, wrestling with his frustration. "If we can't kill the worms, and we can't drive them away with shields or deterrent chemicals, what can we do?" He stared at the planetary ecologist. "Would it be possible to . . . stun them? At least long enough for our crews to make a big haul?"

Haynes caught his breath, and his lips formed a thin smile. "We need to use a different paradigm. And that certainly opens up new avenues of thought." The ruddy-faced man composed himself, as if preparing for a lecture. "With their obvious size and power, the worms are very territorial. We think magnetite grains react with an electrostatic field generated by the worm's body as it moves through the sands, either through friction or from some organ deep inside the creature's body. The larger the worm, the stronger the repelling field it generates—and the greater the territory it claims."

"We have generators of our own," Jesse said. "Could we tune them to a similar frequency? Stake out our own territory and broadcast a boundary so the worm thinks we're a greater rival, making it afraid to approach?"

"We'd have to cover a huge area," Gurney said immediately. "Even with live-rubber shielding, ground-based fields and storm static still short out our equipment. We could never hold a large enough perimeter."

Haynes continued his preoccupied, mysterious smile. "If the environment precludes us from countering those fields externally, perhaps we could attack from *inside* the worm and short out its internal dynamo." Feverishly, the planetary ecologist began sketching on his portable datascreen. "Imagine a shielded drum-sized generator with insulated antennae sticking out, and discharge tips to deliver a short, intense shock."

"Like a depth charge?" Tuek said. "Get the worm to swallow it, then trigger the field?"

"Precisely! Each worm segment has an independent neurological system chained into the overall whole. Thus, we would have to short out each segment. As the worm swallows the charge, the antennae would deliver repeated bursts all the way down."

"Aye, that would kill the leviathan!" Gurney said.

Grinning, Jesse said, "Even if it only puts the worm out of commission for a while, instead of killing it, our harvester crews would have a much longer period to excavate spice."

He looked at Dorothy, seeing the excitement in her eyes, but also a reluctance. She cautioned, "Dr. Haynes, we know you technically work for the Grand Emperor. House Linkam has few funds to divert to your project."

Jesse leaned closer to the scientist. "How much will it cost, Dr. Haynes?"

The planetary ecologist chuckled. "Don't worry, Nobleman. I will have all the equipment and technical assistance I require. Developing a potential new tool for spice harvesting clearly falls within the purview of my assignment, even though the Grand Emperor has no real interest in my experiments. However, even if I give this concept priority, remember that it is a long march from an idea to a functional prototype."

"Then we'd best get started." Jesse looked from his advisors to the sealed door of the conference room, and stood up.

Tuek continued to frown. "I would suggest that we keep this line of investigation confidential. We have enough trouble with Hoskanner spies and saboteurs, and if they learn of a new concept, they will be sure to cause trouble."

"Even to the Imperial planetary ecologist?" Gurney sounded surprised.

Haynes nodded. "The Emperor and the Hoskanners will do whatever they want. I am not so bold to think that my supposed importance will give them a moment's pause. I hate to say this, but I do not always trust the Emperor's motivations."

Dorothy said, "I'm inclined to agree with General Tuek. We don't dare let the Hoskanners discover what we're doing. We've got to let them believe we're hopeless and continuing to flounder." She gave a sly smile. "If they're convinced they've already won, they won't try so hard to defeat us."

# 17

*Time may wear a benign mask, but it is always the faceless enemy, the destroyer of hopes and dreams.*

—THE PROPHET OF CARTHAGE

After more than a year, Jesse had finally begun to develop a "typical day" on hostile Duneworld. Early in the morning, he donned his sealed bodysuit and desert cloak, and went down to the main dining hall where Dorothy and Barri were already waiting for him.

Servants scurried into action, bringing breakfasts covered with clearplaz to prevent the escape not only of heat, but of precious moisture. Developed and marketed by a local entrepreneur, the sophisticated plazware was designed to minimize even the faintest wisps of water loss. When the diner moved his eating utensil toward the plate, the cover slid back just long enough for a bite, then snapped shut. Dorothy had adopted these devices to show that the Linkams understood the value of moisture, that they were not a profligate noble family like the Hoskanners.

Through the plaz lid over the plate, Jesse saw a steaming blue omelet of imported Catalanian eggs prepared with desert peppers, boar bacon, and llantro roots. It was one of his favorite meals. Jesse took a sip of spice coffee, hardly noticing the cinnamon taste of melange. Now that they consumed spice daily, he paid scant attention to it. Strange. On Catalan he had rarely indulged in the substance, and now he couldn't imagine a meal without it. Melange had become as much a part of life on Duneworld as the air and sand.

Outside, he heard a large engine. Ornijets and transports were always coming and going at Carthage's separate landing zones, but this engine sounded much louder. A massive roar filled the skies of the mountain city.

Barri ran to one of the windows. "That's the Emperor's symbol!"

With an uneasy groan, Jesse went to see a hulking and intimidating interstellar craft descending over the company town, one of the largest vessels capable of landing on a planetary surface. An Imperial inspection ship, fully armed and threatening.

No, he realized—this would not be a typical day after all.

❧

WITH LINKAM FINANCES excruciatingly tight, Dorothy authorized no lavish decorations and shut down portions of the mansion. If the Grand Emperor's man had expected to be received in a sumptuous hall, he was sorely disappointed.

Counselor Ulla Bauers twitched his rabbitlike nose and looked around the headquarters building with an irritated expression, thus implying that he had more important things to do and wanted to be on his way. A precise man with front-parlor habits from another age, he wore a carmine-and-gold high-collared robe that would have been the envy of any nobleman. On Duneworld, he looked entirely out of place.

"Hmmm. By Imperial permission, House Linkam has presided over spice operations for a year now," Bauers said in an erudite tone, "but your melange exports have been, ahh, seriously below expectations." He narrowed his eyes dangerously. "I am afraid, Nobleman Linkam, that you are an embarrassment to the Emperor."

Suppressing his anger, Jesse explained, "The Hoskanners left us with inferior equipment. Much of the new machinery I ordered—and paid for—was either defective upon delivery, or delayed by bureaucratic schemes. We have filed a dispute against the Ixian suppliers in Imperial commercial court, but a decision will not be reached until after the challenge is ended." He forced a thin smile, trying not to glare at the overdressed man. "Still, I do have another year to go and no time to lose. I appreciate the Grand Emperor's interest, but we have work to do."

"Hmm-ahh, perhaps you missed certain nuances in the original challenge agreement, Nobleman? Such details are among my specialties." Bauers cleared his throat—not a cough, but a confined disturbance of the larynx. "If the Grand Emperor so directs, he can rescind the challenge at any moment and give Duneworld back to House Hoskanner."

Jesse stiffened. "The Grand Emperor explicitly said there would be no rules."

"Ahh, but the agreement also stated, and I quote, 'This contract shall be subject to Imperial law.'" He offered Jesse a disdainful smirk. "That can mean anything the Emperor decides."

Simmering, Jesse said, "Why would he toy with us in such a way? The Nobles' Council will be outraged if you strip away the challenge without giving me a fair chance."

"It is simple, Nobleman Linkam. The people demand melange, and you haven't shipped enough. We never anticipated that you would fail so miserably. It is inconceivable!" He frowned. "Hmmm, or are you hiding portions of your output? Hoarding melange for black-market suppliers? Your trickle of exports to Renaissance cannot possibly be your entire production. Where are your secret spice warehouses?"

Jesse chuckled. "We keep barely enough for household use."

The ferretlike man arched his eyebrows. "Word has reached me that your freedmen and convict workers are extremely unhappy. Low production and exports mean paltry bonuses for them. Under Hoskanner administration, many of them would have saved enough to go home already. I am informed that Carthage is a tinderbox, and a riot could flare up at any moment. Is this true?"

"Exaggerations spread by a few remaining Hoskanner loyalists," Jesse said dismissively. "A handful of loudmouths have been arrested, most of them convicts with years left on their work sentences. We have the situation completely under control."

"Umm-ahh, when the Hoskanners were here, they faced difficulties, too, but spice flowed like a river. They developed a market all across the Empire, and now the shortage is being felt, as offworld spice stockpiles are depleted. Prices are at record levels."

"Then the nobles will have to tighten their belts and do without the luxury, or pay more for it. The Emperor gets his cut, so he should be happy." Jesse's gray eyes looked like sharp ice chips. "Counselor Bauers, I was never asked to provide any sort of progress reports. In the meantime, my rate of production is my own concern. The only number that matters is the total I deliver at the end of the challenge. If I am to fail, then you can declare my defeat at the end of two years—not a moment before."

"Hmm-ahh. Remember the fine print, Linkam."

"There is more to an agreement than fine print, sir, and more to justice than words. We have clear evidence of Hoskanner meddling throughout the past year. If the Emperor is so anxious for his spice, then he should not have allowed my enemies to hamstring me."

Hearing the approach of boots, Jesse saw Esmar Tuek appear in the doorway. "Excuse me, My Lord. May I speak with you privately?"

"Counselor Bauers was just about to go and order his inspection ship to withdraw to a convenient distance," Jesse said. "He doesn't want to block our spice export vessels."

Bauers said with a sniff, "On the contrary, I, and my ship, will depart only at a time of my choosing. For now, the vessel remains precisely where it is."

Coolly, Tuek nodded. "Very well then, Counselor, my information concerns you as well. My men have scanned the identities of your crewmen who are milling about at the main spaceport landing fields. Are you aware that your ship carries known Hoskanner agents who were evicted from Duneworld a year ago?"

Bauers seemed genuinely surprised. "What?"

"Your specialty may be fine print, but General Tuek's is security," Jesse said with a cautious smile. "He is never mistaken about such matters."

"Ahh, I certainly had no idea any of my crew had ever been to this planet before."

"The Hoskanners undoubtedly fooled you, too," Jesse said, "though you do not look like a man who is easily hoodwinked."

Standing stiffly in his dusty uniform, Tuek added, "Due to the obvious security threat, Counselor, we must insist that your crew remain within the confines of the landing zone for the duration of your stay here. I will assign a cordon of our security troops to assist you in this matter. No member of your crew is to set foot in Carthage or mingle with either the convict workers or freedmen."

Jesse smiled thinly. "You, of course, are welcome to come and go as you please, Counselor Bauers."

"I know nothing of Hoskanner agents." The persnickety man sniffed. "The Grand Emperor has sent me here to inform you that the spice must flow. If you do not show dramatic progress soon . . . hmm, he is not a patient man."

# 18

History has shown that if a noble goes soft, it will be his undoing. To avoid this calamity, he must always maintain an emotional distance from the people around him.

—GRAND EMPEROR CHAM EYVOK III (THE WARLORD EMPEROR)

With Linkam spice production drastically reduced, the hopes of the sandminers had plummeted along with their income. Despite harsh working conditions under the stern Hoskanners, at least back then some of the men had eventually earned enough credits to buy their way off of Duneworld. Now the freedmen were angry with the downturn in the economy, and the convicts saw no chance for going home when they finished their sentences, despite Jesse's promises.

Having little discretionary income, the sandminers could not spend money in the shops and saloons of Carthage, and so the businessmen, water merchants, and wrung-out pleasure women fell on hard times. Even the Catalan staff missed their ocean world. They stared at the empty desert skies and longed for rainfall instead of dust.

House Linkam generated enough capital to keep operating, if just barely, from their meager spice exports, augmented by hard-fought contributions from a handful of noble families. In his precarious financial situation, Jesse had been forced to impose austerity measures in the mansion and in Carthage, thus making life even more difficult for the workers.

He lost much sleep, feeling their misery and discontent, and he wished he had the means to improve their lives. Back on Catalan he had been in touch with his people, and they had loved him. He'd been a good leader, caring for their needs, listening to their problems. But here . . .

Meeting with Dorothy, he discussed many alternatives to ease the burden on the people, but without any financial cushion whatsoever, he had his hands tied. Though it made administration more difficult, he instituted tax relief, forcing his own Catalan staff to work with their salaries postponed. On Dorothy's suggestion, he distributed some of the old stored luxury clothes and trinkets the Hoskanners had left behind, but these superficial items helped little and only served to point out how drab and hard their lives were on Duneworld. The hard-bitten sandminers and townspeople whispered among themselves about Linkam management, asserting that the nobleman's ineptitude was stealing their future.

Out in the desert, every piece of functional harvesting equipment was in use, protected by live-rubber shielding. Extra teams worked without rest in the repair bays to put the spice harvesters and carryalls back into service with all due speed.

Some sandminers had received unrequested furloughs, laid off because there simply wasn't enough functional equipment to put them to work. Left to themselves, bored, restless, and angry, the men continued to grumble, blaming all their troubles on House Linkam. The convicts especially, espousing the increasingly radical teachings of the prison-offshoot Zensunni religion, demanded that Jesse return melange operations to the Hoskanners, "who knew what they were doing."

When thirty-four penal laborers refused to work on their assigned harvester teams, Jesse angrily voided their contracts and sent them back to Eridanus V. Meanwhile, the Imperial inspection ship continued to loom over Carthage. He knew Ulla Bauers was watching everything. . . .

❧

UNDER A HOT and hazy noon sky, Jesse strode through an open marketplace in the center of town. In an effort to disguise himself, he wore the dirty desert cloak of a sandminer, and few people gave him a second glance. As the nobleman of Duneworld, he had been wanting to get out and see some of the common people in their day-to-day activities, instead of viewing them from groundvans or low-flying aircraft. Two plainclothed guards accompanied him in similar attire, though he knew Tuek was behind them somewhere with a larger force, ever conscious of security.

In the crowded bazaar, shopkeepers and vendors shouted for customers to notice their wares. Incense sellers and purveyors of exotic scents wafted small samples of sweet or pungent smoke, which caught the attention of passersby with the enticingly different smells, unlike the more common odor of melange throughout the rest of Carthage.

Behind a thin wire barrier, two old women sat next to dozens of small gray rock pheasants, which they had raised in pens. The women had the birds' heads tucked under their wings and tied in place, forcing them to sleep. The desert birds, native to other arid planets, had originally been brought here by the Hoskanners, one of their better decisions. The pheasants drank very little precious water, and their tender flesh was highly prized (and expensive) on Duneworld. Few spice-miners could afford the delicacy, though they much preferred the fare to bland company rations. When a customer agreed on the price, one of the old women would snap the necks of the chosen birds and hand over the fresh meat in spice-fiber sacks.

As Jesse was about to leave, he saw one of his guards talking into a lapel microphone. The man, who had a sharp chin and small, dark eyes, took Jesse aside, and said to him, "My Lord, a spontaneous rally is taking place on the other side of town, led by a freedman. He is calling for House Linkam to leave the planet."

Outside the market, Jesse met with General Tuek. "I'm going over there," the nobleman announced. "I've been frustrated with the need to speak on my own behalf, and this is my chance."

"I advise against it, My Lord."

"Somehow, that doesn't surprise me." Jesse's eyes twinkled. In a firm voice, he said he wanted to face the demonstrators, talk with them, and let them know that he heard their grievances and would do whatever he could.

"The crowd is in an ugly mood," Tuek said.

"Then it's even more important for me to speak with them." Jesse lifted his chin stubbornly.

"I expected as much," the old security chief said. "I've already sent for forty of our best guards to go with you."

◈

ACCOMPANIED BY THE guards, Jesse headed for a fleet of ground-vans parked in full view of the towering Imperial inspection ship. The unwelcome vessel remained where it had landed a week before, dominating the main spaceport, so that many smaller vessels had to use secondary fields. He wondered if secret Hoskanner agents had somehow incited the minor uprising from behind their barricades. Were they waiting to enjoy his reaction?

From behind the cordon, Ulla Bauers and the other men noticed Jesse, but he ignored them. He took the van's controls himself, letting Tuek's guards find seats or scramble aboard a second vehicle. He roared off in a cloud of Duneworld's ever-present dust and steered along the steep roads to where milling, angry people had gathered. When he dis-

THE ROAD TO DUNE

embarked and strode forward, his phalanx of security men formed a protective wedge to clear a way through the throng. Men in desert bodysuits and women in long robes moved aside, whispering in surprise when they recognized the noble visitor, who now wore the formal cloak of his rank.

With his mind spinning and questing for alternatives, trying to determine what he might say to them, Jesse approached the steps of a large prefab meeting house. A weathered old man stood there shouting, "—better under the Hoskanners!" Jesse recognized him immediately: Pari Hoyuq, the competent captain of a spice harvester that had recently been damaged and remained out of service. *Too much time on his hands*, Jesse thought. *Gurney could have handled this in private, if he'd had a chance.*

Seeing him, Hoyuq's face lit up with intense indignation. "You, Nobleman! Are you going to send more of us back to prison planets?"

Jesse kept walking, forcing himself to remain calm and reasonable. "Are you intending to break your contract, Pari? Like those other men who refused to work in the spice fields?" He climbed the steps to be at the same level as the old sandminer. Alert to danger, Tuek's Catalan security men hurried to protect him, using the vantage to scan the crowd for threats.

Hoyuq said, "I would never refuse work—if work were available! Too many of us have no chance to earn any bonuses. No chance at all. I am a *freedman*. I served my sentence, got my release." He tapped the chevron tattoo on his forehead. "We all want to leave this place, but you Linkams have made that impossible!"

Jesse kept his eyes on the old sandminer, as if this were a private conversation between the two of them. "I already promised you, and all freedmen, that I would pay your passage home—if we win the contest."

Instead of cheers, the reminder evoked only groans and grumbles. The man scowled and leaned closer with his leathery face. "Ha! Nobleman, there's a greater chance of rain falling from the sky! You gave us hope with your empty promise, and we worked hard. We believed you, and for what? You cannot win the challenge, so your promise is empty."

Jesse felt as if a hot knife had plunged into his chest, and he knew how hopeless the situation must seem to these people. In the headquarters mansion, even he and Dorothy could see the numbers and know that it would require a miracle for them to surge ahead of their rivals. Still, he squared his shoulders. "I have not given up, Pari. And neither should you." He turned to face the crowd at last. "Not any of you."

From below, several people shouted. "Life was better under the Hoskanners!"

"No spice, no work, no bonuses—*no reason to be here!*"

"These days, even Eridanus V isn't as bad as the mess you've turned Duneworld into."

"We want the Hoskanners back."

Stiffening, Jesse took a breath to quell his outburst. Then he said, "Ah yes, the Hoskanners. Perhaps you should look more closely at your troubles and turn your anger toward the proper target." He narrowed his eyes. "Wasn't it the Hoskanners who ruined our weather satellites, putting sandminers in danger? Wasn't it Hoskanner spies who sabotaged equipment so that you can't go out to work the spice veins? Wasn't it the Hoskanners who bribed offplanet manufacturers to prevent or delay the delivery of vital machinery? Wasn't it the Hoskanners who diverted water shipments so that prices climbed higher and higher?" He jabbed a finger at them. "Their only goal is to make House Linkam look weak. I'm asking you for fairness, for common decency. Give me a chance to make your lives better."

Old Hoyuq clung stubbornly to his anger. "Then make our lives better, Nobleman. You cast blame easily, but if you want us to believe in a conspiracy against you, prove that you are better than the Hoskanners. Show us with your actions."

Jesse's mind raced, searching for something immediate. He and Dorothy had discussed many possibilities, all of which they had deemed too extravagant or too risky. Right now, though, he did not have the luxury of studying House Linkam's resources, its ledgers. He had to do something before a riot broke out.

Jesse folded his arms across his chest. "Very well. In difficult times, we all ration, we all pull together, and we all share discomfort. Beginning tomorrow morning, I will distribute the water reserves from my own family holdings. Anyone who comes to my home will receive an extra share, until our supplies run out. Henceforth, my daily ration will be the same as yours." At the murmurs of disbelief, his gray-eyed gaze darted from face to face. "I know your money is tight. Therefore, I am also fixing water prices at the level they were when House Linkam came to Duneworld. I will issue a decree to the water merchants."

As he heard the amazed cheers, he knew he had temporarily dodged the worst unrest. The solution could not last, and it might damage the economy of Carthage, but he could not afford to worry about such matters. He had to keep his operations going, one day at a time.

THE WATER SELLERS and importers expressed their outrage at Jesse's price controls by declaring a strike. Shipments had been delayed, their own supplies limited, and they had felt perfectly justified in raising prices as high as the city could bear. The greedy businessmen shut down all operations, locked their doors, and refused to sell water at the low prices House Linkam had set. Several plump and disgruntled water sellers demanded justice outside the mansion, but they got little sympathy from the populace, who knew the merchants had been gouging them.

As promised, House Linkam began distributing water freely to the people of Carthage, all of whom were affected by the bad times. While some were too proud to accept the charity, old freedmen, out-of-business shopkeepers, and widows of sandminers began showing up for assistance; each person who asked received a small ration of water. Drop by drop, the Linkam reserves began to dwindle, but the mood in Carthage improved. Valdemar Hoskanner would never have done such a thing.

Jesse worked inside the mansion's banquet hall, showing his face and letting the people see that he was responsible for this easing of their misery. Esmar Tuek stood at his side, probing eyes alert, surreptitiously scanning every visitor.

When one bearded man reached the head of the line, the veteran held up the scanner, retrieving images from security files and charts of identity points. At a signal from Tuek, two Catalan guards took the man into custody, despite his protestations. "What have I done? You can't seize an innocent man!"

General Tuek held up the scanner screen. "We have detailed files of all Hoskanner sympathizers and suspected saboteurs." He smiled. "Now, the rest of you are welcome to step forward."

A handful of men and women drifted out of line and tried to slip away from the mansion. Tuek sent men after them to make more arrests.

Jesse let his anger show, speaking loud enough for everyone in line to hear him. "Hoskanner agents have already done enough damage to my House, and to all of you. Now they dare to come take the water I intend to give to my loyal workers?"

While the people grumbled, Tuek leaned closer to Jesse. Satisfied, he said with a grim smile, "You can expect to hear from Bauers about this, My Lord. Arresting Hoskanners? He will be incensed."

"No, Esmar. As much as he might want to free those agents, he can't admit to any connection with anyone who may be working for the Hoskanners. However, it does give me a bit of leverage. I'm going to contact him first." Jesse rose to leave. "Our Imperial friend is going to help us break the water sellers' strike, though he doesn't know it yet."

⤙⥾⤚

THE NEXT DAY, in a formal announcement from the steps, Jesse offered an ultimatum to the unruly merchants. "I have no patience for your price gouging when people are suffering. You can survive with decreased profits for a time—as the rest of us have had to. Either accept my terms or depart from Duneworld. If you leave, however, you forfeit all assets and go with nothing."

Predictably, the indignant water sellers stormed over to the huge inspection ship and pleaded with Counselor Bauers to intervene. Smiling with amused helplessness, the man declined. "Hmmm, Grand Emperor Wuda made it clear that Nobleman Linkam can do as he pleases, with no rules or restrictions, in order to produce the maximum amount of spice. Ahhh, my hands are tied because of the edict." His nose twitched.

Before Jesse had issued his hard-line statement, he'd reached a secret deal with Bauers. Though he despised the terms, he saw no alternative but to offer the exposed Hoskanner saboteurs as a bribe, delivering them to the Imperial ship in exchange for the inspector's cooperation. Without admitting any connection to the Hoskanners, Bauers had agreed. Very quickly.

Later, when the water sellers and producers called upon him and pleaded for leniency, Jesse magnanimously granted amnesty. "Now, let's all work together."

It was another short-term victory, but he savored it nevertheless. Finally, he felt a little momentum on his side.

# 19

*Everybody complains.*

—GURNEY HALLECK

On a seemingly quiet evening, Gurney Halleck slipped into the old communal buildings that served as residences for the people Jesse had brought from Catalan. These were the best dwellings in Carthage.

Though he was the spice foreman in charge of freedmen, convict laborers, and Catalan workers alike, Gurney had always liked to socialize with his crews. He came into the Catalan residences hoping to relax for a change. He wanted to listen to quiet talk of the sea and the rain among men he had considered friends back home—men who now served under him as sandminers.

Immediately upon entering the main hall, however, the jongleur sensed a mood more sour than the odor of crowded, unwashed bodies. As the Catalan men organized their gear and supplies for the following day's harsh work out on the sands, they complained of thirst, isolation, grit in everything, sandburn, sunburn, windburn. Gurney had come to expect such grumbling from the convicts or disenchanted freedmen, but not Jesse's loyal men.

"Now, now, what's set you all off tonight?"

Unhappy-looking women in drab desert garb distributed packaged food and drinks. Some of the packs were open, revealing chunks of gray meat with sticks of too-bright vegetables. The men ate with grimy hands, inadvertently adding a seasoning of raw melange to the bland food.

"There's nowhere to *live* on this hellhole, Gurney!" one of the men said. "Not under or above ground, not in rock caves. And look at this stuff!" He prodded the unappetizing preserved food. "What I wouldn't give for some hot fish and lemon stew!"

The workers turned to Gurney, using him as a target for their complaints. "We're so overworked we don't get time to eat in peace, and even on long and dangerous shifts, we still don't harvest enough melange."

Another man hurled a spice shaker against the wall. "Even if we win the accursed challenge, what will our prize be? Will we ever see our homes again?"

"When will Nobleman Linkam reinstitute our wages? It's bad enough being miserable, but to do it for no pay?"

Gurney chuckled. "You know the nobleman's good for it! You have food, water, and a bunk to sleep in. Would you rather I had General Tuek come and tell you stories about how he had to survive during the Lucinan campaign?"

With forced good cheer, like a man hoping to calm a storm by waving his hands against the wind, Gurney sat on top of a metal crate and played his baliset, picking out familiar tunes without singing the words. "Come now, listen." He might have been their spice foreman, but he was also still a jongleur. He began to sing in his most soothing voice.

"In swirling sand,
  With men on the ground,
  Cinnamon filled the air,
  As the worm drew near.

" 'Damn the spice!' he shouted,
  And plunged into danger,
  The bravest of nobles,
  The bravest of men."

But the sandminers didn't want to listen. Instead, they began to throw food and insults at Gurney, forcing him to back toward the door. Even so, it seemed to him like a good-natured release of steam; he had made himself the butt of their dissatisfaction, allowing them to take out their ire on him. He held up his hands. "All right, lads! I'll talk to the nobleman! I'll see what I can—"

Just then, the freedman captain of a spice harvester rushed into the main hall, slamming the heavy moisture-seal door behind him. "Where is the spice foreman? It's happened again!" He unsealed his face mask and knocked dust off his cloak.

The mood shattered. Gurney set his baliset aside and strode forward. "I'm here—what is it?"

"Two more spice harvesters gone, Gurney! Along with half of my mates and the entire crew of the other harvester!" Dirt and dust seemed to ooze from every pore of the man's body, with every agitated exhalation. "I barely made it off that rattletrap carryall alive. The other survivors are in the Carthage infirmary right now. General Tuek told me to find you!" The rest of his words came out in disarray as he described the disaster.

"That leaves us with only seven harvesters!" a man groaned.

Gurney listened, feeling as if he'd been shot in the stomach. He tried to calculate how many men had just been sucked down a worm's gullet. Freedmen, convicts, Catalan refugees. So much loss. He didn't see how House Linkam could survive any more.

He muttered, "Even the sandworms are in league with our enemies."

～⌁～

KNOWN SPIES AND saboteurs should be used as harsh examples, not bargaining chips. Esmar Tuek was not happy with the arrangement his nobleman had made. By releasing the captives to Bauers, Tuek and his interrogators lost the opportunity to obtain important information.

Since their arrival on Duneworld, he'd suspected that someone was feeding the Hoskanners details about what went on inside the Linkam household. His careful questioning of the newly arrested Hoskanner sympathizers and saboteurs had uncovered disturbingly accurate information about finances, habits, and new security measures. He was fully aware of one person who had access to all that information inside the headquarters mansion.

His suspicions turned to Dorothy Mapes, a woman who didn't seem to know her place. She had always been at odds with Tuek, challenging his decisions, using her wiles with Jesse to seize advantages for herself. Though not noble born, she was at the heart of House Linkam's business dealings, tracking productivity, controlling finances, dealing with suppliers who did not fulfill their contracts, influencing Jesse in clever ways.

Tuek had seen ambitious, conniving women manipulate and corrupt Jesse's gullible father and brother. The current patriarch was smarter, tougher, and more practical than his noble predecessors. But still he was a man—and therefore vulnerable. Dorothy knew every detail of the Linkam business, from records of the spice crews to Jesse's work routes and itinerary.

The security chief decided to watch her carefully. She was, potentially, a very dangerous woman. . . .

# 20

Dr. Haynes transmitted a long-awaited message from the forward research base. He had a prototype of his "shock canister" ready for testing against an actual sandworm.

Because of the severe spice-production shortfalls, Jesse decided to gamble everything on the new concept. He would have his other harvesters ready to move if Haynes's device worked as projected. They would wait safely and quietly away from the worm zone while another harvester did its work. In the event that the shock canister failed to stun the sandworm, his standby harvester crews would lose a day of productivity on other fields; if the test worked, though, they might be able to exceed a month's total haul in only a few hours. It was worth the gamble, especially now.

"This is more than a test; it's a huge opportunity," he said to Gurney.

"I don't want to waste it. Are your men prepared for a massive melange harvest?"

"I'm always ready for a massive melange harvest," the spice foreman said, with a gleam in his eyes. He had already mapped out a particularly rich vein for the following day's mining operations. "This field has more than we could take even if the sandworms were on a week-long vacation. I've never dreamed of having the chance—until now."

"Then issue orders to the carryalls. I want them ready to deliver all seven of our remaining spice harvesters for a full-force push."

"If that depth-charge stunner works, laddie."

"Yes, Gurney. *If* it works."

AT THE FORWARD research base, Dr. Haynes proudly displayed a barrel-sized canister that held a powerful static generator. Covered with diamond-hard plating to withstand a worm's gullet, dozens of flexible whiskers sprouted from the device in every direction. Each antenna was insulated with live-rubber shielding and capped with a powerful discharge bulb.

"Judging from readings I took of worm-generated energy fields, this device should pack enough of a jolt."

" 'And the dragon saw that he had been thrown down to the earth.' " Gurney scratched his chin. "Aye, the worm will swallow quite a bitter pill."

Jesse nodded. "Let's get ready. We'll deploy the first spice harvester just like we would on a normal day, so the crews won't suspect. The minute a worm shows itself, we drop the shock canister—and pray."

Dr. Haynes took a solo ornijet to deploy the prototype himself. While Gurney readied the harvester crews on the ground, Jesse joined Tuek in a scout flyer to observe the test. The nobleman felt tense and eager; so much hung on the success of this new technique. He sensed that Counselor Bauers was ready to take drastic action back in Carthage—perhaps even pull the plug on the whole Linkam operation.

They flew up into a shatteringly bright day. The first harvester had already been dispatched to churn through the spice vein, while spotters watched for the arrival of the inevitable worm. "We need sharper eyes than ever before, lads," Gurney transmitted from the desert floor.

This time the spice operations would also serve as bait.

The six other fully crewed harvesters were mystified at the change of plans and complained because they were kept waiting instead of working the fields. No one but Haynes's small team knew about the shock canister.

Tuek guided their flyer above the dust plume generated by the lone harvester. He looked at Jesse with a knowing smile on his red-stained lips as he heard the spice foreman bellowing over the comm system to marshal the men. "Gurney's just a jongleur, but he treats the spice crews like soldiers under his command."

"An apt comparison. We're at war against a dangerous planet as well as the Hoskanners."

"And devil-worms."

The huge mobile harvester went about its work, following a routine that had gone on for more than a year. Usually, the operations reminded Jesse of a swarm of gnats darting in to bite skin, draw a drop of blood, then fly away before a hand could swat them. Now, though, the waiting seemed interminable.

Gripping the flyer's controls, Tuek was clearly uneasy—but not about the test. Something else weighed heavily on the old veteran's mind. Finally, he summoned his courage and said, "My Lord . . . Jesse, there is a matter I must discuss with you."

"I've been wondering what was eating you, Esmar. Out with it."

After only a brief hesitation, the security chief spoke. "I fear your own concubine might be a Hoskanner spy." Before Jesse could even express his shock, Tuek quickly continued, "Someone has been leaking vital details to our enemies . . . when equipment is ordered, the maintenance schedules of our harvesters and carryalls, even guard duty rosters. I learned that much from interrogating the Hoskanner sympathizers. Ask yourself, how many times has Counselor Bauers obtained information he shouldn't have? How often do Hoskanner saboteurs know exactly where to find vulnerable machinery?"

"That doesn't mean we have a traitor, Esmar. Many people have that information. You're a paranoid old fool."

"And you're a lovestruck one. If Dr. Haynes proves his new technique today, it's more crucial than ever that we keep this a secret."

"I have already decided that the crews will be kept isolated to prevent them from passing the word. Nobody in Carthage will know."

"She'll know."

Frowning, Jesse said, "Dorothy was at the original meeting where Dr. Haynes proposed his idea. I have trusted her for twelve years—nearly as long as I've trusted you, Esmar."

The security chief concentrated on his flying, but his shoulders sagged. "Both your father and especially young Hugo lost fortunes, bought expensive trinkets for femme fatales, and allowed themselves to be duped into dangerous romantic intrigues."

"Dorothy's not like that. She is the mother of my son. You'd better have hard evidence if you plan to say any more to me."

Tuek scowled. "No evidence, My Lord, just strong suspicions, which I developed through a process of elimination. It is what I do as your security chief."

Jesse silenced him coldly. "I've heard enough, General Tuek. I refuse to discuss the matter further."

Wrapping his pride around him like thick armor, the veteran spoke not a word as they sat together and waited. It was almost a relief to him when the sandworm came.

"Wormsign!" The spotter's message repeated over all the channels. Workers in the first spice harvester switched to emergency procedures, just as they would on any other day. Gurney would take no chances.

Most of the men didn't know that something was fundamentally different about the current operations.

Tuek indicated the ominous rippling line as the immense creature burrowed straight toward the spice operations, altering the desert landscape with its passage. Jesse spotted a darting movement as a small ornijet streaked down to intercept the worm's path. "That's Dr. Haynes."

The planetary ecologist landed and planted himself halfway between the monster and the spice harvester. Jesse directed Tuek to swoop close to the landing site, in case Haynes needed a rescue. "I've lost enough men and equipment. I'm not about to lose our planetary ecologist, too."

The bottom bay doors of Haynes's ornijet deposited the shock canister onto the dune. The Imperial scientist emerged, going about his activities with brisk but efficient movements while the oncoming worm picked up speed. Perhaps the creature sensed the small craft and intended to gulp an appetizer before charging to the gigantic harvester. . . .

While Jesse watched, circling above with Tuek, the ecologist bent over the prototype, going through a swift checklist, extending the wiry antennae.

"Why isn't he leaving?" Jesse's pulse quickened.

"Dr. Haynes does not leave details to chance."

Finally the ecologist thrust a short pole into the sand next to the diamond-hard canister. Touching his collar, Haynes transmitted, "For insurance, I'm activating one of our static-shield generators. It always drives the creatures into a frenzy."

"Get out of there!"

Haynes switched on the generator. From above, Jesse watched the oncoming worm turn, spraying sand as if the small beacon had enraged it. The monster surged toward the bait, dramatically increasing its speed.

Dashing to his ornijet and scrambling inside, Haynes slammed the access door. The hurtling worm left a wake of tan powder behind it like a stampeding bull, reminding Jesse of the maddened beast that had killed his brother, Hugo. "Doctor, you'd better hurry!"

"Oh, yes, Nobleman. I can hear the worm. I feel the vibrations."

The ornijet lifted off with blast jets. The wings flapped furiously as it gained altitude, first a few meters, then twenty, then fifty.

The static-shield generator continued its call, and the huge worm lunged, its mouth open wide enough to engulf the whole dune. The armored prototype tumbled into the gullet, looking altogether insignificant in the swirl of sand going down.

"The worm's taken it!" Jesse exclaimed. "It's swallowing the charge!"

In the sand-and-air turbulence, Haynes's ornijet dipped and swirled, but the planetary ecologist regained control and soared away.

The shock canister's automatic trigger activated. As the antennae contacted the beast's softer inner flesh, the device unleashed its powerful sting.

The worm swallowed convulsively, and sparks burst out in spectacular, rippling surges. The creature reared and writhed, opening its folded mouth to cough out dust and sand. Sparking loops of discharge lightning crackled from its yawning throat as if the beast had vomited a tiny thunderstorm.

Sparks began to fade from the worm's mouth as the depth charge continued all the way down, blasting one independent ring segment after another. The sinuous body spasmed, rolling on the open dunes. At last, the beast crashed to the ground and lay twitching.

Jesse responded swiftly. "Gurney, have the carryalls bring in the other six spice harvesters! The worm is down. I repeat, *the worm is down!*"

While the sandminers from the remaining harvesters rattled off confused questions, the spice foreman dredged up and transmitted another one of his quotes, which he'd been saving for just such a successful test. "'May their bellies be filled with treasure, O Lord. May their children have more than enough!'"

The planetary ecologist circled around and dropped his ornijet onto the churned, fresh sand next to the hulk of the motionless beast.

"Haynes, what are you doing?" Jesse shouted into the comm.

"This is an unparalleled opportunity, Nobleman. I remind you that my commission still comes from the Emperor, and my assignment is to understand Duneworld. I have never had a chance to see a worm so close. I can learn more in an hour than I have conjectured in the past two years."

"If he stays at the beast's side, he can give us early warning when the worm starts to awaken," Tuek pointed out.

"Exercise extreme caution," Jesse said to Haynes, though he suspected the intensely curious man would do as he pleased anyway.

Safe from the guardian worm, the remaining harvesters were dropped along the rich vein. While a few spotters cruised overhead, alert for storms and other hazards, the sandminers ran out like giddy children on a candy hunt. They could see the giant desert demon lying incapacitated, and they ran out into the rust-powdered sands, digging, scooping, reveling in their unexpected success. Sandminers threw in redoubled efforts, though they could not fight off their joy. Some of them threw handfuls of melange at each other, as if they were at play. The men laughed and threw themselves into the work; after more than two hours of frantic labor, none of them wanted to pause for even a few minutes of rest. Load after load of rich melange filled the cargo containers. Carryalls could not move the bounty away as fast as the men collected it.

All the while, Gurney shouted encouragement, urging them to greater speed, even singing songs. The sandminers were delirious with sudden hope, fully aware of the extravagant bonuses they would at last receive.

"If William English had survived," Jesse said in a low voice, "this one day's haul might have been enough to earn him passage back home."

While the operations continued, Jesse told Tuek to fly him to the fallen sandworm as well. The old veteran frowned, and the stains around his lips made him look as if he had just devoured a large quantity of bloody meat. "You intend to be as foolish as our planetary ecologist?"

Coldly, still stung by the veteran's suspicions of Dorothy, he replied, "It's not often I get to look at a helpless enemy face-to-face. This worm represents as much of a challenge to us as the Hoskanners. Let me feel my moment of victory."

Dutifully, Tuek landed near the lifeless monster. It looked at least a kilometer long. Jesse disembarked and hurried over to the amazed scientist, who stood close to the towering mass. "Is it dead?" The air was filled with the cinnamon redolence of spice.

Haynes had taken scrapings of the hard outer covering of the ring segments. He shook his head. "It'll take far more than that to kill one of these creatures, Nobleman Linkam. This worm won't be any trouble for hours, I suspect. Your crews should have plenty of time to do their work."

"After a year and a half of adversity, we've finally turned the corner." Jesse stared at the enormous sandworm. The sharp smell of cinnamon yelled in his nostrils—raw spice, acrid like the ooze from the sandtrout that had sent English into a drug-induced frenzy.

The leviathan stirred, causing Jesse and Tuek to jump back.

"It's done that several times now," Haynes said. "I think it's having worm dreams."

Before it stopped and settled down again, the creature exhaled a great wind that carried enough vaporous melange to make Jesse dizzy, a sensation that passed as the air cleared. "Even with today's huge haul, I have decided that we'll send only a modest increase to Bauers—just enough to show progress, keep him from shutting us down, but not enough to spark his interest. I want the Emperor and Valdemar Hoskanner to believe we're still struggling."

Tuek gazed up at the massive hulk with a grim expression, as if contemplating how he might wrestle such an opponent. With narrowed eyes and a furrowed brow, the old general turned to Jesse. "You understand that these crews will need to be kept quarantined, My Lord? Now that this trick has worked, if they are allowed back in Carthage, the news will leak, and you can be sure the Hoskanners will try to sabotage what we're doing."

Jesse permitted himself a feisty smile. "We'll erect additional barracks and spice storage facilities in remote places. We'll keep the men busy enough—and earning enough bonuses—to quell their complaints. With only half a year remaining, we need every moment to build up our reserves."

# 21

*The purpose of night is to prune the limbs of yesterday.*

—GURNEY HALLECK,
unfinished poetry

As weeks passed with the sandminers sequestered in hastily erected barracks, far from Carthage's few amenities, House Linkam amassed a significant hoard of melange. Out in the western mountains Gurney established natural warehouses inside rock caves and in camouflaged silos, then posted his most trusted men to guard the treasure.

After each successful worm-stun operation, the isolated workers tallied the spice yield, which translated into bonuses. In less than a month, they had earned as much as they would have banked in half a year under the Hoskanners. Many freedmen sat in amazed disbelief as they realized they finally had a chance to earn passage off this planet.

Some unhappy workers, however, cursed the spice foreman and complained about their quarantine. After several of these disgruntled sandminers tried to escape from a temporary camp and were revealed to be Hoskanner spies, Gurney threw them into a makeshift brig, seized their spice shares, and distributed them among the remaining men.

Meanwhile in Carthage, Jesse used various excuses along with modest increases in the spice he delivered to keep Counselor Bauers at bay. Although Tuek's cordon of soldiers still contained the inspection ship's crew (despite their protests), the Grand Emperor's man could come and go as he pleased. Even so, Bauers learned little and grew increasingly displeased.

No one knew where all the missing spice-harvesting crews had gone. Rumors of underhanded treatment of the men began to spread, and Jesse declined to provide any acceptable explanations.

As he stood in his ship looking out on the city, Counselor Bauers couldn't help smiling to himself, a feral slash that cut across his face. To survive, Jesse Linkam had begun to think like the Hoskanners. . . .

Jesse lay in bed beside Dorothy. Sworn to secrecy about the shock-canister method, she kept an unofficial accounting of how much melange had been gathered. To boost morale, she suggested that Jesse begin quietly providing the exiled spice crews with additional comforts and entertainment, even female companionship, if they wanted it. Jesse also decided to donate his personal chef from the mansion, though Piero Zonn would have even more problems out in a dusty base camp than in the questionable civilization of Carthage. Still, he would be commanded to do what he could for the sandminers; without them, the Hoskanners could never be defeated.

Meanwhile, back in the city, the water reserves of House Linkam had been exhausted. While the people appreciated the generosity, as soon as they began to be turned away their grumbling started once again. Jesse thought of their hardships, feeling guilt because finally his teams were hauling in huge melange harvests, yet he had to pretend to be poor.

With the tighter markets and the higher demand for melange across the Empire, Jesse had Tuek snoop out a few black-market connections. The old veteran was easily able to bring in extra water shipments, using a portion of the never-reported spice hoard to pay for the precious liquid. Thus, Jesse soon reinstituted the water benefits for all supplicants. Times were still hard for the townspeople, but no one in Carthage would go thirsty while he was their nobleman. . . .

After making love that night, Jesse and Dorothy spoke of old times on Catalan, and wished they could be back home. He toyed with the triangular stone of the diagem promise ring on her finger, remembering when he had given it to her out on a lonely reef where they had tied up their boat. The day had been full of intimate moments, romance, and shared dreams. But now Jesse never completely let down his guard in Dorothy's company, troubled by the suspicions Tuek had voiced about her. He held his concubine's firm, warm body against his own, listening to her breathe. Although she lay very still and silent, he knew she was only pretending to sleep so as not to disturb him. How much else was she pretending?

He didn't want to think about it.

AS A TANGERINE dawn profiled the rooftops of Carthage, Ulla Bauers marched to the front arches of the headquarters mansion. Dressed in full Imperial regalia, he strode officiously past the stark, empty pedestals from which all the Hoskanner statues had been so rudely removed.

Jesse greeted him in the entrance hall, but Bauers did not return the smile or the salutation. He scowled ferociously. "Today, I shall watch your sandminers at work. They have not been seen in Carthage for weeks, and most of your crew barracks stand empty. Each time I inquire, you come up with another unbelievable excuse. Hmmm, now, tell me the truth!"

"The workers are out in the desert harvesting spice, Counselor. Just as Grand Emperor Wuda wishes." His voice and wide-eyed expression were full of bewildered innocence.

"Ah, but I *will* see them! Today!"

Trying to look a bit downcast, Jesse responded, "I'm afraid that's impossible. We have suffered great losses of crews and equipment, and every moment counts. All of my men are out either searching for spice veins or trying to harvest them as best they can. You are aware that our exports of spice have increased by more than twelve percent since last month. Why would you question me now?"

Hands on hips, Bauers shot back, spraying spittle with his words, "All well and good, but where are your men working? *Exactly* where?"

A casual shrug. "Out in the dunes somewhere. I can't keep track of their locations. Gurney Halleck is my spice foreman, and I let him choose the most viable veins of melange."

"Stop being evasive with me! I am the Imperial inspector—give me something to inspect! I have received reports of unrest among the Imperial planets, of spice riots and nobles demanding their share of melange, of starship crews petitioning the Emperor for priority distribution."

Jesse raised his eyebrows. "That sounds like quite an exaggeration, Counselor. Our exports are down from the Hoskanner peak, but there is certainly enough melange to fill the most desperate need. Perhaps that implies a bit too much dependence on a luxury drug?"

"Melange is a necessary commodity, not a luxury."

"It still sounds like Hoskanner propaganda. I charge that Valdemar is spreading rumors and causing alarm."

"Hmmm, I assure you these riots are not exaggerations. Thousands have already died. Now tell me where your spice harvesters are!"

Enjoying his guest's discomfiture, Jesse spread his hands. "You could go out looking for them, I suppose, if you consider that to be your Imperial duty. But Duneworld is a big planet, and bad things happen out in the deep desert. Believe me; my son and I almost died out there. The weather can turn on you in an instant." He snapped his fingers. "If you go out into the desert against my advice, I cannot guarantee your safety."

Bauers grew still and cold, reading the implied threat in Jesse's words. "No rules, you mean? You dare to threaten me with the Emperor's words?"

"As you so rightly pointed out, you are an acknowledged expert in contractual matters, in issues of fine print. I am but an inexperienced nobleman faced with a tremendous challenge." He paused for effect. "A challenge, I might add, that I take very seriously."

He ushered the sputtering man out. Jesse knew, however, that Bauers would not give up. He only hoped he could stockpile enough melange before the Imperial inspector discovered his secret.

# 22

A good foreman works hard to guide his crew and get the job done. A good crew follows orders and performs to the best of its abilities. Here, we have failed in both respects.

—GURNEY HALLECK,
incident report

Following the evening meal in the temporary base camp, exhausted sandminers drank their ration of spice beer and shared stories. Inside the sealed mess hall, the cinnamon odor of spice permeated everything.

Though they were far from Carthage and had not seen their homes or families for weeks, most of the sandminers were content enough with their conditions. The new chef found ways to make the prepackaged food much more palatable (though the man huffed about impossible hardships), and each sandminer received double their previous allotment of water. Even the pleasure females were glad to have a small captive audience of customers with credits in their accounts and very little to spend them on. Though the women were dried and leathery, unattractive by most objective measures, the majority of sandminers did not complain.

But some did. The undercurrent never quite disappeared.

One evening while Gurney played the baliset in the communal tent, the men relaxed, dozed, or gambled their shares back and forth in games of chance. The music entertained the crewmen, and the Linkam jongleur enjoyed having a group of listeners every night.

"Toss that baliset over here. It needs to be tuned up," sneered one of the freedmen, Nile Rew. "I'll stomp on it a little with my foot."

Several men laughed. Others told Rew to be quiet.

Gurney forced himself to receive the comment as a joke, though the man's caustic tone suggested otherwise. "I can tune you up the same way."

Rew poured more of the potent spice beer for himself from a spigot attached to the table. As soon as Gurney resumed his music, the edgy freedman swept an arm across the table, sending beer glasses flying. Men cursed him for wasting the precious water in the drinks.

"This place is nothing but a prison! I'm a *freedman,* by all that's holy! With my bonuses, I've already got enough credits to book passage offplanet, but I'm stuck here! For months! Curse the Linkams and their secrets. They have no right to treat us like prisoners." He glared at his fellow sandminers, and shouted to them. "They have no right to keep us here, men. Anyone who wants to go back to Carthage, follow me!"

He lunged for the moisture-seal door which led out to the camp's armorpave landing pad where the ornijets and carryalls were kept. Some of the spicemen chuckled, while a half dozen followed Rew out into the hot night. Despite the large bonuses they were accruing from the remarkable spice harvests, the credits did them no good if they couldn't leave the desert planet—or at least spend them in town.

Gurney stalked after Rew, and a blast of hot wind hit him in the face as he charged through the doorway. The spice foreman plowed toward the disgruntled man, knocking aside several of his drunken followers to get to him. Gurney's movements were as inexorable as an avalanche, and he caught Rew just as he was mounting an ornijet's running board. With a thick forearm, he knocked the surly man to the sand.

Sandminers came out, cheering for Gurney and yelling disparaging comments at Rew, though a handful of men grumbled and moved closer, siding with the surly man. Two of the bedraggled pleasure women watched with pinched expressions, unimpressed with the rowdy behavior.

Rew rose shakily to his feet, then reached into a pocket with surprising speed and brought out a sonic knife. The blade glittered in the camplight.

Gurney backed up a step. "Oh, you want to play, do you?" He drew his own dagger and activated the hilt so that the vibrating edge increased its sharpness beyond that of a diamond razor. "With *me?*"

The spice foreman swung, cutting a buzzing arc through the air. Rew overreacted as he tried to block, but Gurney reversed his own weapon and smacked the freedman's wrist with the butt of the hilt, breaking a thin bone. Rew cried out, and his knife clattered onto the ornijet's running board.

"Enough of this nonsense." Gurney slipped his dagger back into its sheath.

From behind, something struck a hard blow to the back of Gurney's head. He fell, hitting the sand-crusted armorpave surface. He heard a voice, somebody yelling, then rushing footsteps—before he saw a boot draw back just an instant before it struck him in the forehead. . . .

GURNEY WOKE TO a ferocious headache. With his skull pounding and ringing, he had a difficult time focusing on the concerned face of Dr. Cullington Yueh.

"Oh, you gave us quite a scare, friend," said the old battlefield surgeon.

"What are you doing?" Yueh was supposed to be in Carthage, not at the base camp; the doctor knew nothing about the secret deep-desert operations. "You shouldn't be out here."

"Then don't make it necessary for me to come again. When we got the message from your camp saying that you've been unconscious for hours, Nobleman Linkam dispatched me here. Your men were very worried about you!"

"Except for the ones who did this to me." He groaned.

"A few bad apples. Most of your crew are good men, I think. It was like calming a bunch of frantic mothers when I arrived." The surgeon dabbed a pungent-smelling patch on Gurney's aching forehead. "Good thing they called—you might have remained in a coma if I hadn't administered the right drugs."

He gave another, louder groan. "Some doctor! Didn't you bring any pain relievers with you, man?"

The doctor clucked his tongue. "Oh, you already have a full dose. I'm sure your headache will only get worse when Nobleman Linkam gives you a tongue-lashing for not keeping your men under better control."

Still dazed, Gurney mumbled, "What happened?"

"Some of your men escaped and went to town in an ornijet, flying wild. Luckily, because of your crew's warning, General Tuek's security force was able to intercept them as they landed—almost crashed, actually. A pack of drunks."

"Have they talked to anybody?" Alarmed, Gurney tried to sit up, but the old battlefield surgeon pushed him back down.

"Oh, don't you worry. Tuek has them in isolated custody. Your secret is safe."

# 23

*When the world around you is dry as dust, the mere memory of beauty
must suffice.*

—DOROTHY MAPES,
*A Concubine's Life*

Rife with rumors, angry about the spice crews that had been missing for months, the Carthage population blamed everything on
the Linkams. Seeing only meager spice shipments brought back from
the desert and knowing nothing about Jesse's hidden hoard out in the
mountain caves and in camouflaged silos, they felt no hope, only restless rage.

Though Nile Rew and his fellow escapees had been arrested as soon
as they landed their craft, a wild story of forced work camps in the deep
desert had leaked out. Other rumors began circulating about the ex-
travagances of the Linkam household. Jesse continued his free water
stipend, and the people noticed that the nobleman's reserves seemed
inexhaustible; their thoughts turned to suspicion instead of gratitude.

No doubt incited by Hoskanner loyalists, malcontents gathered in front of the headquarters mansion, enraged by some unfounded new rumor. The group seemed to have no leader, which made them even more dangerous as they demanded entry. They carried makeshift weapons, and General Tuek coordinated a defensive operation, which necessitated removing the cordon of soldiers that stood watch around the Imperial ship.

Jesse fumed. How many Hoskanner agents were even now slipping out to infiltrate Carthage all over again? Trapped aboard the inspection vessel for so long, the spies would certainly seize their chance. And the ungrateful townspeople were undoubtedly aiding their efforts, whether willingly or accidentally.

The nobleman looked at the distant faces and felt an anger that matched theirs. Did they not know what was at stake here? "I have already distributed all of our water reserves, Esmar, and paid out of our own spice profits to bring more shipments in. I doubled their rations, gave them all they need. They aren't thirsty—just unhappy." He made a sound of disgust. "Nothing will satisfy them."

Grim, Tuek said, "Sometimes accusations trump goodwill, My Lord. A thirsty man given a drink today will demand another tomorrow. Their memories are very selective, but can any of them say their lives are worse than they were under the Hoskanners?"

"If I gave them an ocean, they would still complain. The only ones truly thirsty are those who have gambled or lost their own rations. I have been more than generous in trying to buy their goodwill. I wanted to be their nobleman, like I was to the people of Catalan. But they spit on my generosity."

From the front of the crowd, a woman shopkeeper shouted, "We demand to see your extravagant conservatory! We know you have it in there."

"Flowers and shrubs!" another woman shouted. "You arrogant bastards!"

The crowd roared; a shrill voice rose above them. "How dare you spill water on plants while our throats are parched!"

Perplexed, the security chief turned to Jesse and said, "A conservatory? Where did that ridiculous rumor start? Hoskanner seditionists, spreading unrest, prodding sore spots." With a gesture, Tuek summoned his armed troops to come forward, their weapons raised.

Deeply concerned, Jesse paled. "The conservatory was Valdemar's; he left it behind. I thought nobody knew about it except for Dorothy and myself."

Tuek's eyes narrowed, adding data to his ever-growing mental catalog. "So, she was one of the few who knew . . . and now someone has leaked it to this mob?"

"Enough, Esmar," Jesse snapped.

Provoked by someone at the rear of the crowd, the people pushed higher on the steps. "We can break our way inside!"

"Stand down, or my men will open fire!" Tuek bellowed.

"You can't shoot us all!" The shouts grew louder, more emotional and incomprehensible.

"I don't want any of these people killed," Jesse cautioned. "Not over something as stupid as this."

"That may be unavoidable, My Lord. I am dutybound to keep you alive." As the people stumbled forward, Tuek ordered three men to drag Jesse to safety, despite his protestations. "Find a secure room for the nobleman." He met Jesse's eyes. "We won't let anyone inside the mansion harm you or your son." Jesse noted that the old veteran pointedly left out Dorothy's name.

At Tuek's command, the loud report of a projectile gun fired into the air should have cowed the people, but instead served as a trigger for the riot. With a cry, more and more dusty men and women rushed up the stairs toward the door.

The Catalan Guards stood shoulder to shoulder. "Prepare for a full barrage!" Tuek yelled so loudly that his voice cracked in the dry air.

"Stop!" A woman's voice came from below the steps, to the side of the main entrance. A previously locked servants' door now stood open, and Dorothy Mapes emerged. "Stop!" For a relatively small woman, she shouted her command with a power that seemed superhuman.

Tuek glared at Dorothy and gestured to four of his men. "Sweet affection, get her out of there!"

Unprotected, she lifted her head with regal dignity and faced the mob, as if she could guard the servants' entrance simply with her confidence."You people have been misinformed! We have given the city of Carthage all our water reserves for distribution to the people. You know this."

"What about the conservatory?"

"We know you're hiding it!"

Tuek's security guards elbowed their way down the stairs, but could not move through the crowd swiftly enough. Jesse tore himself free of his escort and ran back toward the main entrance, trying unsuccessfully to reach his concubine. The men and women were clustered too tightly, jockeying for position and pushing him back.

"Then anyone who wishes to see, come with me," Dorothy yelled over the tumult. She held a hand up. "Twenty of you at a time. I will show you the difference between House Linkam and House Hoskanner."

Before a livid Tuek could stop her, she allowed a group of the protesters inside the mansion.

⁓

WHEN JESSE AND the guards finally caught up with Dorothy and the twenty angry townspeople on the fourth floor, she had led them to the end of a corridor in the south wing. "This was a Hoskanner conservatory!" she said. Holding the full attention of the witnesses, she activated the secret panel, and the moisture-seal door hissed open.

"Look inside and imagine the decadence, the waste of water, the lushness that *Valdemar Hoskanner* hid for his own private amusement.

Imagine how many of your fellow citizens went thirsty because of his self-indulgence."

Within the sheltered greenhouse chamber, only dead plants filled shelves and counters. Dry leaves and dead insects lay scattered about. The air was redolent with the smell of dry decay.

"Nobleman Linkam knows how hard life is here on Duneworld," she continued, "and such waste offends him. When My Lord learned of Valdemar's personal paradise, he shut off all water to this room." Her voice was as firm as a rock formation from the deep desert. "Outraged at the excess, we allowed every plant in the conservatory to die—and the water was passed on to the people of Carthage, making life better for you."

The twenty spectators gazed around, some nervous, some ashamed, some looking completely out of place, as if they didn't know why they had been drawn into the mob in the first place.

One large man still searched for a way to release his pent-up emotions. Dorothy did not flinch, even when confronted by his bulk. "Why won't you let the spice crews come home? What about all the melange you're hiding in the deep desert?"

"Outright lies and destructive rumors." Dorothy waved an arm expansively, sure now that they would believe her. "Just like this."

Tuek's men stood uncertainly in the hall, weapons ready, but the fury had died from this first group of observers. The guards led them outside, while Dorothy remained in the room to await others.

Jesse came to her side. "That was foolish, and dangerous."

"But effective. Would you rather our house guards slaughtered them all?" She gave him a small, hard smile. "Esmar will hate guiding more people in here, won't he? But I keep my word, as you do yourself."

He frowned, but kept his thoughts private. Even Tuek hadn't known about the conservatory—so how had the rumor started in the first place? Of course, he realized: the Hoskanners knew. But they didn't—or *shouldn't*—know about the deep-desert operations. Niles Rew and his unruly escapees had been held in isolated custody, yet still someone had leaked the information. Two damaging secrets had gotten out, at the same time.

Tuek couldn't possibly be right about her. But Jesse found it difficult to dispute the facts. Throughout their tenure here, saboteurs had known about the movement of equipment, the stations of security troops, the orders of new harvesters and carryalls, which were inexplicably delayed. . . .

"What is it, Jesse?" She looked at him, her brow furrowed. Did he see a hint of guilt etched on her face? Could she possibly be hiding something? From him? Now, suddenly, he couldn't be sure.

Dorothy continued to look at him, waiting for an answer. Finally, he turned away. "Nothing."

# 24

*In the Known Universe some of the most inhospitable worlds hold the
most value.*

—REPORT OF THE IMPERIAL RESOURCE BOARD

After the crowd had dissipated—for now—Jesse and Tuek strode
through the corridors of the mansion. The brooding security
chief seemed even more introspective than usual.

Sunlight passed through leaded plaz windows with an intensity that
suggested the level of afternoon heat outside. Members of the household staff were picking up debris and dust in the halls and rooms from
such a large influx of people.

With a glance at Tuek, Jesse said, "We've proved something to them
at least. Valdemar Hoskanner would never have allowed them such access."

"He would have killed everyone in the mob." The veteran did not
sound judgmental. "As I was prepared to do."

"It could have been much worse if not for Dor's quick thinking."

Scowling, the other man rubbed his red-stained lips. "Her foolish bravado, you mean. She put us all in danger." After a long moment, he added, "In my experience, Jesse, rumors begin far from the light of day—but they all start somewhere, an ember of truth that is fanned into flames by an instigator."

He knew the old veteran meant Dorothy. Jesse didn't understand why Tuek had never liked or trusted her. Was it because she had so much influence over the nobleman, while she was only a commoner? "When we came here, Esmar, we fired much of the old domestic staff that worked for the Hoskanners. Some of them could have known about the conservatory. They must have talked."

"But why now, My Lord? At the same time as the rumor about the spice stockpiles in the deep desert? I do not like coincidences." He motioned for Jesse to follow him into a nearby chamber. After they closed the door, the security chief removed a messagestat cylinder from an inside jacket pocket. The ornate cylinder bore an unmistakable Imperial crest.

"I found this on my desk an hour ago," Tuek said. "Counselor Bauers has also heard the rumors of our secret hoard, and he believes them."

"He certainly gets up early."

Tapping the cylinder, Tuek said, "Based on the amount of bluster, I'm confident he doesn't have proof yet. But someone informed him, even before today's mob started spreading rumors. In fact, I have it on good authority that he has already dispatched search teams into the desert."

Jesse felt a chill. "Has Gurney's latest camp been moved?"

He nodded. "I sent an immediate order, and Bauers will only find a few tracks in the sand. We should be able to stay one step ahead of him."

"Then why aren't you smiling, old friend?"

"There's more." The veteran's face darkened. "The Emperor himself is coming here on his private yacht, along with an Imperial military force, to formally confiscate all melange . . . supposedly to preserve

peace. The Emperor plans to strip you of your title . . . and monopoly . . . here."

Jesse had the cylinder open now, scanning the details. Looking up,
he said, "In a contest with no rules, keeping our production levels secret should not have been a problem, but I'm afraid they never had any
intention of letting me win the challenge. The Emperor and Valdemar
had a deal in place before any of this began." He hurled the cylinder
against a stone wall. The cylinder bounced and then rolled on the
floor, making a clatter that seemed to mock him.

"We only have three days to get ready," Tuek said. "Then we will
have to face Grand Emperor Wuda. I hope you're not willing to concede defeat, My Lord."

"Absolutely not, Esmar. But we need to buy ourselves some time."

THAT NIGHT JESSE lay beside Dorothy in bed. Though she slept
peacefully, he remained awake and alert, full of thoughts and doubts
that he didn't want to share with her, or with anyone. Not yet. First he
needed to sort them out himself.

With his proclamation, Bauers had effectively hamstrung the
Linkam hopes. If Jesse revealed the spice he'd been holding in reserve
while exporting only minimal amounts, then the Grand Emperor
would simply take it. No rules. Apparently no justice or fair play, either.

He and Tuek had decided to keep the Emperor's imminent arrival a
secret for now, including from Dorothy.

*In three days I must face the Emperor. Will I lose my title without so much
as a chance to answer his questions?* Jesse suspected, though, that in this
devious trap no answer would ever be acceptable.

He had plenty of questions of his own. Why was the Imperial leader
so desperate for spice? Exports were much less than the Hoskanner
quotas, but enough melange had still gone directly to Renaissance to

more than meet the Emperor's personal needs. Were other noble families agitating for shares of the Duneworld prize? Melange was in wide demand, judging from the Hoskanner production and export records he had seen. But still, wasn't it just a drug—a luxury?

If the Emperor disqualified Jesse from this contest, House Linkam would be ruined. They had mortgaged everything, even borrowing deeply from exploitive noble families who charged crippling interest. Could Jesse leave that in place as a legacy for his son? Barri would be penniless, as weak and insignificant as William English's family had been. The thought of Barri being thrown onto a penal planet like Eridanus V made his stomach roil.

Intellectually, when he assessed the angry powers arrayed against him, Jesse knew he could not win. For a moment he considered just taking his spice hoard and fleeing to another planet. Given the high price of melange, even on the black market, he could buy a planet somewhere on the fringe of the Empire. Take Dorothy and Barri, load a ship, and go renegade.

*The Grand Emperor cannot strip House Linkam if he cannot find House Linkam.* Despite his flouting of rules, even Emperor Wuda could not completely spurn the Nobles' Council. Legalities must be observed.

But unlike his father and brother, Jesse Linkam was not a man to run and hide. Besides, Ulla Bauers would undoubtedly use some tricky legal loophole to hunt down Jesse and his family.

Rage infused Jesse, and fresh determination. He thought of another way.

Leaning across the bed, he kissed Dorothy on the cheek. "I love you, my darling. Always remember that." She murmured the same in return, then drifted back to sleep again with a gentle smile on her face.

*Three days.*

Jesse swung out of bed, dressed quietly, and slipped into the shadowy corridor. He wrote and sealed a terse, irrefutable letter that specifically revoked all of his concubine's authority, stating that Dorothy could no longer be his proxy. And he intentionally named no successor. *Let Bauers wrestle with that little legal wrinkle.*

Because he would leave no explanation, she would be angry, even crushed, but Jesse was confident she could eventually figure out his reasons. He considered waking Tuek and telling the security chief his plans, then decided instead to take this bold action on his own. If they didn't know what he was doing, even an Imperial interrogator could not drag the information from them.

Before long, Jesse was at the controls of an ornijet, speeding over the dark sands toward the forward research base.

# 25

*We are, each of us, capable of anything.*

—VALDEMAR HOSKANNER

Confused, upset, and most of all afraid for her nobleman's safety, Dorothy waited for three days, but no word came from him. Jesse had disappeared in the middle of the night, leaving only a shocking letter that stripped her of all authority. Why? What had she done? Had someone accused her?

No one seemed to know where the Linkam patriarch had gone, and because he had removed her as his proxy, no person could be contacted who was officially in charge of House Linkam. It was an impossible situation. All business seemed to be frozen.

Hardest to deal with were Barri's questions about his father. The boy could sense his mother's concern, but he wasn't completely frightened yet. Jesse had often gone out to the spice fields, though never without telling her first.

If he knew anything about the mystery, Esmar Tuek refused to share information with her. The security chief seemed even more guarded than usual, as if he dreaded what was about to happen. He kept watching the open skies. After reading the severance letter, Tuek had looked at Dorothy with even deeper suspicion. It troubled her to see the strange enmity in his eyes, the subtle hostility in his demeanor. But he was hiding a deep secret of his own behind that hard, inscrutable face; she could read the telltale signs in his body language.

Yet Jesse claimed he trusted the man implicitly. Tuek had now served three heads of House Linkam, and it was not a mere concubine's place to question the relationship between a nobleman and his loyal, if overly zealous, security chief.

Why would Jesse simply leave Carthage? Why hadn't he trusted her enough to explain his strange departure? It was as if he wanted to make himself disappear and hide from everyone, even from her. . . .

And now an unannounced ship was arriving.

Alerted by an office assistant, Dorothy ran out on a sealed-plaz balcony of the mansion. From her high vantage she gazed toward the northern desert, where a heat-addled shape approached, glinting in the midday sun. She hoped it was the ornijet Jesse had taken, or perhaps a larger transport ship from the forward base. Thermal ripples in the air blurred all details.

The approaching craft circled, choosing the best of the various landing fields in the stepped and rocky city. The Imperial inspection ship still dominated the main field, where it had rested for months without moving.

Hearing something behind her, she turned to see Tuek step out on the balcony. Had he been reading her thoughts . . . or spying on her in his irritating manner? She kept her tone cordial but cool. "That ship isn't Jesse coming back, is it, General?"

The old veteran stood stiff and straight, watching the unusual craft land in one of the zones normally reserved for Linkam ships. She had never seen a vessel of such gaudy design. "No, that is not Nobleman

Linkam." He pointed toward the smaller of the two spaceports. "It is Emperor Wuda's personal yacht."

She reeled. The Emperor had come in person! Even under the baking heat of Arrakis, Dorothy felt a peculiar, disturbing coldness. An Imperial arrival could only mean a political coup that would damage House Linkam. "Does Jesse know about this?"

The general smiled slightly with his stained lips. "It is not for me to say what the nobleman knows or does not know." He turned to look at the Imperial yacht as it landed. "Now the fun begins."

⁓

A POMPOUS AND overdressed emissary issued a formal command for Nobleman Jesse Linkam to meet with Grand Emperor Wuda aboard the inspection ship. The tall emissary displayed all the emotion of a robot; he stood in the mansion's great vaulted hall, delivered his words to Dorothy, and then turned like clockwork, preparing to exit.

"I'm afraid that's not possible," Dorothy said, bringing him to a halt. "The nobleman is not currently available." Her voice, though soft, had the effect of a wrench jammed into the man's gears.

Flustered, the emissary searched for a new script from which to recite. "No one is unavailable for the Grand Emperor!"

The man's large stature made Dorothy feel even smaller, but she had seen his type before and had no patience for imagined self-importance."Nobleman Linkam is in the deep desert supervising spice operations. I do not know his exact whereabouts, and I have no way of communicating with him."

"Nobleman Linkam was forewarned of the Grand Emperor's arrival. He should have arranged to be present. Who is his proxy to receive an edict? The formalities must be observed."

"No one. I was formally removed from that position, and the nobleman has not yet appointed a replacement."

The man looked as if he might explode. A sudden bright pleasure warmed Dorothy's heart as she put the pieces together and reviewed the evidence. This was exactly why Jesse had made himself unavailable! He had intentionally terminated her as his representative, leaving a vacuum, which effectively tied the Emperor's hands. If no one could find the nobleman, then no one could deliver legal demands. And no one could make any binding decisions for him.

Dorothy maintained her confident smile. "Spice harvesting is a difficult business, and unforeseen disasters occur with unfortunate regularity." Not a lie . . . in fact, she hadn't told him much of anything. "Though I am not allowed to make binding decisions for Nobleman Linkam, I would be happy to greet the Emperor. Tell him I will be there at the appointed time."

The emissary did not look pleased, but could only agree.

⟆

AFTER PASSING THROUGH the ornamental rock garden where the broken Hoskanner statues had been discarded, Dorothy crossed the armorpave landing field toward the huge inspection ship. Hot yellow sunlight pounded down with the force of weapons fire, but she breathed as calmly as she could, trying to force peace upon herself.

General Tuek insisted on accompanying her, but still held his secrets as tightly as Duneworld gripped the mysteries of melange. How could she react properly to the Emperor if she did not have the information she needed? Why hadn't Jesse explained himself to her before creating the authority vacuum?

Together, they stepped onto a royal purple carpet that had been laid for the Grand Emperor's procession from the ornate yacht at the other spaceport to the enormous inspection vessel. Blown dust and sand had already dulled some of the fabric's brilliant color.

Imperial guards stood at attention on each side of the inspection ship's entrance, where an open lift awaited the visitors. She and Tuek entered an enclosure that verified their identities and scanned for weapons. After being cleared, they stepped through to the lift where Ulla Bauers waited, gazing down the bridge of his nose at them. "Hmmm, since when do a concubine and an old soldier speak on behalf of a House? We specified Nobleman Linkam in person."

Dorothy bristled, but tried not to show her irritation. She glanced sidelong at the stoic veteran; his red-stained lips formed a firm iron line.

"Nevertheless," Tuek said, "we will try to be of assistance."

"Hmm-ahh, we shall see. This way."

The lift took them up twenty-seven levels, deep inside the massive inspection vessel. Dorothy wondered why the Emperor's man needed such an immense ship to keep watch on spice operations. Perhaps much of the size might be puffery to promote an imposing sense of awe for the Emperor. Tuek was convinced that the vessel contained an entire standing army tucked away in soundproof compartments, though he had no proof.

Maybe the Counselor had hoped to seize a huge cargo of spice by military force, leaving the Linkams empty-handed. Packing such a hoard into the ship and delivering it to the Grand Emperor, after skimming a satisfactory percentage for himself, Bauers would reap many rewards.

Dorothy and Tuek followed the overdressed, ferretlike man through a maze of corridors, observation galleries, and rooms without apparent purpose, then into the opulent grand salon. The gilded walls and ceilings were covered with frescoes, some of the finest and most extravagant workmanship she had ever seen. On the far side of the chamber, one of the Emperor's numerous portable thrones had been erected; Inton Wuda undoubtedly had one aboard his personal space yacht as well.

The fat, pale ruler sat high atop the elaborate chair; to Dorothy, he looked like an overstuffed, overdressed doll. Bauers moved forward with a mincing gait that seemed like an intricate court dance. He bowed, then stepped to one side. With a casual gesture, Bauers motioned for the two to approach.

In unrehearsed unison, Dorothy and Tuek bowed, averting their eyes from the most powerful man in the Known Universe, the third Wuda to rule in succession following the Millennial Wars. Nearly lost in bowls of fat, his eyes moved from face to face. When he spoke, his voice seemed too small to come from such an important man. "What is this insignificant delegation? I summoned Nobleman Linkam himself."

"He is not in Carthage, Sire," Dorothy said, keeping her eyes averted. "And he has left no official proxy to act in his stead."

"This is the nobleman's concubine, a mere commoner," Bauers said with a sniff, then added as if it were a joke, "Hmm, and she also serves as the business manager for House Linkam. The former sapho addict is Esmar Tuek, their security chief. Note his red lips, from the sapho cure."

"An odd pair." Wuda scowled and squirmed, as if preparing to rise from his throne in indignation, then deciding it wasn't worth the effort. "What sort of insult is this? When is your nobleman expected back?"

Tuek answered. "We're not certain, Sire. He is working the spice fields with his men, striving to do the best possible job on your behalf."

"If he's working so hard, then where is the melange to show for it?" the Grand Emperor demanded. "His output has been shameful, an embarrassment! All across my Empire, people are clamoring for his head."

Dorothy was sure the Emperor must be exaggerating. "Nobleman Linkam has recently increased production, Sire. Since he has several months remaining in his challenge, he hopes to deliver greater quantities to you soon."

"So he's hopeful, is he? Well, so am I! And whatever *I* hope for holds precedence!"

Dorothy wasn't sure what distinction the Emperor was trying to make, but he had grown quite red in the face. "We will do whatever you command, Sire."

"Of course you will! And don't speak unless you have something in-telligent to say." He snorted, looking disdainfully at the diagem prom-ise ring Jesse had given her. "A concubine business manager! And a worn-out sapho addict!"

Bauers swept in from the side. "Shall I escort them out of here, Sire?"

"Not until you learn exactly where Nobleman Linkam is, so that we may go out and see what he is doing. We flew halfway across the Known Universe to come here. We must take care of this matter promptly and get spice production back to normal. I should never have listened to Nobleman Hoskanner. This whole challenge is nonsense."

"We don't know exactly where our master is," Tuek repeated. Though he spoke the truth, as Dorothy did, it was obvious to both of them that Jesse didn't want to be found.

Dorothy added, "Because of continual danger from worms, spice op-erations shift from day to day."

The Grand Emperor showed his displeasure by putting his face through a variety of unpleasant expressions. "Incompetence, utter in-competence! You don't even know where your nobleman is, and he left no one in charge. No wonder the spice exports have collapsed."

Bauers emitted a wicked chuckle. "Hmm, the disadvantages of hav-ing a commoner for a business manager."

Because the Emperor laughed at the joke, Dorothy and Tuek were forced to chuckle along with him.

As Bauers herded them out of the grand salon, Dorothy noticed a mark on the lower part of his neck, mostly hidden by his voluminous black collar. It looked like a gray tattoo, but she could see only the rounded top of it.

Noting her interest, Bauers quickly got behind her and pushed them toward the doorway.

*Is he hiding something?* she wondered.

# 26

*Sometimes, it is wise not to investigate every mystery you encounter.*

—SANDMINER'S ADMONITION

Two men stood outside the brown barracks dome watching the murk settle in the late afternoon sky. Very soon, Jesse wanted to declare victory by fiat; the only score that would impress Emperor Wuda was an overwhelming amount of melange and the secret of an immensely effective new production technique. He would have to return with so much spice in hand that Valdemar's promises and bribes would look paltry by comparison.

Jesse Linkam would turn the old order of commerce and politics on its ear.

Though Dr. Haynes was technically in Imperial employ, he had agreed to keep all aspects of the shock-canister technology confidential. If Emperor Wuda tried to seize the spice and deny House Linkam its profits and glory, General Tuek already had orders to destroy the designs and all of the supporting work. Now that the idea was out there, however, somebody could re-create it—but that would take a considerable amount of time and effort to accomplish, and the Empire was desperate for spice now. Jesse still maintained the upper hand.

Despite several days of labor that seemed harder than the worst battle he'd ever fought, Gurney Halleck wore an incongruously boyish grin on his lumpy face. The bruise in the center of his forehead was a fading blotch of yellow and purple. "The Emperor's spies may have learned about our stockpiles, laddie, but they have no inkling how *much* spice we've gathered or *how* we did it. The numbers, and our method, would astonish even Bauers himself." The jongleur's grin widened further.

"Exactly how much do we have, Gurney? The last tally I saw, we were approaching eighty percent of our goal."

"Should be well over ninety percent now. Now that we've gotten rid of that bastard Rew and others who were poisoning morale, our sandminers have been working like madmen. To quote an old saying, 'All work and no play . . . makes for bigger bonuses!' I'm awfully proud of the men." The spice foreman narrowed his eyes. "They all deserve a huge reward."

"After we win, I'll be generous until it hurts, Gurney. As soon as the Emperor locates me, he intends to force me to leave Duneworld. Don't think he hasn't already reached a backroom deal with Valdemar Hoskanner. The clock is ticking, and a lot of things could still go wrong." He gazed toward the horizon. The new weather satellites had spotted a storm brewing out there.

"This morning's scouts found a rich vein nearby," Gurney reported. "Maybe the biggest yet. It surfaced sometime during the night. If we use one more shock canister and put all seven spice harvesters on it, we might actually top our production goal. In a matter of hours."

"Only if the weather holds. We've been in communication silence, but the Grand Emperor must have arrived in Carthage by now. He's probably bellowing for me, but we've moved around so much that even Esmar can't figure out where we are."

"Yes indeed. All those storms, static discharges, and faulty Hoskanner equipment." His smile became sly. "No way to track us down. Very difficult to keep effective lines of communication open . . . especially when we don't want to."

"Esmar still thinks there's a standing Imperial army hidden inside that inspection ship. If he's right, I hope they don't stage a military takeover of Carthage." He clenched his teeth. "No rules! That foul Wuda fails to follow his own conditions when it looks as if the contest might not turn out the way he wants."

"He may be Emperor, My Lord, but he is no nobleman. He has no honor."

Jesse shook his head sadly. "You're right."

"The men are tired, and it's late in the day, but we can still deploy a last shock charge and continue spice operations into the night until the storm forces us to halt." Gurney's rough skin looked ruddy in the oddly colored light. "Or we can pack up and wait for tomorrow."

"Each tomorrow holds too much uncertainty. Send out the crews and hope the weather doesn't turn on us. This time, I'll deploy the canister myself. Let's win this game, Gurney."

# 27

*Genuine trust is even rarer than the spice melange.*

—GENERAL ESMAR TUEK,
*Security Briefings*

Restless and unable to sleep because of the Emperor's threats, Dorothy spent part of the night alone in the dry, empty conservatory. It was a silent and private place, though no longer secret. With all the plants dead and brittle, no one had a reason to go in there anymore.

Sitting alone in the darkness, smelling the powdery decay around her, she closed her eyes and imagined the room as it had been when she first saw it, so verdant and moist, an oasis in the barren desert . . . an outrageous display of Hoskanner wealth and power.

But had she and Jesse been correct in killing this little piece of Eden? The plants did not belong here on Duneworld, but neither did she. No human did. The fungi, flowers, and fruit shrubs were a reminder of other places, of more pleasant environments. Was it really a reckless waste of water, as she and Jesse had insisted, or should they have seen it as a sign of hope? The thought of the greenery, moisture, and teeming life was so blissful that she laid her head on the table and drifted off to sleep. . . .

An abrupt shadow superimposed itself on Dorothy's dream. She sat up in alarm, though she didn't know why she felt such urgency. Looking around, she saw nothing out of place, but something was not right. Emerging from the sealed conservatory, she sensed immediately that the mansion was too silent.

The concubine hurried down the wide central staircase to the second level, where she found two of Tuek's guards lying in the hall, arms and legs akimbo like insects sprayed with poison. She froze, listening for any movement, then glided forward to check them for pulses. Both men were alive, but unconscious. Gas? Something incredibly fast-acting, she decided. Sniffing the air, she caught a faint, unusual odor reminiscent of pine and burnt sugar.

As she ran down the corridor, she found more bodies. The night staff had fallen in their tracks. The mansion's sealed ventilation system must have been compromised; a powerful soporific would have done its work in short order. The isolated conservatory, kept secret by Valdemar Hoskanner, used an independent system.

Heart pounding, she raced to Barri's bedchamber. The door to the boy's room was open, and she nearly tripped over Tuek's motionless form sprawled on the floor, his hand gripping a stun gun. Apparently the security chief had suspected something amiss, but not in time to do anything about it.

"Barri!" Stumbling inside, she saw that her son's bedding was in disarray, and expected to find him unconscious like all the others. But he was not there.

*My son is gone!*

Dashing to the window, Dorothy saw three dark forms running through the front rock garden where the Hoskanner statues had been discarded. She judged them to be large men, and they carried a bundle about the size of a young boy. Frantically, she overrode the seals, cracked the casing around the window, and broke it open to the dry night air. "Stop!"

The men looked up at her, but sped onward. They were much too far away for her to catch them. A mother's anguished cry rose on a warm night breeze. Her throat was constricted by a rattling necklace of horror. The ungainly rhythm of her own heartbeats pounded in her ears.

As the dark figures kept running, Dorothy broke her paralysis and hurried back to Tuek's unconscious form, where she wrenched the stunner out of his slack grip. As soon as she reached the open window, she depressed the firing stud without knowing how far the weapon could shoot. Though she sprayed the area, the stunner's beam dissipated into the empty night, and the kidnappers disappeared with the boy. She tossed the useless weapon on the bed.

At once furious and terrified, Dorothy went back and tried to rouse the incapacitated veteran, shaking him as hard as she could. "Wake up, damn you! General Tuek, do your job!" He didn't move. She slapped his face, but he was too deep in unconsciousness. White-hot anger infused her. This man should have protected her son!

"Damn you, damn you, damn you!" She hit him harder across the face, and the triangular diagem of Jesse's pledge ring cut the skin on his rough cheek. Blood trickled down the side of his weathered face, but she didn't care.

Someone with intimate knowledge of the household must have abducted Barri. Everything had been coordinated too perfectly, executed with precision. Inside her head, Dorothy heard the needle-stick noises that came with fear, skin-rasping fingernails followed by a bloom of sound in the murky shadows around her, cutting the stillness of the mansion.

Spinning, she saw Dr. Cullington Yueh sauntering toward her. He had escaped, too! He wore a gas filter over his kindly face and held the gilded ceremonial scalpel in his hand, its razor edge glinting in the low light.

Dorothy's eyes widened with realization. She didn't need to say anything, but looked around for something with which to defend herself. A small statue was out of her reach.

"I don't know how you escaped the gas, Dorothy." He pulled his mask aside and let it hang on his neck. "Oh, my job would have been easier if you'd gone to sleep like the others. Then I . . . I could have . . ."

Her skin grew hot, and she struggled to keep from flying at him with her fists. "*Why,* Cullington? What do you have to gain?" Her words tasted like acid. "Is Barri dead? What are they going to do to him? Tell me—*now!*"

The old surgeon bowed his head in shame and extended his prized ceremonial scalpel to her, handle first. His face was covered with perspiration. "Take my life, I beg you, for I must pay the price of betrayal."

She snatched the weapon, but hesitated before using it. "What sort of trick is this?"

"I had no choice but to allow them in, and now I cannot go on. Kill me. That will put an end to it all. Oh, I'm sure my Wanna is dead anyway."

"What happened to Barri? How can I get him back? *Why would you do this to us?*"

He reeked with dishonor, appeared barely able to stand. "The Hoskanners. They have imprisoned my wife Wanna on Gediprime. They torture her, yet keep her alive. Each time I refuse to perform Valdemar's bidding, they send me new images of her agony."

"You said she was dead!"

"Better if she were." Yueh shook his head. "They forced me to act as their spy and saboteur. But my life—even hers—is not worth all this." He gestured at the comatose forms around them, then crumpled to his knees, his face a mask of misery. Suddenly, he grabbed the scalpel and slashed at his forearm, succeeding only in cutting a long, shallow gash before Dorothy grabbed his weapon hand.

"Cullington! Stop this nonsense!" She fought with him for the scalpel, and finally wrenched it from his sweaty palm, as both of them tumbled to the floor.

Lying defeated beneath her, the old man looked at the bloody surgical blade in her hands, then at her face. "Use the knife, please! If I die, then I am no longer their puppet. Wanna would kill me herself if she knew what I was driven to do."

Dorothy seethed. Tuek had suspected her, but all along Yueh was the real traitor, the clandestine source of information for the enemies of House Linkam. She realized that when the surgeon had tended Gurney Halleck's injury, he had learned the secret of the new spice-harvesting operations.

Information he must have leaked to Jesse's mortal enemies. . . .

"You will not die by my hand, Cullington. Not today. I need to save my son—and you're going to help me do it." She threw the scalpel down the corridor, and it skittered away. The old doctor began to stammer excuses, but she took him by the collar and pulled his sweating face close to hers. Blood from the cut on his arm dripped onto the floor, where thirsty stones absorbed the red wetness. "You're going to do everything I tell you to do. *Everything*, even if it kills you."

Broken, Yueh sobbed, and tears streamed down his sagging face. "Oh, with all my heart, I pledge myself to you. From this day forward, my life begins anew."

# 28

*There are many kinds of storms.*
*Take care not to underestimate any of them.*

—NOBLEMAN JESSE LINKAM

The seven spice harvesters were deployed simultaneously, every able-bodied man ready to operate the factory machinery. After months in exile, they could smell the sharp possibility of success, and it smelled like melange.

After opening the comm line, Jesse spoke to the men. They were already charged with anticipation, and he funneled their hopes, strengthening their collective will. "After today, if we bring in even half as much melange as I hope, you can return to Carthage. Go to your homes, your families, and your well-earned rest." He smiled, hearing an echo of cheers over the speaker. "And, at last, many of you freedmen can leave Duneworld. There's a ticket offplanet for any man who wants it—or a high-paying job for anyone who chooses to stay with me."

He watched the crews in their joyous frenzy as carryalls picked up harvesters and lifted into the sky. He'd never seen the men so eager to hit the sands. "But first, let's fill up those harvesters. This is Duneworld—and the spice is there for the taking!"

With military precision, the carryalls dropped the first industrial vehicles onto the rusty sands. In a matter of moments, the harvesters ratcheted into position and began to dig into the caked desert. Dust plumes churned into the darkening sky. Overhead, circling flyers monitored an oncoming weather front, and satellites mapped its course, unable to project how the storm might shift in its path.

The well-seasoned crews did not allow the weather to slow them. By now, the men had rehearsed the routine enough to be comfortable with working on a high wire over a chasm. Every day entailed hardships and dangers, while small fortunes of melange passed into their personal accounts. Most of the freedmen had already earned enough to buy tickets offworld, and the convict teams saw their passage monies placed in trust, so they could truly leave Duneworld as soon as their sentences ended.

With all the machinery landed in the midst of the reddish vein, the sandminers began loading container after container of fresh, redolent spice, which was processed and compacted, then airlifted away to be added to the dispersed stockpiles.

When the inevitable sandworm finally appeared, it charged in from the northern fringe of the storm, plowing straight at them. Like a fur-whale breaching the Catalan seas, the creature surged above the dunes, a ringed, sinuous body haloed with crackling static electricity.

Since coming to this planet, Jesse had become a competent ornijet flyer, one who was aware of the vagaries of desert weather, cold sinks, thermal updrafts, hot crosswinds, and abrasive sands. Now, as he received the worm spotter's call, he cruised in and adjusted his trajectory to intercept the beast.

"On course," he transmitted to Dr. Haynes on a private frequency. "I'll deploy the canister within safety parameters." Jesse's voice sounded surprisingly calm to his own ears, belying the fear that he felt. His best men and equipment were out there on the spice sands, flirting with disaster.

In the months since they'd begun using Haynes's depth-charge system, only one of the numerous shock canisters had misfired; even then, the highly trained crews had averted catastrophe by evacuating the men and equipment in time. And this was to be the last shock-charge deployed before House Linkam claimed unexpected victory in the great contest. If he defeated the Hoskanners, Jesse could begin to have a normal life again. Success today would guarantee a strong foundation for House Linkam and for his son.

According to plan, Jesse set the small ornijet down on an open expanse of dunes, then disengaged the shock canister and let it settle onto the soft sand. Leaving the engines humming and the wings vibrating, he sprang out and set the device.

Directly overhead, the sky had darkened to an ominous gray-brown soup, the leading edge of an approaching Coriolis storm. Wasplike crackles of static began to jump and pop around his boots, while pebbles bounced along the top of the dune, activated by the discharge that came as a precursor to the Coriolis winds.

Jesse's hands tingled as he planted the static-shield generator next to the canister. *Bait.* When he activated its thrumming field, alarming blue-white flickers rippled through the air. He hurried. With his senses optimized to a frightening level, he saw and heard the worm coming toward him like a maglev train, lured by the tempting song of the generator.

Visible sparks leaped from the wings of his landed craft, dancing in the air. Incredible! After a quick double check of the canister, Jesse scrambled back into the ornijet and lifted into the sky, sending out a burst of exhaust.

He was safely away by the time the sandworm's whirlpool maw gulped the shock canister. A knockout surge shot down the worm's gullet, and the creature rose up, writhing and thrashing at the air. An amazing burst of lightning flashed out of its mouth. A web of tiny shocks curled up and down its outer rings. Balls of white light collected in plasma surges, then flew upward to pop like soap bubbles. St. Elmo's Fire.

Sparks flew in all directions; globes of phosphorescent light erupted like fireworks. The eyeless monster lurched forward, leaped high, and then crashed down onto the uneven dunes, sending reverberations in all directions.

"Well, laddie, *that* was impressive!" Gurney's transmitted voice was exuberant.

"Never seen anything like it," Jesse said over the comm line. Feeling a little shaky, he circled over the downed worm to make sure it was subdued. "We should have a minimum of six hours. Get your crews back to work."

By now, the sandminers knew with a fair degree of accuracy how long each shock canister rendered a worm immobile. Even while stunned, the beasts often twitched and stirred, causing jittery observers to overreact. Accustomed to that, Gurney's excavation crews refused to sound every possible false alarm. Each minute of an early evacuation cut into profits.

The Coriolis storm's thick, brownish nucleus was still a good distance away, but winds were increasing around the spice patch, and would likely force a shutdown before the sandworm recovered enough to be a threat.

Safe from the creature, the sandminers returned to their tasks with redoubled energy, scooping load after load of the spice. Excitement and energy flowed through the men. They knew this could be their last haul before a long and well-deserved respite.

Full of adrenaline-enhanced joy, Jesse landed next to the spice harvesters. He stepped into the mounting breeze to lend a hand, not afraid to get his own hands dirty, just as he'd done on Catalan. If this final excavation pushed them past the Hoskanners, he wanted to be part of it.

The brunt of the angry weather front approached slowly. Gurney monitored the dangerous system, and the sandminers worked with frantic abandon, their hair and clothing whipping in the warm wind. The new weather satellites transmitted detailed updates every fifteen minutes. Unfortunately, the sandminers' attention was focused more on the Coriolis storm than on the motionless sandworm.

As heat-discharges stitched the sky with white-hot barbs, the monster recovered itself with astonishing speed. Rippling its sinuous body, the creature reared up and began to move toward the excavation sites, drawn by the pulsing clamor of seven noisy harvesters.

Alarm shouts went up. Worm spotters, caught off guard, sounded an immediate withdrawal. Gurney bellowed for the carryalls to sweep down and grab the huge harvesters and their cargoes. Darting ornijets dropped to the sand to snatch crewmembers who were too far from their vehicles.

Workers rushed in all directions while static sparks flew from the sand. Jesse swung into action. Had the unexpected storm discharge weakened the shock canister somehow? Perhaps the spectacular light show had bled away the bursts that would normally have knocked out each of the worm's ring segments. That was a question for Dr. Haynes to investigate at some later time. Right now, Jesse and his men needed to fight for their survival.

"Run!" he shouted into the microphone on his collar. "Get aboard anything that flies. Leave the equipment behind—just *get out of here!*" Trying to get to higher ground where the extraction crews could see him, he plunged up a soft slope through sand that clung to his ankles.

The maddened worm thrashed through the dunes, then slammed into the first spice harvester before most of the crew could escape. Only partially attached to the huge machine, the carryall could not wrench the mobile factory free of the sand. As the worm devoured the big harvester, the airborne carryall could not disengage. The carryall crew screamed over the comm as they were dragged underground along with the doomed sandminers.

Wreckage from the harvester and the carryall strewed the sand, but the frenzied creature was not finished. It turned to the other machinery.

Two more carryalls clutched a pair of spice harvesters and successfully lifted them into the sky, flying away with their engines roaring. Over the noise, Jesse heard the keening of the approaching storm. Looking back, he saw the worm abruptly change direction and plunge toward the four remaining harvesters.

Only two carryalls were left. One dropped down, and the locks engaged, grabbing the heavy harvester. Stranded sandminers continued to race in from the dune fields and scramble aboard, but the pilot did not wait. The carryall lifted off, pulling the harvester out of the sand and leaving a dozen men on the ground. The doomed workers turned, mouths open in dismay as the rampaging worm came at them. It gulped the whole field in a single mouthful.

Jesse kept running. He reached the top of a dune and slid down the other side, hoping to put distance between himself and the worm. He smelled sulfur in the air and heard shouts, along with the winds and the crashing turmoil of the worm.

He shouted into the collar microphone again, "Save the men! Any ship that can make a second run, swing back!" He wasn't sure if anyone heard him amid the babble of overlapping commands and screams.

Then, as Jesse scrambled forward, the ground unexpectedly dropped out from beneath his feet. He gasped, flailed with his hands, and saw the powder swirl, sucking him down.

*A sand whirlpool!*

The vortex had his legs now and yanked him into the sand up to his waist, his chest, his shoulders. He cried out one last time, then closed his eyes as the impossibly dry maelstrom swallowed him. He couldn't fight, couldn't escape. It all happened too fast. He felt as if he had dropped over a cliff and fallen into darkness.

No one on the surface had even seen him vanish.

# 29

After the gas wore off and Esmar Tuek crawled his way back to consciousness, he found that the nightmare had only just begun.

He lay on the floor outside the bedroom of young Master Barri. Memories eluded him, lost in a cacophony of questions. He recalled leaving the mansion's security chamber, sensing shadows around him and whisper-quiet movements . . . something so wrong that it made the gray hairs on the back of his neck prickle. He had gone to check on the nobleman's son, heeding his instinctive sense of danger.

Now, as he lay recovering, Tuek remembered his legs going heavy, each breath feeling like a gasp through clogged bellows, his vision and balance spinning. Shouts had sounded around him, oddly muffled through an unseen gauze filling his head. In a blur, the walls and floor had tilted around him as he saw guards sprawled comatose on the floor. Each footstep had felt like lifting a boulder up a steep hill. Staggering toward Barri's bedchamber, Tuek had seen a blur of movement—

And now he awoke on the cool tiles, his cheek pressed against the stone. With strong arms the old veteran levered himself up and sat catching his breath, fighting nausea and a pounding headache. His face hurt, and when he touched his bruised cheek he found a hard crust there and a dab of thick blood from a small cut under his left eye. Someone had struck him.

Anger lit a fuse in his bloodstream. He wrenched himself to his feet and gathered his balance enough to lean against a stone-block wall. Tuek tried to cry out for assistance, but his voice faded like a dry rasp of blown sand against a windowpane. Outside, the light had changed, and it took him a moment to place the time—the edges of dawn! How many hours had he been out cold?

He staggered into the boy's bedchamber, where he saw a plaz window with the seals broken, shockingly open to the dry outside air. The self-cooling sheets on the bed were rumpled, but empty. Master Barri was gone.

When he found a mirror above the boy's vanity, Tuek stared at the small cut on his own face, a distinctive indentation. He considered taking an impression, using investigative tools to reconstruct the weapon that had struck him. Then he recognized the unusual shape of the wound. Dorothy Mapes wore a triangular diagem on her ring.

He drew a breath again and called out, but managed nothing more than a coarse whisper. "Guards! I need assistance!"

Making his way out of the bedchamber, he heard stirrings in the mansion. Groans, curses, and the plaintive calls of alarm wafted through the corridors as stunned household staff and Catalan men at arms struggled to awaken.

"Guards!" he called again, and was pleased to hear the satisfyingly loud voice he produced this time. Almost recovered now, Tuek strode down the corridor, his mind spinning through the immediate steps he would have to take. He would bring all of House Linkam's resources to bear. The nobleman's son was missing, and Dorothy Mapes had something to do with it!

He stopped in his tracks. Looking down, he saw a gilded ceremonial scalpel lying on the floor. Blood on the blade. He bent, but stopped himself from touching it, recognizing immediately that it had belonged to the old household surgeon Cullington Yueh. Why was his blade here? Whose blood was it? Tuek marked the weapon for preservation and analysis. His teams could learn much from the evidence. . . .

Later, after the Catalan Guards had made a complete sweep of the mansion and assessed the damages, one thing became obvious: someone with intimate knowledge of the floor plan had rigged the dispersal of a potent knockout gas through the building's ventilation system.

In addition to the boy, both Dorothy Mapes and Dr. Yueh were missing. Had they been allies? The stunner found inside the boy's bedchamber had been fired enough that the charge pack was nearly depleted. Quick scans verified that Dorothy's fingerprints were on the sharp scalpel, and the blood matched Yueh's. Tuek touched the distinctive wound on his cheek, obviously made by the diagem ring Jesse's concubine always wore.

"If you search more thoroughly," he grimly told his men, "you should find the body of Dr. Yueh." He sank into a hard chair at his security console, but knew it would be days before he allowed himself a full night's sleep. "We have been betrayed."

DR. YUEH ESCORTED a bound Dorothy Mapes past security into the Imperial yacht's plush parlor. Her sharp eyes noticed subtle differences in the ornate cut of this throne from what she had seen on the larger ship. Apparently, Grand Emperor Wuda had many such thrones; perhaps a different artisan had done the work here.

For good measure, she struggled against the bonds that she had instructed Yueh to tie around her arms; the knots were clever, but she could easily work her way free if she wished. It had seemed the only way to get on board the Emperor's ship in time to reach Barri.

"You were not ordered to bring the concubine!" The plump Grand Emperor emerged from behind the throne, as if he had been hiding there. He wore a simple black robe with a high gold collar, which made his skin look even pastier than usual. Two guards emerged from behind columns, one on each side of the visitors. "I want only the son of Nobleman Linkam as hostage."

Dr. Yueh seemed on the verge of collapse. He stammered, "D-don't underestimate her value, S-Sire. The nobleman holds her in extremely high regard. She is the mother of his only son. I believe Nobleman Linkam has a powerful emotional connection with her."

"You mean he *loves* this woman? A commoner? No wonder he is weak." He tittered, and the guards followed suit. "Well, you promised me the boy, and you delivered him. Now, as we agreed, I will use my influence to see what I can do for your poor wife in the Hoskanner clutches."

A flush of gratitude pinkened the old surgeon's milk-pale cheeks. "Thank you, Sire."

"However, I have no use for a mere concubine—especially one who is not of noble birth. She gains me nothing." The Emperor looked at Dorothy with the pouting expression of an insect collector discarding a specimen. "She isn't even that pretty."

Yueh swallowed hard, and uttered the words he had been told to repeat. "Oh, don't underestimate her value, Sire. She may be useful as an additional bargaining chip. The nobleman is very fond of her. It is one of his weaknesses."

She lifted her chin, ignoring the turncoat doctor. "Taking political hostages is expressly forbidden by your own Imperial law, Sire."

The Emperor frowned at her. "As you said, it is my own law. I can make new decrees if the old ones no longer serve me. It won't be difficult to spread the story that the Hoskanners kidnapped your son. Who would disbelieve it?"

Dorothy did not reply. She wanted to think that General Tuek would be able to ferret out the truth, but he had little evidence . . . and plenty of preconceptions against her.

She waited as Emperor Wuda stepped onto the pedestal of his throne and settled his bulk into the seat. He took a long time to make himself comfortable atop a thick gold-and-black pillow.

"I want to see my son," she demanded, using a level of vocal command that made the Grand Emperor flinch and glower.

"So? I want many things as well, and *my* wishes trump yours. We've learned of the large spice stockpile Nobleman Linkam has been hiding from me. In fact, I am amazed—his complaints and excuses had us convinced of his incompetence. And now! If the estimates I'm receiving are accurate, we could ship enough melange to end the spice riots on Renaissance, Jival, Alle, and every other planet." His plump lips formed a humorless smile. "As soon as we find out where he's hiding it."

Dorothy frowned. Spice riots? What was going on out there in the Empire that had been kept hidden from Duneworld? "And you intend to hold my son hostage until Jesse cooperates?"

"And you, too, apparently. Rather simple, wouldn't you say?"

Though she doubted her appeal would help, Dorothy said, "Grand Emperor, you and your comrades call yourselves noblemen. What is noble about kidnapping a nine-year-old boy?"

"A lowborn concubine wouldn't understand the rules of civilized society," he said with a condescending, mocking smile.

The pieces were falling together all around her, but not in expected ways. Why did so many people crave the spice? She redirected her line of inquiry. "Why would you discard centuries of tradition, break established law, and do everything in your power to bring down House Linkam when we are on the verge of winning a challenge that you yourself offered?"

"For melange, of course. The spice is everything."

This still didn't make sense to her. "Why are you so desperate? An Emperor can have at his disposal any drug he chooses."

The flabby leader gripped the armrests of his throne, and leaned forward. "Grand Emperor Inton Wuda is never *desperate* for anything."

Dorothy caught herself, realizing that she had uncovered a weakness he had never meant to reveal. He was obsessed with the spice! What sort of hold did it have on him? She tried to retreat quickly. "Sire, please forgive my choice of words. I am agitated about the danger to Barri Linkam, *my son*, a young *nobleman* in his own right. He deserves every protection that your good offices can afford him."

The Emperor made an annoyed, dismissive gesture. He shifted uneasily on the pillow. "Naturally, he will be protected. He's no good to me dead."

She held her silence, knowing that Jesse was a stubborn man, not given to compromises, even when faced with unfavorable odds. He would not be blackmailed, under any circumstances. She feared what he would do when he learned of the kidnapping.

"Throw the mother into the same room with the brat," said a deep, firm voice that was disturbingly familiar to Dorothy. "If that keeps him quiet, it'll be worth letting her live for now."

At a sound on her left, Dorothy looked in that direction, past Dr. Yueh.

Striding through a doorway, Valdemar Hoskanner smiled smugly at her. Without a word, he took a seat in a chair beside the throne, as if he belonged there.

# 30

*There is always a way to escape from any trap,*
*if one only has the eyes to see it.*

—GENERAL ESMAR TUEK,
*Security Briefings*

Spinning and sliding, Jesse plunged into an empty, suffocating hell. The vortex sucked him downward, seemingly to the very core of Duneworld. His elbows and shoulders banged against oddly smooth rock, as if he were sliding down a stone throat.

Dust clogged his mouth, nose, and eyes. He tried to cough but could hardly breathe. Flailing helplessly, unable to stop the swift, bumpy descent, he was dragged deeper and deeper down an endless waterfall of sand. He had watched William English being sucked to his death. No one had ever emerged alive from a sand whirlpool.

Nevertheless, Jesse struggled for his life.

Though his eyes were squeezed shut and burning from the grit, he saw tiny flashes of light behind his eyelids, followed by blackness deeper than the Stygian realm of sleep. He needed air, but couldn't breathe. Sand rushed past him, roaring and scouring, threatening to suffocate him.

Abruptly, a bubble of exhaled gas and fumes burst around him, pushing away the murderous dust, allowing him one choking breath of sulfurous gases that contained just enough oxygen for him to survive a few seconds longer.

In his fading thoughts, Jesse remembered Barri's determined, optimistic face. The boy always focused on solving problems, striving to make his father proud. As Jesse tumbled, he thought of Dorothy, his beloved concubine. Such a strong-willed woman! His heart ached for her, and he knew she could not possibly have betrayed House Linkam. Esmar Tuek, despite his skills, had to be mistaken about her.

Too often, he had kept his own feelings locked up, not telling her the depth of his love. As the head of House Linkam, he had always tried to be self-sufficient and firm, avoiding the foolish behavior of his father and brother. Regrets cascaded around him, flowing like the sands as he plunged deeper into Duneworld. He wished he could have one last moment with Dorothy, and with Barri.

No excavation would ever find him. He would vanish like so many others. Everyone would assume the sandworm had devoured him. Now, at the culmination of his spice challenge, just when he was about to achieve victory, this capricious planet had stolen it all from him.

In a measure of defiance, Jesse blew one last breath from his lungs with an angry, exhausted shout. Sand and dust coughed out of his mouth—

Unexpectedly, he tumbled through an open void and landed on a soft mound of sand that had rained down from above. The impact was enough to knock the little remaining wind out of him. Stunned and disoriented, he sucked in huge lungfuls of humid air that reeked of bitter cinnamon, like a spice harvester's exhaust stack. But it tasted incredibly sweet in his lungs, breathable air! With his every gasp, the melange essence seemed to reinvigorate his nerves and his muscles.

Jesse rolled over and got to his hands and knees, coughing grit, shaking his dust-encrusted head. He shuddered for a long moment, gulping breaths to replenish the oxygen in his bloodstream. Bits of sand continued to fall like gentle rain on top of him, then stopped.

Questions clamored in his head. Where was he? How far had he fallen?

This deep underground, he had expected to see nothing but inky darkness, yet a faint blue phosphorescence clung to the walls around him, and he could make out a series of tunnels stretching in all directions, a honeycomb labyrinth beneath the dunes. His eyes adjusted surprisingly well.

Jesse struggled to his feet, though his entire body felt bruised, and his arms and legs were scraped raw in places. The spice vapors seemed to enhance his senses and sharpen his vision. Frantically, more energized than he had imagined he could be, he ran through one passageway after another until he grew short of breath. Realizing he could lose track of the original place he had fallen, Jesse tried to retrace his steps, using a sharp stone to scrape a mark on the walls at each intersection. He seemed to be in a crisscrossing network, like blue blood vessels beneath the sand.

Dr. Haynes had postulated that the dune seas of this world had tides and movements, exhalations and fumaroles that hinted at mysteries far beneath the surface. Jesse wondered if he would ever be able to tell the planetary ecologist, or anyone else, what he was seeing here. . . .

With one shaky footstep, then another, he continued to explore the subterranean paths. He needed to find a way *out,* he realized, not his way back to the mound of sand. He had no inkling of which direction he might go or how he might ever get back to the surface. Jesse had fallen so far, he doubted he could climb up the stone throat again. He needed to find a different route—or remain down here forever.

A passageway opened into a large grotto, where the bluish light grew brighter. He could discern shapes around him now—bizarre, alien forms, living things that he had never guessed might exist in the arid vastness, a bizarre wonderland of life and energy.

He heard eerie rustling noises: the movement of spongy forms that rose from the tunnel floor on huge blue stalks with wide, soft leaves. They reminded him of bulbous fungi, plants with rings around their trunks and stalks that swayed and opened up smacking mouths. Their forms hinted strangely of sandworms that were rooted to the ground.

An incomprehensible nursery of exotic fungusoid plants surged and waved around the grotto, piling layer upon fleshy layer. As segmented stems bent over, round orifices coughed out a powdery mist of blue spores that smelled of spice but oddly seemed the wrong color, not reddish or rust-colored at all.

With sparkling eyes, Jesse strolled through the odd subterranean warren. The fungusoid plants drifted like kelp in an ocean current. In a frenzy of fecundity, the stems grew visibly before his eyes, rising taller and taller. Leaves like rounded hands flopped out of the ringed stalks, then fell off and took root themselves, spawning secondary waves of growth.

Jesse continued walking, exploring the freakish milieu. He wondered if his senses had been overloaded by all the melange wafting through the air. He had heard of the bad effects of extreme spice overdose. Was this all a hallucination?

Then he came upon a skeleton. A desiccated, mummified cadaver sprawled on the ground with a tattered sandminer's uniform. Jesse stared, afraid for a moment that he had found William English, but the clothes were wrong. Other men had been lost in the desert, dragged down into sand whirlpools. This victim had not been able to find his way out. . . .

Jesse continued walking and then running, faster and faster. Now, however, he did not get short of breath. Inside his body, Jesse discovered a tremendous, mounting energy—and he covered a great distance through the tunnels, chambers, and grottoes without pausing to rest.

Inside a towering chamber of rock, volcanic light added a yellow-and-orange glow to the pale phosphorescence. Shafts of exhaled brimstone vapors curled upward toward the surface. He realized that he must be standing at the root of one of the fumaroles.

The rubbery spice plants grew even thicker there, clustered around the nourishing gas vents. They rose like overfertilized magical bean-stalks, clogging the passage and seeking a way to the dunes above. . . .

Time faded for Jesse as he moved relentlessly onward, covering many kilometers, with the melange-impregnated air buoying him along. Though he had no way of telling time, he guessed that many hours or even days had already passed. How long could he last down here? He never felt a need to rest, but he did fear that his body would eventually burn out from its hyperprocessed, restless energy. Long-distance space travelers consumed only spice during their journeys across the Known Universe. The substance supposedly gave them all the nourishment they required.

Had word of his death reached Dorothy in Carthage? Did his de-mise mean that his family automatically forfeited the Hoskanner challenge? Or could Barri, as his heir, reap the benefits? He had inten-tionally left no proxy behind, no one who could make binding deci-sions for the household. Would the Emperor just seize it all and ruin House Linkam, much as William English's family had been ruined, generations ago?

*There are no rules.*

Jesse paused in his underground journey, then pushed forward again, regaining his determination and resolve. He was not dead yet. He would not give up. There must be a way out.

Far ahead, he heard a rushing noise as powder tumbled from a new surface opening. A sand whirlpool high above had dropped open to let a flood of sand drain down like time grains through an hourglass. Fumes from another volcanic vent swirled upward like smoke exiting a chimney, and the blue spice plants reached toward the ceiling, groping for a way out.

Jesse stared as a possibility occurred to him. It was a decent chance, he decided—and he knew of no better way out.

As the fleshy growths clustered together, stretching upward like the hands of clamoring beggars, he dove into them. The rising mass of vegetation jostled and lifted. He climbed higher on the spongy flesh, holding on and hoping that the vent in the rocks was wide enough to permit his body to pass.

Around him, he felt the verdant upsurge gain strength as more and more plants shoved toward the surface of the desert planet. One of the nearest fleshy mouths opened like a blossom and exhaled a cloud of choking cinnamon into his face and eyes, but Jesse did not let go. He felt himself being carried upward, gaining speed. The rock walls rushed and scraped past him, cutting his skin as he was pushed higher.

Then, like a drowning man reaching the surface of an ocean, the profusion of growths exploded into open sky, vomiting great gouts of cinnamony, rust-colored powder.

Jesse found himself flying through the air like a rag doll. Moments later, he crashed against the slope of a hard-packed dune. Coughing and shuddering, he scrambled to his feet. Staggering into bright sunlight, he saw the swarm of spice plants still boiling up out of the blow, turning from blue to brown in the air and spraying melange, dumping a rich, reddish carpet in all directions.

As he watched, the fungi withered, dried, and fell into a mat across the sandy ground. Within seconds of exposure to the desiccated air, the spice plants crumbled and flaked, becoming a layer of rich melange.

Sunlight—real sunlight—burned his eyes. Shading his vision with one hand, Jesse felt himself adapting to the outside air. It was daybreak, with lemon yellow and tan hues creeping through the sky.

Lost in the midst of the vast desert, Jesse turned in all directions, trying to spot a landmark. Everything around him looked scoured and clean. The Coriolis storm must have passed. He could not even hazard a guess as to how long he had been gone.

Then, like a miracle, he saw a line of mountains on the eastern horizon and tiny, diamondlike lights in that direction, geometric shapes. He could see them only because his temporarily enhanced vision seemed to have telescopic properties. Jesse identified the oasis and the diamond-shaped plantings, the pillbox water silos, as well as the wedge-shaped main building of Dr. Haynes's research base. Green-planted dunes added a tiny fringe of color before they faded into the endless brown of the desert.

Jesse began to walk across the sand. The desert made distances deceptive, but he had no doubt he would accomplish the trek, no matter how long it took. Even in the brutal heat of midday, he doubted he would need to slow down.

Behind him, his footprints began in the middle of a field of fresh spice and extended in a line, following him straight to the sanctuary of the forward base. The spice had given him new life.

# 31

There are intriguing puzzles all around us. Why waste time solving the wrong ones?

—DR. BRYCE HAYNES,
*Ecological Notebooks*

Aided by the metabolism-enhancing properties of the intense melange to which he'd been exposed, Jesse was already recovered by the time he reached Dr. Haynes's base. Despite a long, grueling trek, he felt strong, and most of his superficial injuries had disappeared. Giddy, he joked with Gurney that he had inhaled an Emperor's ransom of spice with every breath he took in the subterranean realm.

Blustering, laughing, and clapping him on the back with the force of a crashing cargo skiff, the jongleur said, "If it kept you alive, laddie, it was worth more than that!"

Stunned sandminers milled around the research base, still in turmoil from the disaster. Thirty-seven men, two spice harvesters, and one carryall had been lost. *Three days ago.* He had been underground, considered dead, for three days. His safe return was desperately needed good news.

Even though the storm had dissipated, electrostatic charges in the air still interfered with transmissions. The forward base tried to send a signal informing Carthage of Jesse's return, but they heard only white noise in response.

Jesse brooded. "I know how distraught Dorothy and Esmar must be. Gurney, dispatch a fast flyer to carry a message—I don't care if the weather is still unsettled."

The spice foreman raised his uneven eyebrows. "A messenger would give us away. The Emperor won't let you hide. Are you ready to give up the game?"

"It doesn't matter anymore, Gurney. Especially if we have as much spice as you say. I want to end this."

Jesse spent several hours cleaning himself and eating a meal of real food—washed down with water, since he didn't want any of the spice beverages. Afterward, he spent time with his injured and shaken sand-miners, commiserating with them over their losses and congratulating them all for winning a challenge that had seemed impossible from the very beginning. Even with the disaster, Gurney told him the harvesters had gathered enough spice to tip the scales in the final tally. "Success is close at hand, men."

"And I will be true to my word," Jesse told them all. "Once the Emperor acknowledges my claim here on Duneworld, any freedman who wishes to depart will be given passage offplanet, at my expense. House Linkam will also make it worthwhile for those who choose to stay."

Gurney found cause for celebration in the mess hall. "'And he seized all the gold and silver and all the vessels that were found in the house of God. He seized also the treasuries of the king's house.' That we have done, My Lord! According to the final sum, we have beat the bloody Hoskanners, by the grace of the gods and demons. I've already begun to compose a song about it."

"Your songs are always lies or exaggerations, Gurney," Jesse pointed out.

"Ho, but in this case there's no need. The events themselves are fantastic enough."

The surviving sandminers understood the terrific news, though many of them still seemed stunned and broken to have faced such a disaster at their moment of greatest accomplishment. Every one of them had lost friends on the destroyed harvesters and carryall. Jesse looked at them all, feeling their heartache as part of his own. He was the nobleman, responsible for their safety and their future. Even with the thrill of victory, he promised himself that he would never forget the tremendous cost. . . .

Gurney led Jesse outside into the brittle daylight and over to one of the rock-camouflaged storage silos. Dr. Haynes's plantings extended out in broad chevrons of greenery, windbreak lines where scrub fought against the encroaching sands. Gurney said, "It may not be so easy to collect your prize, My Lord, if General Tuek is right about an Imperial army hidden in that inspection ship."

"The Grand Emperor did not come to Duneworld to pat me on the back. We'd better have enough melange to impress him."

Inside the dim cavern of one of their storehouses, the spice foreman stood with his hands on his hips, his square chin tilted up and his face alight with pride. Looking around, Jesse saw crate after crate of compressed raw spice. The containers covered the floor and were stacked to the ceiling.

"This is just a tiny fraction of it. We've tallied up all the caches in caves and hidden in the desert. We beat the Hoskanners by a good margin, and our time is not yet up."

Jesse could not believe the wealth he saw. "Don't forget to count the melange we've already released for distribution over the past two years."

Gurney laughed. "A drop in the bucket compared to the treasure we amassed afterward! I tell you, the Empire is starving for this stuff. We'll get a good price for every speck of it. Of course, the Grand Emperor and his cronies will get their share, but there's plenty left for us."

Jesse hung his head. "No profit is worth the misery we've been through, the people we've lost."

"You were forced into this situation, laddie—and you turned a trap into victory."

"We're not out of the trap yet. Guard our stockpiles with your life, Gurney. As soon as we can arrange for transport and proper security, I'll contact the Emperor's inspection ship and demand that he declare me the winner of this damnable challenge."

"And then Duneworld will be yours."

Jesse's shoulders felt heavy. "Alas, the rains and seas of Catalan would suit me better, Gurney."

WHEN JESSE FINALLY met with the planetary ecologist in his laboratory office, Haynes's eyes were glazed with wonder and fascination. "I must know everything you experienced, Nobleman." He sat at a conference-room table, his hands clasped in front of him, elbows resting on the hard surface. He leaned forward, ready to drink in every word. "You've seen things I only dreamed of. No man has ever returned from a sand whirlpool. No man has ever seen what creates the spice!"

And so, to the best of his ability, Jesse described all that he had witnessed and endured. He paced the room, then relented and poured himself a cup of spice coffee from a sealed urn. The burn of melange in his mouth gave him a delicious thrill.

Haynes took notes and asked probing questions, but mostly he sat and listened. When Jesse finished, the planetary ecologist stared at the chamber wall, his gaze distant, as if his imagination was roaming across the dunes to rich spice fields and worm sands, to gasping fumaroles and hidden tunnels beneath the desert, running like blue veins through a living planet. "Nobleman Linkam, you have helped me complete the working theory I've been developing for so many years."

Inside the room under bright artificial lights, test beds of hardy plants grew, each of them given carefully monitored rations of water. Some of the species looked weak and withering, while others thrived. Jesse inspected some of the strange adaptations to an arid environment.

"And what is your theory?" Jesse asked.

Haynes shook his head, as if suddenly intimidated. "I can't be sure of all the details yet. There are many small threads I still wish to tie together."

"I'm not asking you for a rigorous scientific explanation, Dr. Haynes. At the moment, I'd just like a layman's understanding of this planet that's absorbed so much of my sweat and blood for the past two years."

Haynes surrendered. "I have long suspected a network of tunnels and vents beneath the sand. Until now, I never imagined that they might be part of an elaborate ecosystem, a labyrinth filled with fungusoid 'spice plants,' as you call them. It adds a new foundation to the ecology of Duneworld, which has always seemed sparse and mysterious, with too few components to support a biological web."

"Like only seeing the tip of an iceberg. There is much more to it beneath the surface."

"Exactly."

"But what's the connection between these spice plants, the sandworms, and everything else?" On a flat specimen shelf, small trays contained samples of melange of varying colors and densities; Jesse knew that spice was graded according to quality, though even the lowest form still provided a heady rush. Right now, the smell of the open samples made his nostrils tingle. He leaned closer to sniff.

Haynes looked down at the notes on his datapad. "My theory—and mind you, it is only a theory—is that the spice, the fungusoid plants, the sandtrout, and even the worms are all connected."

Jesse touched a fingertip to the darkest spice sample, tasted it on the tip of his tongue. "You mean mutually dependent on one another? Parasites? Symbiotes?"

Haynes shook his head. "This may be difficult to accept, Nobleman, but I am beginning to conclude they are all aspects of the *same life-form*—phases in a complex growth and development cycle."

"How can that be? Sandtrout, worms, and plants are nothing alike."

"Is a caterpillar like a butterfly? Is a larva like a beetle? A nymph like a dragonfly? The sandworms and spice plants could be—for lack of a more accurate comparison—male and female forms of a bipartite organism. Fungusoid organisms grow, and at a certain climactic point they reach to the surface, where they spew billions of microspores. In the atmosphere, the plants immediately die, as you witnessed. The spice we consume is composed of these microspores mixed with powdery plant residues, distributed by the winds. In turn, the spores germinate and grow, forming tiny creatures that devour the sand plankton and then grow into what we see as sandtrout."

Haynes held up a finger, as if making a place mark in his flow of thoughts. "It's fascinating, if my conjecture is correct. The sandtrout themselves may be the larval forms of the monstrous worms, while some of the little creatures may burrow deep and take root as spice plants. Perhaps each 'male' sandtrout grows into a giant creature, or somehow links together with others of its kind to form a colony organism, since each sandworm ring appears to be autonomous."

"This is all difficult to grasp," Jesse said. "A life cycle so alien, so incomprehensible."

"We are on an alien, baffling planet, Nobleman."

Jesse stopped in front of a row of cages holding kangaroo rats, tiny rodents that went busily about their lives even in confinement. He wondered if they would rather be free out in the desert, like the ones he and Barri had encountered, or if they even had such an awareness.

"Worms seem to guard the spice sands," Jesse said. "Are they preventing other worms from attacking their young? Or preventing our sandminers from stealing the spores?"

Haynes shrugged. "As good an explanation as any. I never suspected that sand whirlpools and fumaroles might be crucial links in the chain of spice distribution. After reaching some catalyst point, a perfect balance of temperature and chemicals, the fungal organisms reproduce in explosive proportions. They draw large amounts of sand—silica—as nourishment or structural material. This, combined with minerals and chemicals in the volcanic gases, triggers even more growth and reproduction. They find an outlet to the air, where they dump their spores and then die."

With a wan smile, the planetary ecologist rested his elbows on the table. "Or the real explanation could be something entirely different, almost beyond human comprehension. I just don't know."

As he poured himself another cup of the strong spice coffee, Jesse thought of all the giant worms they had incapacitated with shock canisters, all the melange they had excavated from rich veins. He took a long drink. "Harvesting so much spice, is there a chance we're destroying a fragile life cycle that has existed here on Duneworld for millennia? Humans have only been on this planet for a few years."

"There's always that chance. I simply don't have enough information yet."

With the vivid images of the amazing underground catacombs before his mind's eye, Jesse set his jaw. "If I'm awarded permanent control of this planet, it may be necessary to curtail our production. We'll have to be good stewards of the land and allow some of the melange fields to lie fallow so that the populations of worms and spice plants can replenish themselves."

The scientist's face became sad. "That will never happen, Nobleman Linkam—not as long as the Grand Emperors and noble families remain in power. Nobles, starship crews, and wealthy merchants have become increasingly dependent upon the spice, and will demand more and more production. It will only get worse, not better."

"Spice may be popular, but I think you're exaggerating its importance."

Haynes shook his head. "Why do you think the Imperial inspection ship came here to intimidate you after only a year? You may have heard rumors of spice riots on Renaissance and other wealthy planets—they are all true."

"I thought that was just Hoskanner propaganda, to stir up resentment against House Linkam." Restless, Jesse found screens that displayed real-time images from the weather satellites. The surface of Duneworld was bland and unremarkable, with few features to help him find the location of the forward research base. Most of the large storms were centered high in the northern hemisphere.

"If anything, Nobleman, those reports minimized the uproar. With Duneworld's exports drastically reduced, the entire Empire is craving this substance. They desire spice more than anything else."

Jesse scowled. "Come now, Dr. Haynes—as valuable as it may be, melange is just a luxury commodity. It would be good for some of the pampered nobles to forget their hedonistic pleasures for a while. Once spice becomes too scarce or too expensive, the people will turn to other vices. The Empire offers plenty of them."

Haynes's voice had a grim edge. "Most noble families are addicted to melange—*fatally addicted*, I fear—and they are just now beginning to realize the fact. That is the dark side of the spice."

"Then they'll have to endure. It'll toughen them up." Jesse's voice grew iron-hard. "Someone will develop treatment plans. Esmar Tuek endured his cure from the sapho drug, which is said to be the worst addiction ever known."

The planetary ecologist shook his head. "Believe me, Nobleman, sapho is child's play compared to melange withdrawal. You do not consume spice extravagantly yourself, but after your recent exposure underground, I fear you may be inextricably bound to it as well. The Emperor is desperately dependent on melange, as are many high-ranking families, and the pilots and crews of starships. If the spice flow stops, the whole Empire will fall into a dark age such as the human race has never known. An entire generation will die from the drastic effects of withdrawal."

Jesse absorbed the startling comments. He tasted the pleasant burning of spice in his mouth and lungs from the saturation underground, from the cups of spice coffee he'd just finished, from the pure sample he'd tasted. Deep inside himself, he already felt an undeniable twinge of longing, not yet a craving but an insistent whisper that suggested how sweet melange would taste right now. Yes, he could envision it becoming an all-consuming personal need.

He thought of the noble families and the Emperor himself panicking because their supplies were cut off. When Jesse had heard his name being reviled due to his apparent failure, such vitriol had not made sense to him, even allowing for Hoskanner rabble-rousing. He had thought that powerful forces were arrayed against him, influential people and alliances working to ensure his failure. Now his fingers tightened into a fist at his side. The Duneworld challenge had been more than a trap. It had widespread consequences that were more severe than he'd ever imagined.

A commotion arose outside the laboratory, and someone pounded on the door. "My Lord," Gurney said, "the messenger's ornijet has just returned! He has news from General Tuek. You'd better hear it."

Sensing something terribly wrong, Jesse hurried to face the man who bore a communiqué from the old security chief. When the messenger handed over the cylinder, Jesse grasped both ends and pulled it apart to display the screen and holographic recording.

The blurry simulacrum of Esmar Tuek looked distraught, his face pummeled with grief and uncertainty. "My Lord, we have been attacked! The headquarters mansion was betrayed from within. All of my men were gassed unconscious—including me. Dr. Yueh is missing, and we fear he has been killed. And . . . your son has been kidnapped."

Jesse wanted to shout at the image, but he knew questions would have no effect upon the recorded hologram. His throat clenched. "There is more, My Lord. It appears that the traitor was none other than your concubine, Dorothy Mapes, who is also missing."

Grabbing the messenger, Jesse said, "You're flying me back to Carthage right now." He looked back at Gurney and barked, "You stay here and defend our melange stockpiles. This sounds like a ploy to steal the treasure from us—and I swear, on the sacred honor of my family, that if the Emperor has harmed my son, he will not live long enough to feel his withdrawal from spice."

# 32

*In every relationship, one party holds leverage over the other. It is simply a matter of degree.*

—GRAND EMPEROR INTON WUDA,
*Proclamations and Ruminations*

lying erratically, the ornijet swept in over the mountains of Carthage, passing above the main spaceport where the huge Imperial inspection ship stood like a fortress. At the secondary spaceport across town, Jesse spotted the Emperor's opulent private yacht waiting.

He directed the nervous pilot to go directly to a small landing zone on the roof of the headquarters mansion. When the ship's wings and engines had settled, Jesse flipped open the angled door and found a solemn-looking Esmar Tuek standing there flanked by a small honor guard.

The old general appeared to have aged decades since Jesse had last seen him. The scab of an odd triangular cut marked one cheek. The reddish stains around his lips seemed different . . . more splotchy. Jesse feared that in his shame and despair Tuek had allowed temptation to overwhelm him. Had he resumed his addiction to the sapho drug?

Tuek bowed his head, his eyes watery and forlorn. He held a small flat case with scuffed corners, as if it had been carried from place to place for many decades. He extended the case, opened the lid. Inside, Jesse saw several medals, Catalan rank insignia, as well as ribbons of longtime service to House Linkam. "I have failed you, My Lord. I do not deserve these tokens of honor. I have shamed you and myself."

"What is this nonsense, Esmar?"

"I hereby resign my post as your security chief. It is my sincerest hope that my successor will not let you down in this crisis, as I have."

Bristling, Jesse made no move to accept the box of medals. His gray eyes flashed as he stepped closer, then shocked Tuek by delivering a quick, sharp slap across the older man's face. "Don't be a fool, Esmar— and don't treat *me* like one! Do you think anyone could have done better than you? I cannot lose your skills and advice, especially now."

"I have no honor, My Lord."

"No one ever gained honor by running away. To regain it, you must help me rescue my son." He glowered at the security chief until Tuek finally lifted his gaze. Looking at the nobleman, the old man flashed a look of anger mixed with hope.

Jesse lowered his voice. "I need you, Esmar. Don't make me ask again. Now, tell me exactly what happened, show me your evidence against Dorothy, and I will judge her guilt for myself."

Tuek's cheek showed a scarlet mark from Jesse's blow. He stood wavering, and finally took a step backward. "As you command, My Lord."

✦

AFTER READING TUEK'S report, Jesse sat alone in a small private office adjacent to his suite, his fingertips touching the papers as he brooded. He could neither believe nor deny the obvious conclusion: There had been a spy in his household. The Emperor and the Hoskanners knew too many secrets, even about the stockpiles of spice. Jesse had trouble believing that his concubine, his business manager, and the *mother of his son* could have betrayed him. His heart told him it wasn't possible.

But the evidence seemed to offer no alternative.

Tuek suspected the kidnapping and betrayal was a Hoskanner plot at its root, because Valdemar feared the Linkam stockpile had grown so large he would lose the contest. It was an act of desperation. Could the Emperor be involved as well? It seemed unlikely . . . but then, a lot of things seemed unlikely.

One of the household servants appeared at the open door of the office chamber, fidgeting and clearing his throat. Jesse looked up with heavy, weary eyes. "I asked not to be disturbed. I must think."

"There is a messenger, My Lord. He is carrying a ransom demand."

Jesse sat up. "Send him in—and call General Tuek immediately."

Tuek arrived within moments, fully clad in his most impressive military uniform. Wearing ominous sidearms and all his badges and medals, he stood beside Jesse as the kidnapper's representative was ushered in.

Jesse was surprised, and then sickened, to see that it was Ulla Bauers. So this was the Grand Emperor's scheme after all! He could have fought the Hoskanners—House against House—but the Emperor had brought an impossible amount of power to bear against him.

Keeping his face hard and unreadable, with his jaw set, Jesse forced out the words. "Why does the Emperor's man participate in this criminal, barbarous act?"

"Emperor Wuda sends his sincere apologies. His embarrassment is acute for being forced to resort to such, hmmm, medieval tactics. But you have left us no choice in the matter. Hmm-ahh, we thought concern for your son would bring you scurrying out of the desert where you had hidden."

"To what purpose?" Jesse demanded. "I have done nothing wrong."

Bauers sniffed. "Your own actions, Nobleman Linkam, are a disgrace. You brought galactic commerce to its knees, but not because of incompetence, as we thought. Instead, we know that you are hiding an illegal hoard of melange. As is clear in Imperial law, all stockpiles belong to the Emperor for distribution as he sees fit."

"Is that the same Imperial law that prohibits taking noble hostages?" Tuek growled, but Jesse motioned for him to be quiet.

With an effort, Jesse composed himself. "My instructions in the challenge were clear and simple: that by the end of two years I was to surpass Hoskanner production amounts. Never was it said that I had to deliver the melange as soon as I harvested it. Though your inspection ship has harassed us for months, I am required only to show you my total *at the end.* We kept our production hidden for good reason. If the Hoskanners knew how close we were to achieving our goal, they would have increased their sabotage attempts. You pride yourself on being a legal expert, Counselor Bauers. What, exactly, have I done wrong?"

"You strangled the flow of spice. Our Empire depends on it. You are a loose cannon, creating turmoil for your own profit. You can no longer be trusted."

"Neither can the Grand Emperor, it seems." Tuek moved to Jesse's side.

Bauers sniffed. "These are the terms: You will immediately deliver all of your spice stockpiles and surrender your operations on Duneworld to Valdemar Hoskanner, who served us efficiently for many years. We cannot risk further instability such as you have aroused."

Jesse met the representative's eyes. "And if I refuse?"

"Hmmm, one cannot say exactly how the Grand Emperor will express his displeasure. However, it seems only your son is readily available to endure his wrath."

"And my concubine?"

"Hmmm, does she hold some value to you? Interesting. If you comply, the Grand Emperor may be, ahh, generous. We could consider her part of the bargain. They are both on his private yacht, and both are uninjured. At present."

Jesse's voice was frozen metal. "You will find, Counselor Bauers, that I do not respond well to coercion."

"Hmmm, just as the Grand Emperor does not respond well to a loss of spice."

Jesse turned to Tuek. "General, while I consider my response, please escort the Grand Emperor's representative to our temporary guest quarters."

With a faint smile, the old veteran nodded. "The small and uncomfortable ones, My Lord?"

"Those will do fine." He looked at Bauers.

Pretending not to be alarmed, the gaudily dressed man said, "Hmm, perhaps I wasn't clear enough, Nobleman. This is not a matter for negotiation. The Grand Emperor wants the spice. No other response will do. Holding me hostage will accomplish nothing."

"Hostage? You are merely a guest . . . a guest who has just threatened to murder my son and—with no legal basis—ordered me to forfeit all of my family wealth. I need a little time to contemplate the treachery of Emperors."

He gestured, and Esmar Tuek brusquely escorted the man away.

THOUGH HE HAD many concerned advisors to assist him, Jesse knew that the terrible decision was his alone to make.

He summoned his security chief to the office chamber, along with the men in charge of monitoring spaceport operations and spice distribution. "The only response to such a terrible ultimatum," Jesse began, "is to find an even greater threat to hold over our enemy. That is what I intend to do."

Tuek's brow furrowed. "That could escalate the situation out of control."

Jesse slammed his fist on the table and rose to his feet. "They threatened to kill my son!" He swept his gaze around the group of uneasy men. When he saw that he had them cowed, he sat down again and repeated in a quieter but more menacing voice, *"They threatened to kill my son."*

"So what will you do, My Lord?" Tuek said. "We are prepared to follow your commands."

Taking a deep breath, Jesse looked toward a window that overlooked the city. Emperor Wuda's yacht, visible on the other side of dwelling complexes and habitation domes, was well guarded. Tuek had proposed a commando operation to swarm the craft with the best Catalan soldiers and snatch the hostage boy. But Jesse could only foresee disaster in such an attempt. So he played another card instead, the ultimate gambit.

"Send a message to Gurney Halleck. Tell him to rig explosives laced with toxic contaminants to all of our spice stockpiles. Be prepared to destroy all one hundred thousand Imperial tons of concentrated melange."

There were gasps and murmurs around the table. Each man knew that such an amount of spice would not only buy offworld passage for the entire population of Duneworld, but would allow them to live like nobles for the rest of their lives.

Tuek nodded slowly. "That will definitely get the Grand Emperor's attention, My Lord. Which security code should I use for the message?"

"No code, Esmar I want the Emperor to hear it. Tell Gurney to rig the spice harvesters and carryalls, too. Let's make it as hard on the Emperor as possible. If people are already rioting for spice, the nobles could overthrow Wuda for this."

"You're pushing back awfully hard," Tuek said quietly.

"It doesn't match the executioner's axe they hold over my head." Jesse narrowed his eyes. He had done what no other person had ever accomplished: He had gone beneath the surface of Duneworld, seen the interconnected spice plants and the network of struggling life in the desert, and returned alive after three days. Now Jesse would deliver an ultimatum to trump all ultimatums. "Next, Esmar, remove all the re-actor drives from our fleet of ships. Build as many crude nuclear war-heads as you can, and disperse them to the richest spice veins in the desert. How many drives do you think we can scavenge in the next few hours?"

The general withheld his questions and calculated. "More than a dozen, perhaps as many as twenty."

Jesse's face was a grim mask of determination. "Good. We need our family atomics."

~~~~~

"KEEP THE CONCUBINE, Emperor," he said in a voice colder than the icecaps on Catalan. As he recorded his message, Jesse spoke with a righteous anger and a raw power that made his threat utterly convinc-ing. "But know this—if you do not release my son unharmed, if you force my hand, I *will* destroy every speck of melange on this planet, now and forever."

He slapped the messagestat cylinder into the hand of an alarmed and chastened-looking Ulla Bauers. "Make no mistake, without my son, without my title, and with the overwhelming debt I have incurred, I have absolutely nothing to lose."

Jesse sent the Counselor scurrying to the Imperial yacht, then sat in the headquarters mansion and waited for the Emperor's response.

# 33

Duneworld is not a dead planet after all, but full of hidden and marvelous
life. Humans, however, can change that in short order.

— DR. BRYCE HAYNES,
*Ecological Notebooks*

From the sun-filtered window in a high tower of the mansion, Jesse
looked across the rooftops and crags of Carthage toward the secondary spaceport. His message had been delivered to the Grand Emperor
six hours ago, but so far the Imperial yacht remained silent and ominous.

Gurney Halleck had sent confirmation that all stockpile silos, hidden cave caches, spice harvesters, and carryalls had been rigged with
conventional explosives and toxic contaminants. Jesse did not doubt
the spice foreman would destroy it all if given the command. In a mad-
deningly cheery voice, Gurney added over the open channel that his
inventory calculations had actually underestimated the stores of
melange—when fully compiled, all the hidden storehouses actually
held an extra four thousand Imperial tons. It was an added twist of the
dagger into the Emperor's side.

Esmar Tuek had used their nuclear engines to create seventeen dirty atomic warheads, which had been dispersed to the richest spice sands, where they could be remotely detonated on a moment's notice.

Emperor Wuda and his advisors knew that Jesse was not bluffing. . . .

Dr. Haynes became frantic when he learned about the desperate tactics. The planetary ecologist sent an urgent message from the forward base. "This is not a game, Nobleman Linkam! The Grand Emperor is deadly serious, and I don't think he'll back down."

"Neither will I."

"Nuclear fallout will destroy the spice cycle, break the biological chain, and make the sandworms and spice plants extinct. You could wipe it all out forever!"

"I hold my son in the highest possible regard," Jesse said icily, forcing the scientist to believe his intent. "If the Emperor harms him, he will pay the price, even if it costs the ecosystem of this planet and the industry on which the Empire is addicted." Abruptly, he terminated the communication and went back to waiting.

With a heavy heart, Jesse understood that if Haynes was correct, if most of the nobility really were fatally addicted to melange—including Jesse himself—then his action would be a death sentence upon most of the leaders in the Empire. The subsequent political turmoil would be unimaginable.

No, Jesse was not bluffing.

He thought of his compliant father and his ridiculous brother. Maybe it was for the best, Jesse thought, if the Known Universe was finally cleansed of the decadent and parasitic noble families. Recent events had proved beyond any possible doubt that "nobles" and "honor" were not necessarily related.

He had meant to win the challenge fairly. He had intended to divulge the shock-canister technique for harvesting larger amounts of spice, present the Emperor with his share of the huge stockpiles, and claim his victory. But House Linkam had never been meant to win.

From the very beginning, the Grand Emperor, House Hoskanner, even much of the Nobles' Council had set him up to fail.

*My enemies underestimated me.*

Looking out on the dusty city and the desert beyond, Jesse longed for greenery as wide as the rice-paddy region of his beloved Catalan. He wanted to hear the trickle of rain and smell the iodine sea, hear the waves crash against jagged rocks, the laughter and songs of fishermen coming in with nets swollen from their catch. He had grown tired of the rattlesnake whisperings of blowing sand on barren Duneworld, and the odors of dust, sweat, and melange.

He ached with grief. Still clinging to an irrational hope that it might have been a trick, that someone had framed Dorothy, he wished she could be at his side. Despite all he had heard, he didn't know if he could live without her.

As the sky shifted into a pastel sunset, soft orange colors glinted off the Emperor's yacht. The first shadows of dusk began to creep outward from the tall mountains. Still nothing but silence.

His heart heavy, Jesse imagined Barri held in a prison cell. And Dorothy, too? Or had she sold her allegiance to the Emperor, to the Hoskanners, or to both? Desperately, Jesse wanted everything back the way it had been a scant two years ago: he, his son, and Dorothy, running the family operations on Catalan, content with realistic ambitions instead of the folly of Duneworld. He had never wanted to come here in the first place. . . .

Without warning, the Emperor's yacht exploded.

The sky lit up in a massive fireball, and Jesse jumped back from the window. A moment after the flash, a resounding boom slammed the thick windows of the observation tower. The shockwave vibrated the plaz as if someone had struck a dulcimer with a heavy mallet. Objects rattled in the room and fell off tables and shelves, crashing to the floor.

At the landing field, a powerful detonation had blasted out the sides of the gaudily armored hull. The white-hot flames of ignited fuel burned like cutting torches, tearing through walls and bulkheads, shattering windowports, spraying debris high into the air. A secondary eruption drove blue-and-orange flames into the inferno, blasting a pillar of fire skyward.

Moments later, Tuek ran into the room, his face florid, his eyes wide. "My Lord, did you see—"

Jesse reeled, breathing hard, unable to find words. He gestured listlessly toward the window. Outside, debris rained from the sky.

The nobleman brought a mounted telescope around and with shaking hands trained it on the landing field. Heavy frameworks bent and tilted, then crashed over into the flames. Several dead Imperial guards lay strewn like broken toys across the armorpave field. Interminable minutes passed before Carthage emergency crews arrived and went to work with chemical extinguishers. The entire yacht was incinerated.

Jesse's knees turned to powder and could no longer support him. He slumped into a chair, almost missing the seat, but caught himself. He sat back, so numb he was unable to weep, and unable to absorb the immense scale of the tragedy.

Dorothy and Barri, both aboard the yacht, had been annihilated in the horrendous conflagration—along with the Emperor.

DURING THE SPICE challenge, Jesse Linkam had fought impossible odds and finally figured out a way to earn his victory. Now he wanted to squeeze until he crushed his enemies. His broken heart was held together only by stitches of revenge.

Despite his grief and shock, Jesse was his own man, more wily than his father or brother had been, more able to survive in the face of adversity. He still had the leverage to escape the numerous traps arrayed against him, but he needed to remain rational and strong, not allowing his emotional side to take over.

From Dr. Haynes, he now understood that control of Duneworld's melange provided more leverage than any other House held. *He who controls the spice controls the Known Universe*, Jesse thought.

With innocent Barri dead, he now stood as the only survivor of House Linkam. He despised the incomprehensible treachery that had rendered him as cold and calculating as any of his so-called "noble" enemies. . . .

Less than half an hour after the explosion, a contrite and distraught Ulla Bauers rushed to the headquarters mansion, as if hoping to prevent Jesse from overreacting to the disaster.

In the austere parlor on the main floor, Jesse regarded the ferretlike man with disdain, wishing Bauers had been killed in the explosion as well. His dark blue coat and billowing shirt had ashes on them, which he tried to brush off as he stood there.

"What do you want?" Jesse's words were like knives. He wanted to kill this wretched Imperial spokesman who had shoved all possible acceptable outcomes over a sheer cliff.

Bauers started to smile, then seemed to think better of it and formed a thin, straight line with his mouth. "I come bearing good news, Nobleman Linkam! The Grand Emperor himself is safe after the horrific explosion of the Imperial yacht. At the last moment, he was informed of a deadly Hoskanner assassination plot upon his person and managed to shuttle over to the inspection ship, just in time. He escaped only moments before the bombs detonated."

"A Hoskanner assassination plot?" Jesse's rough voice oozed skepticism.

"Yes, Nobleman."

"And what about my son and my concubine?"

"Ahh, I am very sorry. Despite rescue efforts, there were no survivors aboard the yacht. How could there have been?"

"Yes," Jesse said, his heart sinking once more. He clenched and unclenched his fists, wanting to strangle the man with his bare hands. "How could there have been? Very convenient, don't you think?"

"The Grand Emperor expresses his deep regret that these discussions

THE ROAD TO DUNE

got out of hand. It was Valdemar Hoskanner who suggested the idea of kidnapping your son. I assure you, the Emperor never intended to harm the boy in any way. You are, after all, his noble cousin."

"Noble? He is not noble! My son is dead because of him."

"Hmmm, a casualty of the foul Hoskanner plot, I'm afraid. Nothing to do with the Grand Emperor. It seems Valdemar planned to kill the Emperor, disgrace the Linkam family, and seize the Imperial throne for himself, along with all spice production. The Emperor was deceived. He is quite pained at the misery you must be going through." Bauers bent in a formal bow. "With sincere apologies, he begs your forgiveness. He wants to make amends, somehow. Provided you release your hoard—after keeping an appropriate profit for House Linkam—you will be allowed to maintain control of spice operations here on Duneworld."

"My son is dead, and the Emperor wishes to bargain with me?" Jesse drew himself up, feeling the burn of anger.

"Your son is dead because of Valdemar Hoskanner."

Jesse wanted to spit. "Really? And what is to become of Valdemar Hoskanner, if he is such a despicable criminal?"

"Ahh, the Grand Emperor has already signed a decree that his House is to be stripped of all power and possessions." The prissy man risked a broad smile. "So you see, Nobleman, justice will be done. From now on, you will have control of all the Duneworld spice operations. The Grand Emperor is willing to offer a great many other concessions, provided of course that you withdraw your threat of destroying the melange hoard and, hmmm, remove all atomics from the spice fields."

Jesse narrowed his eyes. He didn't believe a word of it, strongly suspecting that the Emperor and Bauers had concocted a scheme to frame the Hoskanners—thus they could claim complete innocence while still getting their spice. The Counselor waited in fidgety silence; once, he swallowed so hard it was audible.

But House Linkam would not surrender. Aflame with hatred, Jesse meant to make them pay until it hurt all the way to their bones. The raw Imperial politics they had directed against him would not pass un-noticed, or unpunished. He would make his enemies suffer for their ac-tions. "What will happen to the holdings of House Hoskanner?"

Bauers looked uncomfortable, as if he had hoped Jesse would not think of that detail. "Hmmm, perhaps they should be divided equally between House Linkam and the Grand Emperor."

"Not acceptable," Jesse snapped. "It seems that Valdemar Hoskan-ner killed my only son and heir. The Grand Emperor himself admits this. For my suffering, I claim the right of vengeance. If Valdemar is truly to blame, then all of his holdings are forfeit. To me."

Bauers fidgeted. "Hmm, ah. I shall discuss that with Emperor Wuda."

Jesse leaned forward. "It is not a matter for discussion, Counselor. That is my ultimatum. If you want me to remove the atomic threat from the spice fields and disengage the booby traps from our large stockpiles—" He glanced over at Tuek. "How much spice was it again?"

"One hundred four thousand Imperial tons of melange, My Lord," the old veteran responded. "Packaged, processed, and ready for deliv-ery. Unless you decide to destroy it."

Unblinking, Jesse stared at the Imperial representative. He felt sick inside, knowing that the ache of his personal loss would never go away, regardless of any concessions he received now. He didn't want the spice holdings, control of Duneworld, or the Hoskanner family for-tunes. But he *did* want the Emperor to feel the sting and pay for his part in the tragedy, even if he claimed to have been duped himself. "Do we have a deal?"

The representative bowed slightly. "Agreed, Nobleman Linkam. Accept our congratulations for winning the challenge. You have in-deed surpassed the Hoskanner output, and made your place in history on this day."

Jesse bit back a retort. He would gladly give up his place in history if he could just have his son back.

After Bauers departed, Jesse sat feeling stunned, wanting only to be alone. Old Tuek stood beside him, seemingly filled with words and wanting to comfort his lord. But he remained silent.

Jesse did not feel at all victorious.

# 34

*There is nothing more satisfying than a vanquished foe.*

—VALDEMAR HOSKANNER

Shortly before the Emperor's yacht exploded, Dr. Cullington Yueh had been on board in a "secured" cabin where no outsiders could see him. Certainly, the Linkams would want to kill him as a traitor.

As a result of Yueh's betrayals, Emperor Wuda and the Hoskanners had gotten what they wanted, but the old surgeon no longer believed his wife would be returned to him. Even if Wanna did miraculously survive, he could never admit to his wife what he had done to get her released. The shame of it would be too great.

Responding to a summons from the Grand Emperor, the agitated doctor had been permitted to leave his cabin. Two guards had escorted him into the audience chamber, telling him to wait until Wuda chose to see him. Alone except for his conscience, Yueh fidgeted beside an elegantly adorned porthole, an oval set in a delicately worked gold frame.

Gazing blankly out at the city, the old doctor thought about how the aggressive bastards had met their match in Nobleman Linkam. Instead of bowing to the Emperor's ultimatum after the kidnapping, Jesse had countered with a devastating threat of his own.

Stalemate. The Emperor seemed not to understand the harsh decisions a person might be driven to make when he had nothing left to lose. Yueh knew that all too well himself. He wished he could have been so strong. Now he worried about Barri and Dorothy, and hated himself for his role in what had happened to them. He was supposed to be a healer. How could he ever justify putting their lives at risk?

Now, why was the Emperor taking so long, and why had he summoned Yueh here? The yacht's elegant chamber was silent . . . much too silent.

The doctor had misjudged many things. When he'd arranged for the kidnappers to gain entry to the mansion, he had tried to tell himself that the boy would not be harmed, that Jesse would simply yield, and that everything would work out for the best. But after his own years of service to House Linkam, Yueh should have known the nobleman better than that.

Impatient, he looked down at the armorpave landing field and was surprised to see the corpulent Grand Emperor hurrying away from the yacht, accompanied by the tall and imposing Valdemar Hoskanner, the fidgety and overdressed Bauers, and a small entourage.

A sudden, inexplicable panic swept over Yueh. They had ordered him here and told him to wait, making certain he would stay where he was.

His mind went numb as he sensed terrible forces aligned against him, dark secrets spinning within even darker secrets. Looking toward the chamber entry, he saw that the guards weren't there any longer, either.

Something was going to happen. He had to leave, quickly! Then he remembered his pledge of honor to Dorothy. She and Barri Linkam were being kept in a sealed holding chamber aboard the yacht.

Yueh hurried out into the disturbingly empty main corridor and followed the circular floor plan at a full run. Seeing no one, he went up a level and raced toward the holding compartments. He unsealed the exterior lock and entered a large, unadorned room that dominated the center of the deck.

"Barri!" he called. "Where is your mother?"

At a machine inside, the boy was playing an electronic game, totally preoccupied by it. His unruly brown hair was even more mussed than usual. He looked at the doctor with disinterest, then pointed toward an inside doorway, before turning back to his game. It seemed to be the only thing to keep the alert boy's mind occupied in the austere enclosure.

With a mounting sense of foreboding, Yueh found Dorothy Mapes in a small room. Although her face was red, her mouth drawn, and her chest heaving as if she was shouting, he could not hear a sound. Her hands were pressed against an unseen barrier that separated them, and her eyes held the same panic that he himself felt.

Dorothy pointed urgently at something to the doctor's right, a control panel on the wall. Yueh began pressing the buttons, entering release codes. Suddenly the silence melted away, and he heard Dorothy scream her son's name. "Barri!"

With the containment field released, she fell forward onto the floor, then scrambled to her feet and ran toward the large central room. "Let's go! Barri, come with me—now!"

The boy's expression fell. "Mother! I'm close to winning!" He kept playing feverishly.

Yueh grabbed Barri and jerked him away from the machine. "We need to get off the ship! After they ordered me to stay aboard, I saw the Emperor and Valdemar Hoskanner fleeing the yacht. Oh, something terrible is going to happen!"

"They're trying to assassinate my son!" Dorothy said, as they hurried into the corridor. "He's the heir to House Linkam, and they want him out of the way. When I overheard them, Bauers sealed me in the cell."

Reaching one of the small emergency hatches, they unsealed it and dropped more than a meter to the landing field. Barri stumbled to his knees, but the old doctor helped him up, and the three of them kept going. They ran at breakneck speed across the hot armorpave surface, terrified they would be seen, and shot.

Yueh raced around to the side of a small terminal. Under an overhang behind the building, he husked, "Get down! Maybe they won't see us." He pressed Dorothy and her son into the shelter and huddled beside them.

"I don't see any guards at all," Dorothy said.

A huge explosion cracked the air, and pieces of the Emperor's yacht rained from the sky. Yueh heard fragments pelting the overhang above them, and the thunk-thunk of debris striking the ground.

Barri and Dorothy wanted to flee, but the doctor held them back. "We must stay here and hide, exercising more caution than ever. Our only advantage right now is to let them think they've succeeded."

❦

JESSE STOOD IN the sunlit high tower, his heart and thoughts hardened by grief. The cataclysm had been too sudden, and the immensity of his personal loss had not yet sunk in. During the aftermath he'd tried to keep going, to stay on the course he had set even before knowing the addictive nature of melange.

Now, more than ever, he was willing to do what must be done. He would participate in an Imperial system he hated, playing politics in order to make his enemies squirm, and in the process he would become more and more like them. Back when his secret spice hoard had started mounting every day, along with the conviction that he might actually win the challenge, Jesse had begun to experience a feeling of raw power. It had been heady territory.

And as the reality of losing Barri and Dorothy became inescapable, he concluded that neither his melange stockpile, nor victory in the challenge, nor that feeling of power mattered. Instead, he felt like a beaten man whose only future lay in an empty victory.

The Grand Emperor had offered him a deal, pretending that a hefty reward and continuing control of the spice industry somehow made up for the deaths of Barri and Dorothy. The Emperor thought he'd won, considered himself safe and secure again now that he'd blamed and ruined Valdemar Hoskanner. And Jesse had implied that would be good enough.

Now he felt ill about it.

Opening the moisture-sealed door, he stepped out into the hot, desiccated air on the high balcony. From there, he could use a long-distance transceiver to reach Gurney Halleck, who still waited at the spice stockpile silos, and General Tuek, whose men remained ready at the spice fields with their remote detonation devices on atomic warheads. Neither of them would question any decision Jesse might make.

He depressed the activation button on the communicator. "Gurney, Esmar—I need you to be strong. I need you to do what must be done."

The two men quickly acknowledged, waiting for explicit orders from the nobleman. With a single command, Jesse could obliterate a year's worth of spice production and contaminate the richest melange fields for centuries, perhaps even destroy the spice cycle of the planet. The nobles, the addicts, the hedonists would all die from horrible withdrawal, and the Emperor could shrivel along with them all. If Dr. Haynes was right, the Empire itself could crumble—and Jesse didn't give a damn.

For him, everything had vanished in the single blast aboard the Emperor's yacht.

In front of him on the high balcony, the drop to the tangled streets of Carthage seemed hypnotic. With one easy step, he could plunge over the edge. Noble House Linkam had been doomed from the moment Valdemar had offered the challenge. How had he ever imagined he could stand against such forces?

"Gurney, the booby traps on the stockpiles. I want you to—"

Something caught his eye far below: Three bedraggled forms hurried furtively toward the front entrance of the mansion, as if seeking safety inside. It looked like an old man and two smaller figures.

Jesse's hands gripped the railing, and he lost sight of them as they slipped into the mansion through a discreet servants' entrance.

"My Lord?" Gurney's voice sounded very worried. "What should I do? Do you really want me to—"

"Gurney, stand by!" He looked down again, squinting, feeling his heart pound in his chest and cursing himself for so easily leaping at even a ridiculous thread of hope. He ran back inside and shouted for the house guards.

IN THE RECEPTION hall, a shamefaced Dr. Yueh stood before Jesse Linkam. His eyes downcast, the household surgeon revealed his role in the kidnapping plot and proclaimed Dorothy's innocence. Though the old doctor offered no excuses, the concubine spoke on his behalf, explaining how the Hoskanners had imprisoned and tortured Yueh's wife in order to force his betrayal, and how Yueh had saved them.

Now, Jesse knew that the defeated and disgraced Hoskanners would strike out in vengeful fury before they turned their holdings over to House Linkam. Since the Hoskanners believed the household traitor to be dead in the explosion, Wanna Yueh was no longer of any use to them. With a sinking sensation, Jesse felt sure that Valdemar Hoskanner had already killed the poor woman, and not swiftly or painlessly.

The distraught surgeon said, "I have completed my pledge to your concubine, though that does not make up for my disgraceful deeds. Oh, even Wanna would never have agreed with what I did."

Jesse said in a steady voice, "I have always considered you a decent man, Cullington. You betrayed me and my family . . . but if not through you, my enemies would have found some other way to destroy me. Despite the unconscionable things you did, still my family is alive because of you. I will never forget that you abandoned your loyalty to House Linkam. But I grant you your life."

Yueh kept his gaze down. Tears streamed down the old man's face. "I thank you, My Lord, but no one will grant my Wanna her life. So in the end I gained nothing by betraying you."

Placing a hand on Yueh's shoulder, Jesse said, "Redemption will come for both of us. I promise you that."

# 35

*Wealth and power are the great dividers of men. Those who attain them are not always the victors.*

—NOBLEMAN JESSE LINKAM

J esse waited, but he did not forgive.

Grand Emperor Inton Wuda was a survivor of the highest order, in possession of skills that seemed ingrained into his Imperial lineage. In the aftermath of the thwarted plot, he shifted any shadow of blame away from himself. Jesse did not believe the man for an instant, but he held his tongue. He observed warily, while keeping his family and himself safe.

All culpability for the "spice crisis" conveniently fell on the shoulders of Valdemar Hoskanner and his closest allies. All Hoskanner wealth was stripped away and transferred to House Linkam, as Ulla Bauers had promised, on behalf of the Emperor. The disgraced Hoskanners were left even worse off than William English's grandfather had been.

And the Emperor's "indignant revenge" didn't end there. A pair of unpopular heads of smaller Noble Houses were blamed for starting spice riots on various planets, and their holdings were forfeited to him. Interestingly, their confiscated wealth slightly exceeded what the Linkams received from the dissolution of House Hoskanner.

As a show of good faith, Counselor Bauers offered to take General Tuek on a tour of all levels of the inspection ship. In arranging the visit, the security chief had played the role of a curious aficionado, telling Bauers that House Linkam might use its newfound wealth to build a fleet of such vessels to transport melange cargoes across space. After seeing the interior of the huge ship, the old veteran was relieved to report to Jesse that none of the suspected massed troops were hidden there after all. The vessel's sheer size was apparently only for the purpose of intimidation.

Jesse maintained his distance from the Grand Emperor, as one would from a contagious plague victim. At first, he had thought the pale and overweight leader was an easily manipulated fool, but now he realized how easily Wuda discarded anyone who no longer served his purposes. No doubt, Valdemar Hoskanner had thought the Emperor was wrapped around his finger, and now he'd been ruined. Wuda was the ultimate fair-weather friend. No matter what rewards or promises the Emperor offered, Jesse would never trust him. Never.

For weeks, while representatives wrapped up details of the new agreement, the Emperor remained aboard the inspection ship, which became something of a temporary Imperial capital. He summoned noblemen from far and wide, but Jesse felt little forgiveness toward them, either. Still angry with many of the nobles for forcing him to be their champion and then abandoning him when he needed their help and finances, he pointedly did not invite any of them into the headquarters mansion. Instead, they stayed in improvised guest quarters on the inspection ship and around Carthage, all of them looking hungry for more and more spice.

The noblemen who had provided loans at usurious rates were paid in full, and then turned away from Duneworld; Jesse had silently vowed not to do business with them again. On the other hand, the three poor families who had gambled on House Linkam, by lending all the money they could afford, were well rewarded. Jesse intended to let them participate in some of the spice operations and profits.

In a new agreement hammered out by the Emperor's lawyers, House Linkam would be paid extremely well for managing the melange operations. But when Dorothy led him through the intricacies of the complicated profit-sharing formula, Jesse was not surprised to see that the Grand Emperor's coffers would receive at least twice as much as House Linkam. Even so, the tally for each of them was enormous.

The newfound melange wealth would be more than sufficient to repair all the financial damage that generations of mismanagement had inflicted on House Linkam, while making the family business impregnable. However, Jesse intended to measure success by his own sense of justice, not by mere economic standards.

WHEN THE GRAND Emperor asked to come to dinner at the mansion, Jesse could not turn the man down, nor could he object to his bringing Counselor Bauers along. So one evening, by arrangement, Wuda and his companion swept into the great house with a contingent of personal guards. Leaving the guards out in the corridor, the pair were led by a uniformed servant into the banquet hall.

Already seated for the meal, Jesse gave Dorothy a tight-lipped smile across the long table. They had assumed their customary places of honor, despite the imminent arrival of the important visitors. The Emperor and his man were shown to secondary seats, which displeased each of them, from the downturned expressions on their faces. Still, they said nothing, and smiled when Jesse rose to his feet and greeted them. At the same time, Dorothy stood and bowed stiffly.

"Good evening, gentlemen," Jesse said, and promptly sat back down, as did his concubine. Both of them felt very uncomfortable being in the same room with the shiftless Imperial leader and his equally untrustworthy inspector.

A procession of serving women carried in steaming plates of rock pheasant, along with side dishes. This fowl had become a favorite of Jesse's—at least, as far as desert fare went. They were small birds, so it took three of them to fill each plate. But they were quite succulent, and much enhanced by one of the chef's Catalan recipes.

As the diners ate, hardly a word was spoken. Despite wanting to be civil to these influential men, Jesse was not really in any mood for chitchat, not after all he had been put through. Besides, it seemed to him that Wuda had invited himself, so he should be the one to select the topic of conversation. The four of them exchanged uncomfortable glances around the table, while servants looked on, obviously ill at ease themselves.

When they finished the main course and the plates were taken away, the Grand Emperor said, "There is one final matter of pressing importance. My prosecutors have completed a criminal investigation, and I have decided on appropriate punishments." Reaching for a silver goblet of spice wine, he gazed dispassionately around the table, and took a sip.

Jesse's pulse accelerated as the withering Imperial gaze settled upon him. He wondered if the corpulent leader had found a legal way to break their bargain after all. "Oh?"

The Emperor raised his free hand, and his personal guard contingent left their stations out in the corridor and entered the hall. Six armed men with projectile weapons slung over their shoulders took up positions around the banquet table, two of them behind Jesse, two behind Dorothy, and two behind Bauers. Their royal blue uniforms were highlighted with crimson piping, like a thin flow of blood.

Esmar Tuek burst into the banquet hall, heading a larger force of Catalan house soldiers. Though the Emperor's guards were surrounded by at least three times their number, they did not flinch. Jesse sat rigid and cold, sure that he had been betrayed again.

Calmly, Wuda took another sip of wine and said, "In our universe, nothing is ever as it seems, is it?" He addressed Tuek from his chair. "My guard captain has explained the situation to you, General Tuek?"

"Your captain has given me his word of honor that there will be no tricks. Yet by my sworn duty, Sire, I must hear the promise from your own lips."

"You have my Imperial pledge," Wuda said, frowning impatiently. "No deceptions. No harm will come to Nobleman Linkam or his concubine."

Tuek whispered in Jesse's ear. "We are forced to entertain a highly unwelcome guest, My Lord."

Again, the Grand Emperor raised his hand, and Valdemar Hoskanner strode in, unshackled and wearing extravagant clothes that dripped with golden chains and jewels. He acted as if he still owned the rugged mansion he had built. Hoskanner was followed by six Imperial guards and, behind them, even more of Jesse's own house contingent. At the Emperor's command, another chair was brought to the table, and the vile Hoskanner patriarch was seated next to Bauers.

Jesse glared daggers at his mortal enemy, but the arrogant man did not deign to notice him.

"Now that it's time for dessert," the Emperor announced, "I thought we'd invite my esteemed colleague to join us."

When Jesse looked closer, however, though he tried to appear haughty and in control, Valdemar looked like a cornered animal. His dark eyes darted this way and that, not settling on anyone or anything.

Servers brought in elegant plates of Catalanian layer cake that looked like an intricate cross section of colorful geological strata. It had been a favorite of Jesse's own foppish father, the very dessert that had poisoned him when prepared by the wrong hands.

"Oh, how marvelous!" Wuda exclaimed. "Isn't it magnificent, Valdemar?"

"Yes, Sire. In a . . . rustic fashion."

As the diners consumed sumptuous portions of cake, the Emperor, Bauers, and Valdemar began to exchange casual conversation, while Jesse sat coolly formal. The visitors drank fine red wines, ate sweets, and told old stories. Jesse was disturbed to note relaxation in the voice and demeanor of the beleaguered Valdemar, even after he had supposedly been stripped of all of his possessions.

When the desserts were finished, more wine was poured. Then the Emperor nodded toward the captain of his guard. Four uniformed men took positions behind Ulla Bauers and Valdemar Hoskanner.

The soldiers brought out glittering wire garrotes from their uniforms.

Bauers looked over his shoulder, suddenly alarmed. "Hmm, ahhh, Sire—what is this?"

"So they've found you out, after all." Valdemar's voice was brittle and resigned, as if he had been squeezed of all emotion during his confinement.

Jesse stared in surprise and shock at the Imperial theatrics.

Casually, the Grand Emperor's forefinger pointed from Hoskanner to Bauers like a metronome, back and forth, as if playing a childish game of chance, trying to decide which man to choose. The finger came to rest, pointing directly at Valdemar Hoskanner.

"So," Valdemar said to the plump Emperor. "This is our final exchange?"

"Regrettably so," Wuda said. "You have engaged in behavior unbecoming of a nobleman, and in the process you almost destroyed the spice, Duneworld, and House Linkam. For your unpardonable acts, your Noble House shall forever live in infamy. We are adding your family name to the Imperial Dictionary as an interesting new noun. 'Hoskanner: A disgraced nobleman.'"

Already defeated, Valdemar did not respond.

"Thus I grant you an odd sort of immortality," Wuda said. "At least you have left your indelible mark on history, unlike so many people who are soon forgotten, as if they never lived at all."

With a feral smile, Valdemar tilted his head so that one of the soldiers could more easily slip the sharp wire around his neck. It took only seconds. He slumped, then fell onto the floor, taking the chair over with him.

Across the table, Bauers had turned gray, fidgeting more than ever. The Emperor said in a strangely reassuring voice, "The same fate is *not* in store for you, Counselor."

Bauers looked relieved until the second guard reached down and yanked back his voluminous black collar to reveal a tiny gray tattoo in the shape of a horned cobra, the symbol of House Hoskanner.

Jesse shouted, rising to his feet. From behind him, he heard Tuek and his men engage their weapons.

Dorothy looked at the Counselor's neck. "I saw part of that mark earlier, but I didn't know what it was!"

The Emperor gestured casually, and the guard whipped the garrote around Bauers's throat. The ferretlike man gasped and thrashed. "You said . . . you said I wouldn't . . ."

"I said the same fate is not in store for you. Oh, you'll still be executed, but we won't bother to reserve a place in history for you, Ulla. You'll simply be forgotten." Bauers gurgled and clawed so much that he probably heard little of what the Emperor continued to say.

Looking down the table, Jesse saw that Dorothy did not squirm in her chair as she watched, though her face bore a squeamish expression. She met his gaze, and he saw no pleasure in it, only sadness.

"The whole affair was a debacle from the start," Wuda said to the struggling man, "and you nearly caused my Empire to fall. Your idea of the spice challenge, the threats you advised me to make, your participation in the kidnapping plan."

Bauers kicked and squirmed, tugging on the sharp cord until his fingers were as bloody as his neck.

"I am very sorry, Ulla, but how can I ever accept your counsel again?"

Though Bauers took longer to die, soon the guards dumped his body beside Valdemar's on the floor.

"Well, that was the special dessert I planned," the Grand Emperor said. "Anyone for aperitifs?"

Showing no emotion, though his insides roiled, Jesse summoned a server to bring the after-dinner drinks, while the Emperor's guards dragged the two bodies away.

"Such a shame," the fleshy leader mused. "All this time, I thought he was working for me. I only learned about the tattoo yesterday, and immediately placed him under surveillance. You see, I am as much of a victim in this conspiracy as you are."

"Faulty advice is always dangerous," Jesse said.

"You and I will have to work more closely together in the future, Nobleman," Wuda said. "I assure you, there will be no more problems between us."

"That is my sincere wish." Jesse wanted to say a great deal more, but his prudent side made him keep his silence. He and Dorothy had decided to spend the greater part of the year at his Catalan holdings, leaving Gurney Halleck on Duneworld as spice foreman. They had already begun to make quiet plans to build up the riches and power of House Linkam, and form solid alliances with a few members of the Nobles' Council, to assemble defenses against the scheming Grand Emperor.

In a way, Jesse found it ironic that he was using techniques he had learned from observing Wuda himself. The pasty man had an innocuous appearance but was in reality extremely sharp, observant, and manipulative, with a seemingly inexhaustible repertoire of schemes. His treacheries had folded and tangled together, leaving a difficult trail to follow—one that Jesse would take some time to unravel, if he ever could. This much seemed clear: The way Wuda worked it, he always placed himself in position to rake in the spoils.

If Jesse had lost the challenge, Valdemar would have paid the Emperor huge bribes, and everything would have gone back to the way it had been. When Jesse won instead, the Emperor successfully destroyed the powerful House Hoskanner, which might have posed a threat to his throne. In addition, the challenge forced House Linkam to develop an innovation in spice-harvesting methods that the Hoskanners would never have bothered to attempt. Now melange exports from Duneworld would dramatically increase.

*Wheels within wheels,* Jesse thought. *I have much to learn, to protect my House.*

There were few people in this universe the nobleman could truly trust. He could count them on the fingers of both hands. Or one. Gurney, Esmar, Dorothy. *Dorothy.* A tremendous, undeniable impulse came over him.

When the sweet wines were arrayed before them, the customary choice of three stemmed glasses for each of the diners, Jesse raised a glass and said, "I have an announcement of my own, Sire. A toast to my news!"

"And what is that?" the Grand Emperor inquired in the most erudite of tones, as if he had just deigned to speak directly to an underling.

Knowing that Dorothy had not betrayed him and had only been trying to save their son, Jesse decided to throw caution and time-honored traditions to the winds. He had made the Emperor wealthier than his wildest dreams, and that should put him in a sympathetic mood.

Taking a deep breath for courage, Jesse looked down the table at her. "Dorothy Mapes, you are my concubine, the mother of my son, and my loyal companion, but I'm afraid that is no longer sufficient for me." He spoke as if no one existed in the entire universe except the two of them.

She stared at him, her expression a mixture of sadness and love, as if she knew what he was about to say. She had always said she expected him to choose a woman from a powerful family, joining their Houses in a noble marriage. Now that he had control of Duneworld and all of the melange operations, Jesse would receive many such offers.

Then he stunned her. "Will you become my wife?"

"But . . . that's not possible, Jesse. You know it."

"House Linkam cannot exist without you, my love," Jesse insisted, "and I cannot live without you. The nobles may be addicted to spice and power, but I am addicted to you."

Unexpected tears sparkled in Dorothy's eyes, and Jesse hurried down the table to her. She looked up at him, then became harder and more sensible. "No, Jesse. I am a mere concubine, without any noble blood. You and I can never marry. I will not be the ruin of your great House!"

He turned a sharp, implacable look toward the plump Wuda. "I'm certain our Grand Emperor will give us a special dispensation. As he's told us before, he is the embodiment of Imperial law. The Emperor can change it whenever he sees fit to do so."

Inton Wuda gave a bored wave of assent as he sampled the second liqueur. Obviously, he had expected news of more significance. "I think you're a fool, Linkam, but it's the least troublesome request you have made in some time."

Jesse sipped from a small glass of melange distillate, warming his mouth and throat. Setting the drink down, he held her and looked into her myrtle-brown eyes. "Marrying you may not be the best political path for House Linkam, but forget all that, Dor! After what we've just achieved, we can certainly overcome a few mutterings at court."

She looked at him for a long moment. "If My Lord insists . . ."

He kissed her, and her mouth tasted like spice.

"From this day forward, you shall be known as *Lady* Dorothy Linkam," he said. "True nobility is not a birthright—it must be earned."

# THE ROAD TO
# *DUNE*

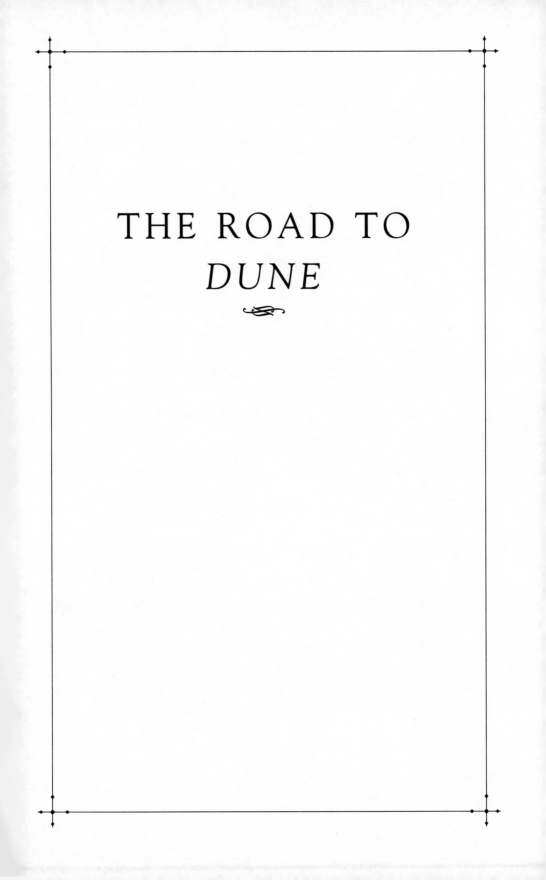

"THEY STOPPED THE MOVING SANDS"

In 1957, Frank Herbert chartered a small plane and flew to Florence, Oregon, to write a magazine article about a research project being conducted by the U.S. Department of Agriculture. The USDA had discovered a successful method of stabilizing sand dunes, planting poverty grasses on the crests of dunes to keep them from encroaching on roads and buildings. Experts were traveling to Florence from all over the world to see the project, since many areas were experiencing problems similar to those occurring in the Sahara Desert, where advancing sands were causing severe damage. Frank Herbert was very excited about the article, which he titled "They Stopped the Moving Sands." He sent a detailed outline to his agent, Lurton Blassingame, along with photographs.

The agent expressed only lukewarm interest and refused to send it out to publishers until it was reworked. Ultimately, Frank Herbert lost enthusiasm for the magazine article, and it was never published. It formed the beginning, however, of more than five years of intense research and writing that would culminate in *Dune*.

Here, for the first time, we are pleased to publish Frank Herbert's notes for the magazine article.

*from the desk of*
FRANK HERBERT

July 11, 1957

Dear Lurton,

Enclosed are some pix to explain an article I'd like to have queried around. Briefly, it involves the control of sand dunes which have been known to swallow whole cities, lakes, rivers, highways. The dunes in these pix for a time threatened part of an Oregon coastal town. Several agencies attacked the problem some ten years ago in a combined operation there. They've come up with the first answer to shifting sands that's known in all history. It's so successful that Israel, Chile, the Philippines and several other nations have sent experts to Oregon to learn how it's done.

Sand dunes pushed by steady winds build up in waves analogous to ocean waves except that they may move twenty feet a year instead of twenty feet a second. These waves can be every bit as devastating as a tidal wave in property damage . . . and they've even caused deaths. They drown out forests, kill game cover, destroy lakes, fill harbors.

Millions of acres of Chilean coast have been made unfit for humans by these shifting sands. Israel fights a constant battle with surrounding deserts. Several Oregon harbors have been plagued by this problem. And there are hundreds of other trouble spots all over the world.

The scientists working on the Oregon coast found that the sand could be controlled completely only by the use of one type of grass that will grow in such places and tie down the sand with an intricate inter-lacing of roots. This grass is extremely difficult to grow in nurseries, and a whole system of handling it had to be worked out. They tried more than 11,000 different types of grass before hitting on this one . . . and they were working against time because of the sand invasion along this stretch of coast.

It makes an exciting story with a very nice conservation twist and some excellent human angles. Let's see if somebody wants it.

I'm still plugging along on the new novel. You'll see it soon.

Best regards,
Frank

THE PROPOSAL:

The small Oregon coastal town of Florence is the scene of an unsung victory in the fight that men have been waging since before the dawn of recorded history. The fight is with moving sand—with dunes.

Sand dunes pushed by steady winds build up waves like ocean waves—except that they may move as little as twenty feet a year instead of twenty feet a second. But these slow motion waves can be every bit as devastating to property as a seismic wave—and the damage can be more lasting.

Wind-driven dunes have swallowed whole cities and towns from ancient times down to modern times. Ask any archaeologist about sand covered Tel Amerna, the city of the Horizon of Aten built by Akhenaton and his wife, Nefertiti, on the Nile banks. Here are only a few of the communities that have fought a losing battle with sand: Murzuk in the Sahara, Washari and a string of other settlements of the Kum-tagh desert in Sinkiang, hundreds of towns along the Hadhramaut coast of Arabia, Inca settlements and more recent ones on the Peruvian and Chilean coast from Trujillo south past Callao and Caldera.

Dunes have swallowed rivers—on the Guinea coast of Africa and in

French West Africa near Njeil—and there are other recorded in-stances.

Dunes have threatened harbors—on Samar in the Philippines, along Africa's Guinea Gulf, along the Inca coast of Peru and Chile—and the port of Siuslaw, Oregon, where the solution was found.

Millions of acres of Chilean and Peruvian coast have been made un-fit for humans by shifting sands. Israel fights a constant battle with sur-rounding deserts. Harbors all over the world are plagued by this problem.

In 1948, several federal and state agencies centered a study of dunes at Florence, Oregon, a town threatened by moving sand. Efforts were focused on the Port of Siuslaw and the Siuslaw River, both in the path of advancing dunes.

It took ten years, but this group, under the direction of Thomas Flippin (work unit conservationist for the Siuslaw Soil Conservation District), has come up with the first enduring answer to shifting sands in all history. It's so successful that Israel, Chile, Egypt, the Philippines and other nations have sent experts to Oregon to learn how to fight their sands.

Briefly, the scientists working the Oregon coast found that sand could be controlled only by use of one type of grass (European beach grass) and a system of follow-up plantings with other growth. The grass sets up a beachhead by holding down the sand in an intricate lacing of roots. This permits certain other plants to gain a foothold. The beach grass is extremely difficult to grow in nurseries, and part of the solution to the dune problem involved working out a system for propagating and handling the grass.

More than 11,000 different types of grass were tried by this group in Oregon before they hit on a way of handling beach grass—and they were working against time because the sand invasion along this stretch was swallowing houses, railroad tracks, Highway 101, the port of Sius-law and a nearby lake . . . and it was drowning out game cover along forty miles of coast.

How the group in Oregon solved the many problems that go into taming the sands and how their solution works make an exciting story with an excellent conservation twist and human interest through the people who won the battle.

July 29, 1957

Dear Frank,

Control of sand dunes may be a story; it is fairly limited in appeal but certainly worth trying if you'll make your outline a little more detailed. You should put it on a page without any date, just an outline, and give the answers to the questions I've written along the margins. We should also know how widespread the use of this grass is now and how rapidly it is being multiplied.

Cordially,

Lurton

(Note: Lurton Blassingame sent two letters with the same date on them.)

July 29, 1957

Dear Frank,

There may be a piece in your battle of the sand dunes but your outline still doesn't indicate it. You give much more space here to telling about the cities the sand has destroyed than you do in telling us how the battle has been won. There's no statement about the size or the number of dunes moving on Florence and Port Siuslaw. We don't know the size of either of these towns. You don't tell us how many miles of road and railroad were destroyed. I presume that the victory has been won and, if so, how far apart are Florence and Siuslaw? This outline is so vague. What has happened to the railroad? If the battle has been won, has the crew gone back to some other kind of work or are they rushing on to fight the moving sand dunes somewhere else in the country?

The outline and the story should deal with the battle to save these towns. If you put in any history, it will be just to let us see how hopeless the battle seemed, since it had never been won before. And the story probably should be tied around the man in charge so that there can be human interest in it. American editors don't give a damn about Murzuk and Kum-tagh; they don't even know what these names mean. If you're going to get an okay for a piece, you're going to have to devote the major space in your outline to interesting a U.S. editor NOW.

Cordially,
Lurton

# THE LETTERS OF
## *DUNE*

On an odyssey to understand his enigmatic father, Brian researched the biography *Dreamer of Dune* and then wrote new Dune novels with Kevin. During this process, we pored over Frank Herbert's notes, correspondence, and drafts. The files were in several locations, spread across more than a thousand miles. Unraveling the mysteries of this legendary author, and of his masterpiece, *Dune*, was formidable and fascinating.

Frank Herbert's correspondence files yielded interesting gems that show an author's passion and his continuing drive to find a publisher for a massive novel that he knew was good but which did not fit into the marketing niches of the time.

FOR YEARS after his initial article idea of "They Stopped the Moving Sands," Frank Herbert toyed with the story about a desert world full of hazards and riches. He plotted a short adventure novel, *Spice Planet*, but set the outline aside when his concept grew into something much more ambitious.

When Herbert finally presented an early draft of *Dune* to Lurton Blassingame in the spring of 1963, the agent wrote back:

April 5, 1963

Dear Frank,

Congratulations! You have a novel that is big in many ways, not only in sheer size, but in ideas and story value. It is not a *Once and Future King* of the future because I think it stumbles too often, but it did make me think of that delightful book.

For some readers it may prove to be too slow and I wouldn't be surprised if some editor asked you to cut. But the main thing right now is to know when you will have in the remainder—or the outline of the remainder. There isn't much science here, but you have a very good adventure story laid in the future and I suppose that is all that matters. That, and the fact that you have done a good job with your characters.

I think this will be called a better book than *Dragon in the Sea* and that has won many songs of praise. I bow three times—and hold out my hands for the rest of the story.

Cordially,
Lurton

Later in the month, Frank Herbert replied, sending additional chapters. He wrote:

The science in these books is essentially broad-focus—the shaping of politics, the transformation of an entire planet, religion (the transformation of an entire people), and does not dwell long on specific single tools—although I'll be surprised if you don't discover that the "stillsuit" concept is a new one, and it plays a key part in the stories. And for that matter, human individuals are treated as ecological *tools*, so what this adds up to is that we're looking at science in a different way here.

I did 70 pages final draft last week (part enclosed) and don't see why I can't duplicate that this week and mail it off to you about next Tuesday. The rest of it can come to you at about the same rate. (Think of it as a weekly serial.)

Blassingame liked the new chapters but said: "I am quite pleased with your story and your way of telling it. Length is the only problem that worries me. I will look forward to more chapters. I find the work very interesting—but how in the world are we going to sell the serial rights when it runs so long?"

The mechanics of Frank Herbert working with his agent were quite different in those days from what they might be today. Blassingame was a hands-on agent, even assisting in the preparation of the manuscript pages before sending them to *Analog* editor John W. Campbell, Jr.:

May 24, 1963

Dear Frank,
I had a call from John Campbell this morning. He is interested in *Dune* and I am seeing him Monday to hear what he has to say.

The original copy went to him last week after I had corrected all pages, deleting, adding and substituting certain pages. In places where one to half a dozen words had been substituted, the

old lines were X'd out and new words either typed above old lines
or printed in by pen.

Here are seven pages to retype. Certainly those pages where
additions have been added in the left margin must be retyped. We
had time only to start page 210, enclosed with returned pages, for
you to follow with the others if you wish. I'm sorry we have no
time to do all the others but I'm sure you will understand. I'd like
to get this carbon copy to Doubleday next week. The margin in-
serts on original copy were typed, the sheet cut and the new lines
scotch taped onto the page and the page folded up at the bottom
to the length of uncut sheets. These pages look OK.

I'm looking forward to receiving the rest of the book!

Cordially,

Lurton

Five days later, Blassingame wrote again, somewhat concerned
about the sheer amount of information Frank Herbert was introducing
at the start of the novel:

One way that might help us solve the problem is to do a little
more with your history with which you precede each chapter of
the book. Opening this novel, you might quote from some ency-
clopedia, "When the Duke Leto inherited Arrakis in the
year____, the planet had no oceans, no streams. In the northern
section, there were the cities (in a few sentences you can tell
about the water problem on the planet for the cities and the
desert). The Duke's reign lasted only____, then the Harkonnens
fell upon him and (here you can add about the wiping out of the
troops, the killing of the Duke, the escape of Paul and Jessica)."

You'll do better than this, but I do think we need to have a little more background on the planet and the situation into which
you plunge us. And your clever use of quotes at the beginning of

each chapter gives you a chance to provide us with this information.

Campbell purchased the story in a matter of days, for serialization in the magazine, paying $2,550 (three cents a word) for it (a net of $2,295 to the author after agent's commission). Early in June 1963, the legendary editor wrote the first of many letters he would exchange with Frank Herbert in ensuing years.

Concerning the leading character, Paul Atreides, Campbell wrote: "Congratulations! You are now the father of a 15-year-old superman!" He then went on for four pages to give suggestions on how to fit the powers of the superhero into the novel, culminating in this comment: "If 'Dune' is to be the first of three, and you're planning on using Paul in the future ones . . . oh, man! You've set yourself one hell of a problem! You might make the next one somewhat more plottable if you didn't give Paul quite so much of the super-duper."

Frank Herbert did not agree, and adhered to his basic view of Paul's powers, in which he had future vision, but with some limitations. Frank wrote a detailed and philosophical five-page response discussing the nature of metaphysics, time, and prescience. After Blassingame read a copy of this response, he wrote to Frank: "I think you did a brilliant job of defending your position. So far [Campbell] has known of only two ways of handling supermen and I hope he will accept your arguments and say that in future he knows of three ways."

Campbell did accept the defense. Five days later, he responded in a three-page letter, continuing the esoteric discussion but adding: "I'm not suggesting you drop Paul's time-scan ability because I dislike it— but because I suspect it might make adequate plotting damn difficult. Your suggestions as to the limitations of the ability are sound."

The interchange between editor and author proved thought provoking in more than just the specific story at hand. A few weeks later, Frank Herbert wrote back to Campbell:

> Your letters on Time set off a prolonged conversation here the other night between Jack Vance, Poul Anderson, and myself. We missed you.
>
> Vance: Past and future as "entities" are merely illusion; the only reality is the now-instant. (This tosses out all Time-travel stories.)
>
> Anderson: Time is related purely to standards of measurement. (Very hard-headed on empirical science.)
>
> Herbert: Time and life are related in a way that does not hold for Time and inanimate objects.
>
> That oversimplifies, but pretty well summates points of view. There was more—much more. A good *Time* was had by all.
>
> As I said, we missed you.

To fit *Analog*'s requirements, Frank Herbert prepared four synopses, which would appear with each of the planned four serializations of *Dune World*, around 85,000 words. Frank wrote: "The synopses, oddly enough, break the book into almost equal parts—four of them. This doubtless comes from lavish use of cliffhangers." Subsequently, he had to modify this to three synopses, as Campbell changed his mind and decided to run the story in three parts.

All the while, Blassingame had been in contact with major publishers such as Doubleday & Co., trying to find one of them to publish the novel in book form. By the summer of 1963, word began to filter back to Frank Herbert that this would be no easy task, primarily because of the length of the book. Most science-fiction novels at the time were only around 50,000–75,000 words, and *Dune* (when the author included more material after the serialization) approached 200,000.

Because of such artificial attitudes, Frank Herbert did not always think highly of New York publishers. One letter attests to this: "As to

Doubleday—if they take it, excellent. If not, there are other publishing houses. I can feel in my bones that the Dune trilogy [the three parts of the original novel now published as *Dune*] is going to be a money maker for whoever publishes it. I always remind myself that editors come and editors go, but writers outlast most of them. (Campbell is a delightful exception, but then he's a writer, too.)"

A week later, Doubleday said they might offer a contract on *Dune World*, but only if it could be cut to 75,000 or 80,000 words. Frank Herbert made changes to the manuscript, but in August, Timothy Seldes of Doubleday withdrew his offer of a contract, saying he had too much trouble with the beginning of the novel: "In fact, I recommend to you the adding up of unfamiliar technology in the first ten pages. It is conceivably a reflection on the story as a whole that, at least to my mind, Mr. Herbert has so much trouble getting into it."

Blassingame had sent the manuscript out to several publishers, and in late October of 1963 it was declined politely by Charles Scribner's Sons. Shortly afterward, Frank Herbert completed Book II of *Dune* ("Muad'Dib"), and sent it off to his agent, with this comment: "I was unhappy to learn that Scribner's rejected *Dune*. The editor's comment that he may have been mistaken (in doing so)—let us hope that's prophetic."

On November 1, 1963, Frank Herbert completed Book III of *Dune* ("The Prophet") and sent it off to his agent with this note: "Here's Book III of the trilogy, the one I think most successful of the series. Let's hope some editors share this judgment."

Blassingame liked the third part but wrote back: "One big obstacle is the division of material. Most trilogies have big time gaps between books or shift viewpoints. Your story is continuous. You really don't have three novels; there is only one big novel. It may have to appear as a single volume." In December, Doubleday asked for a second look at *Dune*, so the agent sent it to them again, cautioning the author: "Your chief trouble is length. Your novel is about twice as long as most other persons' novels . . ."

Just before Christmas of 1963, John W. Campbell wrote to

Blassingame that he liked the new Dune material for serialization in *Analog*, saying: ". . . this is a gee-gorgeous hunk of stuff." He went on to make suggestions about cutting back the prescient powers of Paul Atreides but did not make this a condition of publication. He said that "the major trouble you [have] with the Dune World series [is] getting Paul's psi faculty into focus as a useful, profitable faculty, rather than something that just confused him and everything else."

The new material—another 120,000 to 125,000 words—would require an additional five magazine installments to publish, but Campbell said it was exactly the sort of "swashbuckler" that he wanted for *Analog*.

When Frank Herbert saw the cover art for the first "Dune" issue of *Analog*, he was tremendously impressed and wrote: "Frequently, I have to ask myself if the artist was actually illustrating the story his work accompanied. No so with John Schoenherr. His December cover caught with tremendous power and beauty the 'Dune mood' I struggled so hard to create. It's one of the few such works of which I'd like to have the original."

With equal enthusiasm, John W. Campbell wrote that the cover art was ". . . Schoenherr's sixth attempt, I believe. Getting the feeling of desolation, danger, dryness and action was not easy; the guy earned his pay on that one!"

Frank Herbert and John Campbell talked extensively by phone about the manuscript, and the author won the arguments over the prescient powers of Paul Atreides. Frank had a strong affinity for ESP and had been researching the subject for years, as he explained to his agent:

ESP is one of my interests to the extent that I have done considerable reading on it in what I would call the quasi-scientific end of the field. This includes Rene Sudre's *Para-Psychology* and a considerable amount of J. B. Rhine—including *The Reach of the Mind* and *New World of the Mind*. I've also dabbled in Puharich, the "sacred mushroom" writer.

I'm what you might refer to as an agnostic where ESP is

concerned—a "Doubting Thomas." Some of the writers on this end of the field, such as Fodor and Tassi, are too kookie for my tastes, and I have strong doubts as to the mathematical basis for the statistics of Rhine's tests.

Okay, I'm from Missouri. This does not, however, limit my enjoyment of a good ESP story or stay in my imagination in exploring the "what ifs" of possible mental powers.

In the interaction with Campbell, however, Frank Herbert did take one important suggestion. In the first version of the manuscript, Paul's sister Alia was killed, but the editor talked him into reversing this decision and keeping her alive for future stories. This proved to be wise counsel, as she became one of the most interesting characters in the Dune universe.

(As an aside, Frank also decided to "revive" Duncan Idaho in later novels because the fans liked him so much. The Dune universe would be much poorer without Alia Atreides and the serial gholas of Duncan Idaho.)

In the various drafts of the book, Frank wrote additional chapters, which he eventually trimmed from the manuscript in an attempt to keep the length under control. These lost chapters are published later in *The Road to Dune*.

In late January 1964, Timothy Seldes of Doubleday again declined the novel, writing: "Nobody can seem to get through the first 100 pages (of Book I) without being confused and irritated." A few weeks later, Julian P. Muller of Harcourt, Brace & World also rejected the manuscript, citing "slow spots," "wearying conversations," "bursts of melodrama," and the sheer size of the material. He also said: "It is just possible that we may be making the mistake of the decade in declining *Dune* by Frank Herbert."

In the midst of such rejections, Frank wrote to his agent, insisting: "This is going to be a salable property." More people were beginning to appreciate the story as well. A short while later, the 22nd World Science Fiction Convention (Pacificon II) notified him that *Dune World* (based upon the *Analog* serialization) had been nominated for the prestigious Hugo Award.

In response, Frank Herbert wrote back to the convention:

I really feel very deeply honored that "Dune World" has been nominated for the Hugo. It really is quite a surprise. As a rule, I don't believe writers think about such things. We're too busy writing "the story."

Win, lose or draw, I'm looking forward to seeing you in September. Right now it's back to the typewriter. I'm piled twenty feet deep in work . . . and I love it.

That summer, Blassingame reported continuing problems with placing the novel with a book publisher: "I hope the enormous length of *Dune* isn't going to prevent a sale, but we are still being bothered by it." Saying the novel was "old fashioned in presentation" and in need of cutting, New American Library rejected the manuscript a short while afterward.

At Pacificon II in Oakland, California, *Dune World* was up against *Here Gather the Stars* by Clifford D. Simak (book title *Way Station*), *Cat's Cradle* by Kurt Vonnegut, *Glory Road* by Robert A. Heinlein, and *Witch World* by Andre Norton for the Hugo Award. *Dune World* did not win (*Way Station* did), but John Campbell's *Analog* received a Hugo for best professional magazine. Frank Herbert went to the convention and appeared on Campbell's behalf to pick up the award, which he then shipped to New York. In appreciation for Frank's contribution, the editor wrote: "I want to thank you for helping us get the Hugo this year—in both ways! I told the Committee that either you or Poul Anderson would be the obvious proxies for *Analog*, both being West Coasters, and both being major reasons why the Hugo was coming this way."

Campbell sent payment for the postage, but Frank Herbert wrote back: "It was my honor to pick up your hard-earned Hugo and forward it. The postage was such a small thing, you shouldn't have bothered. However, it did arrive just as #2 Son (Bruce) asked for an advance on his allowance. You may take some satisfaction from the fact that you were there to provide that advance."

Fan letters began to stream in from *Analog* readers, but so did rejection letters from major publishers. E. P. Dutton added their name to a list of turndowns that would eventually reach more than twenty, writing: ". . . something of this size would require a perfectly incredible investment and a list price far in excess of that any science fiction book has ever had before." Citing similar reasons for his rejection, Allen Klots Jr. of Dodd, Mead & Co. added: "It is the sort of writing that might attract a cult and go on forever, but we have not had much luck with science fiction and there is too much of a chance, in our opinion, that this would be lost of its own weight."

Early in 1965, Frank Herbert received good news from a surprising source. Chilton Books, best known for publishing auto repair manuals, made an offer of $7,500 (plus future royalties) to publish the three Dune segments—"Dune World," "Muad'Dib," and "The Prophet"—in a single hardcover. Chilton's farsighted editor Sterling Lanier had tracked the agent down after seeing the story in *Analog*. (Lanier was a science-fiction author himself, and wrote the novels *Hiero's Journey* and *Menace Under Marswood*.)

Lanier wrote that he admired the work and he wanted to publish it in one book, and that he wanted the author to add even more material! He intended to name it all *Dune*, and said he would make contact with Campbell's artist, John Schoenherr, for the cover art. The Chilton offer was quickly accepted. A short while later, Lanier reported: "I have bought Schoenherr's cover of Jessica and Paul, crouching in the canyon, and I think it will make a magnificent and arresting sight."

As *Dune* was being prepared for publication, Frank Herbert wrote to a friend, describing his own writing style:

For *Dune*, I also used what I call a "camera-position" method—playing back and forth (and in varied orders depending on the required pace) between long-shot, medium, close-up and so on. Much of the prose in *Dune* started out as Haiku and then was given minimal additional word padding to make it conform to normal English sentence structure. I often use a Jungian mandala in squaring off characters of a yarn against each other, assigning a dominant psychological role to each. The implications of color, position, word root and prosodic suggestion—all are taken into account when a scene has to have maximum impact. And what scene doesn't if a book is tightly written?

Later, responding to a letter from a fan, Frank Herbert wrote:

My idea of a good story is to put people in a pressure environment. This happens in reality, but life's dramas tend to lack the organization we require of the novel. I hit on the idea of a desert planet while researching a magazine article about efforts to control sand dunes. This led me to other research avenues too numerous to detail completely here, but involving some time in a desert (Sonora) and a re-examination of Islam.

Arrakis is hostile because hostility is an aspect of the environment which produces drama. Typhoons, fires, floods—what these do to people contains the essential elements of good story.

Long novel: it was an experiment in pacing. I'm not sure how successful the experiment, but certainly I realize it violates novel conventions. I did not, however, even consider the violation. I was too concerned with the internal rhythms of my story. Essentially, these rhythms are coital . . . slow, gentle beginning, increasing pace, etc. Also, I chose to end it in a non-Hollywood way, sending the reader skidding out of the story with bits of it still clinging to him. I did not want it neatly tied off, something you'd forget ten minutes after putting it down. Casualness is one of our modern hangups. I don't write casually, and I should be sorry to hear that anyone read me casually. Lest this sound pretentious, let me say that I have no feelings of moral judgment about this way of writing. Good-bad-indifferent? It's just the one I chose.

It's also long because it contains what I call "vertical layers"—many levels at which a reader may enter it (another experiment on my part). You can choose the layer you want and follow that throughout the story. Re-reading, you might choose an entirely different layer, discover "something new" in the story.

My opinion of the novel? First, we'd have to do that semantic thing, define what the hell a novel is; then we'd get involved with analysis of that verb "to be" in our answer, and at the end, we'd be nowhere.

This isn't a thing that submits to analysis. There's no *truth* to be found this way. The novel, as generally understood, simply involves good story, which means "entertainment that instructs." Entertainment. *Dune* has elements of caricature—desert reduction and absurdum; Victorian poses. Is it a novel? It falls within the usual classification. It is representative? I hope not, but feel unqualified to judge.

The novel? Lord, man—give me Occam's razor. You're asking me to be a critic, a role I despise. There's only one useful kind of critic, the one whose tastes are so similar to your own that when he says, "I liked it" you can be sure you'll like it, too. He pre-reads the yearly offerings and keeps you from wasting time on things which he turns down. Unfortunately most criticism is by poseurs. They use their comments about someone else's work as a platform on which to strike poses. What they're really saying is: "Look at me! Look at me!" Most such critics can't write worth a damn in the field they're judging or are afraid to cast their own efforts adrift in the sea of poseurs. I guess the only worthwhile critic is Time. If it endures . . . And what we classify as "the novel" appears to be enduring. What I'm hoping is that it also is undergoing improvement, keeping up with the times.

Another letter from the author contained even more insights: "The way I write a book, I knew better than to send off outline and sample chapters. I compose a book (musical sense)—filling, balancing, emphasizing, re-writing . . . Obviously, the finished product will bear little resemblance to any damned sample!"

◈

AS CHILTON BOOKS prepared for the release of its hardcover volume of *Dune*, Sterling Lanier asked Frank Herbert to help in promoting the book. Using his many friends and newspaper connections, Frank wrote:

August 23, 1965

Dear Sterling,

Enclosed is the list for the 25 books you said your promotion department would mail to help sales on *Dune*. I've been doing a bit of scurrying on this and have an old friend who runs a Tacoma advertising & promotion firm (and who is *very* good) all set to mount a PR campaign for me through the Pacific Northwest. I have plenty of old friends, school chums and the like in key positions (radio and TV commentators, editors, columnists and such) throughout the region. This shouldn't be too difficult.

For San Francisco and Los Angeles—I can be of some promotional help. I'm working on City Lights [bookstore] for a window display and whatever other help they can give in the North Beach "Little Bohemia." When I go back south next month, I'll deliver a few copies to editor friends on the leading papers.

Oh, one more thing—if your promotion department can spare two more copies—I'd like them to go to Robert C. Craig, 3140 E. Garfield, Phoenix, Ariz., 85008. He's the only relative I have who can be of any help in this. He travels throughout the Southwest (Arizona, Texas, New Mexico and Oklahoma) for the USDA and has hundreds of important friends down there.

The book looks beautiful and was out sooner than I expected.

Warmest regards,

Frank

Chilton also produced a two-minute radio spot, which ran on over five hundred radio stations.

September 30, 1965

Dear Mr. Herbert,

Attached is the two-minute script on *Dune* which was broadcast over more than 500 commercial and educational stations, plus 170 Veterans Administration Hospital stations during the week of September 27. Many stations will use it more than once.

The *Inside Books Radio* programs are sponsored by libraries and book stores throughout the country. We believe these broadcasts will broaden the audience for your book among people who are not ordinarily reached by the traditional book media, as well as those who are.

Sincerely yours,

Mrs. Mary Jo Groenevelt

\* \* \*

WEEK OF SEPTEMBER 27
INSIDE BOOKS SCRIPT #4, DO NOT BROADCAST BEFORE
THURSDAY, SEPTEMBER 30

Title: Dune    Author: Frank Herbert
Publisher: Chilton Books, 227 S. 6th Street, Philadelphia.
Price: $5.95    Publication Date: 10/1/65

Time now for our daily look inside the exciting world of books . . .
based on reports we receive from *Publishers Weekly*, the Book Industry
Journal. (sponsor time) One of the most fantastic novels that we've
seen in a long time is *Dune* by Frank Herbert. When we say that *Dune*
is a *fantastic* novel, we mean just that: a work of pure fantasy . . . an exciting science-fiction story that takes place far in the future on a distant planet. Actually, we should have said *several* distant planets . . .
because the story of *Dune* concerns a Duke named Leto who moves
from one planet to another. The planet that he leaves is a rich and fertile one . . . and the planet that he moves to is a terrible desert, with almost no water at all. Duke Leto is the head of a very ancient noble
house, and when he moves from the good planet to the desert planet,
the future of his entire household is put into jeopardy. But he doesn't
really have a choice because he has to follow the orders of the Emperor.
The Emperor has sent Duke Leto far away because he is jealous of
Leto's great wealth and popularity . . . and because he is under the influence of Leto's greatest enemy, an evil baron named Vladimir
(VLAD uh meer) who is the head of a rival noble family. Actually,
Duke Leto's new planet is not *entirely* a wasteland. It's also the only
planet where one can find the most valuable drug that exists . . . a drug
that contains the secret of everlasting life. But if we tell you very much
more about the background of *Dune*, we'll be giving away essential
parts of the story. So let's change the subject a little bit and say that
the real hero of *Dune* is not Duke Leto but his son, Paul, who is only

fifteen years old when the story begins. Paul is not an ordinary child. He is much more sensitive than most . . . and has a particular mental power which sets him apart from all other people . . . a power that he has inherited from his mother, and that allows him to recognize the *real truth* when he finds it. We said at the beginning that *Dune* was an exciting novel, and it is . . . but it's also something more. It's the creation of a whole society of the future, worked out to the very last detail. You might call it a kind of *super* science fiction . . . where the author has even gone so far as to provide a short dictionary of special words that refer to powers and states of being that don't exist—or don't *yet* exist—on our world . . . but that form the very basis of the world of *Dune*. (sponsor time) We've been talking about *Dune* by Frank Herbert. We'll have another Inside Books report for you tomorrow, at this time.

*   *   *

Chilton also sent out an extensive press release, entitled "DUNE Will Never Let the Reader Go":

Frank Herbert's latest novel, *Dune*, is a giant work of literature and a gripping excursion into fantasy.

Because the all-powerful Emperor fears Duke Leto's growing wealth and popularity, the Duke must exchange his lands. Duke Leto Atreides must move from a *planet*, which he owns, to another planet which he has been given in exchange. And the Emperor, Shaddam IV, is the Emperor of the *Universe*. Duke Leto's son, Paul, is so little normal in any way that he is the possible key to all human power and knowledge. The Duke's lady, Paul's mother, is the creature of the Bene Gesserit, the strangest religious matriarchy ever conceived, whose aims are also universal rule.

The answer to all questions lies in a world called Dune, the planet Arrakis, which produces as its sole export Melange, drug of immortality. Arrakis is a world of sand, rock, and heat, where roam armed savages who kill for drops of water.

A book as universal as time, brilliant in scope, and dazzling in narrative, *Dune* is an example of what can be done when an inspired writer turns his eyes *forward* into history rather than back.

Frank Herbert, whose work has been compared to both Aldous Huxley and Edgar Rice Burroughs, is a newspaperman whose published works include *The Dragon in the Sea* and scores of short stories.

\*   \*   \*

Science-fiction luminaries also weighed in. Poul Anderson wrote: "By any standards whatsoever, *Dune* is an important book, and within the science fiction field a major work—a suspenseful story, four-dimensional characters, and a setting worthy of Hal Clement. But there is much more. There is pity, terror, irony, Machiavellian politics, and the best study I have seen of one of the most important and least understood phenomena in history: the messiah. Frank Herbert is not only concerned with the impact of such a prophet on human events. He looks deeper, he asks what it feels like to have a destiny. In so doing, he tells us much about the nature of man."

And Damon Knight wrote: "The highest achievement of a science fiction novelist is the creation of an imaginary world so real, so vivid, that the reader can touch, see, taste, hear and smell it. Arrakis is such a world, and *Dune* is clearly destined to become a science fiction classic."

Then the reviews started coming in. One of the newspapers for which Frank Herbert worked (the *Santa Rosa [CA] Press Democrat*) ran an article titled "Ex-Staffer's Weird Novel": "Frank Herbert, once a Press-Democrat reporter, has been compared to Edgar Rice Burroughs as a spinner of unusual tales. This book is, of course, no exception, and will hold the reader spellbound from beginning to end." *Kirkus* said:

"This future space fantasy might start an underground craze. It feeds on the shades of Edgar Rice Burroughs (the Martian series), Aeschylus, Christ and J. R. R. Tolkien." *Science Fiction Review* claimed that *Dune* "is, I think, the longest science fiction novel ever published as a single book. . . . I won't attempt to sketch the plot; suffice it to say that there should be something in the book for everyone: adventure, psychology, power politics, religion, etc."

Perhaps not surprisingly, the reviewer for *Analog* liked the novel: "*Dune* is certainly one of the landmarks of modern science fiction. It is an amazing feat of creation." However, the reviewer for *The Magazine of Fantasy and Science Fiction* was not so kind: "I don't think any amount of effort or ability could have made this odd hodgepodge of concepts stick together. I cannot possibly trace the many strands interwoven in the novel. . . . This is a long book, and in its major premises quite unworthy of the work put into it."

The *El Paso Times* wrote: "The creation of an imaginary country, complete with flora, fauna, myths, legends, history, geography, ecology and so forth, demands an agile and informed mind. Herbert obviously possesses the requisite knowledge to devise and develop such a concept, but unfortunately his fantasy is more fascinating to him than to the average reader. . . . What with struggling with an 18-page glossary of terms, and concentrating on perfervid prose which makes that of H. Rider Haggard seem austere, it is no easy matter to ingest this 412-page tome."

Early in 1966, the British publisher Gollancz made arrangements to publish *Dune* in hardcover throughout the United Kingdom, while New English Library would do the UK paperback version. In the United States, Chilton sold paperback rights to Ace Books.

Then, on February 17, 1966, Frank Herbert received the news that *Dune* had won the Nebula Award for the best science-fiction novel of 1965, awarded by Science Fiction Writers of America. Damon Knight, president of the organization, wrote to him in advance of the banquet in Los Angeles:

February 17, 1966

Dear Frank,

It is my pleasant duty to tell you that *Dune* has won the best-novel award in the SFWA balloting (as, in my opinion, it richly deserved to do). Please don't shout this from the housetops yet; it is supposed to be under wraps until the March 11 banquet.

I hope you will be able to attend the L.A. banquet and pick up your trophy; if you haven't sent in your reservation yet, it should go to Harlan Ellison. If for any reason you can't make it, please tell Harlan who you would like to accept the award for you.

With personal congratulations & best wishes,

best,

Damon

(He added a handwritten postscript: It would be even nicer if you could come to the New York banquet on the same date, but that's a long way . . . )

On the heels of that message, Harlan Ellison wrote to Frank Herbert:

February 26, 1966

Dear Frank,

I've got to know soonest if you'll make the banquet. We have to give them a final count at the restaurant, at least a week ahead of time, and also the proportion of prime rib dinners to rack of lamb dinners. So letting me know on the 9th is impossible.

Also, since I have won the short story award—and you can keep that news to yourself, fuzzyface—it would be a bit presumptuous of me to accept the novel award for you. It already looks like I bribed the membership. So you'll just have to be there to take it yourself. (In the final event that you cop out on all of us determined to pay homage to your unquenchable ego, I'll arrange to have some notable accept for you, and then ship the effing thing to you; but that is a *last* resort.)

Either way, you'd better fill in the enclosed, and send me a check for your ticket(s) just in case you can make it. If you can't we'll refund the money. Reluctantly, but we'll refund it.

Don't miss it, Herbert. It may be the one chance I get to officially insult you from a podium. Also the program looks to be extraordinarily exciting and maybe even profitable.

Be good. See you at the banquet. Don't disappoint me.

Harlan

Only a few days later, sad news arrived, as Sterling Lanier announced that he and Chilton Books were parting ways. (Though he did not say so, part of this might have had to do with his strong advocation of the immense novel *Dune*, with all of the publication costs involved, and the fact that sales of the book still had not picked up.) The supportive editor wrote:

You have done a fantastic job, and I am deeply proud to have been even remotely associated with you. I honestly feel that my only *real* contribution was to see that the book was a great one and to go out and hunt for it. I had to track it down through the good offices of John Campbell. Arthur Clarke gave you a fantastic writeup, in a letter to me, which we are using in *The Library Journal* along with Faith Baldwin's . . . Hope we meet someday, somewhere.

On March 11,1966, Donald Stanley from the *San Francisco Examiner* reported:

Tonight the [SFWA] meets in Los Angeles. The conventioneers will watch a couple of pilot films by director Gene Roddenberry from next season's CBS series, "Star Trek." The main business, however, will be the presentation of the first SFWA awards in science fiction.

Winner of the prize for best novel is Frank Herbert, a former picture editor at *The Examiner* who left last year to devote full time to writing.

The bearded Herbert used to come prowling into our book department asking for "anything you have on dry climate ecology."

Most visitors want Burdick or O'Hara; Herbert lusted after the desert. T. E. Lawrence, the Koran, Mojave botanicals, all were grist for his arid mill.

Late last year Chilton published the reason for all this sand-etched activity. "Dune" is the name of the novel that took Herbert some half dozen years of researching and writing and which the SFWA jury has chosen for its first award.

In April, Frank Herbert wrote from his study in Fairfax, California, to Damon Knight, who lived in Milford, Pennsylvania: "The Nebula sits on my windowsill now against a background of oaks and bays which are just getting their spring foliage. Please tell Kate [Damon's wife, Kate Wilhelm] (and Mrs. Jim Blish) that there should be an award for the award. Thank God! Someone has at last broken away from the glistening phallic symbols with arms reaching toward heaven. This is a work of art."

("The glistening phallic symbols" was a reference to the Hugo Award—which Frank would also receive later that year for *Dune*.)

EARLY IN 1967, sales of *Dune* began to pick up, and Chilton went back to press for an additional printing. Frank Herbert wrote to his agent: "Book stores in this area can't keep *Dune* in stock—selling out and reordering at a delightful pace. Hope this is a national thing." Indications were good, because by January of 1968 Ace Books went back to press for an additional 25,000 copies of the paperback, too.

By early 1968, Frank Herbert was hard at work on a sequel to *Dune* but was having some difficulty with the title, first choosing *Fool Saint* and then *(The) Messiah,* before settling on *Dune Messiah.* He also considered and discarded the cryptic title *C Oracle,* representing a coracle floating on a sea of time.

John W. Campbell received a copy of the sequel that summer, and he didn't like it at all. In a scathing letter, he wrote: "Paul commits acts of absolute folly—which you seek to explain on the basis of His Vision Requires It . . . Paul winds up as a God That Failed—he winds up, in Fremen terms, which he accepts as a useless-to-the-tribe cripple abandoned in the desert . . . In outline, it sounds like an Epic Tragedy, but when you start thinking back on it, it works out to 'Paul was a damn fool, and surely no demi-god; he loused up himself, his loved ones, and the whole galaxy!'"

Frank Herbert began his major revisions to the manuscript. Some of the alternate or deleted chapters and scenes are included later in *The Road to Dune.*

A month later, Frank completed rewrites and sent them to his agent, who reported back: "I think you did a good job on the revision of the *Dune* sequel. It reads better now than it did before, though it still is not the masterpiece that *Dune* is. I think Campbell will like it now. He has a copy."

But Campbell still didn't like it at all. In a reversal of the experience with *Dune,* at a time when book publishers were vying for the right to publish *Dune Messiah* in hardcover and paperback, the magazine editor took the opposite stance, and refused to serialize it in *Analog.* He wrote:

Herbert's revision of "The Messiah" still didn't satisfy me . . .
In this one, it's Paul, our central character, who is a helpless

pawn manipulated against his will, by a cruel, destructive fate. . . .

The reactions of science-fictioneers, however, over the last few decades have persistently and quite explicitly been that they want *heroes*—not anti-heroes. They want stories of strong men who exert themselves, inspire others, and make a monkey's uncle out of malign fates!

His list of complaints included the following:

. . . Item: If Paul can't "see" where other oracles have muddied the waters of Time—then neither can they "see" where he is working. Because what he does, responding to his vision of the future, alters that future to indeterminacy—the future is unstabilized; it is *not* determinate.

. . . Item: a Hero leader who cuts and runs from the Climactic Battle is not a Messiah—even though, or particularly if, his side actually wins. Neither is he a martyr, nor a Victim of Fate.

Campbell didn't understand and perhaps Frank Herbert didn't explain adequately at the time that his intention was to write an anti-hero book, in order to warn about the dangers of following a charismatic hero. As Brian explained in *Dreamer of Dune:*

*Dune,* the first novel in what would ultimately become a series, contained hints of the direction (Frank Herbert) intended to take with his superhero, Paul Muad'Dib, clues that many readers overlooked. It was a dark direction. When planetologist Liet-Kynes lay dying in the desert, he remembered these words of his father, spoken years before and relegated to the back reaches of memory: "No more terrible disaster could befall your people than for them to fall into the hands of a Hero." And at the end of an appendix it was written that the planet had been "afflicted by a

Hero." . . . The author felt that heroes made mistakes . . . mistakes that were amplified by the numbers of people who followed those heroes slavishly . . .

Among the dangerous leaders of human history, my father sometimes mentioned General George S. Patton, because of his charismatic qualities—but more often his example was President John F. Kennedy. Around Kennedy a myth of kingship formed, and of Camelot. His followers did not question him, and would have gone with him virtually anywhere. This danger seems obvious to us now in the case of such men as Adolf Hitler, who led his nation to ruination. It is less obvious, however, with men who are not deranged or evil in and of themselves. Such a man was Paul Muad'Dib, whose danger lay in the myth structure around him. (pp. 191–192)

Despite Campbell's rejection, *Dune Messiah* was picked up by *Galaxy* magazine, and would run in five installments, in the July–November 1969 issues. It was also picked up in hardcover by G. P. Putnam's Sons, and in paperback by Berkley Books. With sales and accolades on the upswing, an ebullient Frank Herbert wrote to his agent: "*Dune* is hot right now. A sequel is sure to capitalize on that fact. It's required reading in several college lit and psych classes and is referred to on campuses as a 'great underground book.' Are all the publishers in New York asleep at the switch?"

He was not yet earning enough money from his writing to entirely quit working as a newspaperman, but things were heading in the right direction. In a couple of years, *Dune* and *Dune Messiah* would become phenomenal bestsellers and Frank Herbert would be lecturing on college campuses all over the United States. *Dune* would be picked up by the environmental movement for its desert ecology theme, and well-known movie producers would begin knocking on his door.

UNPUBLISHED SCENES

AND CHAPTERS

# INTRODUCTION

~⁊~

While poring over early drafts of the *Dune* and *Dune Messiah* manuscripts, we discovered alternate endings, additional scenes, and chapters that had been eliminated from the final published works.

Prior to its 1965 hardcover publication, *Dune* was serialized in *Analog*, but each segment was limited by the magazine's length restrictions. The editor, John W. Campbell, Jr., worked closely with Frank Herbert to trim scenes and chapters, making them fit into the number of pages that Campbell wanted.

The following chapters were cut in this fashion and then never restored when the novel was published in book form. In one passage here, Frank Herbert mentions that spice has been used for only about a century, but in later versions, he expands the time frame to span many thousands of years. Many details are inconsistent with the published versions, and these scenes should be considered drafts, not "canon."

These are interesting and enlightening additions to the stories and are available here for the first time. The context should be clear to anyone familiar with the early novels.

Some of the chapters from *Dune Messiah* are a radical departure from what was published as the final version, and some of the alternate endings are spectacular and shocking.

# Deleted Scenes and Chapters from
## *Dune*

# PAUL & REVEREND MOTHER MOHIAM

*(Several short scenes from the opening of* Dune*)*

On the inner wall beneath the window was a loose stone that could be pulled out to reveal a hiding place for the treasures of his boyhood—fishhooks, a roll of meta-twine, a rock shaped like a lizard, a colored picture of a space frigate left behind by a visitor from the mysterious Spacing Guild. Paul removed the stone and looked at the hidden end of it where he had carved with his cutterray: "Remember Paul Atreides, age 15, Anno 72 of Shaddam IV."

Slowly, Paul replaced the stone above his treasures and knew he would never remove it again. He returned to his bed, slipped under the covers. His emotion was sad excitement, and this puzzled him. He had been taught by his mother to study a puzzling emotion in the Bene Gesserit fashion. Paul looked within himself and saw that the finality of his goodbyes carried the sadness. The excitement came from the adventure and strangeness that lay ahead.

❧

PAUL SLIPPED OUT of bed in his shorts, began dressing. "Is she your mother?" he asked.

"That's a fool's question, Paul," Jessica said. She turned. "Reverend Mother is merely a title. I never knew my mother. Few Bene Gesserits of the schools ever do; you know that."

Paul put on his jacket, buttoned it. "Shall I wear a shield?"

Jessica stared at him. "A shield? Here in your home? What ever put that idea into . . ."

"Why're you afraid?" he demanded.

A wry smile tugged one corner of her mouth. "I trained you too well. I . . ." She took a deep breath. "I don't like this move to Arrakis. You know this decision was made over my every objection. But . . ." She shrugged. "We haven't time to dally here." She took his hand the way she had done when he was smaller, led him out into the hall toward her morning room.

Paul sensed the oddness of her taking his hand, felt the perspiration in her palm and thought: *She doesn't lie very well, either. Not for a Bene Gesserit she doesn't. It isn't Arrakis that has her afraid.*

❧

PAUL TURNED BACK to the Reverend Mother; thinking of the exposed idea within this test: *Human or animal?*

"If you live as long as I have lived you will still remember your fear and your pain and your hate," the old woman said. "Never deny it. That would be like denying part of yourself."

"Would you have killed me?" he asked.

"Suppose you answer that for yourself, young human."

He studied the wrinkled face, the level eyes. "You would have done it," he said.

"Believe it," she said. "Just as I would've killed your mother in her day. A human can kill what she . . . he loves. Given necessity enough. And there's something always to remember, lad: A human recognizes orders of necessity that animals cannot even imagine."

"I don't see this necessity," he said.

"You will," she said. "You're human, and you will." She looked across at Jessica and their eyes locked. "And when you've brought your hate to a level you can manage, when you've absorbed it and understood it, here's another thing for you to consider: Think of what it was *truly* that your mother has just done for you. Think of her waiting outside that door there, knowing full well what went on in here. Think of her with every instinct screaming at her to leap in here and protect you, yet she stood and waited. Think on that, young human. Think on it. There's a human, indeed, your mother."

SOUNDS FROM THE assembly yard below the south windows interrupted. The old woman fell silent while Paul ran to the window and looked down.

An assemblage of troop carriers was drawing up in review ranks below and Paul saw his father in full uniform striding out for inspection. Around the perimeter of the field, Paul made out the distorted air that spoke of shields activated there. The troops in the carrier wore the insignia of Hawat's special corps, the infiltrators.

"What is it?" the old woman asked.

Paul returned to her. "My father the Duke is sending some of his men to Arrakis. They're here to stand review."

"Men to Arrakis," the old woman muttered. "When will we learn?"

She took a deep breath. "But I was talking about the Great Revolt when men threw out the machines that enslaved them. You know about the Great Revolt, eh?"

"'Thou shalt not make a machine in the likeness of a man's mind,'" Paul answered.

"Right out of the Orange Catholic Bible," she said. "Want to know the trouble with that? It leaves too much unspoken. It's a sop to the counterfeit men among us, the ones who look human but aren't. They look and talk like humans, but given the wrong pressures they expose themselves as animals. And the unfortunate thing is they think of themselves as human. Oh, yes! They think. But thinking isn't enough to qualify you as human."

"You have to think within your thinking," Paul said. "There's no end to it."

She laughed aloud, a quick burst of sound full of warmth, and Paul heard his mother's laughter joining it. "Bless you," the old woman said. "You've a wonderful turn for language, lad, you fill it with meaning."

⋙

"TELL ME TRULY now, Paul, and remember I'm a Truthsayer and can see truth. Tell me: Do you often dream a thing and have the dream happen exactly as you dreamed it?"

"Yes."

"Often?"

"Yes."

"Tell me about another time."

He looked up to the corner of the room. "I dreamed once that I stood in the rain outside and the castle door was locked and the dogs were barking in their cages and Gurney was beside me and Duncan Idaho and Duncan stumbled against me and bruised my arm. It didn't hurt much, but Duncan was so very sorry. And that's how it happened when I was ten."

"When did you dream this?"

"Oh, a long time ago. Before I had a room by myself. It was when I was little and slept in a room with a nurse beside me."

"Tell me another time." There was excitement in the old woman's voice.

SHE CLEARED HER throat. "Those of our numbers who have not attained the status of Reverend Mother know only so much of the search as we tell them. Now, I will tell you a bit more. A Reverend Mother can *sense* what is within her own bodily cells—every cell. We can peer into the cellular core of selfdom, but there we find . . ." She took a trembling breath. "This thing of which I spoke earlier. This emptiness which we cannot face. Fearful it is. The direction that is dark . . . the place where we cannot enter. Long ago, one of us fathomed that a male force is needed to peer into this place. Since then, each of us at attaining the Reverence has seen that this is true."

"What's so important about it?" Paul asked, and his voice was sullen.

"Let us imagine," she said, "that you have a troop carrier with only half its motor. If you find the other half, you'll have the complete unit needed to move your carrier."

"You still have to put them together and make them work," Paul sneered. "May I go now?"

"Don't you want to hear what I can tell you about the Kwisatz Haderach?" Jessica smiled at the Reverend Mother.

Paul said: "The men who've tried to . . . enter this place, are they the ones you say died?"

"There's a final hurdle they seem unable to leap," the old woman said.

His voice was not a child's voice, but old and grim despite its treble pitch: "What hurdle?"

"We can only give you a hint."

"Hint then."

"And be damned to me?" She smiled wryly. "Very well: *That which submits rules.*"

"That's a hint?"

She nodded. "But submitting, you rule."

"Ruling and submitting are opposites," he said.

"Is the place between them empty?" she asked.

"Ohhhh." He stared at her. "That's what my mother calls the tension-with-meaning. I'll think about that."

"You do that."

"Why don't you like me?" Paul asked. "Is it because I'm not a girl?"

The Reverend Mother snapped a questioning look at Jessica.

"I've not told him," Jessica said.

"That's it, then," Paul said. "Can a woman help it if her child's a boy?"

"Women have always controlled what sex their offspring will be," the old woman said. "By acceptance or rejection of sperm. Even when they didn't know the mechanism of it, they controlled it. There's a kind of racial necessity in this, and men must submit to it."

He nodded. "By submitting, we rule."

"That's part of it."

Jessica spoke from behind him: "Yet, humans must never submit to animals."

He glanced at his mother, back to the old woman.

～⅏～

"CONCENTRATE ON YOUR training, lad, all of it," said the old woman. "That's your one chance to become a ruler."

"What about my father?" Paul demanded. "Are we just . . ."

"Your mother warned him," the old woman said. "Specifically against instructions, I might add, but that isn't the first Bene Gesserit rule she ever broke."

Jessica looked away.

The Reverend Mother plunged on without a glance at her. "You naturally love and respect your father. If there's action you can take to guard him, you'll want to take that action. But have you ever thought about your duty to the ones who came *before* your father?"

"Before . . ." The boy shook his head.

"You're the latest in the Atreides line," she said. "You carry the family seed. And when you come right down to it, that's a tenuous thing. There are no other viable members of your line. A once-numerous clan comes to this: If both you and your father die, the name Atreides ends there. Your cousin, the Padishah Emperor, who is Corrino bar Shaddam, will gather the last of the Atreides holdings back into the Regate, a possibility which has not escaped him. Fini Atreides."

"You must guard yourself for your father's sake," Jessica said. "For the sake of all the other Atreides who've come to this . . . to you."

"YOUR MOTHER WILL tell you of these things. They're not in any history books, not the way she'll explain them. But what she tells you, depend on it, lad. Your mother is a container of wisdom."

Paul stared at the hand that had known pain, then at the Reverend Mother. The sound of her voice held a difference from any other voice he had ever heard. The words were as though outlined in brilliance. There was an edge to them that cut through him. He felt that any question he asked her, she would have the answer. And the answer could lift him out of his flesh-world. But awe held him silent.

"Come, come, ask the question," she said.

He blurted it out: "Where did you come from?"

She absorbed the words and smiled. "I've heard it phrased differently," she said. "One youngster asked me: 'How old are you?' I thought that contained a measure of feminine adroitness."

She stared at him. He stared back.

"I came from one of the Bene Gesserit schools. There are many such schools to the power of many. Do you know yet about mathematical powers?"

He nodded.

"Good. Routine knowledge is always useful for communication. We teach another order of knowledge. We teach what you might call 'thingness.' Does that make any sense to you?"

He shook his head no.

"If you graduate, it'll mean something to you," she said.

Paul said, "But this isn't answering my question."

"Where did I come from? I am a Bene Gesserit. Thence, where did Bene Gesserit come from? Well, lad, I have only time to give you the outline. We'll leave it to your mother to fill in the details. Eh?"

He nodded agreement.

"A long time ago," she said, "men had machines that did more things for them than machines do today. Different things. They even had machines that could, after a fashion, think. They had automatic machines to make useful objects. All of this was supposed to have set man free, but, of course, permitted machines to enslave him. One man with the right kind of automatic machine could make many destructive objects. Do you see that?"

He found his voice and ventured sound: "Yes."

She noted the change in him, the increased alertness. "Good, lad. What we didn't have was a machine to make all men good or even to make all men into men. There are many counterfeit men among us, lad. They look human. They can talk like a human. But given the wrong pressure, they expose themselves as animals. The unfortunate thing is, they think of themselves as human. Oh, yes, they think. But thinking isn't enough to make you human."

"You have to think about your thinking," he said. "You have to . . ." he hesitated, ". . . understand how you think."

She had followed his words, mouthing them silently with him. Now, she wiped her eyes, said: "Ah, that Jessica."

"What happened to all the machines?" Paul asked.

"It takes a male to ask that kind of question," she said. "Well, they destroyed them, lad. There was war. Revolution. Anarchy. And when it was over, men were forbidden to make such machines again."

"You aren't telling me where you came from," he said.

She laughed out loud, a quick burst of sound full of warmth. "Bless you, my darling, but I am. You see, there was still the need for some of the things those so-called thinking machines had done. So somebody remembered that certain humans could think in those ways."

"What ways?"

"They could take in all kinds of information and never be at a loss to repeat it. They had what is called eidetic memory. But more than that. They could answer complicated questions. Mathematical questions. Military questions. Social questions. Probability questions. They could swallow all sorts of information and spew out answers when the answers were needed."

"They were human," he said.

"Well, yes they were, most of them."

"What do you mean most of them?"

"It isn't important, lad. Your mother can explain about idiot savants and such if you ask her. But I'm explaining where I came from. This was the way of it. Schools were started to train this special kind of human. One such school was called the Bene Gesserit School. In it was a human who saw the need to separate the humans from the animals. As a stock. A breeding stock. But there was a reservoir of chance human births among the animals because of . . . mixing." She thought she saw his attention waning, and snapped: "Do you understand all this?"

"I know how we pick the best bulls," he said. "It's through the cows. If the cows are brave the bulls will be brave."

"Yes, of course," she said. "It's a general rule. Men are the doers, and human males seek out the Bene Gesserit. Well, lad, the Bene Gesserit School was successful. We produced mostly women . . . breeders. Brave ones. Beautiful ones. But in the new Empire there were only certain ways we could act. Some of the things we did had to remain secret. You know what I'm telling you are secret things, don't you?"

He nodded absently. The secrecy of her manner had been obvious. There were other things troubling him. He voiced one of them: "But I'm a boy."

*Maybe he is the one,* the old woman thought. *So mature for his years. So very perceptive.*

She said: "Men have their uses. And we've always been searching for a special kind of man."

"What kind?"

"Our time is too short," she said. "Your mother will have to explain it. I can say this to you briefly: The man we need will know himself that he is the man. When he learns this of himself, that will be the moment of his graduation."

"You're just putting me off," he said. He felt resentful. The adult world had no more hateful aspect than this form of frustration.

"Yes, I am," she admitted. "But you'll have to take me on faith right now. It's not only impossible for me to answer your question right now, it could be hurtful for you. It's as though the knowledge had to grow within you until the day you feel it flowering. It can't be forced. We think we know the climate it needs, but . . ." She shook her head.

The apparent uncertainty in the old woman's manner shook Paul. One moment she had been the Goddess-source of all knowledge. Now . . . he could see her exposing an area of unknown. And that area concerned himself. He didn't formulate this feeling as words. He only felt it. It was like being lost.

"Time to call in your mother," she said. "You've a busy day ahead of you."

# PAUL & THUFIR HAWAT

Paul continued to stare at the old man. "Thufir, I just thought of something."

"Heh?"

"I really know so little about you."

"What's that?" Hawat stared sharply at Paul, wondering: *Am I being insulted by this cub? Does he doubt my loyalty?*

"I mean I don't know *real* things about you," Paul said. "Like, oh, have you ever been married, or . . ."

"I've had women," the old man growled.

"And children?"

"Like as not."

"But no family."

"My Duke's family is my family."

"It's not the same," Paul said. "You've been so busy with our . . ."

"What I want or need my Duke gives me," Hawat said. "If talk like yours came from a commoner it'd be a headsman offense. You're born to rule, lad, and to accept the services of those whose loyalty you've earned. Being born to it isn't enough, though. You've a deal to learn, too. That's why we're here now and we'd best get down to business." He tapped the papers on the table. "Yueh and your mother and everyone with a scrap of knowledge about Arrakis has been pumping it into you. Now, what do you know about the place?"

# PAUL & GURNEY HALLECK

⌘

Gurney was, in fact, the closest thing to a playmate that Paul knew.

Gurney dropped the weapons onto the exercise table, lined them up, gave them a last examination to be certain they were ready: stunners on safety, buttons secure on the rapier tips, bodkins and kindjals in their blunting sheaths, fresh power charges in the shield belts.

Behind him, Gurney heard the boy moving restlessly, and it occurred to Gurney that Paul was slow to warmth with most people, that few saw anything but a strange irregularity of friendliness beneath the manners. *Like the old Duke,* Gurney thought. *Always conscious of class. And it's a pity because there's so much fun in the boy, too much to be pushed under all the time.* He turned, swinging a baliset off his shoulder, began checking its tune. *There I go again*, he thought. *Filling my mind with fly-buzz when I should be getting down to work.*

❦

"YOU HATE THE Harkonnens almost as much as my father does," Paul said.

"Almost as much," Gurney agreed, and Paul heard the irony. "The Count Rabban at Lankiveil is a Harkonnen cousin. You've heard the tale of Ernso, the goldsmith, captured on Pedmiot and sold to slavery of the Count Rabban . . . with his family held in the same bondage?"

"I've heard you sing the ballad many a time," Paul said.

Gurney spoke to the wall beyond the boy. "Then you'll recall that Ernso was ordered to embellish the handle and blade of the Count's best sword. And Ernso obeyed, but he hid in the design a curse calling on heaven to destroy an evil House."

"Yes." Paul nodded, puzzled. The bloody ballad was not one of his favorites.

"And the design remained hidden there," Gurney said, "until a Court lackey chanced to see it and recognized the script from his childhood. Oh, it was a great joke at Court until word got back to Beast Rabban."

"And for that Ernso was hung by his toes over a chirak nest until dead and his family scattered to the slave pits," Paul said. "I remember the story, but . . ."

"I'd tell you a thing now that's known to very few in this House," Gurney said. "I'm properly called Gurney Halleck Ernson, the son of Ernso."

Paul stared at the rippling of the scar on Gurney's jaw.

"It was Hawat's men brought me off Giedi Prime that time they nearly got the Baron," Gurney said. "I was just a child, but I showed aptitude for the sword, there being motive behind my learning. Duncan

316

Idaho found a way for me to train at his school on Ginaz. I had some large bids for my services when I graduated, lad, but you understand now why I came back to the Atreides and why I'll never leave short of being carried out in the basket."

# PAUL & DR. YUEH

~⊷∾~

That sounds like Hawat," Yueh said, and he smoothed his droop-
ing mustache. "Hawat's gone, I hear. Taken most of the propaganda corps, all the presses. Interesting. I wonder what filmbooks he
has in mind for first publication there. The Harkonnens, you know,
didn't use much printed matter on Arrakis. They relied on the persua-
sion of the sword."

"My father does things differently," Paul said.

"Indeed," Yueh said. And he straightened the Suk School's silver
ring that bound his hair at the shoulder.

"My mother says you have some Bene Gesserit training," Paul said.
"Does the Suk School have Bene Gesserit teachers?"

"No." Yueh dropped his hand to his lap. "My . . . Wanna . . . she was

Bene Gesserit. A wife teaches a husband much even when he is not deep-trained . . . and when she's Bene Gesserit . . ." He shook his head.

"Is she . . . dead?" Paul asked.

Yueh swallowed in a dry throat. *He has pity for me. I do not want his pity!*

"Yes," he said. And he thought: *I pray it is true. Let her be dead, and in that death, free of Harkonnens. Yet, I cannot be sure until I face the Baron in our own tahaddi alburhan. The challenge of the proof. My eyes shall see it.*

"I'm sorry," Paul said. And he thought: *Perhaps that's why he makes me uneasy. He's a man with a terrible grief. I must be kinder to him. Mayhap my father could get him a woman.*

"I must leave in a few minutes," Yueh said. "But we really haven't studied much, have we? It's all this upset. We'll get back to regular lessons and a full schedule . . . on Arrakis."

"Things are pretty mixed up," Paul said. "And there's all this huddling within our four walls because our forces are depleted by the ones we've sent on ahead. My father says we're not very vulnerable here, though, because many of the Great Houses pray for the Harkonnens to violate the Convention. That'd make the Harkonnens fair game to anyone who wanted to hit them in force."

"It *is* best to stay indoors, though," Yueh said. "I hear they blasted a hunter-seeker out of the orchard last night."

# PAUL & DUKE LETO ATREIDES:
## THE SPACING GUILD
## & THE GREAT CONVENTION

B ut first let us consider Salusa Secundus. Forgive me if I seem to deal in the obvious. I wish to be certain you see the matter as I see it."

And Paul took a deep breath, thinking: *At last he's going to tell me how we can win.*

"The popular idea," the Duke said, "is that our civilization is a scientific one, based on a Constitutional Monarchy in which even the lowliest may gain high position. After all, new planets are being discovered all the time, eh?"

"Hawat says new Terranic planets are as rare as hen's teeth and that dispensation of them is a Royal monopoly," Paul said. "Except for the ones we don't know about that the Spacing Guild keeps for itself."

"I'm glad to hear you quoting Hawat so much," the Duke said. "It bespeaks a native caution in you. But I doubt that the Guild holds any planets. I don't think they like living on the dirt . . . out in the open. I've ridden Guild ships to Court and elsewhere several times. You don't see much of the crews except on viewscreens, but what you do see gives you the clear impression that they despise planet-bound humans."

"Then why do they deal with us at all? Why not just . . ."

"Because they understand ecology," the Duke said. "They know they have a nice safe niche in the scheme of things. It's cheaper to depend on us for raw materials and those products they don't care to manufacture . . . or cannot—such as melange. Their philosophy is *Don't Rock the Boat*. They'll transport us and our products for a profit. Anywhere, anytime—just as long as it doesn't endanger them. The same service offered to all at the same price."

"I know that, but it's still puzzling," Paul said. "I remember that Guildsman who came here when we contracted for the extra rice shipments. He gave me a picture of a landing frigate and . . ."

"He wasn't a Guildsman," the Duke said. "He was just an agent for the Guild, born and raised on a planet as we were. A true Guildsman has never been seen on dirt to my knowledge."

"It seems strange that the Guild doesn't just move in and take over the worlds," Paul said. "If they control all the . . ."

"They chose their path," the Duke said. "Give them that. They know what any Mentat knows—there's a great deal of responsibility in ruling, even when you do it poorly. The Guild has shown many times it doesn't want that responsibility. They like what they are, where they are."

"Hasn't anyone ever tried to compete with them?" Paul asked.

"Many times," the Duke said. "Competing ships never come back, never arrive anywhere."

"The Guild destroys them!"

"Probably. Then again, perhaps not. And the Guild does provide general transportation services at a reasonable price. It's only when you get into the special services that the cost goes up."

"They just destroy anyone who tries to compete with them," Paul said.

The Duke frowned. "What would you do if a rival House set up next door to you and started competing for your world—openly, no holds barred?"

"But the Convention . . ."

"Hang the Convention! What would you do?"

"I'd throw every thing I had against them."

"You'd destroy them." The Duke tapped a finger on the table for emphasis. "Now, let us not forget something, a fact you've been told often enough: Ours is a feudal society, each world vulnerable from space. That's the real reason for the Great Convention. A planet is vulnerable from space, and the Guild will transport anything anywhere anytime for a price. If they carry a cargo of short-range frigates, as they'll carry ours to Arrakis, and those frigates bomb out a world, the information on who did it is also available . . . for a price. This is the Great Convention, the Landsraad, our only true agreement—to unite and destroy anyone who attempts such a thing."

"Well, what about renegades?" Paul asked. "If . . ."

"Hasn't anyone explained these things to you before?" the Duke demanded. He sighed. "When a renegade buys Guild silence, there are two requirements. He may not be fleeing after major violation of the Convention, and he may never again contact a central world—in any way. Otherwise, all bets are off. That's part of the agreement between Guild and Landsraad. Things aren't all one-sided. We share certain rules with the Guild."

"I've heard all this before," Paul said, "and read about it and asked about it. But it still seems . . . wrong. There's . . ."

"A man's promise is no better than his motives for keeping it," the Duke said. "The agreements don't bother you; it's the motives."

"That's it!" Paul said.

"What holds the Universe together?" the Duke said. "Why aren't we all renegades? One word, son: trade. Each world, each group of worlds, has something unique. Even Caladan's pundi rice is unique to Caladan. And there are people who want it, who cannot get it anywhere else. It's a superb food for babies and old people, you know . . . soothing, easily digested."

"Trade?" Paul asked. "That doesn't seem enough."

"It isn't for the wild adventurers and the rebels," the Duke said. "But for most people it is. We don't rock our boat, either. And *that's* why we're accepting Arrakis. *There's* a planet that's not only unique, but pricelessly so, and in a way that the Harkonnens and the Imperium do not suspect."

*There it is again*, Paul thought, *that hint at something in our favor.*

"What is it they don't suspect?" Paul asked. "You and Hawat keep hinting at . . ."

"Paul . . ." The Duke hesitated, staring hard at his son. "This is a most vital thing. I . . . but, no, it's time you assumed more responsibilities."

# BARON HARKONNEN & PITER DE VRIES

Y ou say I've not seen death," Piter said. "You are so wrong. Once, I saw a woman die. She fell from the third balcony of our home into the courtyard where I was playing. I was only five, but I can still recall that I thought she looked like an odd green sack as she fell. She was wearing green, you see."

The Baron, noting the odd change in Piter's manner, said: "Many women do, Piter. Women die every day."

"This one was my mother," Piter said. "Oh, it meant little to me at the time. She was merely one of the many concubines around the palace. It was only on reflection years later that I drew significance from the event."

"Ahhhh," said the Baron, "and what was that significance?"

"The person falling is already dead," Piter said. "The falling and the death are thoroughly anticlimactic. The event of true importance is the instant of toppling—then you can push or rescue the person about to fall. You control destiny."

The Baron scowled, wondering: *Does this fool threaten me? Is he saying he could oppose me in the matter of the Duke?*

"Then what of Duke Leto?" the Baron asked. "Could there be a change in his destiny?"

"Baron, that you should ask!" Piter said. "The Duke . . . ah, the Duke—he is already falling. An event of total unimportance, the Duke."

## New Chapter:
## FROM CALADAN TO ARRAKIS

*(Paragraph-by-paragraph word counts in margin suggest this chapter was cut due to length, per Campbell's request for serialization in* Analog, *and never restored.)*

◆───

*How such a mass of misinformation as Wingate's book, "Mentat, Guild and Shield," could command so wide an acceptance is difficult to understand. The shield is pictured as a simple device (once you've learned its secret), easily maintained and enabling the righteous to defend themselves from all attack. The Guild comes through as a disembodied group of angels waiting in space for the day they can introduce universal Utopia. And the Mentat! Wingate's Mentat is a golem, without any redeeming warmth. According to Wingate, when you put information into the Mentat, a sort of machine-encased-in-flesh spews out answers untainted by human emotions.*

—FROM THE HUMANITY OF MUAD'DIB BY THE PRINCESS IRULAN

The Atreides frigate lay clamped in a long rack in the womb of the Guild ship. Racked around it lay other frigates, some bearing House crests that required memory trance for Paul to recall—so distant and small they were. And then wedged and packed around and between the frigates stretched a jumble of cargo lighters, pickup satellites, jumpdump boxes, yachts and freight gliders . . . and many shapes for which Paul had no association.

He had watched through the lounge viewscreens as *his* frigate was warped into the monstrous globe of the Guild ship. The first glimpses of that gigantic hold's contents had stunned Paul with the realization that movement of Atreides people and freight could be only a small part of this ship's task.

Caladan was only a minor waystop!

Now, the Guild ship had linked its communications system to the frigate's, and the screen above Paul's floater chair remained dark except for an occasional witch flickering as a voice came from the attendant speakers with instructions.

"Atreides party, do not attempt to leave your ships . . . Communication with members of your party in other vessels is available through our shipsystem and under rules of Guild secrecy . . . In the event of a contract-covered emergency aboard your vessel, activate the *red op* circuit with which you have been provided . . . You will experience strange sensations on and within your flesh as we resume way. Those of you who have never before spaced in a Guild ship please do not be alarmed. These sensations are a natural and harmless part of the first shipdrive moments . . . The Atreides party will be happy to know that they have been picked up by a Guild highline ship. You will be at your destination within a subjective day and a half . . ."

And Paul thought woefully of his father's hope to get a complete rest in deepsleep during the crossing.

The voice from the screenspeakers interested Paul. He detected the controlled modulation of *soothers* and *convincers* in its tones. They were broadband but beautifully executed. There was no sign of the face or flesh of a Guildsman behind that voice, though. Except for the witch flicker, probably sympathetic sonals, the screen remained dark. And Paul thought of the old stories about *space adaptation*, that the men of the Guild had developed long and supple limbs with prehensile toes, that they were totally depilitated, that they had grown extra limbs, that they . . .

Paul laughed at himself. *Perhaps I'll get some accurate data someday,* he thought.

One of Gurney's men, Tomo, entered the lounge through the door beneath the screen. He was a stocky man with barrel chest, heavy arms, a round face held carefully emotionless. He nodded to Paul. "Mr. Halleck's respects, M'Lord. He asked me to tell you that you may repair to the control cone as soon as all danger's past and we're well under way. Duke's orders, M'Lord."

"Thank you, Tomo," Paul said. "Would you convey my regrets to Mr. Halleck? My mother has asked that I remain here until she returns."

The man bowed. "At once, M'Lord." He backed out the way he had come, sealed the door.

Paul glanced up at the telltale glitterings in the room's corners where spyeyes scanned the area for those in the control cone, and he smiled. Gurney had sent the man as a gesture of human reassurance. Paul eased his position in the chair, turning stiffly against the artificial gravity.

*Only a day and a half to Arrakis*, he thought.

He lay back and the chair accommodated itself to the change. There was a lesson to review, a deep lesson from his mother with all its peculiar Mentat overtones. The decision to continue with his training had not been difficult. It had been almost as though some force within himself had made the decision for him. Paul sank into the lesson-review-awareness, sensing the way the lesson linked itself to related data within his mind.

Three quick breaths triggered it. He fell into the floating state . . . focusing the consciousness . . . aortal dilation . . . avoiding the unfocused mechanism of consciousness . . . to be conscious by choice . . . blood enriched and swift flooding the overload regions . . . one does not obtain food, safety or freedom by instinct, yet some humanoid creatures long to be animals . . . *Harkonnen is a beast of prey* . . . animal consciousness does not extend beyond the given moment nor into the idea that its victims may become extinct . . . the animal destroys and does not produce . . . the animal pleasures remain close to the sensation level and avoid the perceptual . . . true human requires a frame of reference, a background grid through which to see his universe . . . bodily integrity comes through nerve/blood flow according to the deep awareness of cell needs . . . man's necessity is for a universe of experience that makes logical sense, yet logic seduces awareness . . . all things/cells/beings are impermanent . . . one strives for the flow-permanence within . . .

Over and over within Paul's awareness the lesson rolled, and at its hub lay the single conceptualization:

*The human being can assess his circumstances and judge his limitations within those circumstances, all through a mental programming, never risking his flesh until an optimum course has been computed. The human being may do this within the compression of elapsed time so short that it may be called instantaneous.*

# BLUE-WITHIN-BLUE EYES

W e've started a research project on this condition of blue eyes,"
Hawat said. "It's a condition not totally unfamiliar off Ar-
rakis, of course. You'll recall the scannos on that creature of the
Harkonnens, Piter Vries."

"The Mentat," Leto said.

"Would that he bore some other title," Hawat said. He shrugged.
"The contention with some is that this condition of blue eyes is a de-
rivative of radiation from the Arrakeen sun. The chief argument is
comparison with the fact that the sun of Tressi is reputed to give a yellow cast to eyes of fifth-generation humans born there."

"Piter Vries is Arrakeen?" Leto asked.

"Not according to the best information available, sire." Hawat
turned away, paced across the room and back, his old shoulders bent,

the leathery skin of his face seamed with the intensity of his concentration. "One of the entrepreneurs we smoked out had an amateur biological laboratory, several cages containing kangaroo rats in a sealed ecological system. Records attached said the rats had been born in this sealed system on non-Arrakeen stock, never removed from the system, and fed only spice. They were maintained in an area sealed away from all local radiation, yet they all had the blue eyes. They were fed exclusively on the spice, mind you."

"Others have said it might be the spice causing this condition," Leto said.

"But others haven't kept records of a succession of such experiments wherein the spice was eventually withdrawn from the creatures and they died rather than revert to normal diet." He stopped his pacing, stared up at the Duke. "Died with every evidence of narcotic withdrawal symptoms."

The Duke wet his lips with his tongue. "It doesn't seem possible. I've never heard of such a thing. Many people use mélange regularly. It's part of *our* diet, Thufir. Surely, we'd have heard reports of withdrawal symptoms before now. I, myself, have gone without spice for . . ." He shook his head. "Well, I've . . . Dammit, Thufir! I know I can use the stuff or leave it alone."

"Can you, sire?" Hawat asked softly.

"But I . . ."

"Has anyone who can afford regular use of mélange ever put withdrawal to the test?" Hawat asked. "I'm not talking about the casual, middle-class users. I'm talking about the uppers who can easily afford it and know its proven geriatric qualities, the ones who take it daily in large quantities as a delightful medicine."

"That would be monstrous," Leto said.

"It wouldn't be the first time a slow poison has been marketed under the guise of a public benefit," Hawat said. "I invite you, sire, to remember the history of the use of saturial, of semuta, of verite, of tobacco, of . . ."

331

# JESSICA & DR. YUEH:
## THE SPICE

It's more than that," she said. "Tuek had advance agents in here. Those guards outside now are his men. I can smell violence about this place."

"Are you sure about the advance agents?"

"Do not forget, Wellington, that I frequently act as the Duke's secretary. I know many things about his business." She compressed her lips, spoke thinly. "I sometimes wonder how much the Bene Gesserit training figured in his choice of me."

"What do you mean?"

"A secretary tied to one by love is so much safer, don't you think?"

"Is that a worthy thought, Jessica?"

She shook her head. "Perhaps not." She continued to stare at the sere landscape. "But still I know there's danger here, and not from the populace. After all, they'll soon rejoice that they're freed from the Harkonnen yoke . . . most of them. But the Harkonnens will have left some who . . ."

"Oh, come, come, now!"

She glanced at him, looked away. "I know that all the Duke's hatred of the Harkonnens isn't empty. The old feud is very much alive. The Harkonnens won't be content with holding the power at Court. This new duchy wasn't just a plum they threw us to buy an end to the feud." She nodded. "I've had time to think about it. They won't rest until the Duke and his line are destroyed."

"This is a very rich plum, Jessica."

"And there's poison in it. The plum offered in such a way that we had to take it. The Baron cannot forget that Leto is a cousin of the Emperor while the Harkonnen titles came out of a pocketbook. He will not forget that my Duke's great-great-grandfather had a Harkonnen banished for cowardice at Corrin."

"You're becoming morbid, Jessica. You've had *too much* time to think during this journey. You should be busy with things that hold your interest."

"You're very kind to try to spare me, old friend," she said. "But I cannot keep my mind from wondering at the things I see." She smiled wanly. "Tell me about the spice trade. Is it really as rich as they say?"

"Mélange is the costliest spice ever known. It's bringing six hundred and twenty thousand credits the decagram on the open market right now."

She turned away, crossed to one of the empty bookcases, rubbed its glistening surface. "Does it really make people live longer?"

He nodded. "It has some geriatric qualities, yes, because it aids digestion. It sets up a protein digestive balance that helps you get more energy out of what you eat."

"It tasted like cinnamon to me the first time I ate it," she said.

"Sometimes it's cut with cassia or cinnamon," he said, "but it does have some cinnamic aldehyde of its own, and eugenol. That's why many say it smells like cinnamon."

"But it never tastes the same twice," she protested. "I've never had a satisfactory explanation for that."

"You know there are only four fundamental tastes?" he asked.

"Certainly. Acid, bitter, salt and sweet."

He inclined his head toward her. "It is the characteristic of mélange that it can blend odd pairs of taste and make them acceptable to the tongue. Some hold that it's a *learned* flavor."

"The body, learning that a thing is good for it, then interprets the flavor always as pleasurable," she said. "That is what you mean?"

"Yes. And for that reason it's also slightly euphoric."

"How does it grow? Is it a plant?"

"Well, the Harkonnens kept the biology of mélange under wraps, but a few facts have leaked out. Apparently, it is fungasoid, and it must grow violently under the proper conditions."

"Which are?"

"We do not know. Attempts to grow it artificially have failed for unknown reasons. And because of the sandworms [he saw her shudder] it has been impossible to study the spice thoroughly in situ."

"So it's a fungus."

"Not exactly. It has some of the properties of fungus, we believe. But it's much more complicated than that. The phenol chain with its odd bifurcation, for example. How can that come from a fungus? And there's a cymene counterpart. Mélange is a fascinating chemical-botanical problem. We can say little more."

"See how I have to pry for technical information?" she said. "Aside from my secretarial duties, the Duke does not expect me to be intelligent."

"Is he aware that you are?"

# PAUL & JESSICA

*(In hiding after the hunter-seeker attack)*

❧

What does it mean that you are Bene Gesserit, Mother?"

*He has inherited my perceptivity,* she thought, and said: "That is the name of the school where I was trained."

"I know that, Mother. But it means something different, too. When my father, the Duke, is bothered by something you have done he says 'Bene Gesserit' like a swear word."

She couldn't suppress the smile that twisted her lips. "And what is it about me that bothers your father, the Duke?"

"When you thwart him. I have heard him call you 'a Bene Gesserit witch.'"

Silent laughter shook her.

Paul's face remained sturdily somber. "Will you teach me the secret things you know, Mother?"

Jessica breathed a silent prayer to Sister Nartha and the oath of succession. *I was careless and have a son instead of a daughter,* she thought. *No! I was not careless. I knew how much my Duke wanted a son. But still it is a son . . . of a Bene Gesserit witch.*

"I will teach you some of the things I know," she said.

He stared at her, dissatisfied with the answer, then: "Now I know how my father, the Duke, feels about you sometimes," he said.

She kept her wry feeling of humor from showing on her face, but still he sensed it.

"We are not amused," he said.

And suddenly she saw a veil parted into the future. *If he lives he will be a great ruler,* she thought. *He has the perceptivity, the quickness, the deep intelligence, but above all else, he has the dignity.*

She spoke formally: "I am sorry if I have offended my son," she said. "I beg the prerogative of my privacy."

"You had that without begging it," he said. A tiny smile twitched the corners of his mouth. "I beg the prerogative of your indulgence."

She rumpled his hair, her eyes smarting with unshed tears. "Did you come here to protect me, darling?"

"Of course. My father, the Duke, has told me to protect you when he is away. I would do it anyway, but all must obey the Duke."

"You are very right," she said. Then: "How will we know when it is safe to leave here?"

"I told Dr. Yueh that I would find you and close a door upon us until he signaled with our knock." Paul turned, rapped on the wall—three raps, a pause, two, then three more.

"That was sensible of you." She turned away, clasping her hands tightly until she felt pain in her knuckles. Death traps . . . deadly peril for her Duke and her son and she herself sought as payment to a traitor. Which traitor? Who was the trusted lieutenant?

"If we are safe in this room, you should relax, Mother," said Paul.

She nodded, turned a smile of false brightness on him. "What have you and Dr. Yueh been up to?"

"We've been looking at a filmbook about our planet. Did you know that down in the desert they have giant sandworms?"

"Yes, I read about them."

"They've killed a lot of dunemen—that's what they call the spice hunters. And they've swallowed whole spice factories."

"I imagine they're pretty horrible."

"And they have winds here that blow six and seven hundred kilometers an hour!"

"As hard as that?"

"And it blows sand that cuts right through metal and everything. And sometimes it gets so hot it melts plastics, because of the friction."

She gnawed at her lower lip, thinking: *What a hideous place!*

Paul said: "The filmbook said this is the driest known terra . . . terraform planet."

"That's why we have to be so careful with water," she said.

"Oh, Dr. Yueh says this house has lots of water. There's a big tank under it."

"But still we must be careful with water. It's so precious here. People even pay their taxes in water."

Paul piped up, "Dr. Yueh says there is a saying on Arrakis. 'Polish comes from the cities, wisdom from the desert.'"

And she thought: *Leto, where are you? You're in danger. But you know that, of course.* And she felt a moment of panic about the room around her. What if Lady Fenring's reassurance about this room were wrong? But, no. Bene Gesserits didn't make that kind of mistake.

"I wish I could go after the spice with my father, the Duke," said Paul.

"He will send his men after the spice," she said. "He won't go himself."

"Not even once?"

"Perhaps. But the spice desert's much too dangerous a place for a boy."

"I'm almost twelve."

"I know, darling, but men need years of special training before they go out on the sand."

"I could learn."

"Maybe when you grow up."

"I'll study. Will you tell Dr. Yueh to get me all the books there are about our planet? I want books even about the time before they found the spice."

"We'll get all we can find," she said.

"Until Dr. Yueh showed me the filmbook I thought we'd always had the spice," he said.

She smiled in spite of her fears. "Only for about a hundred years." And then she thought: *But that is always when you're almost-twelve.* And she remembered that there was a time in her youth when enthusiasm was less a word than a world and less a world than a universe.

Paul said: "Before they found the spice, Arrakis was just a place where they studied about plants and things that grow where it's really dry."

"His Imperial Majesty's Desert Botanical Testing Station," she said. And she wondered: *Where is Dr. Yueh? Haven't the guards destroyed that seeker yet? And what other dangers must we face when we leave this room?*

Paul pulled at his chin.

*How like Leto he is when he's serious,* she thought. And she suddenly realized that Paul was talking just to distract her, to take her mind from her worries.

"His Majesty had many creatures brought here," said Paul. "And plants. They have a mutated form of wild buckwheat that people eat here."

"*Eriogonum deserticole,*" she said. "That's the botanical name for the wild buckwheat."

He studied her face. "You know all about Arrakis, don't you?" he said.

She looked on him fondly, warming her love of him at his effort to distract her. "I know some things about our new home. They brought the plants and animals here to condition this place for humans. Most of the new ones came from Earth. The dry climate plants are called erophytes. I have a filmbook about useful xerophytes. I'll see that Dr. Yueh has it for you tomorrow."

Still, he studied her face. "Don't worry, mother. The guards will take care of the dangers outside. Pretty soon they will come for us. I'll protect you until then."

She put an arm around his shoulder, turned to the tall reach of filter glass that faced the southwest. Out there, the sun of Arrakis had moved well on toward sunset.

Paul put his hand over hers on his shoulder.

# ESCAPE FROM THE HARKONNENS: WITH DUNCAN AND LIET-KYNES AT THE DESERT BASE

*(Paul and Jessica's first sanctuary, after the fall of Arrakeen)*

Jessica stepped over the doorsill into a windowless laboratory. Paul followed his mother, glanced back at the ornicopter his mother had commandeered to bring them. How peremptory she had been to the Duke's guard! He knew she'd used the Voice, and already he was beginning to think in Bene Gesserit terms.

Jessica studied the long room in which they found themselves. It was a civil place full of angles and squares. The room contained about a dozen people in green smocks. Most of them were working at a long bench along one wall—watching dials, fiddling with instruments. There was the smell of ozone, and semi-muted sounds that suggested furious activity: machine coughs, the horse-whinnies of spinning belts and multidrives. She saw cages with small animals in them stacked against an end wall.

"Dr. Kynes?" she said.

A figure at the bench turned. He was a thin man (*like most of the dehydrated pods we've seen on this planet*, she thought).

"I am Dr. Kynes," he said. He spoke with a clipped-off precision, and looked that kind of man. Jessica immediately catalogued him as one whose words could be expected to come out razor apt, rasping off any fuzzy edges of meaning.

*Good*, she thought. *That kind are generally honest.*

"I am Lady Jessica and . . ." She indicated Paul, ". . . this is my son, Paul, the ducal heir."

Momentary tenseness showed in a tightening of Dr. Kynes' jawline. The others turned from the bench, caution in their movements. Machine sounds hummed away to silence. Into this void there came a thin animal squeak from the cages. It was cut off abruptly as though in embarrassment.

"We are honored, Noble Born," said Kynes.

*Noble Born! They all make that mistake*, Jessica thought. *Ah, well, let it pass.*

"You seem very busy here," she said.

"What is this place, Mother?" Paul asked. He stared around him at the people who still watched dials, adjusted instruments. It reminded him somewhat of Dr. Yueh's laboratory, but there was more equipment to this place.

"Visits of royalty are uncommon here," Kynes said. "We were . . . unprepared. Please forgive the . . ."

"I thought this place had been abandoned," she said. "Isn't this one of the old desert biological stations? I saw it on the Duke's chart. I thought this was the place he was supposed to visit tomorrow."

Kynes flicked a glance back to the bench, wet his lips with his tongue, returned his attention to her.

"No one told us you were coming," he said. "The . . ." He shrugged.

Jessica glanced once more around the room, recognizing the activity now for what it was: they'd been cleaning up some sort of last minute tests or work of that sort! They'd been preparing to pull all this out of here in a preparation for Leto's visit!

Paul tugged at her arm. "May I go look at the animals down there in the cages?"

She looked at Kynes.

"Oh, they're quite safe," Kynes said. "Just don't stick your fingers in the cages. Some of the kangaroo rats will bite."

"You will stay beside me, Paul," she said. She recognized the plane-tologist's uneasiness. She stared at him, allowing his nervousness to grow. "I like to see things the way they really are," Jessica said. "That's one reason I sometimes arrive unannounced."

Kynes' face darkened. He glanced out the open door at the orni-copter, the two men standing beside it.

And Jessica realized another thing: Kynes had been expecting some-one to arrive. Otherwise he'd have made more of a stir about the 'copter. His own transport probably, or more of his workers. She al-lowed a cold smile to pass over her face, looked out the door.

"Idaho!" she called. "Come here, please."

She saw Idaho speak to the native pilot, then advance across the sand, through the door. He looked very impressive with his chest shield and currassier weapons. His attitude toward Jessica betrayed ex-treme deference. He was extending himself in good behavior, fighting the shame of his drunkenness.

"Idaho," she said, "there's something unusual going on here. Keep a careful watch on these people. The Duke will want to know about this."

Idaho swept a hard glance around the room. He was the trained killer letting the people here know he could smash them and they couldn't so much as scratch him. "Yes, My Lady," he said.

Kynes swallowed. "My Lady, you don't understand. This is . . ."

"Yes," she said. "What is this?"

Paul looked up at Duncan Idaho, tried to imitate Idaho's hard glance around the room. His own body shield was in full force. He could feel the faint tingling around his forehead where the field was strongest.

"My Duke is very generous to those of his subjects who are truthful and honorable with him," she said. "He is otherwise, I assure you, with people who lie to him or attempt to cheat him."

Kynes chewed his lower lip, tried to explain some of his dignity. "My Lady, in all due respect, but this station is still part of the Emperor's reg . . ."

"And the Emperor has been told, I'm sure, that this station was abandoned," she snapped. "Don't play games with me!"

She sniffed and detected cinnamon! It was so faint behind the ozone odor that only her trained senses caught it. The spice! They were doing something here that concerned the spice! And the ozone was meant to kill the smell. Now, with her senses at full alert, she gestalted the place. She knew she'd be able to sort out the impressions later, get an accurate line on their experiments.

"Really, My Lady," Kynes said. "We're all simple subjects of . . ."

"You have been experimenting with the spice," she accused.

Kynes and his workers froze, staring at her. Their fear was so thick it was like a palpable substance in the room.

Jessica relaxed, smiled. "The Harkonnens forbade it, certainly," she said. "But don't any of you simpletons realize my Duke is not a Harkonnen, that he might have other ideas about such research?"

She saw the first dawning hope in Kynes' eyes, glanced at Idaho. "You can relax, Idaho. We've just run into a symptom of the Harkonnen disease. They haven't had the Atreides antidote yet."

Paul looked at his mother, back to Kynes. How had she known about the spice? It must be her special training, he realized. But how? The knowledge that she could do such a thing as this and that he might learn how to do it firmed his resolution. *I will learn,* he told himself.

Kynes said, "But . . ."

"Don't try to make excuses," she said. "We're familiar with what happens in a Harkonnen fief." She glanced at the workbench, pulling one fact from the gestalt impression, and she thought: *Let them think we're omnipotent.* She said: "You've been tracing the bifurcation of the phenol chain. Good. Tell your people to go on with their work. The Duke will want a full report on your progress."

Kynes sagged. Every line of his face betrayed submission. If she even knew the direction of their research . . .

"Tell your people," Jessica repeated. "My Duke rewards this sort of activity . . . especially if it's successful. And one thing more: You can discard your ideas about abandoning this place. It appears to be an excellent site for such work. It's near the spice sands. It's a place where you won't get casual visitors . . ." She smiled. "We're not casual visitors."

Chuckles came slowly around the room, they told her much. *The way a person laughs shows you where his tensions are,* went a Bene Gesserit axiom. One of the men in the room had only seemed to chuckle. She marked him for later investigation, said: "Is there somewhere we may talk without disturbing your workers or being disturbed ourselves, Doctor?"

Kynes hesitated, inclined his head. "My office, Noble Born." He gestured toward a door at the end opposite the animal cages.

"Paul, you stay with Idaho," Jessica said. "I won't be long. You may look at those animals if you wish, but mind the Doctor's warning. Some of those creatures bite."

No need telling them to wear shields at all times, she thought. She gave Idaho the casual hand signal that told him to disregard her order to relax, for him to remain on alert. Idaho blinked acknowledgement. And she noted as she accompanied Kynes toward the door to his office that one of the workers crossed the room, closed the outside door. The worker was the one with the non-chuckle.

Kynes' office was square, about eight meters to a side. Curry-colored walls were broken by a single line of reel-files and a portable scanner screen. There were no windows. Almost in the center of the room sat a squat desk with a milk-glass top shot full of yellow bubbles. Four suspensor-field chairs ringed the desk. There were papers on the desk held down by a small block of sand-etched marble.

*Where did they expect to hide all this stuff?* she wondered. It was a wedge-shaped building driven into a cliff. Then she realized that this room must have another exit, possibly an entire wall that swung aside. She'd noted when they were coming down in the 'copter that the structure squatted against a cliff. *A cave in the cliff!* she thought. *How efficient.*

Kynes indicated a chair. She sat down.

"There are no windows," she said.

"Up here this close to the shield wall we get some of the high winds," he said. "They run 700 kilometers an hour and even higher. Some of them spill over into this little pocket. We call it the rain of sand. It doesn't take long under that kind of sandblasting for a window to become opaque. We depend on scanner eyes which can be shielded."

"I see." She adjusted her chair to lower resistance. "I brought my son up here, Doctor, because someday he'll rule Arrakis. He must learn about it. We were told this place had been judged safe for the Duke's visit. I therefore considered it safe for my son and me."

"You are perfectly safe here, My Lady," Kynes said.

She spoke with a dry bitterness: "No one is *perfectly* safe anywhere."

Kynes lowered his eyes.

"I understand you've been on Arrakis quite a number of years," she said.

"Forty-one years, My Lady."

"As long as that?"

He met her eyes, looked past her. "I was educated at Center, and came here as my first assignment, My Lady. It was a family tradition. My father was here before me. He was Chief of Laboratories when Arrakis was still His Imperial Majesty's Desert Botanical Testing Station."

She liked the way he said "My father."

"Did your father discover the spice?"

"He did not discover the spice, but the discovery was made by men working under him," Kynes said. He looked down at the desk. "This was his desk."

There was such a sense of pride and devotion in his voice, that Jessica felt the pulse of it with her special awareness.

"Please sit down, Dr. Kynes," she said.

Kynes' throat worked. He looked around the room, obviously embarrassed. "But, My Lady . . ."

"It's quite all right," she said. "I'm only the Duke's bound concubine, the mother of his heir, but it'd still be all right were I Noble Born. You're a loyal man, Dr. Kynes, and honorable. My Duke respects such as you, and we relax the usual ceremony among those we trust." She pointed to the chair across from her. "Please sit down."

Kynes took the chair, adjusting it to its highest resistance so that it supported him stiffly on its edge.

"You're still operating under an Imperial grant?" she asked.

"His Majesty very kindly supports our work."

"Which is?" She smiled. "For the record, that is."

He returned her smile, and she saw the beginning of relaxation in his attitude. "It's mostly dry land biology and botany, My Lady. And we do some geological work—core drilling and testing, things like that. You never really exhaust the possibilities of an entire planet."

"Does His Majesty know the *other* work you do?"

"I don't know quite how to say this, My Lady."

"Try," she said.

"We don't actually conceal anything from the Imperium," he said. "The records are all kept. We make regular reports as required. And we have quite proper authorization for all our projects. We . . ."

She began to laugh. "Kynes . . . Kynes," she said. "You are marvelous. The system is marvelous. And the Imperial Court is so far away."

Kynes spoke stiffly: "We are loyal subjects of the Imperium, My Lady. Please don't try to twist what I . . ."

"Twist? You disappoint me, Kynes."

"What we discover is for the good of the Imperial Regate," Kynes said. "It's not as though . . ."

"I want you to keep one thing foremost in your mind, Dr. Kynes." She permitted a sharpness to creep into her voice. "You are now a subject of the Atreides Duchy. My Duke gives the orders here. He, too, is a loyal subject of the Imperium. And he knows how records may be kept, and the required reports made, and the proper authorizations obtained for *his* projects."

*Now,* she thought, *let's see if there's any steel in him.*

A sour expression turned down the corners of Kynes' mouth. "And the Court *is* so far away. A minor planetologist could be dead and buried, all properly authorized, by the time the Court discovered it."

"You've been too long under the Harkonnens," she said. "Didn't you learn anything except fear and suspicion?"

"Oh, the pattern's clear enough," he said. "My Lady."

"What pattern?"

"The army of tame killers, the subtle pressures and the not so subtle ones." Kynes gripped the arms of his chair until his fingers were white. "I had hoped that this time . . ." He shook his head. "This planet could be a paradise! But all you and the Harkonnens ever think about is grubbing money out of the spice!"

She spoke dryly: "And how is our planet to become a paradise without money?"

Kynes blinked at her.

"As with most visionaries," she said, "you see very little outside your vision."

Kynes chewed his lower lip. "My Lady, I know I've spoken bluntly, but . . ."

"Let's understand each other," she said. "My Duke is not in the habit of destroying valuable men. Your . . . ah . . . sharp words merely show your value. They prove there's steel in you that the Harkonnens didn't take the temper out of. My Duke has need of steel."

Kynes drew a deep breath, hunted the corners of the room with his eyes.

"How can you be sure I speak the truth?" she asked. A wry smile touched her mouth. "You can't be, of course, until it's too late, until after you're committed to an irrevocable decision. But the Harkonnen way offered you no hope at all, did it?"

He shook his head, staring at her.

"I, too, can speak bluntly," she said. "My Duke has his back to the wall. This fief is his last hope. If he can build Arrakis to a strong and secure Duchy, there will be a future for the Atreides line. He comes from Caladan, a planet that was a natural paradise. Too soft, perhaps. Men lost their edge quite easily there."

"My Lady, there was talk of Harkonnen agents left behind." The words were wrenched from him as though he were trying to say more and could not.

"Of course there were agents left behind!" *And now we find out about him,* she thought. "Do you know any of those agents?"

Kynes glanced at the door, wet his lips with his tongue. "No, My Lady. Of course not. I have very little contact with the world outside my work."

*He's lying,* she thought. And the thought pained her more than it should have. She sighed. Another time, perhaps. And Tuek would have to be told of this man's knowledge, of course. Again, she sighed.

"What does your Duke really want of me?" Kynes asked.

*Well, why not change the subject?* she thought. "Can the spice grow artificially?" she asked.

Kynes pursed his lips. "Mélange is not an ordinary . . . that is, it's possible . . . unless . . . you see, I suspect there's a symbiotic relationship between the worms and whatever produces the spice."

"Oh?" She found herself surprised by the idea. *But why not?* she asked herself. *We know of stranger relationships.* "What evidence of such symbiosis do you have?"

"It's very tenuous, My Lady, I agree. But each worm defends its own sector of spice sands. Each seems to have a territory that . . . well . . . you see, we have only one preserved specimen . . . it's in another . . . location. The capture of that specimen was quite a project, you may . . ."

"You have a live worm?"

"Oh, no! It's quite dead. Preserved. We stunned it with a chemical explosion, dug down and killed each ring with repeated applications of high-voltage electricity. Each ring had to be killed separately."

She noted the increased alertness in Kynes, the animation as he warmed to his subject. "Is it a large one?" she asked.

"Quite small, really. It's only about eighty meters long and some fifteen meters in diameter. They grow much larger in the deep desert—ten times that size. We caught this one in the high latitudes where the sand cover on the basic rock is rather thin. They're rare in that region, of course, and, I might add, so is the spice rare there. You never find the worms this far north." He gestured around him. "Too much rock and there are the mountains between us and the desert. *And* there's no evidence of spice in these latitudes."

"Just because there's no spice where there are no worms," she said, "that doesn't . . ."

"But there's other evidence," he said. "My examination of our specimen suggests a complicated relationship. It is very difficult to find true knowledge about the deep desert. Factory crawlers, aircraft, anything that's forced down in the deep desert and unable to get away stands little chance of survival. Your only hope is rescue . . . and that as fast as possible unless you can hold out on one of the rather rare outcroppings of substratum. There are a predictable number of personnel disappearances every year."

"Ah, the uses of statistics," she murmured.

"What, My Lady?"

"The ubiquitous sand," she said. "And you spoke of making it a paradise."

"Well, My Lady, with sufficient water and . . ."

The door behind Kynes slammed open onto reeling violence, shouting, the clash of steel, and wax-image faces grimacing. Jessica found herself on her feet, staring at Idaho's blood-pitted eyes, claw hands around him, arcs of blurred steel chopping. She saw Paul crawling past Idaho . . . the orange fire-mouth of a stunner. Paul had his small knife, the poison one, in his hand, flicking it, flicking it . . . at the people who clawed at Idaho and himself.

In a different version of the scene:

Our first move," Paul said, "should be to recover our Family Atomics. They're . . ."

"What of your father's . . . body, his water?" Kynes asked.

Paul sensed hidden meaning in the question, said: "My father died with honor."

"You know this without knowing the manner of his death?"

"I know it."

"I think perhaps you do, yet the Harkonnens . . . still have his water."

"The Harkonnens will overlook his water," Paul said. "They don't follow the Arrakeen Way. My father's water will escape into the air and soil of Arrakis, become a part of Arrakis, just as I will become a part of Arrakis."

"Fremen will hesitate to follow a man who has not recovered his father's water."

"I see," Paul said.

"You asked for my counsel, sire."

"Could you suggest a way of recovering my father's . . . water?"

"A force is being formed now to recover our own bodies from Arrakeen. They could be told to recover your father, also. If they're successful, a token battle with the leader of this band, you being victorious, would restore the pattern of things."

"But that's not the best way," Paul said.

"No. The best way is for you to do it yourself."

"Our Family Atomics are in Arrakeen," Paul said. "They're shielded and hidden deep underneath our residency there, planted directly in line with the house's power plant and masked by that plant."

*He does not hesitate to tell this man anything,* Jessica thought. *He knows he has the loyalty. Indeed, what an Emperor my son would make.* She pushed the thought aside, warning herself: *I must not become infected by his scheme!*

"On Arrakis," Kynes said, "the water is more important."

"In the Imperium, a Family's atomics are also important," Paul said. "Without them, you lack an unspoken bargaining point."

"The suicide threat," Kynes said, and his voice was bitter. *"I will shatter your planet."*

"Without the atomics," Paul said, "one is not quite a Great House. But then . . ." He gestured to the crysknife hilt partly concealed beneath the robe at Kynes' waist. ". . . is a Fremen a Fremen without his knife?"

A smile touched Kynes' lips, white teeth glistening within his beard.

## New Chapter:
## THE FLIGHT FROM KYNES'S DESERT BASE

⟡

In the cave's blackness, Jessica felt that her life had become sand curling in an hourglass, running faster and faster . . . There were no more luminous arrows to guide them—only a slit in rock that she felt with her hands. The slit gave out into night with the sound of a sandstorm keening overhead, and the fall of sand on her outstretched hand. Her eyes tried to force light from memory, but found only the empty present.

"What is it?" Paul asked. "Where are we?"

"It's the end of the tunnel," she said. She tried to speak calmly, helping preserve his courage. "You saw that last arrow?"

"There was a sign on it," he said. "What did it mean?"

"Square within a square," she said. "That means 'end of path.' It's a Bene Gesserit symbol." And she wondered at the mystery of it. How had Kynes or whoever had made this place known to put a Bene Gesserit symbol there? *The end that is a beginning.*

"What do you feel when you put your foot out?" Paul asked.

"There's a drop-off of some kind," she said. "I can't feel the bottom of it. We'll have to wait for dawn unless we can find some light."

"I feel sand blowing," he said. "And there's dust in my nose."

"If only we had shields. You know, I blamed Idaho for not offering you his shield," she said.

"Lump-lump-lump-lump!"

It was a fluttering sound, directionless in the dark. *Somewhere* out there. Jessica held herself motionless except for a hand that reached out and gripped Paul's shoulder. Fingernails of terror scraped along her nerves.

"What's that?" Paul whispered.

"Chireeep!" It came from the inky dark.

"Maybe something blowing in the wind," she said. "Be quiet and listen."

The waiting moment was packed with a sense of movements. Every sound had its own dimension. They were so tiny, the little movements. Realization flooded through her, squeezing fear into controllable size. The ungainly thumping of her heartbeats evened, shaping out the moments of time. She forced inner calmness.

"It's little animals, or perhaps birds," she said. "They were all around us and we frightened them."

And she realized that this cave must have been a storm sanctuary for creatures from the desert.

"What was that other sound?" Paul asked.

"I don't know," she said. "Whatever it was . . . it was out there . . . quite a ways."

She felt Paul move under her hand. Her son's first hope was to melt into the protective coloration among the people here, to sink back into the people. But first they had to find them.

"I feel some kind of handle on the wall over here," he whispered.

"Careful," she said. She moved her hand along his arm, groped fingers over his and onto cold metal: a bar in a vertical slot. The bar had been pushed to the top of its slot.

"It felt like a hydraulic latch," Paul said. "The kind they have on shipboard for airtight doors."

*Airtight*, she thought. *Sandtight*.

Gently, she pulled down the bar.

A crack of luminosity opened before them—a vertical rectangle.

"It *is* a door," Paul whispered.

"Shhhh," she cautioned.

She pushed the door and it swung wide onto more blackness broken by two puddles of radiance beyond the opening. She recognized the glowing spots for what they were—footswitches.

"Inside," she ordered. "Stay close. Keep hold of me."

They slipped through the doorway, and she pulled it closed behind. The sound of the sandstorm dropped to a distant mewing. The air around them felt old—touched with dust . . . and faintly cinnamon.

Jessica probed into the black with her senses, felt no living thing except themselves.

"What're those two glowing pieces?" Paul whispered.

She spoke aloud, shaping confidence into her tone. "Footswitches. This must be where the 'copter's hidden, the one Dr. Kynes said was at the end of the tunnel." She extended an arm, moved it to set up air currents, sensed a gross object. "Be careful you don't bump into it."

"I'm thirsty," Paul said.

"Maybe there'll be water in the 'copter," she said. She took his shoulder, crept forward to the puddles of radiance on the floor: two glowing circles enclosing black designs. One held a rayflash—it was a light switch. The other was bisected by a straight line—a door control. She touched the rayflash with her toe.

Light drove back the darkness.

Jessica darted her glance around the revealed room, testing it. The ornicopter was there in front of them, sealed beneath a transparent cover. Around it, an irregular space had been carved from the native rock and closed away from the outside by a flat expanse of metal. The place was just big enough to maneuver around the squat shape of the ornicopter.

"It's a big one," Paul said. "I wonder . . ."

She motioned him to silence, listening: The faint shrilling of the storm was punctuated now by interval chirps, a tiny whistling. Some of the sound came from above and behind them. She turned, looked up at broken rock.

"What's that?" Paul whispered.

"I don't . . ."

A flurry of birdwings shocked her to silence. A feathered shape shot across the room over their heads, darted into a cranny on the opposite wall. The chirping whistles arose to a new height, slowly died away.

"A bird," she sighed. "It has a nest in there."

"It looked like a little owl," Paul said. "But how could it get in here?"

"There's dust," she said. She pointed to the cover on the ornicopter and to the floor. "There must be a small hole in the rocks somewhere." She moved forward to the shield over the ornicopter. "Help me uncover this thing."

Dust filled the air as they rolled back the cover. Paul sneezed. And Jessica recalled the precautionary lectures on this planet. *Nose filters,* she thought. *We'll have to find nose filters somewhere.* She slipped into the 'copter, tested one set of its twin controls.

Paul, right behind her, looked up from an examination of the panel and the interior walls. "It has no battle shield," he said.

"It's not a battle craft," she said. She looked left and right at the spread of wings, the delicate metal interleaving that could open to lift them in a soaring glide or compress for jet-driven speed.

"What're those things on the rear seat?" Paul asked.

She turned, followed the direction of his pointing finger. Two low mounds of black fabric. She had taken them for cushions, saw now that they were shaped to fit a human back, that they had adjustable straps—packs. She reached back, flipped one over. It was surprisingly heavy and gave off a gurgling sound. Orange lettering came into view. She read it aloud: "Emergency use only. Contents: stilltent, one; literjons, four; energy caps . . ."

"Literjons," Paul said. "That's what it said on a water machine at the landing field. 'Fill literjons here.' Could that mean water?"

"Yes." She continued reading, feeling the rigors of this planet press in on her with every word: "Energy caps, sixty; recaths, two; burnooses, two; distrans, one; medkit, one; digger, one; sandsnork, one; stillsuits, two; repkit, one; baradye pistol, one; sinkchart, one; filtplugs, eight; paracompass, one; instructs, one."

"What's a recath?" Paul asked.

"I don't know," she said. She dropped her attention to the handwritten addition, below the printing, and in the same orange: "Fremkit, one; thumpers, four."

Paul said. "Thumper?"

"I suppose there'll be an instruction manual," she said. Out of the pack's ziptop came a micro-manual with a magnifier and glowtab for turning the miniscule pages.

"Stilltent," Paul read. "Saaaay . . . it reclaims the water that evaporates from your body." He bent over the book, reading: "Breath reclamation—breathe through the dry-pass tube at all times. Remember, if your stay in the desert may be extended, that all moisture must be conserved. Make sure you wear the recath and its collection bottle at all times. See instructions for correct use of catheter equip . . ." He glanced down the page. "Mother! Do we drink . . ."

"Hush," she said. "If it's purified, water is water. What do you think we drank on the spaceship coming here?"

"But . . ."

"Go on reading," she ordered. *When my water is gone*, she thought, *Paul will still have some left*. "Our lives depend on how well we learn this. You'll see here, it says people have worn catheters for months at a time without ill effect, but we can expect some irritation from them at first."

"I don't like it," he said. His voice sounded sullen.

"What don't you like?" she asked. "Living?"

He looked up at her, then back to the book. Presently, he bent over it, reading and examining the things from the pack.

Stillsuits. They were like a tent, only to be worn at all times.

Nose filters. She showed him how to install them.

Within an hour they had finished the manual and followed its instructions, escaping out to the open sands. They wore the light plastic stillsuits beneath sand-colored robes. A stilltent covered them with its snorkel protruding upward along a rock face.

Only a rough package marked "fremkit" remained to be examined from Jessica's pack. She opened it. Out puffed a pastel blue kerchief that fluttered gauzily as she lifted it. Beneath the kerchief lay what appeared to be a knife in a sheath and a small package marked thumpers. On the thumper package was scrawled: "See instructions for calling sandworms inside."

"Calling a sandworm," Paul said. "Who'd want to?"

"I don't know," she said. She pulled the knife from its sheath. The blade was about twenty centimeters long, four-edged, and made of some milkwhite cloudy substance. She held it up, looked down the point. It had a cross-section in the shape of a shallow X and the tip was pierced by a hair-sized hole.

*Poison?* she wondered.

The handle felt warm and resilient beneath her fingers. She hesitated on the point of squeezing the handle, decided against it. She put the knife back in its sheath for later examination when they were out of the tent.

There remained now the flat little case labeled distrans, which was a distress transmitter, and the baradye pistol. She slipped the transmitter back into the pack, hefted the pistol. The instructions said it could be fired into the sand and would spread a patch of orange dye about twenty meters in diameter.

"What's this?" Paul asked. He lifted a tiny booklet out of the fremkit.

Jessica took it, opened it to the first page.

Handwritten!

The script was small but legible without the magnifier. The glowtab picked out the words. She read, and as she read, excitement grew in her. Not so much for the instructions contained there, but for what they implied.

It opened with two prayers:

"God give us water in torrents that we may bring forth vegetation and grain and gardens luxuriant."

And:

"May the fire of God set a cooling light over thy heart."

It was called, she read, "The Kitab al-ibar, the *azhar* book, giving the *ayat* and *burhan* of life. Believe on these things and al-lat will not burn you."

She turned the page.

"What is it?" Paul asked.

She spoke as she read: "It's a book telling how to live in the desert on the things of the desert. How to use the things you find in the desert." She turned another page, read a sentence, and looked up at him. "Paul, a thing like this couldn't *be* unless there were an entire culture behind it."

"What do you mean?"

"There are people who live in the desert, or at least on the edges of it, people who call themselves 'Fremen,' probably meaning Free-men." She looked at him. "If we could find them. If . . ." She turned back to the book, continued reading.

Paul turned, opened his own pack, burrowed in it for his own fremkit.

She spoke absently as she read: "Be careful of the knife in there. I think it has a poison tip."

Presently, both of them were reading: two little glowtab spots in the glowglobe dusk of the tent.

Paul looked up through the transparent end of the tent. He pointed to a cluster of stars. "That's the constellation of the Mouse. Its tail points north."

"There's much to learn," she said. She adjusted the filtertube over her mouth, glanced at him. "Do you still have the gun Dr. Yueh gave you?"

He patted the sash beneath his robes.

"I presume Gurney has instructed you on such weapons."

"Yes. Why?"

"If we meet . . . when we meet these Fremen, they may not accept strangers easily."

"And they might not expect a child to be armed," he said. He touched the shield stud beneath his robes. "Nor shielded."

"In case the need arises," she said.

And Paul thought: *She is right. Grown men might not suspect I'm no longer a child.*

She straightened, listening. "Hear that?"

"I don't hear anything," he said.

"The absence of a thing is as important as its presence," she said. "Never forget that."

"The storm," he said. "I can't hear the wind." He looked back at the packs, flicked his tongue across his lips, thinking of the water. But if the storm . . . if it was still dark out there. They needed darkness.

Jessica watched his face in the instant it took these thoughts to flick through his mind. She felt sadness and approval at the look of adult decision on his features.

"It'll still be dark outside," he said. "Best we take advantage of it."

She spoke with a crisp edge to give him confidence. "Right. Strap yourself in while I see to the door."

"I can do that," he said.

# MUAD'DIB

꒰ᗺ꒱

**M**ovement caught Paul's attention. He stared down through smoke bushes and weeds into a wedged slab sand surface of moonlight inhabited by an up-hop, jump, pop-hop of motion.

"Kangaroo mice!" he hissed.

Pop-hop-hop!

Into shadows and out.

Paul untied the line around him, slipped out of his pack. He reached down to the ground for a handful of pebbles.

Jessica watched him, wondering.

Paul moved forward. He stayed in shadows, creeping—graceful cat movements.

Slam!

The handful of pebbles hurtled into the sand clearing. Two tiny creatures lay writhing. He was on them in one lithe pounce—cracked their necks.

Slowly, Paul looked back up at his mother. His burnoose was a grey sliding of motion.

*The hunter,* she thought. *The animal. Now, he must return to humanity. He must do it by himself.*

"We won't starve," Paul said.

"Indeed we won't," she agreed.

"They have blood," he said. "It's . . ." He shook his head. "Well, if we have to . . . if we can't find water."

She nodded.

He looked down at the mice, one in each hand. "They were so beautiful," he said.

Jessica smiled. Her cracked lips hurt with the movement.

"They'll save our lives," he said, "if we can't find other food. I'll never forget them."

She nodded. He was coming back.

"We'd best make a fire to cook them," he said.

"Above all, the human is practical," she said.

"What?"

"Nothing, dear. I'll help gather twigs for the fire. We can make it here against the cliff where it won't be seen very far."

Deleted Scenes and Chapters from
*Dune Messiah*

# ORIGINAL OPENING SUMMARY
## FOR *DUNE MESSIAH*

愛

The Bene Gesserits operated for centuries behind the mask of a semi-mystical school while actually carrying on a selective breeding program among humans. When the program appeared to reach its goal they held their inevitable "trial of fact." The records of that trial in the case of the Prophet Muad'Dib betray the school's ignorance of what it had done.

It may be argued that they could examine only such facts as were available to them and had no direct access to the person of Muad'Dib. But the Bene Gesserits had surmounted great obstacles and their ignorance here goes deeper.

The program had as its target the breeding of a person they labeled the Kwisatz Haderach, meaning "the one who can be many places at once." In simpler terms, what they sought was a human with powers of mind that would permit him to understand and use higher-order dimensions.

The school's proctors had the Mentat example from which to start. The typical Mentat, after his training, can solve many problems simultaneously. He investigates long chains of logic and circumstances and, to an observer, seems to arrive at his conclusions in a split second. As many Mentats have testified, however, the internal sensations of the computing process frequently are such that he may feel he has taken millennia to solve the given problems. One of the first steps in training Mentats is teaching them awareness of this Time trick.

Muad'Dib, according to many of the Bene Gesserit tests, was the one they sought. He was born Paul Atreides, son of the Duke Leto, a man whose bloodline had been watched carefully for more than a thousand years. His mother, the Bene Gesserit concubine, Lady Jessica, was a natural daughter of the Baron Vladimir Harkonnen and carried gene-markers of supreme importance to the program.

Lady Jessica had been ordered to produce an Atreides daughter. The plan was to inbreed such a daughter with Feyd-Rautha Harkonnen, a nephew of the Baron. The high probability here was that they would have a Kwisatz Haderach or near–Kwisatz Haderach in the next generation. But Paul Atreides appeared a generation early when the Lady Jessica deliberately defied her orders and bore a son.

These two facts alone should have alerted the Bene Gesserits to the possibility that a wild variable had entered their plans. But there were other indications which they virtually ignored.

1) Paul Atreides as a youth showed ability to predict the future. His prescient visions were accurate, penetrating, and defied four-dimensional explanation.
2) The Reverend Mother Gaius Helen Mohiam, the Bene Gesserit Proctor who tested Paul's humanity, testified that he surmounted more agony in the test than any other human of record. She failed to make special note of this.

3) When the Atreides Family moved to the planet Arrakis, the Fremen population of that planet hailed Paul as a prophet, "the voice from the outer world." The Bene Gesserits were well aware that the rigors of such a planet as Arrakis, with its lack of open water, its vast deserts, its emphasis on basic needs for survival, produce a high proportion of sensitives. The Fremen reaction was another clue the Bene Gesserits ignored.

4) When the Harkonnens, aided by the Sardaukar soldier-fanatics of the Padishah Emperor, reoccupied Arrakis, killing Paul's father and most of his troops, Paul and his mother disappeared. But almost immediately there were reports of a new religious leader among the Fremen, a man called Muad'Dib who was again hailed as a prophet. The reports stated clearly that he was guarded by a new Reverend Mother of the Sayyadina rite, "who was the woman who bore him." Fremen records available to the Bene Gesserits stated clearly that their legends of the prophet contained these words: "He shall be born of a Bene Gesserit witch."

(It may be argued that the Bene Gesserits had sent their Missionaria Protectiva onto Arrakis centuries earlier to implant something like this legend as a safeguard should any members of the school be trapped there and need sanctuary, and that this legend of the Lisan al-Gaib was properly to be ignored. But this is true only if you grant that they were correct in ignoring the other clues about Paul-Muad'Dib.)

5) When the Arrakis affair boiled up, the Spacing Guild made overtures to the Bene Gesserits. The Guild hinted that its Navigators, who used the spice drug of Arrakis to produce the limited prescience necessary to guide spaceships through the void, were "bothered about the future." This could only mean they saw a nexus, a meeting place of countless delicate decisions, beyond which the path was hidden. This was a clear in-

dication that some agency was interfering with higher-order dimensions!

(The Bene Gesserits were well aware that the Guild could not interfere directly with the vital spice source because Guild Navigators already were dealing somewhat with higher-order dimensions such that the slightest misstep could be catastrophic. It was a known fact that Guild Navigators could see no way to take control of the spice without producing just such a nexus. The obvious conclusion was that someone of higher-order powers was taking control of the spice source.)

In the face of these facts, one is led to the inescapable conclusion that the Bene Gesserits' behavior in this affair was a product of a higher plan of which they were completely unaware.

This is the Summa prepared by her own agents at the request of Lady Jessica immediately following the Arrakis affair. The candor of this report amplifies its value far beyond the ordinary.

# New Chapter:

## ALIA & THE DUNCAN IDAHO GHOLA

∽҂∾

*These things I tell you: the sequential nature of real history cannot be re-*
*peated precisely by prescience. We grasp incidents cut out of the chain.*
*That is why I deny my own powers. Eternity moves. It inflicts itself upon*
*me. Let my subjects doubt my majesty and my oracular visions. Let them*
*never doubt eternity.*

—DUNESDAY PROVERBS

It occurred to Alia, studying the ghola in her audience chamber, that
he was a religious unknown. The way he serenely surmounted the
turmoil around him filled her with disquiet.

There were mother-memories of Duncan Idaho within her grasp
and she consulted them for a clue to this creature whose flesh had been
a friend's. With a growing sense of suspicion she realized how she'd
leaned on pre-judgments.

Alia-Jessica had always thought of Duncan as a man who could be
recognized for what he was—not by lineage or planet of origin but of
and by himself: stalwart, isolated, self-supporting. It was the way with
many who'd been friends of House Atreides.

Now, she rejected all preconceptions. This was not Duncan Idaho.
This was the *ghola.*

She turned slightly on the altar steps, looking across the ghola at the Guild navigator and his attendants. The ambassador, swimming in his container of orange gas, gave every appearance of being satisfied with a situation which should not satisfy him.

"Did you hear me correctly, Ambassador Edric?" she demanded. "My suspicions are not to be taken lightly. Perhaps I should order you held prisoner while we seek out and destroy your frigates."

"Let me remind the sister of the Emperor that I am an ambassador," the guildsman said. He turned, reclining in his tank, a buoyant figure with hooded eyes which stared up at her. "You cannot threaten my person and escape the consequences. Every civilized man in the Empire will oppose you if this is your choice."

"Mentat," Alia said, "what is this prattle?"

As she spoke, she knew what the ambassador meant. There was a limit to the force even the most powerful could apply without destroying themselves.

"Do you truly need me to tell you?" Duncan asked.

She shook her head. The evidence lay all around and she wondered why she hadn't seen it before this. A Bene Gesserit axiom arose in her mind like a fish surfacing in turbulent waters: "Concentrate on one sense at the expense of the others. This is a danger. Avoid it." Oracular vision was a sense, she realized. It had blinded her to what could be seen with the naked eye. The primitive forms lay all around her—in money, in culture, in social usages. And the populace was sinking beneath government, being conscripted.

No populace would permit that.

Every misuse of power would be held against the government, stored up until it exploded in one violent overturning.

Alia, staring down at the Guild ambassador, realized she was looking at a martyr. He had been prepared—anointed. He was the sacrifice the Guild offered on the altar of its bid for power.

"So that's the way it is," Alia said. "Then by the power invested in me by the Emperor, I invoke a formal trial. Let the Landsraad judges be summoned. Choose your defender, guildsman."

The ambassador flopped over in sudden agitation, turned his face away from her. *The witch!* he thought. She had always been more dangerous than her brother.

"There is a Fremen saying," Alia said. "'It should not be necessary to pay to gain justice.' To this, let me add that it should not be necessary to pray, as well. Whom do you choose for defender?"

Duncan saw the guildsman give a subtle hand signal to an attendant, leaped to place himself between the group on the audience chamber floor and Alia. It was an instinctive motion which surprised even him.

As he moved, Duncan saw something hurtle from the ambassador's attendants toward Alia. With a blurring reflex, Duncan swept his hand across the thing's path, felt the horned calluses on the heel of his hand strike sharp metal. Something buzzed, clattering to the floor. It flopped there like a wounded fish, and he realized they'd dared hurl a hunter-seeker at the Emperor's sister! The realization accompanied his own reflexive leap as he stamped on the thing, smashing it before it could find warm flesh and burrow into a vital organ.

The chamber erupted in violence around him.

The Fremen guard had plunged as one man onto the Guild entourage.

Knots of struggling battle swayed around the room, churning, rolling—the glitter of knives, grunts, shouts.

Duncan's gaze took in the scene as he whirled, swept Alia into his arms and plunged with her toward the protective seclusion of the passage behind the dais.

But Alia rolled out of his grasp, her knife in hand, and for an instant he thought she was going to sink the blade into him, but she gasped, "Hold!"

"You must get to a safe place!" he insisted, moving to put himself between her and the violence.

An odd smile twisted her mouth and she said: "I command you to step aside, Duncan. It's safe enough here." She gestured and he sensed the sudden silence of the chamber, turned.

Bloody robes, mounded figures lay scattered across the floor. Only Fremen guards remained standing, their chests heaving from the exertion. Remarkably, the guildsman's tank stood unmarked amidst the carnage, the ambassador reclining in his orange gas, arms folded across his chest, eyes intent upon Alia.

"You can do no more than kill me," he said, and there was a strange feeling of emotion in the artificial voice.

"Is that so?" Alia asked. She gestured imperiously to a guard captain, said: "Bring me a lasgun."

"No!" Duncan blurted.

"Do as I command," Alia ordered.

The guard captain hesitated. "The Guild swine may have a shield in that tank," he said.

"M'Lady," Duncan said. "Touch a lasgun beam to a shield and the entire city will go up in the explosion."

"And the Guild will be charged with using atomic weapons against House Atreides," she said. "Who can tell a lasgun-shield explosion from the blast of a fusion bomb?"

"I care not how I die," the ambassador said. "Knife, lasgun beam— however you choose. Offend the law in any way you wish. You have slain my attendants and aides. I know what's in store for me."

"Do you now?" Alia asked. The guard captain placed the black rod of a lasgun in her hand.

She took it without looking, descended the steps to the chamber floor, avoided a body, stopped beside the ambassador's tank.

"Do you have a shield?" she asked, voice conversational.

"I have a shield," the guildsman admitted, voice tight, "but it's turned off. I'll not put the Guild in your hands that easily."

Duncan, following Alia, put a hand on her arm. "Can you believe him, M'Lady?"

"What do you think, Duncan?" She glanced at him, eyes oddly veiled.

Duncan took a deep breath, put his Mentat awareness to her question. Not likely this man would use a shield. This was a dedicated guildsman. He'd die before betraying his own kind.

"It isn't likely, M'Lady," Duncan said. "But must you kill him?"

"You object?" Alia asked. She glanced around at the remains of the violence in the chamber. "Some of my guards died at this creature's bidding."

"I do not participate in public homicide," Duncan said.

"What manner of man are you?" Alia demanded. "You offered your own body to protect me, yet you will not agree to the destruction of my enemies."

"Savagery has been taken out of me," Duncan said.

She touched his cheek. "But you have flesh."

"Do not kill this one, M'Lady," Duncan said. "I know it is the wrong thing to do."

"I command here," she said. "Do you admit that?"

"Yes!"

"Then stand aside."

Reluctantly, every muscle objecting, he obeyed.

Alia turned, adjusted the lasgun for short range, aimed at the guildsman's tank, pressed the trigger.

A hole perhaps two centimeters in diameter appeared in the transparent stuff of the tank. Wisps of orange gas emerged, trailed upward in the vagrant air currents of the chamber.

There was a sudden pungency of mélange in the room.

Alia returned the lasgun to the guard captain, kept her attention on the Guild ambassador. Edric the Steersman swam unharmed in his tank, eyes intent on Alia.

She waited without speaking.

As though they were controlled from outside himself, the ambassador's eyes went to the hole in his tank and the orange gas escaping there.

"Do you smell the spice, Duncan?" Alia asked.

"His air must be saturated with it," Duncan said. He studied the orange gas diffusing into the audience chamber.

"You witch!" the ambassador blurted. "Kill me and have done with it!"

"Kill you?" she asked. "Without a trial? Do you take me for a barbarian?"

The ambassador's chest was heaving. "You don't know what you're doing," he protested.

"Don't I?" she asked.

"I should've turned on my shield!" Edric snapped.

"You really should have," Alia said. "Whom do you choose for your defender?"

"Seal my tank this instant!" Edric said.

"Seal it yourself," Alia said.

Abruptly, the guildsman placed a webbed hand against the hole in his tank, fumbled in the pouch at his waist.

Alia slid the crysknife from its sheath at her neck. Her Fremen guards stiffened. The crysknife carried sacred implications and there were outworlders present. Alia appeared unaware of the disquiet among her guards. She reached out the knife point. Light glimmered from the milky blade. Slowly, deliberately, she thrust the knife into the ambassador's palm where it lay exposed against the lasgun hole.

With a piercing yell, the guildsman jerked his hand away from the hole, held up a bloody palm.

Alia withdrew the reddened blade tip, held it up for Duncan to see.

"Human blood, I'll bet you," she said. And she extended the blade toward one of her guards, said: "Bannerjee, wipe this blade clean and take the wiping to a techman. I want this blood analyzed. I would know what humanity it shares with me . . . and how it differs."

Edric the Steersman had produced a cloth from his pouch. He wrapped his injured hand, stuffed another piece of material into the hole in his tank.

"What do I share with you?" he demanded, glaring at Alia. "I share the common bondage of all life. But the dark memories of your savagery—I no longer share those!"

"I think you have another bondage which is not common," Alia said. "What think you, Hayt?" she demanded, glancing at Duncan.

Instead of answering, the ghola said: "Why do you call me that?"

"Hayt?" she asked. "Is that not how you're called?"

"Yes." The answer was filled with reluctance.

"Can you answer my question?" she asked.

Duncan nodded. "The air this guildsman breathes is saturated with mélange. That says much about him."

"Those capsules we see him pop into his mouth so frequently," Alia said, "do they not add to the picture?"

"More of the spice, I'd say," Duncan agreed.

"The dosage with which this guildsman maintains himself staggers the imagination," Alia said. "How do you compute this?"

Duncan took a deep breath, his manner growing remote in Mentat withdrawal. Presently, he said: "The steersmen of the Guild use the spice to heighten their prescient powers. Without it they cannot divine the safest paths for their heighliners to course through space. In their duties, they must use more and more and more mélange . . ."

"The dosage requirements must increase at a rate which is compounded by a pressure of their need," Alia said. "It is a thing which both my brother and I have sensed."

"You are fools!" Edric raged.

Alia turned, studied the guildsman swimming in his tank. The orange gas had thinned and he appeared pale hanging there in his suspensors.

"Have you chosen your defender?" she asked.

"I choose the Reverend Mother you hold prisoner," Edric snapped. "Gaius Helen Mohiam!"

"Very well," Alia said. She turned to the guard captain. "The ambassador is to be held in custody under constant visual guard until his trial," she said. "I wish daily reports on his activities. Meanwhile, you will drain the gas from his tank and have it subjected to analysis. Replace the gas with the pure air of Arrakis."

"You cannot!" the guildsman protested. "You mustn't."

"Why not?" Alia asked. "Will it kill you?"

"You know it won't," he hissed, bringing his face close to the transparent wall of his tank.

"It will blind his oracular vision," Duncan said.

"You have no human feelings!" Edric said. Extreme agitation shook his body.

"Human feeling?" Alia asked. "What is this birdflap about human feeling? When you've failed, you fall back on this intense inner thing which is outraged by violence. Hah! Let me tell you something, gambler, human feeling's a feeble argument which labels the loser. You failed to measure the consequences, gambler."

"What did you call me?" Edric asked, shock apparent in his voice even through the transponders.

"Gambler!" Alia said. "I pay you a compliment."

"You can't be serious," Edric protested.

"Gamblers and ecologists are the only ones who truly *measure* consequences," Alia said. "We of the oracles are always gamblers. We're a step beyond politicians and businessmen, I give you that."

The guildsman shook his head, a fish-motion that sent tremors down his body. "I beg of you not to take the spice from my air," he pleaded.

"With what would you buy that boon?" Alia asked.

"Buy?"

"My brother's government is always willing to bargain," Alia said.

"Buy?" Edric repeated, his voice louder.

"When you come down to it," Alia said in a reasonable tone, "all government is business. 'Fortune passes everywhere,' as my father often said." She glanced sideways at Duncan, found his metallic eyes hidden by closed lids. It gave him an odd, more human look, a figure in repose. Ghola substance was masked.

As though he felt her glance, Duncan opened his eyelids. The metal orbs glistened as they turned toward her.

"Governments always conveniently overlook their own inequities," he said. "This I was taught. Do you not see how you play your enemy's game?"

Anger sent color into Alia's cheeks.

"There are some questions you may not ask!" she snapped.

"When force closes the mouth of inquiry," Duncan said, "that is the death of civilization."

Alia glared at him, brought her quickened breathing under control. Platitudes!

Edric was staring at the ghola. The guildsman twisted his body around, attention focused on the pair beside his tank.

"Hayt," Edric said, "will you help in my defense?"

Alia whirled. "You presume too much, Ambassador!"

"Do I?" Edric asked, studying Duncan.

"Indeed you do," Duncan said. "I was a gift to House Atreides, freely given, freely accepted. You no longer have demands upon my services."

"My brother must be notified at once," Alia said, speaking softly. "His judgment is, after all, the one which must prevail."

"You take the law too lightly," the guildsman snarled. "Its language is plain enough that even the lowliest citizen can understand it."

"The language of the law," Alia said, "means only what my brother says it means."

With an air of finality, she turned away, motioned her guards to close behind, strode to the dais. There, she turned. "Hayt," she said, "you will accompany me."

Duncan shrugged, fell into step with the guards.

He could hear other guards behind him taking the guildsman's tank into tow, moving it down the chamber. Still more guards, he realized, would be hurrying to collect the bodies and reclaim their water.

Alia's men were, after all, Fremen.

# New Chapter:
## THE HUMAN DISTRANS

*(The character Otmo was changed to Korba*
*in the published version of* Dune Messiah.)*

⌘

He found the guard swarming in the parade yard, a scene of frantic confusion with rumors passing from mouth to mouth in a clamorous, intimidating babble.

Both moons were up and full, but they were on the windowless side of the passage by which Paul returned to the Keep. The hall had been left in darkness broken only by a single shaft of light from the door to the Interrogation Salon. Lack of illumination in the approach was a Security rule. Darkness made one a difficult target.

Word had preceded him on the fight at Otheym's house, and now there were loud cries from the guard area as it was learned the Emperor had returned. Guardsmen wavered into view from the Salon with the light behind them.

Two of Stilgar's men carried Bijaz between them ahead of Paul. The dwarf's short legs couldn't be allowed to slow down the Imperial party. Bijaz, recovered from his fright, was darting glances all around, eyes alert and inquiring.

"Get the Council of Naibs here at once," Paul commanded as he entered the Salon. "And turn down those lights except for that corner over there." He gestured. "We'll question Bijaz there."

"You do not question a human distrans," Bijaz said, a dignity in his manner which made some of the guardsmen laugh.

"Listen to him, now," one of them said. "Would you listen to him?"

"Put him down," Paul said. "Stilgar? Where is Stilgar?"

"Gone for the Naibs, Sire," said a man behind him.

Paul recognized Bannerjee's voice, glanced back, said: "Have you a distrans recorder ready?"

"All ready, Sire." Bannerjee gestured to an aide who carried a thin recorder tube, its shigawire reel glistening in the end.

Paul looked back at the dwarf, who stood now between two impassive guardsmen, glowglobes bright above them. Beads of perspiration stood out on Bijaz's forehead. The dwarf seemed now a creature of odd integrity, as though the purpose fashioned into him by the Tleilaxu was projected out through the skin. There was power beneath this mask of cowardice and frivolity, Paul realized.

"Do you truly work as a distrans?" Paul asked.

"Many things work as a distrans, Sire," Bijaz said. "Anything with a voice and a nervous system can be a distrans. You should know this. You know everything."

"None of that," said the guardsman on Bannerjee's left side, nudging him.

Paul thought of the code word Otheym had imparted by inference—the name of the one killed: Jamis. He felt reluctance to utter the word, to test it on the dwarf. There seemed a demeaning of humanity to use a man as a distrans, even such a man as this.

"Set the recorder for immediate translation," Paul said.

The guardsman beside Bannerjee adjusted his instrument.

"Jamis," Paul said.

Bijaz stiffened. A thin keening sound issued from his lips. His eyes were glazed. The keening wavered and twisted.

Paul stared at the recorder as a piping voice began to issue from it. The voice was very slow with long pauses as though spoken out of great weariness. "Tibana was an apologist for Socratic-Christianity," the thin voice said. "He was probably a native of IV Anbus who lived between the 8th and 9th Centuries, likely in the reign of the Second Corrino. Of Tibana's writings, only a portion survives from which this fragment is taken—'The hearts of all men dwell in the same wilderness.' It is a thing to consider when you contemplate treachery."

Paul glanced around at the uncomprehending faces of his aides and companions. He had not told them the information Bijaz held and they didn't know what to expect. Names—would the names of any present be uttered now by this dwarf?

"The Fremen of the deep desert have revived the blood sacrifice to Shai-Hulud," the recorder piped in time to Bijaz's keening. "They say the Emperor and his sister are one person, one being back to back, half male, half female."

Paul saw eyes turn toward him. He felt suddenly that he existed in a dream controlled by some other mind, and that he might momentarily forget this to become lost in the convolutions of that mind.

"Emperor and sister must die together to make the myth real," the recorder piped. "The words of Otmo the Panygerist are preached in the secret ceremonies. 'Muad'Dib is the Coriolis storm,' they say. 'He is the wind that carries death in its belly. Alia is the lightning which strikes from sand in the dark sky.' And they shout: 'Blow out the lamp! Day is here!' It is the signal they learn for the attack."

Paul thought of the ancient ritual, mystical, tangled with folk memories, old words, old customs, forgotten meanings—a bloody play of ideas across Time. Ideas . . . ideas . . . they carried a terrifying power.

They could blot out civilizations or become a blazing light in the mind to illuminate lives across the span of centuries. He looked at the face of the dwarf, seeing youthful eyes in an old face. Eyes of total blue! The dwarf was a mélange addict, then. What could that mean? He studied the eyes, total blue at the center of a network of knobby white lines which ran to the hollows below the temples. Such a large head. All seemed to focus on the pursed mouth from which that monotonous high whine continued to issue.

*The names,* Paul thought. *Get to the names.*

"Among the Naibs," the recorder piped, "the traitors are Bikouros and Cahueit. There is Djedida, secretary to Otmo."

All around him, Paul felt the guardsmen stiffening as they grasped the import of what was occurring here. Bannerjee took a half step forward to stand glaring down at the dwarf.

*Bannerjee, too?* Paul wondered. He was obsessed by a feeling of threat. Bikouros, Cahueit, Djedida!

"There is Abumojandis, the aide to Bannerjee," Bijaz said. "And Eldis . . ."

Motion erupted beside Paul, a thing he had expected, but not in the form it took. Bannerjee, whirling, placed himself between Paul and the aide with the distrans recorder. The aide had lifted the recorder like a weapon aimed at Paul. A burst of flame darted from the instrument, catching Bannerjee full in the waist. The piping voice of the distrans was stilled but the keening of Bijaz continued as Paul hurled a sliver knife from the sheath in his left sleeve. The knife seemed to sprout from the aide's throat. Bannerjee staggered back into Paul's arms, muttered: "M'Lord, I failed you."

The aide was on the floor, arms outstretched and held by guards, dead eyes staring at the ceiling. Paul recognized the man then: Abumojandis, a Fremen of Balak Sietch from the deep desert. Otheym's list was true, then—traitors.

Medics pulled Bannerjee from Paul's arms.

Paul grew aware that Bijaz was going on with that monotonous keening. The distrans recorder remained silent.

"Someone get another recorder!" Paul snapped. "And see if you can shut that creature up!"

Even as he spoke, he knew the dwarf could not be silenced until the message had run its course. It would be a one-way thing: start it and let it run. They'd have to begin again.

"Get him into the other room," Paul said.

The new flurry of motion his orders had set off was interrupted by the arrival of the Naibs, the Fremen council of Sietch leaders. Stilgar led the procession. He was in his formal robes now, a grim figure beneath a shock of black hair. His craggy face, massive nose and rock-hewn cheekbones held an expression of wary alertness.

"M'Lord," he said. "What is . . ."

Paul silenced him with a wave of the hand, searched the procession. Bikouros and Cahueit were not among the others.

"Where are Bikouros and Cahueit?" Paul demanded.

"They have gone to the desert to deliver an observer for the Qizarate," Stilgar said. "They left while we were . . . in the city."

"The observer," Paul asked. "Who?" As he spoke, he knew who it would have to be.

"Why," Stilgar said, "Otmo has dispatched his own assistant, Dje-dida."

"So they have chosen to run for it," Paul said. He noted that the medics had brought a stretcher for Bannerjee, caught the eye of one of them.

"He will live, M'Lord," the medic said. "It was a cutterray the traitor used and your knife caught the scum in time."

"That man used his body to shield me," Paul said. "See that he lacks for nothing."

"Yes, M'Lord." They went out with the stretcher.

"There are traitors among the Naibs," Paul said. "Bikouros and

Cahueit among them. And Djedida. I do not expect you will catch them, but send after them, all the same."

Stilgar turned to obey.

"And seek out Eldis," Paul added.

"The keeper of your prison, Sire?" Stilgar asked, turning back.

"Do you know of another Eldis?" Paul asked.

"But that one is with the party going to the desert," Stilgar said. "He spoke of a visit to . . ."

"Get after them!" Paul barked.

"At once!" Stilgar hurried from the room.

Paul looked at the assembled Naibs in their rich robes. They were something far different from what they had been in the Sietch days. They stared back at him, not speaking.

In each case, Paul felt the figure of the real Fremen Naib had been blotted out under an image of an uninhibited hedonist, a man who had sampled pleasures most men could never imagine. He saw their glances straying toward the doorway where Bijaz had been taken. The keening voice of the dwarf went on and on. Some of the Naibs looked at the windows which opened into one of the Keep's walled gardens. The glances were uneasy. They disliked buildings, these men. No exotic pleasures could change that. They felt unnatural in the confinement of space built above the ground. Give them a proper cave, one cut from the rock of Arrakis by Fremen hands, and they relaxed.

Paul scanned the faces of Hobars, Rajifiri, Tasmin, Sajid, Umbu, Legg . . . all of them, names so important in Fremen life that they were firmly attached to places on Dune: Umbu's Sietch, Rajifiri's Sink . . .

He focused on Rajifiri, remembering the rough and bearded commander of the Second Wave in the Battle of Arrakeen, found that Rajifiri had become an immaculate fop dressed in a Parato silk robe of exquisite cut. It was open to the waist to reveal a beautifully laundered ruff and embroidered undercoat set with glittering green gems. A purple belt held the waist, its edges studded with golden rivets. The sleeves poking through the slit armholes of the robe had been gathered into rivulet-ridges of dark green-and-black fabric.

The green-and-black said he wore the colors of and was loyal to the House of Paul Atreides. Paul wondered now if that loyalty went much below the laundered silk.

The keening of the dwarf dwindled down to silence.

Briefly, Paul explained the situation to the Naibs, watching their faces for a reaction that would betray the inner man to a trained awareness. There were too many of them to watch all at once, though, and the situation was clouded over with intense emotions, an excitement akin to that of battle. He could see that excitement kindling old patterns in the Naibs. Some of the dross from his Empire began to peel off them.

They began calling for attention, protesting their loyalty.

He silenced their sharp comments with a wave of his hand, said: "You will wait here and watch through the doorway while we go on with our questioning of the dwarf."

As he turned to go into the other room, there was a stir off to the right. The heavy-shouldered form of Stilgar came thrusting through the press of Naibs.

"They're being pursued, M'Lord," he said, stopping in front of Paul. "I must say that were I the one pursued, you'd not catch me . . . and there are men as wise in the desert with this group."

"You sent men who'll think as they think?"

Stilgar raised his eyebrows.

"Sorry, Stil," Paul said. "Of course you did. What'll these fugitives do?"

"You know the answer to that, Sire, as well as I."

Paul nodded. This deadly crew would have friends off-planet, friends in the Guild, in the Bene Gesserit, perhaps even in the Landsraad. His enemies off-planet, Paul knew, would do everything they could—short of exposing themselves—to dull the Emperor's power. Getting a pack of fugitives off Arrakis would be a thing they could attempt.

"Give them two days and they'll be gone off Arrakis," Paul said.

"Hadn't we better go back to questioning this human distrans?" Stilgar asked. He nodded toward the other room.

Paul turned on a heel, led the way. Bijaz sat on a low divan against the opposite wall, feet crossed beneath him, a look of repose on his large features. In spite of the apparent relaxation, there was a charismatic alertness about him that reminded Paul of an ancient idol. The guards beside Bijaz stiffened to attention. One of them came forward diffidently with a distrans recorder.

Stilgar took it, examined it, nodded to Paul.

Bijaz met Paul's gaze, grinned. "Hai, hai," he said. "Have you learned a lot?"

*He doesn't realize we've missed most of his message,* Paul thought.

"We'll go through it again," Paul said.

"And what'll be gained by that?" Bijaz asked. "The message is the same."

"We want to check its veracity," Stilgar said.

"And who's that big lout asking after truth?" Bijaz asked.

Stilgar stiffened, put a hand to his knife.

"Doesn't he know the Emperor should seek victory and not truth?" Bijaz asked, tipping his head slyly to the left.

"Watch your tongue or I'll cut it out," Stilgar growled.

Bijaz shot a look of questioning fright at Paul. "Would you permit that, Sire?"

"What if he caught you when I wasn't around?" Paul asked, trying to lighten the mood.

But Stilgar only shook his head sharply, said: "It's no time for jokes, M'Lord. Let's get on with it."

Paul took a deep breath, said: "Jamis."

At the key word which should have sent him back into a trance, Bijaz merely blinked, continued staring at Paul.

"Jamis," Paul repeated.

No response.

"Why do you invoke the name of our departed comrade?" Stilgar asked.

"It's the distrans key," Paul said. And again: "Jamis."

Bijaz remained alert and staring.

"Your distrans has been cleared," Stilgar said, glancing warily around at the guardsmen. "The message is erased."

"How was it done, Bijaz?" Paul asked, quelling a sense of frustrated rage.

"I felt head sickness when the assassin made his move against you," Bijaz said.

"An erasure signal in the distrans recorder," Paul said. "That means they were more than ready to slay me." He nodded to himself, turned and in a low voice told Stilgar what Otheym had said about Otmo the Panygerist.

"A traitor?" Stilgar asked. "That one?" His brows came down in a heavy scowl. "I'll have him on a slow knife."

"No." Paul shook his head. "We've lost the message Bijaz carried and . . ."

"Then we'll get it from Otmo—the hard way if need be," Stilgar said.

"Do you think they're not prepared for such a thing?" Paul asked.

"Then how . . ."

"There are other ways to smoke out our enemies," Paul said. "What time is it, Stil?"

"Be dawn soon." He looked back to the faces of the Naibs crowded in the doorway. "Why, M'Lord?"

"The stone-burner," Paul said. "Summon a Convocation of the Landsraad here, with the Naibs taking part . . . and a Guild Observer."

"There'll be no evidence the burner contained atomics, Sire," Stilgar said. "The whole thing's turned to slag by now and how can we show a background radiation which differs from . . ."

"It was a stone-burner," Paul said. "There's no other way to fire a stone-burner. Someone's playing a very dangerous game. There'll be traces of how it was brought here. It left a track as clear as a bird in mud."

"Bird in mud, M'Lord?"

"Never mind, Stil," Paul said. "The thing can be tracked. A Guild heighliner brought it here; that's the important thing to remember. The Guild will have to answer to the Landsraad. Not a trade agreement will be signed or honored until . . ."

"The spice, M'Lord," Stilgar said.

"Of course we'll stop all the shipments of the spice," Paul said. "Let's see how they like that. When they run out of spice, not a ship will run anywhere in our universe. And we ship no spice until the culprits are handed over to us."

"Unless they've a substitute," Stilgar said.

"Not likely," Paul said.

Bijaz began to giggle.

Paul turned toward the dwarf, noting how the creature had caught the attention of everyone in the room.

"How they'll wish on the morrow they had no teeth," Bijaz sputtered between giggles.

"What in the name of the worm does he mean by that?" Stilgar demanded.

"Without teeth they'll be unable to gnash," Bijaz said, his voice reasonable.

Even Stilgar chuckled. Paul stood silent, watchful.

"Who do you mean by *they*?" Paul asked.

"Why, Sire," Bijaz said, "the ones who planted that stone-burner on you. Could it be they wanted you to stopple the spice?"

## New Chapter:
## CONSPIRACY'S END

*(This dramatically changes the end of the* Dune Messiah *story.)*

*My enemies can always dissemble. They can always dissemble. There are limits even to an Emperor's law.*

—MUAD'DIB AND HIS LAW, STILGAR'S COMMENTARY

Edric stared through the small, field-blocked communications hole into the adjoining cell. Ennui and a profound fatalism gripped him. The Reverend Mother paced restlessly back and forth in the confinement there, virtually ignoring a visitor.

Irulan sat on the Revered Mother's bed, hands folded in her lap. Her blond hair had been tied in a severe knot at the neck and there was a look of bloodless austerity about her features.

"I have done precisely as I was instructed," Irulan said. Could she flee to the children and take them?

The Reverend Mother cast a warning look toward the door where the guards stood, looked around the cell at the places where listening devices probably had been planted. She sniffed. The smell of the place annoyed her.

388

"It doesn't mater what they hear now," Irulan snapped. "If he wishes to continue ruling, he must come to me on my own terms."

"Your terms?" the Reverend Mother inquired in a slyly insinuating tone.

"His concubine, his link to the Fremen, is no more," Irulan said.

"You're sure?" the Reverend Mother asked, not looking at Irulan. Something was wrong, and she could feel it with the limited oracular ability which spice addiction gave her.

"Security communications never lie," Irulan said. "She is dead. There are two brats, but they have no status."

"They have whatever status he gives them," the Reverend Mother said.

As though she had not heard, Irulan said: "And he will be forced to free you. He is an astute politician, my husband. The days of the spice monopoly are numbered, and he knows it. He must give concessions, compromise. There is no way out for him."

"Your husband," the Reverend Mother sneered.

"He will be my husband completely now," Irulan said, voice smug. "That is one of the concessions we will require."

"Will we now?" the Reverend Mother asked. She caught sight of Edric's face through the communications hole. "What say you, Guildsman?"

"The days of the spice monopoly *are* numbered," Edric said, "but I don't believe it's coming out as we wished."

"What do you see in the future?" the Reverend Mother demanded. "What's going wrong?"

Edric shook his head. What did it matter? They could not change the thing now. Far too late for that.

"You're supposed to be a Steersman, a living oracle," the Reverend Mother pressed. "What do you see?"

Again, Edric shrugged. An unaccustomed sense of kindness held him silent.

"You call yourself a living oracle," Irulan sneered, "yet you cannot know all the things I have done or will do."

Edric bent to peer directly at her. "You should not be here, M'Lady," he said. "The guards will pass you out of here. Go while there is still time."

"What nonsense is this?" the Reverend Mother demanded, sensing the unspoken communication in Edric's words.

"This is a dangerous place," Edric said. "It is about to become even more so."

"You prattle," the Reverend Mother said, but her voice lacked conviction. She moved fretfully back and forth in the cell, agitated by restless stirrings of her own prescience.

"You have seen something," Irulan accused, getting up to stare back at Edric through the hole.

The Reverend Mother pulled her away. "He has seen nothing but his own liver spots swimming on his eyes! Isn't that true, Steersman?"

"Perhaps," Edric agreed, the ennui again dominant.

"Well, what is it?" the Reverend Mother demanded.

"What is it?" Edric asked. He shook his head. He missed the spice-saturated air of his tank. There was a hunger in his cells that no stomach could feed.

"What have you seen?" the Reverend Mother barked.

"He is dead," Edric said.

"Dead?" Irulan asked. "Who is dead?"

"The Atreides," Edric said.

The Reverend Mother had come to a full stop facing the communications hole. She nodded to herself. "So that's it," she muttered. "So that's how it's to be."

"It means he has defeated us, you know," Edric said.

"Nonsense!" Irulan snapped. She glared at him, detesting the orange face, the spice-glazed blue of the tiny eyes.

"Clever, clever, clever . . ." the Reverend Mother muttered.

"It can't be true," Irulan said. There were tears in her eyes.

"Clever, clever . . ." the Reverend Mother said.

"It is true," Edric said. "He is dead. He went into the desert to die. He has gone to Shai-Hulud, as they say in this forsaken place."

". . . clever, clever . . ." the Reverend Mother said, shaking her head.

"Not clever!" Irulan stormed. She turned her glare on the Reverend Mother. "If he has done this, it's foolish!"

"Clever," the Reverend Mother argued.

"It was the action of a child!" Irulan stormed. "You'll be sorry when I'm gone! It's a thing a child . . ."

"And we are about to be sorry," Edric said.

"Not the action of a child," the Reverend Mother said.

"But why would he take his own life?" Irulan demanded.

"Why not?" Edric asked.

"Indeed, why not?" the Reverend Mother said. "He had but one life to spend. How else could he spend it to such advantage? It was clever. It was the supreme act of intelligence. We are undone by it. I am filled with envy."

"M'Lady," Edric said, looking at Irulan, "do you have a religion?"

"What are you talking about?" Irulan asked. She put a hand to her cheek, stared back at him defensively.

"Listen," Edric said.

In the sudden silence, Irulan grew aware of a faint roaring sound, a pulse of many noises.

"What is that?" she asked.

"A mob," the Reverend Mother said. "They've been told, eh?" She glanced at Edric.

"Why should you ask if I have a religion?" Irulan insisted.

"They blame you," Edric said. "They say you killed Chani and this killed Muad'Dib."

"What . . . how . . ." Irulan rushed to the cell door, rattled it. But the guards were gone.

"They're investigating the noise," Edric said. "It's too late, anyway."

"Why do you ask if I have a religion?" Irulan shouted, rushing back from the door to stare through the communications hole.

The Reverend Mother pulled her back, gestured toward the bed. "Sit down."

"Religion helps at times," Edric said. "It's . . ."

"Never mind," the Reverend Mother said, shaking her head.

The roaring sound had grown louder. They could make out individual voices now.

"I demand to be let out of here," Irulan said in a small child voice.

"Once I asked him about religion and his god-orientation," Edric said, looking at the Reverend Mother. "It was an interesting conversation."

"Oh," the Reverend Mother said. "What did you ask?"

"Among other things, I asked if god talked to him."

"And he said?"

"He said all men talk to god. And I asked him if he was a god."

"I'll warrant he had a devious answer for that one," the Reverend Mother said. She had to raise her voice above the increasing clamor.

"He told me that some say so."

The Reverend Mother nodded.

"And I asked him," Edric said, "if he said so. And he said that very few gods in history ever lived among men. I taxed him with not answering my question, and he said: 'So I haven't . . . so I haven't.'"

"I wish I'd known that," the Reverend Mother said.

"Why won't they come and let me out of here?" Irulan demanded from her position seated on the bed.

The Reverend Mother moved to the bed, sat down beside Irulan, took one of her hands. "Never mind, child. You are about to become a saint."

They gave up talking then because the cell had become the inside of a terrifying drum, a battering ram pounding on the door.

Presently, the door shattered, slammed back, and the mob poured through. The first of them died rather abruptly, but a mob is numberless. Eventually, they prevailed and tore the cell's occupants limb from limb.

*[FH handwritten note: Reverend Mother can't flee, too old. Perhaps she delays the mob for Irulan to escape?]*

# BLIND PAUL IN THE DESERT

*(This was the original ending to* Dune Messiah.*)*

Abruptly, he sat up, looked around him in the green gloom of the stilltent. The fremkit pack lay at his feet. He felt contained by the tent and these few possessions. The fremkit held his attention. Such a small pile of human artifacts. They were, though, part of his ability to stay alive in this place. It was very curious. A great deal of death had gone into the experience which had created these few things . . . yet, they represented life. He considered abandoning some of the items in the kit. Which ones, he wondered, might prove most definitely fatal by their absence? The baradye pistol? He drew it from the pack, tossed it aside. Not the pistol. Why should he want to lay down a marker pattern in the sand, a visible call for help?

His probing fingers encountered a scrap of spice paper. He brought it into the light, read it: an official proclamation on the necessities to be packed in a fremkit and the order of their insertion. An official proclamation! He realized he must've signed it. Yes, there it was: "By order of Muad'Dib." But he had no memory of the signing.

"It shall be the solemn duty of the official in charge . . ."

The plodding, self-important language of government enraged him. He crumpled the paper, hurled it aside. What had happened, he wondered, to the dutiful sounds, the clean meanings that screened out nonsense? Somewhere, in some lost where, they had been walled off, sealed up against chance rediscovery. His mind quested, Mentat fashion. Patterns of knowledge glistened there. Mermaid hair might wave thus, he thought, beckoning . . . beckoning the enchanted hunter into emerald caverns . . .

With an abrupt start, he drew back from the ruh-chasm that invited him to plunge into catatonic forgetfulness. So, he thought, the Mentat computation said he should disappear within himself. Reasons? Sufficient. He had seen them in the instant of escape. His life had seemed then to stretch out as long as the existence of the universe. Prescience already had granted him an infinity of experiences. But the real flesh condensed, lay finite and reduced his emerald cavern to a stilltent beginning to drum with the pulse of a wind. Sand chattered like pecking birds against taut surfaces.

Paul scrambled to the door, unsealed it, slipped out and scanned the desert, saw the obvious stormsign: tan gusts, no birds, the abrasive-dry smell of dust. He sealed his stillsuit and tried to peer through the brown haze concealing the distances. A vortex of winding dust lifted out of the haze far off in the bled. It told Paul what lay beneath. He pictured the storm, a giant worm of sand and dust—two hundred or more kilometers of rolling, hissing violence. It had come a long way without hindrance, building up speed and power. It could cross six hundred or more kilometers of desert in an hour. If he did no more than stand here, that storm would come to him, cut the flesh from his bones, etch his bones down to pale splinters. He would become one with the desert. The desert would fulfill him.

It occurred to Paul then to wonder about life's insistent seeking after death. Wonder moved him. He decided that he could not let the planet simply take him. There could be no giving up to destiny for an Atreides, not even in the full awareness of the inevitable.

There'd be no time to salvage the tent, Paul saw. He reached in, grabbed the fremkit, sealed its cover, carried it dangling from one hand as he scrambled over the rock ridge to the lee side. Survival required a niche sheltered from that storm, but there wasn't a break in the rocks on this side. Another storm had scoured the surface here into a smooth concavity down which he slid to the encroaching sand. Fremen had other resources, though. He chose the siff curve of a dune, ran toward it. As he reached the crest, the wind gusted. It tumbled him, rolled him, hissing and pouring sand over onto the slipface. The storm pursued him as he fell. In the valley of the dunes, he burrowed into the sand, fighting for inches, his right hand hampered by the straps of the fremkit. A sandfall from the crest slid around him, trapping his feet. Dust had clogged his stillsuit filters. He spat out the mouthpiece, pulled the robe over his head as another sandfall buried him.

In the abrupt dimming of the stormsound, Paul hunched his shoulders, made himself a small space into which to drag the fremkit. He found the compaction tool in it by feel, built himself a sandwalled nest. Presently, he had room enough to get out the snorkel. The air already was heavy with his exhalations. He drilled the snorkel at a downwind slant upward through the sand, feeling for the surface, for air. When he found it, the filters had to be blown free, and thereafter needed clearing on almost every alternate breath.

It was a mother of a storm up there. He had been right in its path, dead center. There might be a hundred feet of sand through which to burrow free when it passed. He listened to the distant keening of wind coming through the snorkel. Would a worm come to the sound of his burrowing? he wondered. Was that how it would be?

Paul sat back against the hard-packed wall of his nest, kept the snorkel mouthpiece between his teeth. Blow to clear it . . . inhale, exhale, inhale . . . blow to clear . . .

The fremkit glowtabs were green jewels beside him, the only radiance in the darkness which confined him. Was this to be his tomb? Paul wondered. He found the thought vaguely humorous. It was a mouse nest for Muad'Dib, for Muad'Dib the jumping mouse.

For a while, it amused him to compose epitaphs in his head. He died on Arrakis. He was tested here and found to be human . . .

And he thought of how his followers would refer to him when he had gone beyond their reach. They'd insist on speaking of him in terms of seas, he knew. Despite the fact that his life was soaked in dust, water would follow him into the tomb.

"He foundered," they'd say.

*Never again to see rain*, he thought. *Or trees.*

"I'll never again see an orchard," he said. His voice sounded thinly resonant within the sand nest.

Fremen would see rain, he knew. And many orchards finer than the ones at Tabr Sietch.

The thought of Fremen with muddy feet struck him as a curious thing.

Water.

Moisture.

He remembered the dew market where the water sellers had met in Arrakeen. They were disbanded now, destroyed by the changes which dripped from the hands of Muad'Dib.

Muad'Dib, the foreigner whom they hated.

Muad'Dib was a creature from another world. Caladan—where was Caladan? What was Caladan to a man of Arrakis? Muad'Dib carried a subtle, alien chemistry into the cycles of Arrakis. He disturbed the secret life of the desert. Sun and moons of Arrakis imposed their own rhythms onto the desert. But Paul Atreides had come. Arrakis had welcomed him as a savior, called him Mahdi and Muad'Dib . . . and given him a secret name, Usul, the base of the pillar. None of this changed the fact that he was an interloper, product of other rhythms, poison to Arrakis.

Interloper.

Weren't all men interlopers, though? he asked himself. They put on a mask of words, a persona, and they went out into the wild space, cluttered the universe with their stellar migrations.

Paul shook his head in the darkness.

He had uncluttered the universe somewhat. Men would remember Muad'Dib's Jihad for that, at least.

He grew aware that the snorkel was silent. Had the storm passed? He blew on the mouthpiece to clear it of dust. No keening of wind came down the tube.

*Let a worm come,* he thought. *I must at least try to die up there in the open, standing on my planet.* He took the compaction tool from the fremkit, began boring a slanting burrow upward. Sand rasped and fell around him while he worked. Sand scraped against the fremkit as he pulled it up behind him with a pack strap caught on one foot—a trick Otheym had taught him.

But Otheym was dead now, crisped in the searing blast of the stoneburner. One of Otheym's tricks for survival lived on, though. Otheym had learned it from someone before him. And someone else before that had passed it along. Simple thing, but vital: don't lose your fremkit, don't let it slow your digging; carry the thing along by one of its straps hooked over a foot.

Paul felt that his foot was really another man's foot far back in the history of Dune. He remembered a day in his beginnings on this planet, before the Fremen had found him and trained him. He had lost a fremkit, the key to survival. He and his mother could have died there in the desert without the tools represented by that kit. Her prana bindu training had saved them then—the training which went into the depths of the mind and to the smallest muscle.

He realized abruptly that he had been ashamed of his mother for most of his life on Arrakis. She was a Bene Gesserit. She carried the hated blood of the Harkonnens who had killed his father. But before her there had been others—countless humans, each with a figurative foot hooked in the strap of a figurative fremkit.

While his mind worried over such thoughts, he had burrowed very near the surface, Paul knew. Now, the cautious breaking out onto the surface. A Fremen was virtually helpless in this moment. Anything might await him out there, deadly enemies attracted by the sounds of digging.

Cautiously, he probed upward to the slope of dune that he knew must be near. Instinct told him of that nearness.

Daylight came with a burst of tumbling sand.

Paul waited, listening, probing with every sense.

No shadows crossed the hole—only grey sky darkening away toward sunset. There was a strong smell of spice, though, a touch of chill air onto his cheeks where the stillsuit hood left his skin exposed. A zephyr hissing of sand granules came to his ears—a background carrier wave of sound. He pressed an ear to the burrow wall—no distant roar of a worm, no thumping, no dislodging of sand from careless feet.

Paul fitted his noseplugs into place, sealed his suit carefully, secured his fremkit and slid out of the burrow onto the windward slope of a dune. The sand was firm, compacted hard by the wind here. It felt crusty under his feet. The zephyr picked up fluttering bits of something from the crest above him. Brown flakes fell all around. Paul captured one, held it to the filters, inhaled the powerful, giddy aroma of fresh melange. He swept his gaze over the slope. The desert all around him was thick with spice—a fortune in melange, a real spice pocket up from the deeps. He threw the flake of spice into the air, climbed up the duneface through drifts of melange.

Near the crest, he listened with ear against the sand. No wormsound came from the desert in spite of the noise he'd made burrowing to the surface.

*Perhaps there are no worms in this region*, he thought.

Just below the crest, he lay flat, crept up Fremen fashion, peered all

around. Abruptly, he froze and lay motionless as the sand geysered beneath a dune downwind. A hooded man climbed out onto a dune
there. Others followed—more than twenty figures. They concentrated
their attention briefly on the sky to the northeast, then began spreading out across the dune in a familiar pattern. They were going to call a
worm, he saw. Occasionally, they paused, glanced to the northeast.

Paul studied the horizon in that direction, saw the glistening sunset,
underlighted pinpoints which had caught the troop's attention: 'thopters. Paul counted four of them spread out in a search pattern and
headed toward the Fremen atop the dunes. The 'thopters drew near
and the troop waited, heads down.

A single 'thopter detached itself, climbed over the Fremen, banked
above Paul. The thunder of its wings stirred the melange into a minia-
ture storm. It curved around downwind, banked for a landing.

Abruptly, the Fremen band whirled. Maula pistols were jerked from
beneath their robes; the muzzles tracked the landing 'thopter. Its pilot
apparently saw the menace. He spread his wings, jetted away in a steep
climb.

All four ships took up a stacked formation, circled once more over
the troop, went dipping and gliding back to the northeast.

*They saw me,* Paul thought, *but they thought I was a member of this
troop.* He studied the Fremen. They were spreading out now in a familiar wide-armed deployment. No doubt who they were or what they
were doing: these were wild Fremen, renegades who refused to fit into
the ecological pattern which was transforming their planet. And now
they were preparing to summon a worm for a ride into the deep desert.

One member of the troop, an obvious leader, called out to his companions from a dunetop. A man detached himself from the band, sped
across the dunes with a thumper. His feet kicked up tiny spurts of dust
and sand. The whole desert passed into night while he ran, leaving the
first moon with its sharply outlined handprint pattern dominating the
sky.

The thumper began to beat out its summons: "Lump-lump-lump-

lump." It was a sound as much felt through the sand as heard. If a worm lay within range of that sound, it would come raging and hissing through the sand to be trapped as a steed for the Fremen troop.

Could he join them? Paul wondered. A Fremen could abandon sietch, friends and family only for special reasons of honor. Another tribe was bound to consider those reasons and, finding them sufficient, accept the renegade . . . provided they had no urgent need for his water. The water burden took precedent over all else.

But these were renegades who opposed the actions of Muad'Dib. These were men who'd gone back to the blood sacrifice and the old rites. They'd be sure to recognize him. What Fremen didn't know the features of Muad'Dib? Here were men who'd sworn on Fremen honor to fight the changes being wrought on Arrakis. They might slay Muad'Dib out of hand, offer his life as sacrifice in their rite.

He heard the faint sand-hiss then, first warning that a worm answered the thumper summons. The clapper-driven device still sounded from the dunes out there beneath the moonlight. There was no sign of the troop, though. They had blended themselves into the desert to wait.

The worm came from the southwest past the island of rocks. It was a good-sized one riding partly out of the sand—about a hundred meters long. Its crystal teeth flashed in the moonlight as it curved toward the irritant thumper. Paul could see the rippling of its driving segments.

A shape rose from the dunes as the worm passed. Maker hooks glistened as they drove into a segment of the worm. In the same instant, the creature swallowed the thumper, silenced it. The troop went up on its hooks then, turning the worm with a casual grace as they opened its segments. Goaders darted back along the high back as the worm rose farther from the sand. The beat of the goads drummed out in a frenetic rhythm. The worm picked up speed.

Paul turned to watch them go.

The worm was headed back on its own track. The robes of the riders strung out along its back whipped in the wind of its passage. Their voices wafted back to Paul, growing fainter as the rock outcropping hid them: "Hyah! Hyah! Hyah! Hyah! . . ."

Paul waited against the duneface until the sounds faded away, blended with the natural sounds of the night. He had never before experienced such a profound sense of loneliness. The troop of wild Fremen had taken the last of human civilization away with them. Only the desert remained.

He came curiously to the realization that he no longer cared where he was in the universe. He felt that he had lived a preassigned role and come to the end of it without an audience. There should be applause, he thought, but there's no audience. Well-remembered stars occupied their positions in the sky, but they no longer represented directions to him nor could he think of them as signposts. There was merely space all around him laid out against an enormous background of Time. The stars peered past him and through him like the empty eyes of his subject peoples. They were the sealed eyes of ignorance, always seeking to avoid their responsive status as human senses. They were the eyes from which nothing escaped.

For a few minutes, he listened to and identified the night sounds around him. This desert teemed with life which had adapted to it. He had not adapted. His body was mostly water. That water was a poison which could sicken a worm. If a worm devoured too many men, it died.

Presently, he pushed himself away from the dune, climbed up to the siff crest, struck out along the track of the worm. He knew why he had chosen this path and inwardly he laughed at himself for it. Life had passed here. Men had passed here. Outside this track lay a dreadful isolation where no passage was recorded.

Sometime during the night, he came to the realization that Chani had been the moon of his premonition. She had been the one to fall from the sky with that terrifying sense of loss. He stopped, still unable to shed tears. There was only the ache of tears without their release. He drew a libation of water from his catchpockets, poured the water on the sand as an offering to Chani and the moon.

The gesture helped and he went on along the worm track, not bothering to mask his passage in a stride of broken rhythm. At a point in the depressed early hours, he realized he had left the fremkit somewhere behind. It didn't matter. Paul-Muad'Dib was an Atreides, a man of honor and principle. He could not become the monster-of-possibility the vision of the future had revealed. That could not be permitted.

Slowing as weariness crept over him, Paul followed the worm track into the wasteland. Prana bindu training kept his feet moving long after another would have fallen. Even when dawn came, he marched onward. All through the day, he marched. And into the next night.

On the second day there was no marcher.

Only the wind blowing sand across barren rocks of the basement complex. Rivulets of sand ran around the tiniest extrusions, twisting, changing . . . ever changing.

# SHORT STORIES

# INTRODUCTION

Considering the immensity of the Dune universe, we often have trouble keeping each novel from getting too big. There are so many potential story lines and intriguing ideas to explore. This wealth of material leaves many side stories that can be told, hors d'oeuvres to accompany the exotic main course.

When we published "A Whisper of Caladan Seas" in 1999, it was the first new piece of Dune fiction published since Frank Herbert's death thirteen years earlier. It appeared in *Amazing Stories* magazine, and the issue promptly sold out; even back issues are no longer available. This story takes place concurrent with the Harkonnen attack on the desert city of Arrakeen in Frank Herbert's original novel *Dune*. Afterward, we wrote the three Dune prequel novels, *House Atreides*, *House Harkonnen*, and *House Corrino*.

By the time we turned to the *Legends of Dune* trilogy that chronicles the epic Butlerian Jihad, we were introducing Dune fans to history ten thousand years prior to the events in *Dune* itself. We felt this warranted an appetizer to ease readers into a whole new epoch that would span 115 years.

"Hunting Harkonnens" is our short-story introduction to the world of the Butlerian Jihad. During one of our book-signing tours, we found ourselves waiting for several hours in the Los Angeles train station. There, while sitting on an uncomfortable wooden bench larger than a church pew, we brainstormed "Hunting Harkonnens." In this preliminary tale, which lays the foundation of the holy war between humans and thinking machines, we introduced readers to the ancestors of the Atreides and the Harkonnens, and to the evil machines with human minds that Frank Herbert mentioned in *Dune*.

Passing a laptop computer back and forth, the two of us blocked out the story in detail, scene by scene. Then, like team managers picking baseball players during a draft, we each chose the scenes that most interested us. Shortly after returning home from the tour, we wrote our parts of the story, swapped computer disks, and rewrote each other's work, sending the changes to each other by mail and fax until we were satisfied with the end result.

Our second Jihad short story, "Whipping Mek," is a bridging work between the first and second novels in the trilogy, *The Butlerian Jihad* and *The Machine Crusade*. The story is set at a vital point in the nearly quarter-century gap between the events in these two novels, and fleshes out a pair of key tragic figures from later parts of the story.

An even longer time passes between the second and third novels in the series, decades in which remarkable changes take place in the long war against thinking machines. In our final bridging short story "The Faces of a Martyr," the surviving main characters have altered dramatically and we portray some of the driving events that set up the final battle between humans and their mortal enemies in *The Battle of Corrin*.

# A WHISPER OF CALADAN SEAS

*Arrakis, in the year 10,191 of the Imperial calendar.*
*Arrakis . . . forever known as Dune. . . .*

The cave in the massive Shield Wall was dark and dry, sealed by an avalanche. The air tasted like rock dust. The surviving Atreides soldiers huddled in blackness to conserve energy, letting their glowglobe powerpacks recycle.

Outside, the Harkonnen shelling hammered against the bolt-hole where they had fled for safety. Artillery? What a surprise to be attacked by such seemingly obsolete technology . . . and yet, it was effective. *Damned effective.*

In pockets of silence that lasted only seconds, the young recruit Elto Vitt lay in pain listening to the wheezing of wounded, terrified men. The stale, oppressive air weighed heavily on him, increasing the broken-glass agony in his lungs. He tasted blood in his mouth, an unwelcome moisture in the absolute dryness.

His uncle, Sergeant Hoh Vitt, had not honestly told him how severe his injuries were, emphasizing Elto's "youthful resilience and stamina." Elto suspected he must be dying, and he wasn't alone in that predicament. These last soldiers were all dying, if not from their injuries, then from hunger or thirst.

*Thirst.*

A man's voice cut the darkness, a gunner named Deegan. "I wonder if Duke Leto got away. I hope he's safe."

A reassuring grunt. "Thufir Hawat would slit his own throat before he'd let the Baron touch our Duke, or young Paul." It was the signalman Scovich, fiddling with the flexible hip cages that held two captive distrans bats, creatures whose nervous systems could carry message imprints.

"Bloody Harkonnens!" Then Deegan's sigh became a sob. "I wish we were back home on Caladan."

Supply sergeant Vitt was no more than a disembodied voice in the darkness, comfortingly close to his injured young nephew. "Do *you* hear a whisper of Caladan seas, Elto? Do you hear the waves, the tides?"

The boy concentrated hard. Indeed, the relentless artillery shelling sounded like the booming of breakers against the glistening black rocks below the cliff-perch of Castle Caladan.

"Maybe," he said. But he didn't, not really. The similarity was only slight, and his uncle, a Master Jongleur . . . a storyteller extraordinaire . . . wasn't up to his capabilities, though here he couldn't have asked for a more attentive audience. Instead the sergeant seemed stunned by events, and uncharacteristically quiet, not his usual gregarious self.

Elto remembered running barefoot along the beaches on Caladan, the Atreides home planet far, far from this barren repository of dunes, sandworms, and precious spice. As a child, he had tiptoed in the foamy residue of waves, avoiding the tiny pincers of crabfish so numerous that he could net enough for a fine meal in only a few minutes.

Those memories were much more vivid than what had just happened. . . .

❧

THE ALARMS HAD rung in the middle of the night, ironically during the first deep sleep Elto Vitt had managed in the Atreides barracks at Arrakeen. Only a month earlier, he and other recruits had been assigned to this desolate planet, saying their farewells to lush Caladan. Duke Leto Atreides had received the governorship of Arrakis, the only known source of the spice melange, as a boon from the Padishah Emperor Shaddam IV.

To many of the loyal Atreides soldiers, it had seemed a great financial coup—they had known nothing of politics . . . or of danger. Apparently Duke Leto had not been aware of the peril here either, because he'd brought along his concubine Lady Jessica and their fifteen-year-old son, Paul.

When the warning bells shrieked, Elto snapped awake and rolled from his bunk bed. His uncle, Hoh Vitt, already in full sergeant's regalia, shouted for everyone to hurry, *hurry!* The Atreides house guard grabbed their uniforms, kits, and weapons. Elto recalled allowing himself a groan, annoyed at another apparent drill . . . and yet hoping it was only that.

The burly, disfigured weapons master Gurney Halleck burst into the barracks, his voice booming commands. He was flushed with anger, and the beet-colored inkvine scar stood out like a lightning bolt on his face. "House shields are down! We're vulnerable!" Security teams had supposedly rooted out all the booby traps, spyeyes, and assassination devices left behind by the hated Harkonnen predecessors. Now the lumpish Halleck became a frenzy of barked orders.

Explosions sounded outside, shaking the barracks and rattling armor-plaz windows. Enemy assault 'thopters swooped in over the Shield Wall, probably coming from a Harkonnen base in the city of Carthag.

"Prepare your weapons!" Halleck bellowed. The buzzing of lasguns played across the stone walls of Arrakeen, incinerating buildings. Orange eruptions shattered plaz windows, decapitated observation towers. "We must defend House Atreides."

"For the Duke!" Uncle Hoh cried.

Elto yanked on the sleeve of his black uniform, tugging the trim into place, adjusting the red Atreides hawk crest and red cap of the corps. Everyone else had already jammed feet into boots, slapped charge packs into lasgun rifles. Elto scrambled to catch up, his mind awhirl. His uncle had pulled strings to get him assigned here as part of the elite corps. The other men were lean and whipcord strong, the finest hand-picked Atreides troops. He didn't *belong* with them.

Young Elto had been excited to leave Caladan for Arrakis, so far away. He had never ridden on a Guild Heighliner before, had never been close to a mutated Navigator who could fold space with his mind. Before leaving his ocean home, Elto had spent only a few months watching the men train, eating with them, sleeping in the barracks, listening to their colorful, bawdy tales of great battles past and duties performed in the service of the Atreides dukes.

Elto had never felt in danger on Caladan, but after only a short time on Arrakis, all the men had grown grim and uneasy. There had been unsettling rumors and suspicious events. Earlier that night, as the troops had bunked down, they'd been agitated but unwilling to speak of it, either because of their commander's sharp orders or because the soldiers didn't know enough details. Or maybe they were just giving Elto, the untried and unproven new comrade, a cold shoulder. . . .

Because of the circumstances of his recruitment, a few men of the elite corps hadn't taken to Elto. Instead, they'd openly grumbled about his amateur skills, wondering why Duke Leto had permitted such a novice to join them. A signalman and communications specialist named Forrie Scovich, pretending to be friendly, had filled the boy with false information as an ill-conceived joke. Uncle Hoh had put a stop to that, for with his Jongleur's talent for the quick, whispered story—

always told without witnesses because of the ancient prohibition—he could have given any of the men terrible nightmares for weeks . . . and they all knew it.

The men in the Atreides elite corps feared and respected their supply sergeant, but even the most accommodating of them gave his nephew no preferential treatment. Anyone could see that Elto Vitt was not one of them, not one of their rough-and-tumble, hard-fighting breed. . . .

By the time the Atreides house guard rushed out of the barracks, they were naked to aerial attack because of the lack of house shields. The men knew the vulnerability couldn't possibly be from a mere equipment failure, not after what they'd been hearing, what they'd been feeling. How could Duke Leto Atreides, with all of his proven abilities, have permitted this to happen?

Enraged, Gurney Halleck grumbled loudly, "Aye, we have a traitor in our midst."

Illuminated in floodlights, Harkonnen troops in blue uniforms swarmed over the compound. More enemy transports disgorged assault teams.

Elto held his lasgun rifle, trying to remember the drills and training sessions. Someday, if he survived, his uncle would compose a vivid story about this battle, conjuring up images of smoke, sounds, and fires, as well as Atreides valor and loyalty to the Duke.

Atreides soldiers raced through the streets, dodging explosions, fighting hard to defend. Lasguns sliced vivid blue arcs across the night. The elite corps joined the fray, howling—but Elto could already see they were vastly outnumbered by this massive surprise assault. Without shields, Arrakeen had already been struck a mortal blow.

ELTO BLINKED HIS eyes in the cave, saw light. A flicker of hope dissipated as he realized it was only a recharged glowglobe floating in the air over his head. Not daylight.

Still trapped in their tomb of rock, the Atreides soldiers listened to the continued thuds of artillery. Dust and debris trickled from the shuddering ceiling. Elto tried to keep his spirits high, but knew House Atreides must have fallen by now.

His uncle sat nearby, staring into space. A long red scratch jagged across one cheek.

During brief inspection drills while settling in, Elto had met Gurney Halleck and the other important men in Duke Leto's security staff, especially the renowned Swordmaster Duncan Idaho and the old Mentat assassin Thufir Hawat. The black-haired Duke inspired such loyalty in his men, exuded such supreme confidence, that Elto had never imagined this mighty man could fall.

One of the security experts had been trapped here with the rest of the detachment. Now Scovich confronted him, his voice gruff and challenging. "How did the house shields get shut off? It must have been a traitor, someone you overlooked." The distrans bats seemed agitated in their cages at Scovich's waist.

"We spared no effort checking the palace," the man said, more tired than defensive. "There were dozens of traps, mechanical and human. When the hunter-seeker almost killed Master Paul, Thufir Hawat offered his resignation, but the Duke refused to accept it."

"Well, you didn't find all the traps," Scovich groused, probing for an excuse to fight. "You were supposed to keep the Harkonnens out."

Sergeant Hoh Vitt stepped between the two men before they could come to blows. "We can't afford to be at each other's throats. We need to work together to get out of this."

But Elto saw on the faces of the men that they all knew otherwise: they would never escape this death trap.

The unit's muscular battlefield engineer, Avram Fultz, paced about in the faint light, using a jury-rigged instrument to measure the thickness of rock and dirt around them. "Three meters of solid stone." He turned toward the fallen boulders that had covered the cave entrance. "Down to two and a half here, but it's dangerously unstable."

"If we went out the front, we'd run headlong into Harkonnen shelling anyway," the gunner Deegan said. His voice trembled with tension, like a too-tight baliset string about to break.

Uncle Hoh activated a second glowglobe, which floated in the air behind him as he went to a bend in the tunnel. "If I remember the arrangement of the tunnels, on the other side of this wall there's a supply cache. Food, medical supplies . . . water."

Fultz ran his scanner over the thick stone. Elto, unable to move on his makeshift bed and fuzzed with painkillers, stared at the process, realizing how much it reminded him of Caladan fishermen using depth sounders in the reef fishing grounds.

"You picked a good, secure spot for those supplies, Sergeant," Fultz said. "Four meters of solid rock. The cave-ins have cut us off."

Deegan, his voice edged with hysteria, groaned. "That food and water might as well be in the Imperial Palace on Kaitain. This place . . . Arrakis . . . isn't right for us Atreides!"

The gunner was right, Elto thought. Atreides soldiers were tough, but like fish out of water in this hostile environment.

"I was never comfortable here," Deegan wailed.

"So who asked you to be *comfortable?*" Fultz snapped, setting aside his apparatus. "You're a soldier, not a pampered prince."

Deegan's raw emotions turned his words into a rant. "I wish the Duke had never accepted Shaddam's offer to come here. He must have known it was a trap! We can never live in a place like this!" He stood up, making exaggerated, scarecrowlike gestures.

"We need water, the ocean," Elto said, overcoming pain to lift his voice. "Does anybody else remember *rain?*"

"I do," Deegan said, his voice a pitiful whine.

Elto thought of his first view of the sweeping wastelands of open desert beyond the Shield Wall. His initial impression had been nostalgic, already homesick. The undulating panorama of sand dunes had been so similar to the even patterns of waves on the sea . . . but without any drop of water.

Issuing a strange cry, Deegan rushed to the nearest wall and clawed at the stone, kicking and trying to dig his way out with bare hands. He tore his nails and pounded with his fists, leaving bloody patterns on the unforgiving rock, until two of the other soldiers dragged him away and wrestled him to the ground. One man, a hand-to-hand combat specialist who had trained at the famous Swordmaster School on Ginaz, ripped open one of their remaining medpaks and dosed Deegan with a strong sedative.

The pounding artillery continued. *Won't they ever stop?* He felt an odd, pain-wracked sensation that he might be sealed in this hellhole for eternity, trapped in a blip of time from which there was no escape. Then he heard his uncle's voice. . . .

Kneeling beside the claustrophobic gunner, Uncle Hoh leaned close, whispering, "Listen. Let me tell you a story." It was a private tale intended only for Deegan's ears, though the intensity in the Jongleur's voice seemed to shimmer in the thick air. Elto caught a few words about a sleeping princess, a hidden and magical city, a lost hero from the Butlerian Jihad who would slumber in oblivion until he rose again to save the Imperium. By the time Hoh Vitt completed his tale, Deegan had fallen into a stupor.

Elto suspected what his uncle had done, that he had disregarded the ancient prohibition against using the forbidden powers of planet Jongleur, ancestral home of the Vitt family. In the low light their gazes met, and Uncle Hoh's eyes were bright and fearful. As he'd been conditioned to do since childhood, Elto tried not to think about it, for he too was a Vitt.

Instead, he visualized the events that had occurred only hours before. . . .

⤜⧓⤛

ON THE STREETS of Arrakeen, some of the Harkonnen soldiers had been fighting in an odd manner. The Atreides elite corps had shouldered lasguns to lay down suppressing fire. The buzzing weapons had filled the air with crackling power, contrasted with much more primal noises of screams and the percussive explosions of old-fashioned artillery fire.

The battle-scarred weapons master ran at the vanguard, bellowing in a strong voice that was rich and accustomed to command. "Watch yourselves—and don't underestimate *them*." Halleck lowered his voice, growling; Elto wouldn't have heard the words if he hadn't been running close to the commander. "They're in formations like Sardaukar."

Elto shuddered at the thought of the Emperor's crack terror troops, said to be invincible. *Have the Harkonnens learned Sardaukar methods?* It was confusing.

Sergeant Hoh Vitt grabbed his nephew's shoulder and turned him to join another running detachment. Everyone seemed more astonished by the unexpected and primitive mortar bombardment than by the strafing attacks of the assault 'thopters.

"Why would they use artillery, Uncle?" Elto shouted. He still hadn't fired a single shot from his lasgun. "Those weapons haven't been used effectively for centuries." Though the young recruit might not be well practiced in battle maneuvers, he had at least read his military history.

"Harkonnen devils," Hoh Vitt said. "Always scheming, always coming up with some trick. Damn them!"

One entire wing of the Arrakeen palace glowed orange, consumed by inner flames. Elto hoped the Atreides family had gotten away . . . Duke Leto, Lady Jessica, young Paul. He could still see their faces, their proud but not unkind manners; he could still hear their voices.

As the street battle continued, blue-uniformed Harkonnen invaders ran across an intersection, and Halleck's men roared in challenge. Impulsively, Elto fired his own weapon at the massed enemies, and the air shimmered with a crisscross web of blue-white lines. He fumbled, firing the lasgun again.

Scovich snapped at him. "Point that damn thing away from me! You're supposed to hit *Harkonnens!*" Without a word, Uncle Hoh grasped Elto's rifle, placed the young man's hands in proper positions, reset the calibration, then slapped him on the back. Elto fired again, and hit a blue-uniformed invader.

Agonized cries of injured men throbbed around him, mingled with frantic calls of medics and squad leaders. Above it all, the weapons master yelled orders and curses through twisted lips. Gurney Halleck already looked defeated, as if he had personally betrayed his Duke. He had escaped from a Harkonnen slave pit years before, had lived with smugglers on Salusa Secundus, and had sworn revenge on his enemies. Now, though, the troubadour warrior could not salvage the situation.

Under attack, Halleck waved his hands to command the entire detachment. "Sergeant Vitt, take men into the Shield Wall tunnels and guard our supply storehouses. Secure defensive positions and lay down a suppressing fire to take out those artillery weapons."

Never doubting that his orders would be obeyed, Halleck turned to the remainder of his elite corps, reassessing the strategic situation. Elto saw that the weapons master had picked his best fighters to remain with him. In his heart, Elto had known at that moment, as he did now thinking back on it, that if this were ever to be told as one of his uncle's vivid stories, the tale would be cast as a tragedy.

In the heat of battle, Sergeant Hoh Vitt had shouted for them to trot double-time up the cliffside road. His detachment had taken their weapons and left the walls of Arrakeen. Glowlamps and portable illuminators showed firefly chains of other civilian evacuees trying to find safety in the mountainous barrier.

Panting, refusing to slacken their pace, they had gained altitude, and Elto looked down on the burning garrison city. The Harkonnens wanted the desert planet back, and they wanted to eradicate House Atreides. The blood-feud between the two noble families dated all the way back to the Butlerian Jihad.

Sergeant Vitt reached a camouflaged opening and entered his code to allow them access. Down below, the gunfire continued. An assault 'thopter swooped along the side of the mountain, sketching black streaks of slagged rock; Scovich, Fultz, and Deegan opened fire, but the 'thopter retreated—after marking their position.

As the rest of the detachment raced inside the caves, Elto took a moment at the threshold to note the nearest artillery weapons. He saw five of the huge, old-style guns pounding indiscriminately at Arrakeen—the Harkonnens didn't care how much damage they caused. Then two of the mighty barrels rotated to face the Shield Wall. Flames belched out, followed by far-off thunder, and explosive shells rained down upon the cave openings.

"Get inside!" Sergeant Vitt shouted. The others moved to obey, but Elto remained fixated. In a single stroke, a long line of fleeing civilians vanished from the cliffside paths, as if a cosmic artist with a giant paintbrush had decided to erase his work. The artillery guns continued to fire and fire, and soon centered on the position of the soldiers.

The range of Elto's full-power lasgun was at least as long as the conventional shells. He aimed and fired, pulsing out an unbroken stream but expecting little in the way of results. However, the dissipating heat struck the old-fashioned explosives in the loaded artillery shells, and the ragged detonation ripped out the breech of the mammoth cannon.

He turned around, grinning, trying to shout his triumph to his uncle—then a shell from the second massive gun struck squarely above the entrance to the cave. The explosion knocked Elto farther into the tunnel as tons of rock showered down, striking him. The avalanche sent shock waves through an entire section of the Shield Wall. The contingent was sealed inside. . . .

AFTER DAYS IN the tomblike cave, one of the glowglobes gave out and could not be recharged; the remaining two managed only a flickering light in the main room. Elto lay wounded, tended by the junior medic and his dwindling supplies of medicinals. Elto's pain had dulled from that of broken glass to a cold, cold blackness that seemed easier to endure . . . but how he longed for a sip of water!

Uncle Hoh shared his concern, but was unable to do anything else.

Squatting on the stone floor off to his left, two sullen soldiers had used their fingertips to trace a grid in the dust; with light and dark stones they played a makeshift game of Go, a carryover from ancient Terra.

Everyone waited and waited—not for rescue, but for the serenity of death, for escape.

The shelling outside had finally stopped. Elto knew with a sick certainty that the Atreides had lost. Gurney Halleck and his elite corps would be dead by now, the Duke and his family either killed or captured; none of the loyal Atreides soldiers dared to hope that Leto or Paul or Jessica had escaped.

The signalman Scovich paced the perimeter, peering into darkened cracks and crumbling walls. Finally, after carefully imprinting a distress message into the voice patterns of his captive distrans bats, he released them. The small creatures circled the dusty enclosure, seeking a way out. Their high-pitched cries echoed from the porous stone as they searched for any tiny niche. After frantic flapping and swooping, at last the pair disappeared through a fissure in the ceiling.

"We'll see if this works," Scovich said. His voice held little optimism.

In a weak but valiant voice, Elto called his uncle nearer. Using most of his remaining strength, he propped himself on an elbow. "Tell me a story, about the good times we had on our fishing trips."

Hoh Vitt's eyes brightened, but for only a second before fear set in. He spoke slowly. "On Caladan . . . Yes, the old days."

"Not so long ago, Uncle."

"Oh, but it seems like it."

"You're right," Elto said. He and Hoh Vitt had taken a coracle along the shore, past the lush pundi rice paddies and out into open water, beyond the seaweed colonies. They had spent days anchored in the foamy breakwaters of dark coral reefs, where they dove for shells, using small knives to pry free the flammable nodules called coral gems. In those magical waters they caught fan-fish—one of the great delicacies of the Imperium—and ate them raw.

"Caladan . . ." the gunner Deegan said groggily, as he emerged from his stupor. "Remember how *vast* the ocean was? It seemed to cover the whole world."

Hoh Vitt had always been so good at telling stories, supernaturally good. He could make the most outrageous things real for his listeners. Friends or family made a game of throwing an idea at Hoh, and he would make up a story using it. Blood mixed with melange . . . a great Heighliner race across uncharted foldspace . . . the wrist-wrestling championship of the universe between two dwarf sisters who were the finalists . . . a talking slig.

"No, no more stories, Elto," the sergeant said in a fearful voice. "Rest now."

"You're a Master Jongleur, aren't you? You always said so."

"I don't talk about that much." Hoh Vitt turned away.

His ancestral family had once been proud members of an ancient school of storytelling on the planet Jongleur. Men and women from that world used to be the primary troubadours of the Imperium; they traveled between royal houses, telling stories and singing songs to entertain the great families. But House Jongleur fell into disgrace when a number of the itinerant storytellers were proven to be double agents in inter-House feuds, and no one trusted them any longer. When the nobles dropped their services, House Jongleur forfeited its status in the Landsraad, losing its fortunes. Guild Heighliners stopped going to their planet; the buildings and infrastructure, once highly advanced, fell into disrepair. Largely due to the Jongleur's demise, many entertainment innovations were developed, including holo projections, filmbooks, and shigawire recorders.

"*Now* is the time, Uncle. Take me back to Caladan. I don't want to be here."

"I can't do that, boy," he responded in a sad voice. "We're all stuck here."

"Make me *think* I'm there, like only you can do. I don't want to die in this hellish place."

With a piercing squeak, the two distrans bats returned. Confused and frustrated, they fluttered around the chamber while Scovich tried to recapture them. Even they had been unable to escape. . . .

Though the trapped men had held out little hope, the failure of the bats still made them groan in dismay. Uncle Hoh looked at them, then down to Elto as his expression hardened into grim determination.

"Quiet! All of you." He knelt beside his injured nephew. Hoh's eyes became glazed with tears . . . or something more. "The boy needs to hear what I have to say."

ELTO LAY BACK, letting his eyes fall half-closed as he readied himself for the words that would paint memory pictures on the insides of his eyelids. Sergeant Vitt sat rigid, taking deep breaths to compose himself, to center his uncanny skill and stoke the fires of imagination. To tell the type of story these men needed, a Master Jongleur must calm himself; he moved his hands and fingers in the ancient way, going through the motions he'd been taught by generations of storytellers, ritualistic preparations to make the story good and pure.

Fultz and Scovich shifted uneasily, and then moved closer, anxious to listen as well. Hoh Vitt looked at them with glazed eyes, barely seeing them, but his voice carried a gruff warning. "There is danger."

"Danger?" Fultz laughed and raised his grimy hands to the dim ceiling and surrounding rock walls. "Tell us something we don't know."

"Very well." Hoh was deeply saddened, wishing he hadn't pulled strings to get Elto assigned to the prestigious corps. The young man still thought of himself as an outsider, but ironically—by staying in the line of fire and destroying one of the artillery weapons—he had shown more courage than any of the proven soldiers.

Now Hoh Vitt felt a tremendous sense of impending loss. This wonderful young man, filled not only with his own hopes and dreams but also with those of his parents and uncle, was going to die without ever achieving his bright promise. He looked around, at the faces of the other soldiers, and seeing how they looked at him with such anticipation and admiration, he felt a moment of pride.

In the hinterlands of Jongleur, a hilly rural region where Hoh Vitt had grown up, dwelled a special type of storyteller. Even the natives suspected these "Master Jongleurs" of sorcery and dangerous ways. They could spin stories like deadly spiderwebs, and in order to protect their secrets, they allowed themselves to be shunned, hiding behind a cloak of mystique.

"Hurry, Uncle," Elto said, his voice quiet and thready.

With intensity in his words, Sergeant Vitt leaned closer. "You remember how my stories always start, don't you?" He touched the young man's pulse.

"You warn us not to believe too deeply, to always remember that it's only a story . . . or it could be dangerous. We could lose our minds."

"I'm saying that again to you, boy." He scanned the close-pressed faces around him. "And to everyone listening."

Scovich made a scoffing noise, but the others remained silent and intent. Perhaps they thought his warning was only part of the storytelling process, part of an illusion a Master Jongleur needed to create.

After a moment's hush, Hoh employed the enhanced memorization techniques of the Jongleurs, a method of transferring large amounts of information and retaining it for future generations. In this manner he brought to mind the planet Caladan, summoning it in every intricate detail.

"I used to have a wingboat," he said with a gentle smile, and then he began to describe sailing on the seas of Caladan. He used his voice like a paintbrush, selecting words carefully, like pigments precisely mixed by an artist. He spoke to Elto, but his story spread hypnotically, wrapping around the circle of listeners like the wispy smoke of a fire.

"You and your father went with me on week-long fishing trips. Oh, those days! Up at sunrise and casting nets until sunset, with the golden tone of the sun framing each day. I must say we enjoyed our time alone on the water even more than the fish we caught. The companionship, the adventures and hilarious mishaps."

And hidden in his words were subliminal signals: *Smell the salt water, the iodine of drying seaweed . . . Hear the whisper of waves, the splash of a distant fish too large to bring aboard whole.*

"At night, when we sat at anchor alone in the middle of the seaweed islands, we'd stay up late, the three of us, playing a fast game of tri-chess on a board made of flatpearls and abalone shells. The pieces themselves were carved from the translucent ivory tusks of South Caladan walruses. Do you remember?"

"Yes, Uncle. I remember."

All the men murmured their agreement; the Jongleur's haunting words were as real to them as to the young man who had actually experienced the memories.

*Listen to the hypnotic, throbbing songs of unseen murmons hiding in a fog bank that ripples across the calm waters.*

The shroud of pain grew fuzzy around Elto, and he could feel himself going to that other place and time, being carried away from this hellish place. The parched, dusty air at first smelled dank, then cool and moist. As he closed his eyes, he could sense the loving touch of Caladan breezes on his cheek. He smelled the mists of his native world, spring rain on his face, sea waves lapping at his feet as he stood on the rocky beach below the Atreides castle.

"When you were young, you would splash in the water, laughing and swimming naked with your friends. Do you remember?"

"I . . ." And Elto felt his voice merge with the others, becoming one with them. "We remember," the men mumbled reverently. All around them the air had grown close and stifling, most of the oxygen used up.

Another one of the glowglobes died. But the men didn't know this. They were anesthetized from their pain.

*See the wingboat cruising like a razorfin under dazzling sunlight, then through a warm squall under cloudy skies.*

"I used to body surf in the waves," Elto said with a faint smile of wonder.

Fultz coughed, then added his own reminiscences. "I spent a summer on a small farm overlooking the sea, where we harvested paradan melons. Have you ever had one fresh out of the water? Sweetest fruit in the universe."

Even Deegan, still somewhat dazed, leaned forward. "I saw an elecran once, late at night and far away—oh, they're rare, but they do exist. It's more than just a sailor's story. Looked like an electrical storm on the water, but alive. Luckily, the monster never came close." Though the gunner had been hysterical not long before, his words held such an awed solemnity that no one thought to disbelieve him.

*Swim through the water; feel its caress on your body. Imagine being totally wet, immersed in the sea. The waves surround you, holding and protecting you like a mother's arms. . . .*

The two distrans bats, still loose from the signalman's cages, had clung to the ceiling for hours, but now they swayed and dropped to the floor. All the air was disappearing in their tomb.

Elto remembered the old days in Cala City, the stories his uncle used to tell to an entranced audience of his family. At several points in each of those tales, Uncle Hoh would force himself to break away. He had always taken great care to remind his listeners that it was *only a story.*

This time, however, Hoh Vitt took no breaks.

Realizing this, Elto felt a moment of fear, like a dreamer unable to awaken from a nightmare. But then he allowed himself to succumb. Though he could barely breathe, he forced himself to say, "I'm going into the water . . . I'm diving . . . I'm going deeper . . ."

Then all the trapped soldiers could hear the waves, smell the water, and remember the whisper of Caladan seas. . . .

The whisper became a roar.

IN THE VELVET shadows of a crisp night on Dune, Fremen scavengers dropped over the ridge of the Shield Wall into the rubble. Stillsuits softened their silhouettes, allowing them to vanish like beetles into crevices.

Below, most of the fires in Arrakeen had been put out, but the damage remained untended. The new Harkonnen rulers had returned to their traditional seat of government in Carthag; they would leave the scarred Atreides city as a blackened wound for a few months . . . as a reminder to the people.

The feud between House Atreides and House Harkonnen meant nothing to the Fremen—the noble families were all unwelcome interlopers on their sacred desert planet, which the Fremen had claimed as their own thousands of years earlier, after the Wandering. For millennia these people had carried the wisdom of their ancestors, including an ancient Terran saying about each cloud having a silver lining. The Fremen would use the bloodshed of these royal houses to their own advantage: the deathstills back at the sietch would drink deeply from the casualties of war.

Harkonnen patrols swept the area, but the soldiers cared little for the bands of furtive Fremen, pursuing and killing them only out of sport rather than in a focused program of genocide. The Harkonnens paid no heed to the Atreides trapped in the Shield Wall either, thinking none of them could have survived; so they left the bodies trapped in the rubble.

From the Fremen perspective, the Harkonnens did not value their resources.

Working together, using bare callused hands and metal digging tools, the scavengers began their excavation, opening a narrow tunnel between the rocks. Only a few dim glowglobes hovered close to the diggers, providing faint light.

Through soundings and careful observations on the night of the attack, the Fremen knew where the victims would be. They had uncovered a dozen already, as well as a precious cache of supplies, but now they were after something much more valuable, the tomb of an entire detachment of Atreides soldiers. The desert men toiled for hours, sweating into the absorbent layers of their stillsuits, taking only a few sipped drops of recovered moisture. Many water rings would be earned for the moisture recovered from these corpses, making these Fremen scavengers wealthy.

When they broke into the cave enclosure, though, they stepped into a clammy stone coffin filled with the redolence of death. Some of the Fremen cried out or muttered superstitious prayers to Shai-Hulud, but others probed forward, increasing the light from the glowglobes now that they were out of sight of the nighttime patrols.

The Atreides soldiers all lay dead together, as if struck down in a strange suicide ceremony. One man sat in the center of their group, and when the Fremen leader moved him, his body fell to one side and a gush of water spewed out of his mouth. The Fremen tasted it. Salt water.

The scavengers backed away, even more frightened now.

Carefully, two young men inspected the bodies, finding that the uniforms of the Atreides were warm and wet, stinking of mildew and damp rot. Their dead eyes were open wide and staring, but with contentment instead of the expected horror, as if they had shared a religious experience. All of the dead Atreides soldiers had clammy skin . . . and something even more peculiar, revealed when the Fremen cut them open.

The lungs of these dead men were entirely filled with water.

The Fremen fled, leaving their spoils behind, and resealed the cave. Thereafter, it became a forbidden place of legend, drawing wonder from anyone hearing the story as it was passed on by Fremen from generation to generation.

Somehow, sealed inside a lightless cave in the driest desert, all of the Atreides soldiers had *drowned*. . . .

# HUNTING HARKONNENS
## A *Tale of the Butlerian Jihad*

〜〽〜

The Harkonnen space yacht left the family-held industries on Hagal and crossed the interstellar gulf toward Salusa Secundus. The streamlined vessel flew silently, in contrast to the fusillade of angry shouts inside the cockpit.

Stern, hard-line Ulf Harkonnen piloted the yacht, concentrating on the hazards of space and the constant threat of thinking machines, though he kept lecturing his twenty-one-year-old son, Piers. Ulf's wife, Katarina, too gentle a soul to be worthy of the Harkonnen name, asserted that the quarrel had gone on long enough. "Further criticism and shouting will serve no purpose, Ulf."

Vehemently, the elder Harkonnen disagreed.

Piers sat fuming, unrepentant; he was not cut out for the cutthroat practices his noble family expected, no matter how much his father tried to bully him into them. He knew Ulf would browbeat and humiliate him all the way home. The gruff older man refused to consider that his son's ideas for more humane methods might actually be more efficient than the inflexible, domineering ways.

Clutching the ship controls with a death grip, Ulf growled at his son, "*Thinking machines* are efficient. Humans, especially riffraff like our slaves on Hagal, are meant to be used. I doubt you'll ever get that through your skull." He shook his large, squarish head. "Sometimes, Piers, I think I should clean up the gene pool by eliminating you."

"Then why don't you?" Piers snapped, defiant. His father believed in forceful decisions, every question with a black-or-white answer, and that belittling his son would drive him to do better.

"I can't, because your brother, Xavier, is too young to be the Harkonnen heir, so you're the only choice I have . . . for the time being. I keep hoping you'll understand your responsibility to our family. You're a noble, meant to command, not to show the workers how soft you can be."

Katarina pleaded, "Ulf, you may not agree with the changes Piers made on Hagal, but at least he thought it through and was trying a new process. Given time, it might have led to improved productivity."

"And meanwhile the Harkonnen family goes bankrupt?" Ulf held a thick finger toward his son as if it were a weapon. "Piers, those people took terrible advantage of you, and you're lucky I arrived in time to stop the damage. When I provide you with detailed instructions on how our family holdings are to be run, I do not expect you to come up with a 'better' idea."

"Is your mind so fossilized that you can't accept new ideas?" Piers asked.

"Your instincts are faulty, and you have a very naïve view of human nature." Ulf shook his head, growling in disappointment. "He takes after you, Katarina—that's his main problem." Like his mother, Piers had a narrow face, full lips, and a delicate expression . . . quite different from Ulf's shaggy gray hair framing a blunt-featured face. "You would have been a better poet than a Harkonnen."

That was meant to be a grave insult, but Piers secretly agreed. The young man had always enjoyed reading histories of the Old Empire, days of decadence and ennui before the thinking machines had conquered many civilized solar systems. Piers would have fit into those times well as a writer, a storyteller.

"I gave you an opportunity, son, hoping that I could depend on you. But I have my answer." The elder Harkonnen stood, clenching his large, callused fists. "This whole trip has been a waste."

Katarina caressed her husband's broad back, trying to calm him. "Ulf, we're passing near the Caladan system. You talked about stopping there to investigate the possibility of new holdings . . . maybe fishing operations?"

Ulf hunched his shoulders. "All right, we'll divert to Caladan and take a look." He snapped his head up. "But in the meantime, I want this disgrace of a son sealed in the lifepod chamber. It's the closest thing to a brig onboard. He needs to learn his lesson, take his responsibilities seriously, or he will never be a true Harkonnen."

AS HE SULKED inside his improvised cell, with its cream-colored walls and silver instrument panels, Piers stared out the small porthole. He hated arguments with his stubborn father. The rigid old ways of the Harkonnen family were not always best. Instead of imposing tough conditions and harsh punishments, why not try treating workers with respect?

*Workers.* He remembered how his father had reacted to the word. "Next you'll want to call them employees. They are *slaves!*" Ulf had thundered as they stood in the overseer's office back on Hagal. "They have no rights."

"But they deserve rights," Piers responded. "They're human beings, not machines."

Ulf had barely contained his violence. "Perhaps I should beat you the way my father beat me, pounding contrition and responsibility into you. This isn't a game. You're leaving now, boy. Get on the ship."

Like a scolded child, Piers had done as he was commanded. . . .

He wished he could stand toe to toe with his father, just once. Every time he tried, though, Ulf made him feel that he had let the family down, as if he were a shirker who would waste their hard-won fortunes.

His father had trusted him to manage the family holdings on Hagal, grooming him as the next head of the Harkonnen businesses. This assignment had been an important step for Piers, with complete authority over the sheet diamond operations. A chance, a test. The implicit understanding was that he would operate the mines as they had always been run.

Harkonnens held the mining rights to all sheet diamonds on sparsely populated Hagal. The largest mine filled an entire canyon. Piers recalled how sunlight played off the glassy cliffs, dancing on the prismatic surfaces. He had never seen anything so beautiful.

The cliff faces were diamond sheets with blue-green quartz marking the perimeters like irregular picture frames. Human-operated mining machines crawled along the cliffs like fat, silver insects: no artificial intelligence, and therefore considered safe. History had shown that even the most innocuous types of AI could ultimately turn against humans. Entire star systems were now under the control of diabolically smart machines, and in those dark sectors of the universe, human slaves followed the commands of mechanized masters.

At optimal spots on the shimmering cliffs, the mining machines would lock onto the surface with suction devices and separate the diamond material with sound waves at natural points of fissure. Holding diamond sheets in their grasp, the dumb machines would make their way back down the cliff to loading areas.

It was an efficient process, but sometimes the sonic cutting procedure shattered the diamond sheets. Though once Piers gave the slaves a stake in the profits, such mishaps occurred much less frequently, as if they took greater care when they received a vested interest.

Overseeing the Hagal operation, Piers had come up with the idea of letting the captive gangs work without typical Harkonnen regulations and close oversight. While some slaves accepted the incentive program, a number of problems did surface. With reduced supervision, some slaves ran away; others were disorganized or lazy, just waiting for someone to tell them what to do. Initially, productivity dropped, but he was sure the output would eventually meet, and even exceed, previous levels.

Before that could happen, though, his father had made an unannounced visit to Hagal. And Ulf Harkonnen wasn't interested in creative ideas or humanitarian improvements if profits were down. . . .

His parents had been forced to leave their younger son, Xavier, on Salusa with a pleasant old-school couple. "I shudder to think how the boy will turn out if *they* raise him. Emil and Lucille Tantor don't know how to be strict."

Eavesdropping, Piers knew why his manipulative father had left his little brother with the Tantors. Since the aging couple was childless, wily Ulf was working his way into their good graces. He hoped the Tantors might eventually leave their estate to their dear "godson" Xavier.

Piers hated the way his father used people, whether they were slaves, other nobles, or members of his own family. It was disgusting. But now, trapped inside the cramped lifepod chamber, he could do nothing about it.

PROGRAMMING MADE THE thinking machines relentless and determined, but only the cruelty of a human mind could generate enough ruthless hatred to feed a war of extermination for a thousand years.

Though they were kept in reluctant thrall by the pervasive computer mind Omnius, the cymeks—hybrid machines with human minds—often bided their time by hunting between the stars. They would capture feral humans and bring them back to slavery on the Synchronized Worlds, or just kill them for sport. . . .

The leader of the cymeks, a general who had taken the imposing name of Agamemnon, had once led the group of tyrants that conquered the decaying Old Empire. As implacable soldiers in the cause, the tyrants had reprogrammed the subservient robots and computers to give them a thirst for conquest. When his mortal human body grew old and weak, Agamemnon had undergone a surgical process that removed his brain and implanted it within a preservation canister that he could install into various mechanical bodies.

Agamemnon and his fellow tyrants had intended to rule for centuries . . . but then the artificially aggressive computers stepped into power when they saw the chance, exploiting the tyrants' lack of diligence. The Omnius network then ruled the remnants of the Old Empire, subjugating the cymek tyrants along with the rest of already-downtrodden humanity.

For centuries, Agamemnon and his fellow conquerors had been forced to serve the computer evermind, with no chance of regaining their own rule. Their greatest source of amusement was in tracking down stray humans who had managed to maintain their independence from machine domination. Still, the cymek general found it a most unsatisfactory venting of his frustrations.

His brain canister had been installed inside a fast scout vessel that patrolled areas known to be inhabited by League humans. Six cymeks accompanied the general as their ships skirted the edge of a small solar system. They found little of interest, only one human-compatible world composed of mostly water.

Then Agamemnon's long-range sensors spotted another vessel. A *human* vessel.

He increased resolution and pointed out the target to his companions. Triangulating with their combined detection abilities, Agamemnon discerned that the lone ship was a small space yacht, its sophisticated configuration and style implying that its passengers were important members of the League, rich merchants . . . perhaps even smug nobles, the most gratifying victims of all.

"Just what we've been waiting for," said Agamemnon.

The cymek ships adjusted course and accelerated. Connected through thoughtrodes, Agamemnon's brain flew his ship-body as if it were a large bird of prey, zeroing in on his helpless target. He also had a terrestrial walker stored aboard, a warrior form that could be used for planetary combat.

The first cymek shots took the League vessel completely by surprise. The doomed human pilot barely had time to take evasive maneuvers. Kinetic projectiles scraped the hull, pounding one of the engines, but the ship's defensive armor protected it against severe damage. Cymek ships swept past, strafing again with explosive projectiles, and the human yacht reeled, intact but disoriented.

"Careful, boys," Agamemnon said. "We don't want to destroy the prize."

Out on the outskirts of League space, far from the Synchronized Worlds, the feral humans obviously hadn't expected to encounter enemy predators, and the captain of this vessel had been particularly inattentive. Defeating him would be almost embarrassing. His cymek hunters would hope for a better challenge, a more entertaining pursuit . . .

The human pilot got his damaged engine back on line and increased speed down into the isolated system, fleeing toward the water world. In his wake, the human launched a flurry of intensely bright explosive shells, which caused little physical damage, but sent pulses of confusing static through the machine sensors of the cymek ships. Agamemnon's cymek followers transmitted a series of imaginative curses. Surprisingly, the human victim responded in a gruff, defiant voice with equal venom and vigor.

Agamemnon chuckled to himself and sent a thought-command. This would be more fun. His attack ship burst forward like a wild and energetic horse, part of his imaginary body. "Give chase!" The cymeks, enjoying the game, swooped after the hapless human vessel.

The doomed pilot flew standard maneuvers to evade the pursuers. Agamemnon held back, trying to determine if the human was truly so inexperienced or just lulling the cymeks into an unwarranted sense of ease.

They plummeted toward the peaceful blue world—Caladan, according to the onboard database. The world reminded him of the blue irises his human eyes once had. . . . It had been so many centuries, the cymek general could recall few details of his original physical appearance.

Agamemnon could have transmitted an ultimatum to the pilot, but humans and cymeks knew the stakes in their long-simmering war. The space yacht opened fire, a few pathetically weak blasts designed for shoving troublesome meteoroids out of the way rather than defending against overt military action. If this was a nobleman's ship, it should have much more serious offensive and defensive weapons. The cymeks laughed and closed in, perceiving no threat.

As soon as they approached, though, the desperate human pilot launched another flurry of explosives, apparently the same as the gnat-bite bombs he had launched previously, but Agamemnon detected slight fluctuations. "Caution, I suspect—"

Four proximity mines, each a space charge ten times as powerful as the first artillery, detonated with huge shock waves. Two of the cymek hunters suffered external damage; one was completely destroyed.

Agamemnon lost his patience. "Back off! Engage ship defenses!"

But the yacht pilot fired no more explosives. With one of the surviving cymeks moving only sluggishly, the human could easily have taken him out. Since he did not, the human prey must have no further weapons available. Or was it another trick?

"Don't underestimate the vermin."

Agamemnon had hoped to take the feral humans captive, delivering them to Omnius for experiments or analysis, since "wild" specimens were considered different from those raised for generations in captivity. But, angry at the pointless loss of one of his overeager companions, the general decided it was just too much trouble.

"Vaporize that ship," he transmitted to his five remaining followers. Without waiting for the other cymeks to join him, Agamemnon opened fire.

INSIDE THE LIFEPOD, Piers could only watch in horror and wait to die.

The enemy cymeks pounded them again. In the cockpit, his father shouted curses, and his mother did her best at the weapons station. Their eyes betrayed no fear, only showed strong determination. Harkonnens did not die easily.

Ulf had insisted on installing the best armor and defensive systems available, always suspicious, always ready to fight against any threat. But this lone yacht could not withstand a concerted attack from seven fully armed and aggressive cymek marauders.

Sealed inside the dim compartment, Piers could do nothing to help. He watched the attacking machines through the porthole, sure his family could not hold out long. Even his father, who refused to bow to defeat, looked as if he had no tricks remaining to him.

Sensing the imminent kill, the cymeks streaked closer. Piers heard repeated thumps reverberating in the vessel. Through the hatch porthole, Piers saw his mother and father gesturing desperately at one another.

Another cymek blast finally breached the protective plates and damaged the yacht's engines as the vessel careened toward the not-close-enough planet with broad blue seas and white lacings of cloud. Sparks flew on the bridge, and the wounded ship began to tumble.

Ulf Harkonnen shouted something at his wife, then lurched toward the lifepod, trying to keep his balance. Katarina called after him. Piers couldn't figure out what they were arguing about; the ship was doomed.

Cymek weapons fire rocked the vessel with a dull concussion, sending Ulf skidding across the deck. Even the augmented hull armor could not withstand much more. The elder Harkonnen struggled to his feet at the lifepod hatch, and Piers suddenly realized that his father wanted to unlock the chamber and get both of them inside with their son.

Piers read his mother's lips as she shouted, "No time!"

The lifepod's instrument panel flashed and began running through test cycles. Piers hammered on the hatch, but they had sealed him inside. He couldn't get out to help them.

While Ulf tried frantically to work the hatch controls, Katarina raced for the panel on the wall and slapped the activation switch. While Ulf turned to his wife in astonishment and dismay, Katarina mouthed a desperate farewell to her son.

With a lurch, the lifepod shot into space, away from the doomed space yacht.

Acceleration threw Piers to the deck, but he scrambled to his knees, to the observation port. Behind him, as the lifepod tumbled recklessly through space, the cymek marauders opened fire again and again, six angry thinking machines combining their destructive power.

The Harkonnen ship erupted in a sequence of explosions into a dazzling fireball, which dissipated into the cluttered vacuum . . . snuffed out along with the lives of his parents.

Like a cannonball, the lifepod tore into the atmosphere of Caladan, spraying red sparks of reentry as it zoomed toward the blue oceans on the sunlit side of the planet.

Piers struggled with the crude emergency controls in an effort to maneuver, but the small ship didn't respond, as if it were a machine rebelling against its human master. At this rate of speed, he couldn't possibly survive.

The young Harkonnen heir took an agonized breath and tapped pressure pads to alter the thruster pattern. He had little experience in piloting, though his father had insisted that he learn; previously, the skill had not been a priority for Piers, but now he had to figure out the systems without delay.

Looking back, he saw he was being pursued by one of the cymek fighter ships. The spray of reentry sparks increased, like iron filings from a grinding stone. The pursuer's exploding projectiles rocked the atmosphere around him without making direct hits.

Piers sped low over an isolated landmass toward a snowy mountain ridge, with the vicious cymek on his tail, still shooting. Sparkling glaciers girdled the jagged peaks. One of the enemy's kinetic projectiles hit a high ridge, shattering ice and rock. Piers closed his eyes and boldly—without a choice—flew through the debris, heard it pummeling the lifepod. And he barely survived.

Just after he scraped over the ridge, he heard a tremendous explosion and saw the sky behind him light up in a flash of bright orange. The mechanical pursuer had gone out of control. Destroyed, just like his parents and their spacecraft. . . .

But Piers knew there were other enemies, and probably not far away.

⌘

AGAMEMNON AND HIS cymeks clustered around the space yacht's wreckage in unstable orbit, while mapping the trajectory of the single ejected lifepod. They marked where it crossed the atmosphere, how fast it descended, and where it would probably land. The general was in no hurry—after all, where could the lone survivor go on this primitive world?

Without orders, though, the one cymek damaged by proximity mines shot after the lifepod, hungry for revenge. "General Agamemnon, I intend to make this kill on my own." Angrily, the cymek leader paused, then agreed. "Go, you get the first shot. But the rest of us won't wait for long." The cymek leader held the rest of them back until he could finish his analysis.

Agamemnon played the distress signal the noble pilot had transmitted shortly before his destruction. The words were encoded, but not with a very sophisticated cipher; the cymek's onboard AI systems translated it easily. "This is Lord Ulf Harkonnen, en route from our holdings at Hagal. We are under attack by thinking machines. There is not much chance we will survive."

*Such amazing powers of prediction.* Agamemnon assumed the survivor aboard the lifepod must also be a member of the noble family, if not the lord himself.

A thousand years ago, when Agamemnon and his nineteen co-conspirators had overthrown the Old Empire, a group of outlying planets had banded together to form the League of Nobles. They had defended themselves against the tyrants, maintaining their defense against Omnius and his thinking machines. Computers did not hold grudges or gain vengeance . . . but the cymeks had human minds and human emotions.

If the survivor in the lifepod down on Caladan was a member of the defiant League of Nobles, the cymek general wanted to participate personally in his interrogation, torture, and ultimate execution.

Within minutes, however, he received a last-second transmission just before the cymek pursuer crashed on the surface.

"A foolish mission. Next time I want it done right," Agamemnon said. "Go; find him before he can hide in the wilderness. I give the hunt to the four of you—and a challenge. A reward to the cymek who finds and kills the prey first."

The other cymek ships streaked away from the debris field, heading like hot bullets into the cloudy skies. The human escapee, unarmed in his barely maneuverable lifepod, certainly would not last long.

⌒⌒

ABRUPTLY THE LIFEPOD shuddered, and a warning siren sounded. Digital and crystal instruments sparked on the panel. Piers tried to interpret them, adjusting the clumsy controls of the careening vessel, then looked up through the porthole to see brown-and-white slopes ahead, bleak frozen hillsides with patches of snow, dark forests. In the last instant, he pulled up, just enough—

The lifepod scraped tall, dark-needled trees and crashed into high tundra covered by only a thin blanket of snow. The impact bounced the pod back into the air, spinning it around for a second plunge into the patchy forest.

In his energy harness, Piers rolled and shouted, trying to survive but expecting the worst. Cushioning bubblefoam squirted all around him just before the first impact, padding his body from the worst injuries. Then the pod crashed again, ripping up snow and frozen dirt. The pod finally came to rest, groaning and hissing.

The bubblefoam dissolved, and Piers picked himself up and wiped the fizzing slime from his clothes and hands and hair. He was too shaken to feel pain and couldn't take the time to evaluate his injuries.

He knew his parents were dead, their ship destroyed. He hoped his blurred vision was from blood in his eyes, not tears. He was a Harkonnen, after all. His father would have struck him across the cheek for showing cowardly emotion. Ulf had managed to damage the enemy in a fruitless attack, but there were still more cymeks up there. No doubt they would come hunting for him.

Piers fought down panic, turned it into a hard, instant assessment of his situation. If he had any hope of surviving, circumstances forced him to respond with decisiveness, even ruthlessness—the Harkonnen way. And he wouldn't have much time.

The lifepod contained a few survival supplies, but he couldn't stay here. The cymeks would zero in on the vessel and come to finish the job. Once he ran, he would have no chance to return.

Piers grabbed a medical kit and all the ration packs he could carry, stuffing them into a flexible sack. He popped the lifepod's hatch and crawled out, smelling the smoke and hearing the crackle of a few gasping fires ignited by the heat of impact. He took a deep breath of cold, biting air; then, closing the hatch behind him, he staggered away from the smoking pod, crunching through slushy snow into the meager shelter of dark conifers. He wanted to get as far away as possible before pausing to consider his next step.

In a situation like this, his father would have been concerned about the family holdings, the Hagal mines. With Piers and his parents gone, who would run the business and keep the Harkonnen family strong? Right now, though, the young man was more worried for his own survival. He had never fit in with family business philosophies anyway.

Hearing a high-pitched roar, he gazed into the sky and saw four flaming white trails coming toward him like targeted munitions. Cymek landers. Hunters. The machines with human minds would track him down in the desolate wilderness.

As the danger suddenly came closer to home, Piers saw he was leaving deep tracks in the snow. Blood dripped from a nasty cut on his left wrist; more scarlet splashed from another injury on his forehead. He might as well be leaving a roadmap for the enemy to follow.

His father had said it in a stern, impatient voice, but the lesson was valuable nevertheless: *Be aware of all facets of a situation. Just because something is quiet does not mean it isn't dangerous. Do not trust your safety at any moment.*

Under the trees, listening to the roar as cymeks converged over his pod's crash-down coordinates, Piers slathered wound sealant on his injuries to stop the bleeding. *A moment's hurry can cause far more damage than a moment's delay to plan ahead.*

He abruptly changed direction, selecting a clear area where trees had sheltered the ground from the snow and rocks. He moved over the rocky surface in a deliberately chaotic course, hoping to throw off pursuit. He had no weapons, no knowledge of the terrain . . . and no intention of giving up.

Piers climbed higher up the sloping ground, and the snow grew thicker where the trees became sparse. When he reached a clearing, he caught his breath and looked back to see that cymek landers had converged at his lifepod. Still not far enough away, and still without any place to run.

Watching in horrified fascination, Piers saw mobile, resilient walker-forms emerge from the landed ships: adaptable mechanical bodies to carry cymek brain canisters across a variety of environments. Like angry crabs, the cymeks crawled over the sealed wreckage, using cutter claws and white-hot flamers to tear open the hull. When they found no one inside, they literally ripped the lifepod apart.

The walker-forms stalked around the pod, their optic threads gleaming with a variety of sensors. They scanned his footprints in the snow, moved to where their prey had paused to apply his medical pack. The cymek scanners could easily pick up his footprints in the dirt, thermal traces from his body heat, any number of clues. Unerringly, they set out across the bare ground toward where he had chosen to flee.

Chiding himself for the momentary panic that had made him leave such an obvious trail, Piers broke into a full run uphill, always looking for a place to hide, a weapon to use. He tried to ignore his hammering heart and his difficulty breathing in this cold, rugged environment of Caladan. He crashed into another thicket of the dark pines, always climbing. The slope became steeper, but because of the dense conifers, he couldn't see exactly where he was going or how close he might be to the top of a ridge.

He saw sticks, rocks, but nothing that would be an effective weapon against the mechanical monsters, no way to defend himself against the horrific machines. But Piers was, after all, a Harkonnen, and he would not give up. He would hurt them if he could. At the very least, he would offer them a fine chase.

Far to his rear, Piers heard crashing sounds, cracking trees, and imagined the cymeks clearing a path for their armored bodies. Judging from the smoke, they must be setting the forest on fire as well. Good— that way they would ruin the subtleties of his trail.

He kept running as the ground became rockier, with patches of ice spreading out on steep slopes. Precariously balanced snow clung to the mountain, ready to break loose at any moment. The trees at this elevation were bent and twisted, and he smelled a foul sulfurous taint in the air. At his feet he saw tiny bubbling puddles, suffused with yellow.

He furrowed his brows, pondering what this could mean. A thermal area. He had read about such places in his studies, esoteric geological anomalies that his father had forced him to learn before sending him to the mining operations on Hagal. This would be a region of volcanic activity with hot springs, geysers, fumaroles . . . a dangerous place, but one that offered opportunities against large opponents.

Piers ran toward the strong smell and the thickening mist, hoping this would give him an advantage. Cymeks did not use eyes like humans did, and their sensors were delicate, sensitive to different parts of the spectrum. In some cases, it gave the machine pursuers an incredible advantage. Here, though, with the wild plumes of heat and the rocky, sterile ground, the cymeks could not use their scanners to pick up residual traces from his footprints.

He raced through the misty, humid no-man's-land of rocks, snow patches, crusty bare earth, trying to throw off pursuit and seeking a place to hide, or defend. After hours of headlong flight, he collapsed on a warm boulder encrusted with orange lichen next to a hissing steam vent. More than anything else, he wanted to curl up under a rocky overhang next to one of the hot springs and remain hidden long enough to sleep for a few hours.

But cymeks did not require sleep. All of their life-support needs were taken care of with restorative electrafluid that kept them alive in their preservation canisters. They would keep pursuing him without pause.

Piers cracked open the food rations and gobbled two high-energy wafers, but he forced himself to set off again before he felt any resurgence of stamina. He had to press his advantage, not lose any ground.

Using his hands and feet now, Piers climbed steeper rocks. His fingers became powdery with yellow sulfur. He chose the steepest terrain, hoping it would prove difficult for the cymek walker bodies, but it also slowed him down.

The wind began to pick up, and Piers felt it against his face, alternating blasts of warm and cold. The mists cleared in patches, and suddenly the landscape was revealed around him. He looked back toward the last remnants of conifer forests, jutting rocks, and the bubbling mineral pools far beneath him.

Then he saw one of the cymek walker-forms, alone, stalking him. The other three must have separated, circling in their hunt, as if it were some sort of game. The mechanical body glistened silver in the sudden wash of afternoon light. Searching.

Piers knew he was exposed and unprotected on the rocky slope; he slammed his body tight against the rocks, hoping to remain unseen. But within seconds, the cymek had targeted its prey. The mechanical walker unleashed a fiery projectile, a splattering globule of flaming gel that missed Piers and struck the rock with clinging fire.

He scrambled up the rock, finding a new surge of energy. Scuttling rapidly, the cymek negotiated the rough slope, no longer wasting time on the tedious job of tracking the human.

Piers was trapped, with precipitous drop-offs and hot sulfurous pools on the left and right and a steep, smooth snowfield crusted with yellow contaminants above him. Once he got to the top of the ridge, perhaps he could throw rocks, somehow dislodge the cymek below him. He saw no other option.

Clawing with his hands and struggling for footholds, Piers worked his way up the slick glacier field. His shoes punched through the crust, sinking into cold snow up to his knees. His fingers soon grew numb and red. The frigid air seared his lungs, but he scrambled faster, farther. His domineering father would have sneered at him for worrying about mere physical discomfort in a time of such urgency. The glacier seemed to go on forever, though he could see the top, a sheer razor edge on the crest.

The machine hunters must have split up, and perhaps he had eluded the other three among the thermal plumes and crumbling rocks. Unable to find his tracks, they would be combing the ground . . . relentless, as machines always were. Only one of the cymeks had found him, apparently by accident.

Even so, a single monstrous enemy was more than enough to kill him, and this one would be in radio contact with the others. Already they must be coming this way. But this one seemed eager to kill Piers all by itself.

Below, the cymek reached the base of the ice field, scanned for a moment, and then scuttled up. Its long legs stabbed into the snow, climbing faster than any human could hope to run.

The cymek paused, rocked back, then launched another gelfire projectile. Piers burrowed into the snow, and the hot explosive ripped a crater barely an arm's length away from him. The violent impact caused the steep and precarious snowfield to tremble and shift. Around him, the crust began to break apart like a peeling scab. Taking a chance, he kicked at one of the hard slabs of packed snow, hoping to send it tumbling down to strike his enemy, but the frozen surface jammed tight, squeaking and groaning, then falling silent. With a deep breath, he climbed upward again.

As the cymek closed the gap, Piers noticed a rocky outcropping that protruded from the snow. He would scramble up there and make his stand. Maybe he could throw boulders at the machine, though he had no illusions about how effective that would be.

*Only a fool leaves himself without options*, Ulf Harkonnen would have said.

Piers grumbled at the memory. "At least I survived longer than you did, Father."

Then, to his astonishment, at the crest of the glacier he saw a group of figures that looked . . . *human*! He counted dozens of people who stood at the top of the snowfield. They shouted incomprehensible curses at the cymek.

The silhouetted strangers lifted large cylinders—weapons of some sort?—and began to beat on them. Loud booming sounds echoed across the mountains like thunderclaps, explosions. *Drums.*

The strangers pounded on their noisemakers. They had no apparent rhythm at first, but then the pulses combined into a resonance, an echoing boom that set the whole snowfield trembling.

Cracks widened atop the ice, and the glacier began to shift. The massive cymek walker struggled for purchase as the frozen ground began to slide.

Seeing what was about to happen, Piers dove for the rock outcropping, sheltering himself in a pocket walled off by thick stone on each side. He held on just as the snow broke free with a hissing, tumbling roar.

The avalanche struck the cymek like a white tidal wave, bowling over the walker-form, knocking and battering it against other rocks. As the enemy machine crashed down the slope, Piers closed his eyes and waited for the rumbling roar to reach its crescendo and then taper off.

When he finally emerged, amazed to be alive, the air itself sparkled with ice crystals thrown into the sky. While the snowpack undoubtedly remained unstable, the strange people charged pell-mell down the broken snow and ice, yelling excitedly like hunters who had just bagged an impressive quarry.

Still unable to believe what he was seeing, Piers stood atop the boulders. And then he spotted the twitching and battered cymek far down the slope, toppled onto its back. The avalanche had struck it with a destructive force equivalent to a heavy weapon. The cymek had been bashed, dented, and twisted, but still its mechanical limbs attempted to haul the walker-form upright.

Although the primitive humans wore drab survival garb made of scavenged materials, they carried sophisticated tools, more than just spears or clubs. Four young natives—scouts?—hurried to the edge of the broken ice field and the trees and they kept watch, wary of other cymeks.

The remaining humans fell like hyenas upon the crippled cymek, wielding cutters and grappling wrenches. Was the mechanical hunter calling for help from its three comrades? The natives quickly bashed the transmitter antennas on the walker body; then, with startling efficiency they dismantled the walker's struggling legs. The cymek weapon arm flickered in an attempt to launch another flaming projectile, but the Caladan primitives quickly disconnected the components.

From the cymek's speakerpatch came a volley of angry threats and curses, but the humans paid no attention, showing no fear. They worked diligently to disconnect the hydraulics, fiber cables, neurelectronics, setting each piece aside like valuable scrap material. They left the cymek's brain canister exposed, the traitorous human mind disembodied once again, though this time not by its own volition.

Numb, Piers looked at the oddly harmless-looking canister that held the cymek's mind. The natives did not destroy it immediately, but seemed to have other plans. They held it up like a trophy.

Full of questions, Piers made his way down the shifting surface of broken snow. The natives looked up at him as he approached, showing curiosity without threat. They spoke a gibberish language that he could not comprehend.

"Who are you?" Piers asked in standard Galach, hoping that someone here would understand him.

One of the men, a gaunt old fellow with a short reddish beard and lighter skin than his companions, gestured toward Piers in happy victory. He stood in front of Piers, pounded himself on the chest. "Tiddoc."

"Piers Harkonnen," he responded, then decided to simplify, "Piers."

"Good, Piers. Thank you," he said in recognizable Galach, but with a thick accent. Seeing the young man's surprise, Tiddoc spoke slowly, as if fishing the right words out of his memory. "Our tongue has Galach roots from the Zensunni Wanderers, who fled the League long ago. For years I worked in cities of the noblemen, performing menial tasks. I picked up words here and there."

Paralyzed and immobile, the captured enemy cymek continued to snarl insults through an integrated speakerpatch as the Caladan natives used two of the amputated walker legs as support rods, lashing the brain canister so that it dangled between the poles like some captured wild beast. Two of the strongest-looking natives put the metal rods over their shoulders and began to march back up the slope. The other natives gathered up the components they could carry and climbed the rough mountainside.

"Come with us," Tiddoc said.

Piers had no option but to follow them.

AS PIERS FOLLOWED the rugged men uphill, one of his knees throbbed with each step, and his back stiffened until it burned. He had not yet had time to accept the deaths of his parents. He missed his mother, for her kind attentions, her intelligence. Katarina had saved his life, launching the lifepod before the cymeks could destroy the space yacht.

In a way, Piers even missed his father. Despite Ulf's gruffness, he had only wanted the best for his sons, harshly focused on his responsibilities for Harkonnen holdings. Advancing the family fortunes was always paramount. Now it seemed that his little brother, Xavier, was all that remained of the Harkonnen bloodline. Piers had little hope that he would ever get away from Caladan . . . but at least he had survived this long.

He limped up the steep slope, trying to keep pace with the agile natives. Inside its preservation canister, the evil cymek brain sloshed as the primitives carried it. Staticky shouts came from the canister's speakerpatch, first in standard Galach, then in other languages. Tiddoc and the natives seemed to find it amusing.

The natives paid little attention to the disembodied brain, except to glare at it and bare their teeth. The red-bearded old man was the most demonstrative. In addition to menacing facial expressions, he made threatening gestures with a cutting tool, swinging it close to the canister's sensors, which only served to agitate the captive brain more. Obviously they had encountered cymeks before and knew how to fight them.

But Piers was concerned about the other three mechanical hunters. They would not give up the pursuit—and once they found the avalanche site and the dismantled walker-form, the cymeks could track the natives here. Unless the captured one had not been able to signal for help before the avalanche had swept it away. Cymeks did not like to admit weakness.

Piers looked around for any fortifications the people had made. Ahead, overhanging ice formed a giant roof that sheltered a settlement. The primitives had made their camp in a large area melted out by thermal vents in the ground. Women and children bustled among rock huts, performing chores, pausing to look at the approaching party. The people wore thick clothing, boots, and hats lined with fur from unknown local animals. Piers heard the yelping of animals, saw furry white creatures near the dwellings.

Beyond the shelter of the overhang, steam roiled up through thick layers of ice and snow, accompanied by heat bubbles from mudpots and geysers. As Piers followed the tribe down narrow rock steps toward the settlement, he marveled at the stunning contrast of fire and ice, even as he cast constant worried glances over his shoulder to make sure he saw no sign of the other cymek hunters. Occasional droplets rained down from the frozen ceiling of the dome, slowly melting, but when Piers looked up at the blue ice overhead, he decided the glacier—and the settlement—had been here for a long time. . . .

When abrupt darkness fell like a curtain drawn in front of the sun, the native Caladan women used jagged pieces of wood to build a large fire on a rocky area at the center of the settlement. Scouts went out on patrol to keep watch for enemy machines while the rest of the tribe settled down to celebrate. The men brought hunks of fresh meat from other hunts and speared them on long metal spits over the fire.

They placed the captive cymek's brain canister off to one side, in the ice, and ignored it.

Speaking to one another in their guttural tongue, the natives sat on furs around the fire and passed the food around, sharing with their visitor. Piers found the meat too gamey for his liking, but he finished a large hunk, not wanting to insult his hosts. He was famished, and supplemented his meal with part of a ration bar he had salvaged from the lifepod; he offered the rest of the packaged food to his rescuers, and they eagerly accepted.

Still, the urgency gnawed at him. Even among so many other people, he did not feel safe, and he tried to convince the old leader that the danger had not gone away. "There are more cymeks, Tiddoc. I think they're hunting me."

"We already killed one," he said.

"But what about the others? They are still out there—"

"We will kill them, too. If they bother with you. Cymeks have little patience. Lose interest quickly. Are you so important to them? My people know that we are not." He patted Piers's wrist. "We have scouts. We have defenses."

Following the meal, Tiddoc and his people sat around the story fire, telling ancient parables and adventures in their native tongue. During the sharing, the tribesmen passed around gourds of a potent beverage. Wrapped in a fur to ward off the chill air, Piers drank, and felt warm in his belly. At intervals, the old man translated for Piers, relating tales of the downtrodden Zensunni who had fled the machine takeovers, as well as slavery in the League of Nobles.

A little tipsy, Piers defended the League and their continuing fight against the thinking machines, though he sympathized with the unpleasant plight of the Buddislamic slaves on Poritrin, Zanbar, and other League worlds. While Tiddoc struggled to translate, Piers told of epic battles against the evil Omnius and his aggressive robots and cymeks.

And, with a thick voice, he told how his own ship had been destroyed, his parents killed. . . .

THE ROAD TO DUNE

Tiddoc gestured to the cymek brain canister. "Come. The feasting is done. Now we finish our machine war. The people have been looking forward to this." He shouted something in his own language, and two men lifted the canister by its improvised poles. The cymek grumbled from its speakerpatch, but it had run out of effective curses.

Several women lit torches from the central fire and led the way up a path from the dripping glacier overhang. Full of good cheer, the natives marched away, carrying the impotent enemy brain. The cymek hurled threats in every language it could think of, but the primitives only laughed at it.

"What are you doing?" the cymek demanded. Controlling its last functional thoughtrodes, the disembodied brain twisted in its container. "Stop! We will crush you all!"

Piers followed them over a ridge and down a slope to where the air reeked of sulfur and the porous rock grew warm underfoot. Carrying the helpless cymek, the group paused at a steaming hole in the rock and stood chattering and laughing. They held the brain canister over the ominous opening.

Piers bent closer to the hole, curious, but Tiddoc yanked him away. The red-bearded elder wore an eerie smile in the torchlight.

A rumble sounded deep below, and with a preliminary spurt of hot spray, a geyser erupted, a scalding jet that parboiled the cymek's brain. The enemy's curses turned to shrieks, followed by babbling sounds and disjointed pain that trickled out of the damaged speaker-patch.

When the geyser subsided, the delirious cymek cried and gibbered. Moments later the geyser erupted again, and the speakerpatch unleashed hideous howls that sent shudders down Piers's spine.

Even though this monster had tried to kill him, had taken part in the murder of his parents, Piers could not tolerate hearing its misery anymore. When the boiling jet subsided again, he took a rock and smashed the speaker, disconnecting it.

But the natives continued to hold the agonized brain over the geyser hole, and when the scalding spray gushed out a third time, the cymek screamed in silence, until it was boiled alive in its electrafluid.

The natives then cracked the canister open on a rock and devoured the hot, cooked contents.

⤳≈⤵

THE ROCK HUT was warm and marginally comfortable, but Piers slept poorly, unable to put the horrific images out of his mind. When he finally dreamed, he saw himself strapped to poles while the natives held him over the geyser hole. He heard boiling water rushing toward him, and he awoke with a scream caught in his throat.

Outside, he heard only the howl of an animal, then silence.

Then mechanical sounds.

He stumbled to the entrance of the hut and peered outside into the cold, sulfur-smelling air. Now the furry guard animals howled. The primitives shouted and stirred in their encampment. The scouts had been watching.

In a slit of grayish, misty sky between the ground and the icy overhang Piers saw four aircraft approaching with insect-machine noises, their engines glowing in the predawn sky. *Cymeks!*

Tiddoc and the natives fled their stone huts, grabbing torches, weapons. Piers ran out, anxious to help. He had lost the other two cymek hunters in his flight the previous day, but the sophisticated thinking machines had combed the landscape with their scanners until they finally picked up his trail . . . which had led the monsters here.

The cymek ships landed in the nearby rock field and opened hatches, each one disgorging an armed walker body. The crablike warrior machines marched downslope with alarming speed. Ahead, the primitives scattered, hooting, waving torches, taunting the enemy.

One of the cymeks launched a rocket of gelfire, which exploded and collapsed part of the arched, glacier ceiling. Shards of ice tumbled down, smashing the evacuated stone huts.

Tiddoc and the villagers scampered out of the way as if it were a game, gesturing for Piers to follow as they hurried along the path they had taken the night before, onto the geyser field. In daylight Piers saw that it was a broad, gently sloped area of boiling mudpots and hot springs. Fumaroles and geysers belched repeatedly, filling the air with foul steam and heat plumes. Shouting, cursing, the people split up, following instinctive routes across the crusty ground. The natives' supposed panic was a strangely organized action, like a cat and mouse game. Were they luring the enemy? They seemed to have a plan, a hunt of their own.

Piers ran along with them, ducking as the four cymek walkers shot projectiles into the hissing thermal area. Their mechanical bodies plodded forward like heavy spiders on the uncertain ground. For sophisticated machines, their aim was terrible. The cymeks' optic threads and thermal sensors must be nearly blinded in the chaos of heat signatures.

Tiddoc hurled a spear, which clanked on the head turret of the largest cymek walker. It was an ineffective weapon, designed to distract and provoke the cymek, rather than damage the walker body. The leader ran ahead, hooting, luring the cymek onward.

Agitated, the largest machine-creature bellowed through a speaker-patch, "You cannot escape Agamemnon!" The other three cymeks scrambled along behind it.

Piers shuddered. All free humans knew the famous general of Omnius's army, one of the brutal original tyrants.

With a lucky shot, one of the enemy machines blasted a young man who danced too close to the weapon arm, and his twitching, burning body writhed on the ground. The Caladan natives, looking angry and vengeful, tightened their ranks and worked harder against the cymeks. They tossed homemade explosives that exploded with smoke and fire and a loud concussion, leaving scorch marks on the cymek bodies. The machines with human minds did not slow in their progress.

Light-footed, the primitives raced across the volcanically active area. The cymeks, oblivious to the trap, charged after their prey, smashing salty encrustations, pursuing the natives into the reeking mists. They shot more blobs of gelfire, fired explosive projectiles. Another daring man died, his chest blasted into a smoking crater.

Tiddoc and the natives kept hooting and shouting, defiant. Two of the smaller cymeks surged forward into a crater-pocked geyser field. The waving, taunting primitives stopped and turned, expectant.

The thin shell of hardened ground cracked, split. The two mechanical walker-forms tried to skitter backward, but the surface gave way beneath them, breaking apart. Both cymeks plunged through the dangerous ground and tumbled screaming into roiling sulfur cauldrons.

Piers joined Tiddoc and the other humans in their loud cheer, which was squelched when a third native, a long-haired young woman, was cut down by hot projectiles.

Unexpectedly, a furious geyser blast rocketed out of the ground next to a third cymek attacker, scalding the brain canister. Its thoughtrodes damaged, the mechanical behemoth veered away and stumbled around in confusion. The cymek fell to its articulated knees, the electrafluid in its stained brain canister glowing blue as it focused its mental energy.

Tiddoc tossed a small, homemade explosive onto the ground, like a crude grenade. The detonation caused no further damage to the armored walker, but the ground crust fractured. While the wounded mechanical enemy reeled, disoriented, the surface gave way. The third cymek joined the others in the molten mud.

Agamemnon kept advancing toward the retreating humans, as if scorning his incompetent underlings. The lead cymek stalked unwavering toward old Tiddoc. The red-bearded man and his companions threw their spears and more crude explosives, but the mechanical general did not flinch. Behind them and on the sides lay superheated soil, while the immense cymek blocked their only avenue of escape.

On impulse, Piers ran in front of the lead cymek, shouting to distract him. He snatched up a discarded spear and thumped it against one of the tall walker legs. "Agamemnon! You murdered my parents!"

To his surprise, the cymek general swiveled his head turret, and thermal sensors locked onto the upstart human's form. "A feisty one!" the monster said with considerable amusement. "You are the vermin we have been chasing."

"I am a Harkonnen nobleman!" Piers swung the spear like a cudgel at the brain canister. He struck the thick armor plaz with a blow hard enough to rattle his bones—but he left only a tiny nick on the protective canister.

The cymek bellowed a laugh. One of Agamemnon's clawed legs grabbed Piers, yanked away the spear. The young man felt the sharp claw tighten around his torso. He was dimly aware of Tiddoc howling—

Then suddenly the crust gave way beneath the heavy cymek walker. Frothing mud gushed upward, and Agamemnon tumbled into a boiling geyser pit, still clutching his human victim. The claw loosened, just barely, and Piers scrambled on top of the body, trying to shield himself from the heat, to grab the rough rock of the pit's edge. Superheated steam blasted upward, eradicating all signs of Piers and the last machine invader.

❦

ALIVE AND ANGRY, Agamemnon reinstalled himself in an intact spaceship lander and departed from the watery world. With his heavily protected walker body, he had clamped onto the edges of the fuming pit, endured the steam blasts without falling into the molten mud.

The verminous people rallied, hurled more explosives at him, and Agamemnon despised himself for being forced to retreat. With his hydraulics already damaged—and his foolish neo-cymeks all wiped out— his walker-form limped and scuttled back to the landed spacecraft, leaving the tribe behind. Systems onboard his ship reconfigured his brain canister to the controls; he discarded the ruined walker body, leaving it as scrap on the surface of cursed Caladan.

The only survivor of his cymek squad, Agamemnon left the unremarkable world behind. He would return to Earth, and the computer evermind Omnius, and make his report. At this point, he was at liberty to create whatever explanation he chose. Omnius would never suspect him of lying: Such things simply did not occur to the all-pervasive computer. But the cymek general had a human brain. . . .

As Agamemnon flew out into open space, he would have enough time to think of appropriate explanations and shift the blame. He would include a version of the events in his ever-growing memoirs recorded in the machine database.

Fortunately, the all-powerful and all-seeing evermind simply wanted information and an accurate recounting of all events. Making excuses was a purely human weakness.

ON THE LEAGUE capital world of Salusa Secundus, a young boy looked up at dark-skinned Emil Tantor, a wealthy and influential nobleman. They stood on the front lawn of the sprawling Tantor estate, with the tallest buildings of the city visible in the distance. It was early evening, with lights twinkling on in the palatial homes that dotted the hills.

Ulf Harkonnen's distress signal had finally been intercepted, and Emil Tantor had brought the boy the terrible news about his parents and brother. More casualties in the long-standing war against the thinking machines.

Young Xavier Harkonnen bowed his head, but refused to cry. The kindly nobleman touched his shoulder and spoke deep-throated, gentle words. "Will you have me, and Lucille, as your foster parents? I think it is what your father wanted when he left you in our care."

Xavier looked into his brown eyes, nodded.

"You'll grow into a fine young man," Tantor said, "one to make your brother and parents proud. We will do our best to raise you right, to teach you honor and responsibility. You will make the Harkonnen name shine in the annals of history."

Xavier gazed beyond his foster father up to the faint stars glimmering through the dusk. He could identify some of those stars, and knew which systems were controlled by Omnius and which were League worlds.

"I will also learn how to fight the thinking machines," he said. Emil Tantor squeezed his shoulder. "I will defeat them one day."

*It is my purpose in life.*

ON A DARK night in the bright snowfield and dark pines, the Caladan primitives sat on furs around a roaring fire. Keeping their oral tradition alive, they repeated the ancient legends and stories of recent battles. The elder Tiddoc sat beside the foreigner accepted among them, a hero with bright eyes and waxy, horribly scarred skin. A man who had fought single-handedly against a cymek monster and fallen into a scalding hot opening . . . but had crawled out alive, clinging to the battered cymek walker-form. Piers gestured with one hand; the other—burned and twisted into uselessness—hung limp against his chest. He spoke passionately in the ancient Buddislamic tongue, halting as he struggled for words and then continuing when Tiddoc helped him.

Caladan was his home now, and he would live the rest of his life with these people, in obscurity. No escape seemed possible from such a remote place, except through the stories he told. Piers kept his audience enthralled as he spoke of great battles against the thinking machines, while he also learned the Songs of the Long Trek, chronicles of the many generations of Zensunni Wanderings.

As his father had realized, Piers Harkonnen had always wanted to be a storyteller.

# WHIPPING MEK
## A Tale of the Butlerian Jihad

When the armored Jihad warship arrived, the population of Giedi Prime expected news of a great victory against the evil thinking machines. But with only a glance at the battle-scarred vessel, young Vergyl Tantor could tell that the defense of Peridot Colony had not gone at all as planned.

On the crowded fringe of Giedi City Spaceport, Vergyl rushed forward, pressing against the soldiers stuck there like himself: wide-eyed green recruits or veterans too old to be sent into battle against Omnius's combat robots. His heart hammered like an industrial piston in his chest.

He prayed that his adoptive brother, Xavier Harkonnen, was all right.

The damaged battleship heaved itself into the docking circle like a dying sea beast beached on a reef. The big engines hissed and groaned as they cooled from the hot descent through the atmosphere.

Vergyl stared at the blackened scars on the hull plates and tried to imagine the kinetic weapons and high-energy projectiles that combat robots had hurled at the brave jihadi defenders.

If only he had been out there himself, Vergyl could have helped in the fight. But Xavier—the commander of the battle group—always seemed to fight against his brother's eagerness with nearly as much persistence as he fought the machine enemy.

When the landing systems finished locking down, dozens of egress hatches opened on the lower hull. Middle-ranking commanders emerged, bellowing for assistance. All medically qualified personnel were called in from the city; others were shuttled from across the continents of Giedi Prime to help the wounded soldiers and rescued colonists.

Triage and assessment stations were set up on the spaceport grounds. Official military personnel were tended first, since they had pledged their lives to fight in the great struggle ignited by Serena Butler. Their crimson-and-green uniforms were stained and badly patched; they'd obviously had no chance to repair them during the many weeks of transit from Peridot Colony. Mercenary soldiers received second-priority treatment, along with the refugees from the colony.

Vergyl rushed in with the other ground-based soldiers to help, his large brown eyes flicking back and forth in search of answers. He needed to find someone who could tell him what had happened to Segundo Harkonnen. Worry scratched at Vergyl's mind while he worked. Perhaps everything was all right . . . but what if his big brother had been killed in a heroic rally? Or what if Xavier was injured, yet remained aboard the battered ship, refusing to accept help for himself until all of his personnel were tended to? Either scenario would have fit Xavier's personality.

For hours, Vergyl refused to slow down, unable to fully grasp what these jihadi fighters had been through. Sweating and exhausted, he worked himself into a trancelike stupor, following orders, helping the wounded, burned, and despairing refugees.

He heard muttered conversations that told of the onslaught that had wiped out the small colony. When the thinking machines had at-tempted to absorb the settlement into the Synchronized Worlds, the Army of the Jihad had sent its defenders there.

Peridot Colony had been but a skirmish, however, like so many oth-ers in the dozen years since Serena Butler had originally rallied all hu-mans to fight in her cause, after the thinking machines had murdered her young son, Manion. *Xavier's son.*

The ebb and flow of the Jihad had caused a great deal of damage to both sides, but neither fighting force had gained a clear upper hand. And though the thinking machines continued to build fresh combat robots, lost human lives could never be replaced. Serena gave passion-ate speeches to recruit new soldiers for her holy war. So many fighters had died that the Jihad no longer publicly revealed the cost. The strug-gle was everything.

Following the Honru Massacre seven years earlier, Vergyl had in-sisted on joining the Jihad military force himself. He considered it his duty as a human being, even without his connection to Xavier and the martyred child, Manion. At their estate on Salusa Secundus, his par-ents had tried to make the young man wait, since he was barely seven-teen, but Vergyl would hear none of it.

Returning to Salusa after a difficult skirmish, Xavier had surprised their parents by offering a waiver that would allow underage Vergyl to begin training in the Army. The young man had leaped at the oppor-tunity, not guessing that Xavier had his own plans. Overprotective, Se-gundo Harkonnen had seen to it that Vergyl received a safe, quiet assignment, stationed here on Giedi Prime where he could help with the rebuilding work—and where he would stay safe, far from any pitched battles against the robotic enemy.

Now Vergyl had been in Giedi City for years, rising minimally in rank to second decero in the Construction Brigade . . . never seeing any action. Meanwhile, Xavier Harkonnen's battleships went to planet after planet, protecting free humanity and destroying the mechanized legions of the computer evermind Omnius. . . .

Vergyl stopped counting all the bodies he'd moved. Perspiring in his dark green uniform, the young construction officer and a civilian man carried a makeshift stretcher, hauling a wounded mother who had been rescued from her devastated prefab home on Peridot Colony. Women and children from Giedi City hurried among the workers and wounded, offering water and food.

Finally, in the warm afternoon, a ragged cheer penetrated Vergyl's dazed focus, just as he set the stretcher down in the midst of a triage unit. Looking up, he drew a quick breath. At the warship's main entrance ramp, a proud military commander stepped forward into the sunshine of Giedi Prime.

Segundo Xavier Harkonnen wore a clean uniform with immaculate golden insignia. By careful design, he cut a dashing military figure, one that would inspire confidence and faith among his own troops as well as the civilians of Giedi City. Fear was the worst enemy the machines could bring against them. Xavier never offered any observer reason for uncertainty: Yes, brave humanity would eventually win this war.

Grinning, Vergyl let out a sigh as all his doubts evaporated. Of course Xavier had survived. This great man had led the strike force that liberated Giedi Prime from the enslavement of cymeks and thinking machines. Xavier had commanded the human forces in the atomic purification of Earth, the first great battle of Serena Butler's Jihad.

And the heroic officer would never stop until the thinking machines were defeated.

But as Vergyl watched his brother walk down the ramp, he noticed that his footsteps had a heavy, weary quality, and his familiar face looked shell-shocked. Not even a hint of a smile there, no gleam in his gray eyes. Just flat stoniness. How had the man gotten so old? Vergyl idolized him, needed to speak with him alone as a brother, so that he could learn the real story.

But in public, Segundo Harkonnen would never let anyone see his inner feelings. He was too good a leader for that.

Vergyl pushed his way through the throng, shouting and waving with the others, and finally Xavier recognized him in the sea of faces. His expression lit with joy, then crashed, as if weighed down by the burden of war memories and realizations. Vergyl and his fellow relief workers hurried up the ramp to surround the brave officer, and escorted him into the safety of Giedi City.

⟿❦⟿

ALONG WITH HIS surviving sub-commanders, Xavier Harkonnen spent hours dispensing reports and debriefing League officials, but he insisted on breaking away from these painful duties to spend a few hours with his brother.

He arrived at Vergyl's small home unrested, eyes bloodshot and haunted. When the two of them hugged, Xavier remained stiff for a moment before weakening and returning his dark-skinned brother's embrace. Despite the physical dissimilarities that marked their separate racial heritage, they knew that the bonds of love had nothing to do with bloodlines and everything to do with the loving family experiences they had shared in the household of Emil and Lucille Tantor. Taking him inside, Vergyl could sense the tremors Xavier was suppressing. He distracted Xavier by introducing him to his wife of two years, whom Xavier had never met.

Sheel was a young, dark-haired beauty not accustomed to receiving guests of such importance. She had not even traveled to Salusa Secundus to meet Vergyl's parents or to see the Tantor family estate. But she treated Xavier as her husband's welcome brother, instead of as a celebrity.

One of Aurelius Venport's merchant ships had arrived only a week before, carrying melange from Arrakis. Sheel had gone out this afternoon and spent a week's pay to get enough of the expensive spice to add to the fine, special dinner she prepared.

As they ate, their conversation remained subdued and casual, avoiding any mention of war news. Weary to the bone, Xavier barely seemed to notice the flavors of the meal, even the exotic melange. Sheel seemed disappointed, until Vergyl explained in a whisper that his brother had lost much of his sense of taste and smell during a cymek gas attack, which had also cost him his lungs. Although Xavier now breathed through a set of replacement organs provided by a Tlulaxa flesh merchant, his ability to taste or smell remained dulled.

Finally, as they drank spice-laced coffee, Vergyl could no longer withhold his questions. "Xavier, please tell me what happened at Peridot Colony. Was it a victory, or did the"—his voice caught—"did the machines defeat us?"

Xavier lifted his head, and gazed far away. "Grand Patriarch Iblis Ginjo says that there are no defeats. Only victories and . . . moral victories. This one fell into the latter category."

Sheel squeezed her husband's arm sharply, a wordless request that he withdraw the question. But Vergyl didn't interrupt, and Xavier continued, "Peridot Colony had been under attack for a week before our nearest battle group received the emergency distress call. Settlers were being obliterated. The thinking machines meant to crush the colony and establish a Synchronized World there, laying down their infrastructure and installing a new copy of the Omnius evermind."

Xavier sipped spice coffee while Vergyl put his elbows on the table, leaning close to listen with rapt attention.

"The Army of the Jihad had little presence in this area aside from my warship and a handful of troops. We had no choice but to respond, not wishing to lose another planet. I had a full shipload of mercenaries anyway."

"Any from Ginaz? Our best fighters?"

"Some. We arrived faster than the thinking machines expected, struck them swiftly and mercilessly, using everything we had. My soldiers attacked like madmen, and many of them fell. But a lot more thinking machines were destroyed. Unfortunately, most of the colony towns had already been trampled by the time we got there, the inhabitants murdered. Even so, our Army of the Jihad drove in—and by a holy miracle we pushed back the enemy forces." He drew a deep, convulsing breath, as if his replacement lungs were malfunctioning.

"Instead of simply cutting their losses and flying away, as combat robots usually do, this time they were programmed to follow a scorched-earth policy. They devastated everything in their wake. Where they had gone, not a crop, structure, or human survivor was left behind."

Sheel swallowed hard. "How terrible."

*"Terrible?"* Xavier mused, rolling the sound of the word on his tongue. "I cannot begin to describe what I saw. Not much was left of the colony we went to rescue. Over a quarter of my jihadis lost their lives, and half of the mercenaries."

Shaking his head sadly, he continued. "We scraped together the pathetic remnants of settlers who had fled far enough from the primary machine forces. I do not know—nor do I want to know—the actual number of survivors we rescued. Peridot Colony did not fall to the machines, but that world is no longer of any use to humans, either." He heaved a deep breath. "It seems to be the way of this Jihad."

"That is why we need to keep fighting." Vergyl lifted his chin. His bravery sounded tinny in his own ears. "Let me fight at your side against Omnius! Our army is in constant need of soldiers. It's time for me to get into the real battles in this war!"

Now Xavier Harkonnen seemed to awaken. Dismay flashed across his face. "You don't want that, Vergyl. *Not ever.*"

VERGYL SECURED AN assignment working aboard the Jihad warship as it underwent repairs for the better part of two weeks. If he couldn't fly off and fight on alien battlefields, at least he could be here recharging weapons, replacing damaged Holtzman shield systems, and strengthening armor plating.

While Vergyl diligently performed every task the team supervisors assigned to him, his eyes drank in details about how the ship's systems functioned. Someday, if Xavier ever relented and allowed him to participate in the Holy Jihad, Vergyl wanted to command one of these vessels. He was an adult—twenty-three years old—but his influential brother had the power to interfere with anything Vergyl tried to do . . . and had already done so.

That afternoon, as he checked off the progress of repairs on his display pad, Vergyl came upon one of the battleship's training chambers. The dull metal door stood half open, and he heard a clattering and clanging of metal, and the grunting sounds of someone straining with great effort.

Rushing into the chamber, Vergyl stopped and stared in astonishment. A battle-scarred man—a mercenary, judging from his long-haired, disheveled appearance—threw himself in violent combat against a fighting robot. The machine had three sets of articulated arms, each one holding a deadly-looking weapon. Moving in a graceful blur, the mechanical unit struck blow after blow against the man, who defended himself perfectly each time.

Vergyl's heart leaped. How had one of the enemy machines gotten on board Xavier's battleship? Had Omnius sent it as a spy or saboteur? Were there others spread out around the ship? The beleaguered mercenary landed a blow with his vibrating pulse sword, causing one of the mek's six arms to drop limply to its side.

Letting out a war cry, knowing he had to help, Vergyl snatched the only weapon he could find—a training staff from a rack by the wall—and charged forward recklessly.

The mercenary reacted quickly upon hearing Vergyl's approach. He raised a hand. "Hold, Chirox!"

The combat mek froze. The mercenary, panting, dropped his fighting stance. Vergyl skidded to a halt, looking in confusion from the enemy robot to the well-muscled fighter.

"Don't alarm yourself," the mercenary said. "I was simply practicing."

"With a *machine?*"

The long-haired man smiled. A spiderweb of pale scars covered his cheeks, neck, bare shoulders, and chest. "Thinking machines are our enemies in this Jihad, young officer. If we must develop our skills against them, who better to fight?"

Awkwardly, Vergyl set his hastily grabbed staff on the deck. His face flushed hot with embarassment. "That makes sense."

"Chirox is just a surrogate enemy, a target to fight. He represents all thinking machines in my mind."

"Like a whipping boy."

"A whipping mek." The mercenary smiled. "We can set it to various fighting levels for training purposes." He stepped closer to the ominous-looking combat robot. "Stand down."

The robot lowered its weapons-studded limbs, then retracted them into its core, even the impaired arm, and stood waiting for further commands. With a sneer, the man slammed the hilt of his pulse sword against the mek's chest, knocking the machine backward a step. The optic-sensor eyes flickered orange. The rest of the machine's face, with its crudely shaped mouth and nose, did not move.

Confidently, the man tapped the metallic torso. "This limited robot—I dislike the term *thinking machine*—is totally under our control. It has served the mercenaries of Ginaz for nearly three generations now." He deactivated his pulse sword, which was designed to scramble sophisticated gelcircuitry. "I am Zon Noret, one of the fighters assigned to this ship."

Intrigued, Vergyl ventured closer. "Where did you find this machine?"

"A century ago, a Ginaz salvage scout came upon a damaged thinking machine ship, from which he retrieved this broken combat robot. Since then, we've wiped its memories and reinstalled combat programming. It allows us to test ourselves against machine capabilities."

Noret patted the robot on one of its ribbed metal shoulders. "Many robots in the Synchronized Worlds have been destroyed because of what we learned from this unit. Chirox is an invaluable teacher. On the archipelago of Ginaz, students pit their skills against him. He has proved to be such a repository of information to utilize against our enemy that we mercenaries no longer think of him as a thinking machine, but as an ally."

"A robot as an ally? Serena Butler wouldn't like to hear that," Vergyl said guardedly.

Zon Noret tossed his thick hair behind his head like the mane of a comet. "Many things are done in this Jihad without Serena Butler knowing. I wouldn't be surprised to learn of other meks like this one under our control." He made a dismissive gesture. "But since we all have the same goal, the details become insignificant."

To Vergyl, some of Noret's wounds looked only freshly healed. "Shouldn't you be recuperating from the battle, instead of fighting even more?"

"A true mercenary never stops fighting." His eyes narrowed. "I see you're an officer yourself."

Vergyl let out a frustrated sigh. "In the Construction Brigade. It's not what I wanted. I'd rather be fighting, but . . . it's a long story."

Noret wiped sweat from his brow. "Your name?"

"Second Decero Tantor."

With no flicker of recognition at the name, Noret looked at the combat mek and then at the young officer. "Perhaps we can arrange a little taste of battle for you anyway."

"You would let me . . . ?" Vergyl felt his pulse quicken.

Zon Noret nodded. "If a man wants to fight, he should be allowed to do so."

Vergyl lifted his chin. "I couldn't agree more."

"I warn you, this may be a training mek, but it is lethal. I often disconnect its safety protocol during my rigorous practices. That is why Ginaz mercenaries are so good."

"Still, there must be fail-safes, or it wouldn't be much good as an instructor."

"Training that entails no risk is not realistic. It makes the student soft, knowing he is in no danger. Chirox is not like that, by design. He could kill you."

Vergyl felt a rush of bravado, hoped he wasn't being foolish. "I can handle myself. I've gone through Jihad training of my own." But he wanted a chance to prove himself, and this combat robot might be as close to the fight as he ever got. Vergyl focused his hatred on Chirox, for all the horrors the fighting machines had inflicted upon humanity, and wanted to smash the mek into scrap metal. "Let me fight it, just as you were doing."

The mercenary raised his eyebrows, as if amused and interested. "Your choice of weapons, young warrior?"

Vergyl fumbled, looked at the clumsy training staff he had grabbed. "I didn't bring anything but this."

Noret held his pulse sword up for the younger man to examine. "Do you know how to operate one of these?"

"That looks like one we used in basic training, but a newer model."

"Correct." Noret activated the weapon and handed it to the young man.

Vergyl hefted the sword to check its balance. Shimmering arcs of disruptive energy ran along the surface of its blade.

He took a deep breath and studied the combat mek, who stared back at him dispassionately, its eyelike optic threads glowing orange . . . waiting. The sensors shifted direction, watched Noret approach, and prepared for another opponent.

When the mercenary activated the mek, only two of the six mechanical arms emerged from the torso. One metal hand clasped a dagger, while the other was empty.

"It's going to fight me at a low difficulty setting," Vergyl complained.

"Perhaps Chirox just wants to test you. In actual combat, your adversary will never provide a resumé of his skills beforehand."

Vergyl moved carefully toward the mek, then shifted to his left and circled, holding the pulse sword. He felt moisture on his palm, loosened his grip a bit. The mek kept turning to face him. Its dagger hand twitched, and Vergyl jabbed at the robot's weapon with the electronic sword, hitting it with a purple pulse that caused the robot to shudder.

"Looks like a dumb machine to me." He had imagined combat like this. Vergyl darted toward his opponent and struck the torso with the pulse sword, leaving a purple discoloration on the metal body. He tapped a blue button on the weapon's handle until it reached the highest pulse setting.

"Go for the head," Noret counseled. "Scramble the robot's circuits to slow him. If you strike Chirox just right, he will need a minute or two to reconfigure."

Again Vergyl struck, but missed the head, sliding down to the armored shoulder. Multicolored sparks covered the mek's outer surface, and the dagger dropped from its mechanical grip to clatter on the floor of the training chamber. A wisp of smoke rose from the robot's hand.

Excited, Vergyl moved in for the kill. He didn't care if anyone needed this fighting unit for training. He wanted to destroy it, to burn it into molten remains. He thought of Serena, of little Manion, of all the slaughtered humans . . . and of his own inability to fight for the Jihad. This scapegoat mek would have to do for now.

But as he stepped forward, suddenly the flowmetal of the robot's free hand shifted, reshaping itself and extruding a short sword with barbs on the blade. The other hand stopped sparking, and a matching weapon also formed there.

"Careful, young warrior. We wouldn't want the Army to lose your construction skills."

Feeling a surge of anger at the remark, Vergyl snapped, "I'm not afraid of this machine."

"Fear is not always unwise."

"Even against a stupid opponent? Chirox doesn't even know I'm ridiculing him, does he?"

"I am just a machine," the mek recited, its synthesized voice coming from a speaker patch. Vergyl was taken aback, thinking he had caught just a hint of sarcasm in the robot's voice. Like a theatrical mask, its face did not change its expression.

"Chirox doesn't usually say much," Noret said, smiling. "Go ahead, pound him some more. But even I don't know all the surprises he might have in store."

Vergyl moved back to reassess his opponent. He studied the robot's bright optic threads as they focused on the pulse weapon.

Abruptly, Chirox lunged with the barbed short sword, exhibiting unexpected speed and agility. Vergyl tried to dodge the blow, but did not move quickly enough, and a shallow gash opened on one of his arms. He went into a floor roll to escape, then glanced at the wound as he leaped back to his feet.

"Not a bad move," Noret said, his tone casual, as if he didn't care whether the robot killed Vergyl. Killing was both sport and profession to him. Maybe it took a harsh mindset to be a mercenary for Ginaz, but Vergyl—endowed with no such harshness—worried that he had gotten into this situation on impulse and might be facing a challenge more difficult than he was ready for. The combat mek kept advancing with jerking, unpredictable speeds, sometimes lunging with an astonishing fluidity of motion.

Vergyl darted from side to side, striking repeated blows with the pulse sword. He executed proficient rolls and considered attempting a showy backflip, but didn't know if he could pull it off. Failure to properly execute a move could prove fatal.

One of his pulse blows struck the panel box on Chirox's side, making it glow red. The robot paused. A thin, agile arm emerged from the robot's torso and adjusted something inside.

"It can repair itself?"

"Most combat meks can. You wanted a fair shot at a real machine opponent, didn't you? I warned you about this robot."

Suddenly Chirox came at Vergyl harder and faster than before. Two more arms extruded from the body core. One held a long dagger with a jagged tip for snagging and ripping flesh. The other held a shimmering branding iron.

Zon Noret said something in an anxious tone, but the words blurred. The entire universe that Vergyl had known up to this point faded, along with all unnecessary sensory perception. He focused only on survival.

"I am a jihadi," Vergyl whispered. He resigned himself to fate and at the same time decided to inflict as much damage as he could. He recalled a pledge that even the Construction Brigade had to memorize: "If I die in battle against the machines, I will join those who have gone to Paradise before me, and those who follow." He felt a near-trancelike state consume him and remove all fear of death.

He plunged into battle, flailing away, striking the pulse sword against the mek, discharging the weapon repeatedly. In the background, someone shouted words he couldn't make out. Then Vergyl heard a loud click, saw a flash of color, and bright yellow light immersed him. It felt like a blast from a polar wind and froze him in place.

Immobilized, helpless, Vergyl shuddered, then toppled. He fell for what seemed like a great distance. His teeth chattered, and he shivered. He didn't seem to land anywhere.

Finally he found himself looking up into the robot's gleaming optic sensors. Totally vulnerable.

"I can kill you now." The machine pressed the jagged tip of the long dagger against Vergyl's neck.

The combat mek could thrust the blade through his throat in a microsecond. Vergyl heard shouts, but could not squirm away. He stared up into the implacable optical sensors of the robot, the face of the hated machine enemy. The thinking machine was going to kill him— and this wasn't even a real battle. What a fool he had been.

Somewhere in the distance, familiar voices—two of them?—called out to him. "Vergyl! Vergyl! Shut the damn thing off, Noret!"

He tried to lift his head and look around, but could not move. Chirox continued to press the sharp point against his jugular vein. His muscles were paralyzed, as if frozen inside a block of ice.

"Get me a disruptor gun!" He recognized the voice at last. Xavier. Somehow, incongruously, Vergyl worried more about his brother's disapproval than dying.

But then the mek straightened and removed the dagger blade from his throat.

He heard more voices, the thumping of boots, and the clattering of weaponry. Peripherally, Vergyl saw movement, and crimson-and-green jihadi uniforms. Xavier shouted commands to his men, but Chirox retracted the jagged dagger, his other weapons, and all four arms into his torso. The fiercely glowing optic threads dulled to a soft glimmer.

Zon Noret placed himself in front of the robot. "Don't shoot, Segundo. Chirox could have killed him, but didn't. He is programmed to take advantage of a weakness and deliver a mortal blow, yet he made a conscious decision against it."

"I did not wish to kill him." The combat robot reset itself to a stationary position. "It was not necessary."

Vergyl finally cleared his head enough to push himself into a stiff sitting position. "That mek actually showed . . . compassion?" He still felt dazed from the mysterious stun blast. "Imagine that, a machine with feelings."

"It wasn't compassion at all," Xavier said, with a contentious scowl. He reached down to help his brother to his feet.

"It was the strangest thing," Vergyl insisted. "Did you see the gentleness in his eyes?"

Zon Noret, intent on his training mek, looked into the machine's panel box, studied instrument readings, and made adjustments. "Chirox simply assessed the situation and went into survival mode. But there must have been something buried in his original programming."

"Machines don't care about survival," Xavier snapped. "You saw them at Peridot Colony. They hurl themselves into battle without concern for personal safety." He shook his head. "There's something wrong with your mek's programming, a glitch."

Vergyl stared over at Chirox, caught the gaze of the glowing optic threads. In the depths of the lights, the young construction officer thought he detected a flicker of something animate, which intrigued and frightened him at the same time.

"Humans can learn compassion, too," Chirox said, unexpectedly.

"I'll run him through a complete overhaul," Noret said, but his voice was uncertain.

Xavier stood in front of Vergyl, checking him for serious injuries. Then he spoke in a shaky voice as he led his brother out of the training chamber. "That was quite a scare you gave me."

"I just wanted to fight a real enemy for once."

Xavier looked deeply saddened. "Vergyl, I fear that you will have your chance, eventually. This Jihad will not be over anytime soon."

# THE FACES OF A MARTYR

*A Tale of the Butlerian Jihad*

❧

I'm sorry," Rekur Van said to his fellow Tlulaxa researcher as he slipped the knife deftly through the victim's spine, then added an extra twist. "I need this ship more than you do."

Blood seeped around the slender steel blade, then spilled in a final dying gush as Van yanked the knife back out. His comrade jittered and twitched as nerve endings attempted to fire. Van tumbled him out the hatch of the small vessel, discarding him onto the pavement of the spaceport.

Explosions, shouts, and weapons fire rang through the streets of the main Tlulaxa city. The fatally wounded genetic scientist sprawled on the ground, still shuddering, his close-set eyes dimming as they blinked accusations at Rekur Van. Discarded, like so many other vital things . . .

He wiped the blood on his garments, but his hands remained sticky. He would have time to launder the clothes and clean his skin, once he escaped. Blood . . . it was the currency of his trade, a genetic resource filled with useful DNA. He hated to waste so much of it.

But now the League of Nobles wanted blood. *His* blood.

Though he was one of the most brilliant Tlulaxa scientists and well connected with powerful religious leaders, Van had to flee his home-world to escape the lynch mobs. Outraged members of the League blockaded the planet and swept in to extract their justice. If they caught him, he could not begin to imagine the retribution they would inflict upon him. "Fanatics—all of you!" he shouted uselessly toward the city, then sealed the hatch.

With no time to retrieve his priceless research documents and forced to leave his personal wealth behind, Van used his bloodstained hands to operate the stolen ship's controls. Without a plan, wanting only to get off the planet before the vengeful League soldiers could seize him, he launched his vessel into the sky.

"Damn you, Iblis Ginjo!" he said to himself. It gave him very little consolation to know that the Grand Patriarch was already dead.

Ginjo had always treated him as a lower form of life. Van and the Grand Patriarch had been business associates who depended on each other but shared no feelings of trust. In the end, the League had discovered the horrific secret of the Tlulaxa organ farms: missing soldiers and Zensunni slaves were cut up to provide replacement parts for other wounded fighters. Now the tables had turned. All of the Tlulaxa were in turmoil, scrambling for their lives to escape the League's indignant vengeance. Flesh merchants had to go into hiding, and legitimate traders were run off of civilized worlds. Disgraced and ruined, Van was now a hunted man.

But even without his laboratory records, his mind still carried vital knowledge to be shared with the highest bidder. And sealed in a pocket he took with him a small vial of special genetic material that would allow him to start over again. If he could only get away . . .

Reaching orbit in his stolen ship, Van saw powerful javelin battleships manned by angry jihadis. Numerous Tlulaxa vessels—most of them flown by inexperienced and panicked pilots such as himself—streaked away in a pell-mell fashion, and the League warships targeted all Tlulaxa craft that came within range.

"Why not just assume we're *all* guilty?" he snarled at the images, knowing no one could hear him.

Van increased acceleration, not knowing how fast the unfamiliar ship could go. With the end of his sleeve, he wiped away a blot of drying blood on the control panel so he could read the instruments better. The League javelins took potshots at him, and an angry voice over the commline.

"Tlulaxa craft! Stand down—surrender or be destroyed."

"Why not use your weapons against the thinking machines?" Van retorted. "The Army of the Jihad is wasting time and resources here. Or have you forgotten the real enemies of humanity?" Surely any supposed Tlulaxa crimes were minimal compared to decades of devastation by the computer evermind Omnius.

Apparently, the javelin commander did not appreciate his sarcasm. Exploding projectiles streaked silently past him, and Van reacted with a sudden lurch of deceleration; the artillery detonated some distance from its intended target, but the shockwave still put his stolen ship into a spin. Flashing lights and alarm signals lit the control panels in the cockpit, but Van did not send out a distress signal. Noiselessly, he tumbled out of control, playing dead—and the League ships soon left him to hunt other hapless Tlulaxa escapees. They had plenty of victims to choose from.

When the League battleships were finally gone, Van felt he was safe enough to engage stabilizers. After several exaggerated attempts, he compensated for the out-of-control rolling and got his ship back on course. With no destination in mind, intent only on escaping, he flew out of the system as far and as fast as he could go. He did not regret what he was leaving behind.

For most of his life, Van had worked to develop vital new biological techniques, as had generations of his people before him. During the Jihad, the Tlulaxa had made themselves fabulously wealthy, and presumably indispensable. Now, though, Serena's fanatics would raze the original organ farms, destroying the transplant tanks, and "mercifully" putting the donors out of their misery. Short-sighted fools! How the League would complain in coming years when eyeless or limbless veterans wailed about their injuries and had nowhere else to go.

The myopic League idealists didn't consider practical matters, didn't plan well at all. As with so many things in Serena Butler's Jihad, they chased unrealistic dreams, were driven by foolish emotions. Van hated those people.

He grasped the ship's control bar as if to strangle it, pretending it was Iblis Ginjo's thick neck. Despite a full résumé of despicable acts, the Grand Patriarch had succeeded in keeping his own name clean while shifting blame onto an old, hard-bitten war hero, Xavier Harkonnen, and the whole Tlulaxa race. Ginjo's ever-scheming widow falsely portrayed her fallen husband as a martyr.

The League could steal the "honor" of the Tlulaxa people. Mobs could take their wealth and force his people to live as outlaws. But the betrayers could never take away Rekur Van's special knowledge and skills. This scapegoat was still able to fight back.

Finally, Van made up his mind where he should go, where he should take his secret and innovative cloning technology, as well as viable cells from Serena Butler herself.

He headed out past the boundaries of League space to find the machine worlds, where he intended to present himself to the evermind Omnius.

❧

ON SALUSA SECUNDUS, capital of the League of Nobles, a screaming, unruly crowd set fire to the figure of a man.

Stony silent, Vorian Atreides stood in the shadows of an ornate arch, watching the crowd. His throat was clenched so tightly that he could not shout his dismay. Though he was a champion of the Jihad, this wild throng would not listen to him.

The effigy was a poor likeness of Xavier Harkonnen, but the mob's hatred for him was unmistakable. The mannequin dangled from a makeshift gibbet above a pile of dry sticks. A young man tossed in a small igniter, and within seconds outstretched flames began to consume the effigy's symbolic Army of the Jihad uniform—like the one Xavier had been so proud to wear.

Vorian's friend had devoted most of his life to the war against the thinking machines. Now an irrational throng had found a uniform and used it to mock him, stripping it of all medals and insignia, in much the same way Xavier had been stripped of his rightful place in history. Now they were burning him.

As the fire caught, the figure danced and smoldered on the end of its tether. Raucous cheering rattled the windows of nearby buildings, celebrating the death of a traitor. The people considered this an act of vengeance. Vor considered it an abomination.

After Vor learned how brave Xavier had exposed the Tlulaxa organ farms and brought down the treacherous Grand Patriarch Ginjo, he had rushed to Salusa. He'd never expected to witness such an appalling and well-orchestrated backlash against his friend. For days Vor had continued to speak out, trying to stop the hysterical anger from striking the wrong target. Despite his high rank, few came to his support. The smear campaign against Xavier had begun, and history was being rewritten even while it was still news. Vor felt like a man standing on the beach in a Caladan hurricane, holding up his hands to ward off a tidal wave.

Even Xavier's own daughters bowed to pressure and changed their names from Harkonnen to their mother's surname of Butler. Their mother Octa, always quiet and shy, had withdrawn in misery to the City of Introspection, refusing to see outsiders. . . .

Wearing street clothes to conceal his identity, Vor stood among the crowd, unnoticed. Like Xavier, he was proud of his service in the Army of the Jihad, but in the mounting emotional fervor this was no time to appear in uniform.

Over the course of the long Jihad, Primero Vorian Atreides had engaged in many battles against the thinking machines. He had fought at Xavier's side and achieved tremendous, but costly, victories. Xavier was the bravest man Vor had ever known, and now billions of people despised him.

Unable to tolerate the spectacle any longer, Vor turned away from the throng. Such mass ignorance and stupidity! The ill-informed and easily manipulated multitude would believe whatever they chose to. Vorian Atreides alone would remember the brave truth about the Harkonnen name.

❧

THE INDEPENDENT ROBOT stepped back to admire the new sign mounted on his laboratory wall. *Understanding Human Nature Is the Most Difficult of All Mental Exercises.*

While considering the implications of the statement, Erasmus shifted the expression on his flowmetal face. For centuries his quest had been to decipher these biological creatures: They had so many flaws, but somehow, in a spark of genius, they had created thinking machines. The puzzle intrigued him.

He had mounted various slogans around his laboratory to initiate trains of thought at unexpected times. Philosophy was far more than a game to him; it was a means by which he improved his machine mind.

*It Is Possible to Achieve Whatever You Envision, Whether You Are Man or Machine.*

To facilitate his better understanding of the biological enemy, Erasmus performed constant experiments. Strapped onto tables, confined within transparent tanks, or sealed within airtight cells, the robot's current round of subjects moaned and writhed. Some prayed to invisible gods. Others screamed and begged for mercy from their captor, which showed just how delusional they were. A number bled, urinated, and leaked all manner of fluids, discourteously messing his laboratory. Fortunately, he had subservient robots as well as human slaves to restore the facility to an antiseptic and orderly state.

*Flesh Is Just Soft Metal.*

The robot had dissected thousands of human brains and bodies, in addition to conducting psychological experiments. He tested people with sensory deprivation, causing extreme pain and unrelenting fear. He studied the behavior of individuals as well as crowd activities. Yet through it all, despite his meticulous attention to detail, Erasmus knew he continued to miss something important. He could not find a way to assess and collate all the data so that it fit within a comprehensible framework, a "grand unified theory" of human nature. The behavioral extremes were too far separated.

*Is It More Human to Be Good? Or Evil?*

That sign, next to the new one, had posed a conundrum for some time. Many of the humans he had studied in detail, such as Serena Butler and his own ward Gilbertus Albans, demonstrated an innate human goodness filled with compassion and caring for other creatures. But Erasmus had studied history and knew about traitors and sociopaths who caused incredible damage and suffering in order to gain advantages for themselves.

No set of conclusions made sense.

After thirty-six years of Serena Butler's Jihad, the machines were far from victory, despite computer projections that said they should have crushed the feral humans long ago. Fanaticism kept the League of Nobles strong, and they continued to fight when any reasoned consideration should have led them to surrender. Their inspirational leader had been martyred . . . by her own choice. An inexplicable act.

Now, he finally had a fresh opportunity, an unexpected new subject that might shed light on hitherto unexplored aspects of humanity. Perhaps when he arrived, the Tlulaxa captive would provide some answers. After all, the foolish man had fallen into their laps . . .

Rekur Van had brashly flown into Synchronized space controlled by the thinking machines, and transmitted his demand to see Omnius. The Tlulaxa's bold arrival was either part of a complicated trick . . . or he genuinely believed he had a worthwhile bargaining chip. Erasmus was curious as to which it was.

Omnius wanted to destroy the Tlulaxa ship outright; most humans trespassing in Synchronized space were either killed or captured, but Erasmus intervened, eager to hear what the well-known genetics researcher had to say.

After surrounding the small vessel, robotic warships escorted it to Corrin, center of the Synchronized Worlds. Without delay, armored sentinel robots marched the captive directly into Erasmus's laboratory.

Rekur Van's angular gray-skinned face was pinched into a scowl that flickered between haughtiness and fear. His dark, close-set eyes blinked rapidly. He wore a braid down to his shoulder and tried to look confident and nonplused, but failed completely.

Facing him, the autonomous robot preened in his plush, regal robe, which he wore to make himself impressive in the eyes of his human slaves and test subjects. He fashioned a nonthreatening smile on his flowmetal face, then glowered, trying out another expression. "When you were captured, you demanded to see Omnius. It is strange for the great computer evermind to receive commands from such a diminutive human—a man both small in stature and in importance."

Van lifted his chin and sniffed haughtily. "You underestimate me." Reaching into the folds of his stained and rumpled tunic, the Tlulaxa withdrew a small vial. "I have brought you something precious. These are samples of vital cells, the raw materials of my genetic research."

"I have done a great deal of my own research," Erasmus said. "And I have many samples to draw from. Why should yours interest me?"

"Because these are original cells from *Serena Butler* herself. And you have no technology or techniques to grow an accelerated clone of her, as I do. I can create a perfect duplicate of the leader of the Jihad against thinking machines—I'm sure you can think of a use for that."

Erasmus was indeed impressed. "Serena Butler? You can re-create her?"

"Down to her exact DNA, and I can accelerate her maturity to whatever point you wish. But I have planted certain . . . inhibitors . . . in these cells. Little locks that only I can open." He continued to hold the vial tantalizingly in the laboratory's light, where Erasmus could see it. "Just imagine how valuable such a pawn could be in your war against humans."

"And why would you offer us such a treasure?"

"Because I hate the League of Nobles. They turned against my people, are hunting us down at every turn. If the thinking machines grant me sanctuary, I will reward you with a brand-new Serena Butler, to do with as you wish."

Possibilities flooded Erasmus's mental core. Serena had been his most fascinating human subject ever, but his experiments and tests on her had come to a grinding halt once he'd killed her unruly baby. After that, she was no longer cooperative. For decades, the robot had wished for a second opportunity with her—and now he could have it.

He imagined the dialogues they might have, the exchanges of ideas, the *answers* to all his pressing questions. He studied another slogan on the wall. *If I Can Think of the Ultimate Question, Will It Have an Answer?*

Fascinated, Eramus clasped Van's shoulder, causing the Tlulaxa to grimace in pain. "I agree to your terms."

THE GRAND PATRIARCH'S widow sent him a formal invitation, and Vorian Atreides knew it was not an idle request.

The message was delivered by a captain of the Jihad Police, which in itself carried an implied threat. But Vor chose not to be intimidated. He donned many of the medals, ribbons, and decorations he'd been awarded over the course of his long and illustrious career. Although he'd grown up among thinking machines as a trustee, Vor had later become a Hero of the Jihad. He didn't want Iblis Ginjo's pretentious wife to forget for one second who she was dealing with.

Camie Boro-Ginjo had married Ginjo for the prestige his name offered, but it had been a loveless union between loveless people. Camie had every intention of turning her husband's spectacular death to her own political gain. Now, inside the same offices where the Grand Patriarch had formulated so many of his nefarious schemes, she sat beside the bald, olive-skinned Jipol commandant, Yorek Thurr. Vor steeled himself for whatever this dangerous pair might be planning.

Smiling prettily, Camie directed Vor's attention to a model on a display platform, a small-scale rendition of a grandiose monument. "This will be our shrine to the Three Martyrs. Anyone who glimpses it cannot help but be filled with fervor for the Jihad."

Vor eyed the arches, the huge braziers to carry eternal flames, and the three colossal figures inside, stylized representations of a man, woman, and child. "Three Martyrs?"

"Serena Butler and her child, murdered by the thinking machines, and my husband Iblis Ginjo, slain by the treachery of humans."

Vor could barely suppress his anger. He turned to leave. "I will have no part in this."

"Primero, please hear us out." Camie raised her hands in a placating gesture. "We must address the extreme turmoil in the League, the horrible murder of Serena Butler by the thinking machines, and the tragic death of my husband due to the plot hatched by Xavier Harkonnen and his Tlulaxa cohorts."

"There are no facts to prove Xavier's culpability," Vor said, his voice brittle. Camie had been primarily responsible for the blame-shifting and mudslinging. He was not afraid of her, or of her henchman. "Your assumptions are false, and you have stopped looking for the truth."

"It has been proven to my satisfaction."

Thurr rose to his feet. Though shorter in stature than Camie, he had the coiled strength of a cobra. "More to the point, Primero, it has been proven to the satisfaction of the League citizens. They need their heroes and martyrs."

"Apparently they need their villains as well. And, if you cannot find the correct culprit, you create one—as you did with Xavier."

Thurr meshed his fingers together. "We don't wish to engage in an acrimonious debate, Primero. You are a great military strategist, and we owe many of our victories to you."

"And to Xavier," Vor said.

The Jipol commandant continued without responding to the comment. "We three important leaders must work together to accomplish important goals. None of us can be mired down by bruised feelings and traditional grieving. We must keep the populace focused on winning our Holy Jihad and cannot afford arguments that divert us from the real enemy. You persist in raising questions about what happened between Xavier Harkonnen and the Grand Patriarch, but you do not realize the damage you're doing."

"The truth is the truth."

"The truth is relative, and must be taken in the context of our larger struggle. Even Serena and Xavier would agree that unpleasant sacrifices are warranted if they help to achieve the goals of the Jihad. You must stop this personal crusade, Primero. Stop casting doubts. You only harm our cause if you don't keep your feelings to yourself."

Though Thurr's words were spoken calmly, Vor read the implied threat in them and suppressed a fleeting urge to strike the man; this Jipol commandant had no comprehension of honor or truth. No doubt, Thurr had the power to see that the Primero was quietly assassinated . . . and Vor knew he would do it if he considered it necessary.

Still, the Jipol commandant had struck a solid blow, reminding him of his friends' intentional sacrifices. If Vor destroyed the public confidence in the Jihad Council and the League government as a whole, the political repercussions and social turmoil could be considerable. Scandals, resignations, and the general uproar would severely weaken the solidarity the human race needed in order to face the thinking machines.

Omnius was the only enemy that mattered.

Vor crossed his arms over his heavily medaled and ribboned chest. "For now, I will keep my opinions to myself," he said. "But I don't do it for you and your power plays. I'm doing it for Serena's Jihad, and for Xavier."

"Just so long as you do it," Camie said.

Vor turned to leave, but paused at the door. "I don't want to be anywhere around when you unveil your Three Martyrs farce, so I'm heading for the front lines." Shaking his head, he hurried away. "Battles I can understand."

ON THE MAIN machine world of Corrin, years passed, and a female child grew rapidly into adulthood, her cloned life accelerated by Rekur Van. Erasmus regularly visited his laboratories full of moaning experimental subjects, where his new Serena Butler was taking shape nicely.

Among the tormented human subjects, the Tlulaxa researcher seemed quite at home. Van was himself an interesting person, with opinions and attitudes dramatically different from those Erasmus had observed in the original Serena or in Gilbertus Albans. Even so, the intense scientist had an unusual perspective: entirely self-centered, twisted by irrational hatred and spite toward the feral humans. In addition, he was intelligent and well trained. A good mental sparring partner for Erasmus . . . but the robot pinned his hopes on the return of Serena.

During her prolonged development, Van used advanced machine instructional technology to fill her head with misinformation, false memories mixed with details of the real Serena's life. Some of the data took hold; some of it needed to be implanted again and again.

When he had the opportunity, the robot engaged his new Serena in tentative conversation, anxious for the forthcoming days when he could debate with her, provoking her ire and her fascinating responses—just as it had once been. But though she looked like an adult, Rekur Van insisted that the clone's preparation was not complete.

And after all this time, Erasmus was growing impatient.

At first, he had assumed the discrepancies from the Serena he had known were inconsequential, the difference between a juvenile and the woman she would ultimately become. But as the clone approached the equivalent age at which he had known Serena, Erasmus became increasingly disturbed. This wasn't at all what he had expected.

Sensing that he could no longer justify further delays, the Tlulaxa researcher rushed his final preparations. Dressed again in his regal robe, Erasmus arrived to observe as the Serena clone completed several days of immersion in an experimental cellular deceleration chamber, to slow the aging process. Her development had been stretched and pushed, and her weak biological body had endured incredible rigors.

The Tlulaxa had been anxious to prove his claims, but Erasmus reconsidered now. Thinking machines could wait for centuries, if necessary. Perhaps, if he decided to make another clone, he would allow that one to grow normally, since this experimental acceleration might have introduced flaws. The independent robot had extremely high expectations for his renewed interactions with Serena Butler. He did not want anything to get in the way.

As the gummy fluids drained and the female clone stood naked and dripping before him, Erasmus scrutinized her through several spectral regimes, using his full complement of optic threads. A long time ago, through his many surveillance systems, the robot had seen the original Serena naked many times; he had been present when she'd given birth to her frustrating infant, and he had personally performed the sterilization surgery on her so that the pregnancy problem could never occur again.

Now Rekur Van came forward, leering unpleasantly, to give her a physical examination, but Erasmus lifted the little Tlulaxa out of the way. He did not want Van to interfere with what should have been a special moment.

Still dripping from the tank, Serena didn't seem to care about her nudity, though the original would no doubt have been offended: just one of many personality variations that the robot noticed.

"Do I please you now?" Serena asked, blinking her lavender eyes. She stood seductively, as if trying to lure a potential mate. "I want you to like me."

An artificial scowl formed on Erasmus's flowmetal face, and his optic threads gleamed dangerously. Serena Butler had been haughty, independent, intelligent. Hating her captivity among the thinking machines, she had debated with Erasmus, searching for any chance to hurt him. She had *never* tried to please him.

"What did you do to her?" Erasmus turned to the Tlulaxa. "Why did she say that?"

Van smiled uncertainly. "Because of the acceleration, I had to guide her personality. I shaped it with standard female attitudes."

"Standard female attitudes?" Erasmus wondered if this unpleasant, isolated Tlulaxa man understood human women even less than *he* did. "There was nothing 'standard' about Serena Butler."

Van appeared increasingly uneasy, and he fell silent, deciding not to attempt further excuses. Erasmus remained more interested in the clone. This woman looked like Serena, in her soft, classically beautiful face and form, in her amber-brown hair, and in her unusual eyes.

But she wasn't the same. Only close enough to tickle his own memories of her, of the times they had spent together.

"Tell me your beliefs about politics, philosophy, and religion," the robot demanded. "Express your most impassioned feelings and opinions. Why do you think that even captive humans deserve to be treated with respect? Explain why you believe it is impossible for a thinking machine to achieve the equivalent of a human soul."

"Why do you wish to discuss such subjects?" She sounded almost petulant. "Tell me how you would like me to answer, so that I can please you."

As soon as the clone spoke, she shattered his fond remembrance of the real Serena. Though she looked exactly like Serena Butler, this simulacrum was very different in her internal makeup, the way she thought, the way she behaved. The cloned version had no social conscience, no spark, no glimmer of the personality that had become so familiar to him, and which had caused him so much interesting trouble. The real Serena's rebellious attitude had triggered an entire Jihad, while this poor substitute lacked any such potential.

Erasmus noted the difference in the glint of her eyes, in the turn of her mouth, in the way she threw her wet hair over her shoulder. He missed the fascinating woman he had known.

"Put your clothes on," Erasmus said. Looking on from one side, Rekur Van appeared alarmed, obviously sensing the robot's disappointment.

She slipped into the garments he had provided, accentuating her feminine curves. "Do you find me pleasing now?"

"No. Unfortunately, you are unacceptable."

With a blur of his flowmetal arm, Erasmus struck a swift, precise blow. He didn't want her to suffer, yet he did not want to look at this flawed clone ever again. With all his robotic strength, he drove the sharp edge of his shaped metal hand into the base of her neck, and decapitated her as easily as he might cut a flower in his greenhouse gardens. She made no sound as her head tumbled away and her body fell, spraying blood on his clean laboratory floor.

Such a disappointment.

On his left Rekur Van made a choking sound, as if he had forgotten how to breathe. The Tlulaxa man stumbled backward, but sentinel robots stood all around the laboratory chambers. The numerous tortured experimental subjects moaned and chattered in their cages, tanks, and tables.

Erasmus took a step toward the genetics researcher. Van held up his hands and his expression telegraphed what would occur next. As usual, he would try to worm his way out of any responsibility. "I did everything possible! Her DNA matches perfectly, and she is the same in every physical characteristic."

"She is not the same. You did not know the real Serena Butler."

"Yes! I met her. I took the tissue samples myself when she visited Bandalong!"

Erasmus made his flowmetal face a bland expressionless mirror. "You did not *know* her." This Tlulaxa's ability to perfectly re-create Serena Butler had been overstated, at best. As in the robot's own attempts to imitate the paintings of Van Gogh to the finest detail, the copy never approached the original's perfection.

"I have many more cells. This was just our first attempt, and we can try again. Next time, I'm sure we'll take care of the problems. That clone was different only because she never shared the real Serena's life experiences, never faced the same challenges. We can modify the virtual reality teaching loops, make her spend more time immersed in sensory deprivation."

Erasmus shook his head. "She will never be what I want."

"Killing me would be a mistake, Erasmus! You can still learn much."

Staring at the Tlulaxa, the inquisitive robot noted how objectively unpleasant he was; apparently, all of his condemned breed were similar. Van had none of the noble attributes of character that could be found in so many people of other races. The little man might have some value after all, providing a new window on the dark side of human nature.

He was reminded of one of his thought-provoking signs. *Is It More Human to Be Good? Or Evil?*

The robot's flowmetal face formed into a broad smile.

"Why are you looking at me that way?" Van asked, nervously.

At a silent, transmitted signal from Erasmus, the sentinel robots came closer to surround the Tlulaxa man. Van had no place to run.

"Yes, I can learn from you, Rekur Van." He turned, his plush robe swirling, and signaled for the sentinel robots to seize the man. "In fact, I already have several very interesting experiments in mind. . . ."

The Tlulaxa screamed.

❧

FIXING HIS GAZE forward, Vorian Atreides sat stiffly on the bridge of the flagship. Over the past week, his assault force had been cruising across space. Soldiers and mercenaries continued their specialized drills. To the last man, they counted the days until reaching their next destination.

As the fleet entered Synchronized space, Vor mentally tallied all the weapons and firepower, all the soldiers and Ginaz mercenaries he would bring to bear against the thinking machines in the next great battle. He had not heard of the target planet before, but nevertheless Vor intended to conquer it and destroy the machine scourge.

*Politics be damned. Out here is exactly where I belong.*

For years after the death and defamation of Xavier, Vor had thrown himself into the struggle against Omnius. He fought one accursed machine enemy after another, striking in the sacred name of humanity.

Vor felt instilled with the holy determination of Serena, and of Xavier as well. Their strength allowed him to carry the Jihad forward. Always forward. He vowed anew to crush every thinking machine in his path. He would leave the next planet a blackened blister if there was no other way, despite the loss of unfortunate human slaves who served Omnius. By now, the Primero had learned to accept almost any cost in blood, just as long as it counted as a victory against the machines.

His two dearest friends had become martyrs in their own fashion. They had known what they were doing and had been willing to make great sacrifices, not only of their lives, but of their memories as well, allowing myths to replace truth, for the sake of the Jihad.

In a private message, Serena Butler had begged Vor and Xavier to understand the personal sacrifice she was making. Later, Xavier made his own sacrifice in order to stop the Grand Patriarch's predatory organ

488

farm scheme with the Tlulaxa, saving thousands of lives in the process. Xavier's decision to leave Iblis's name untarnished was unselfish and heroic: he knew full well how much harm would befall the Jihad if its Grand Patriarch was proven to be a fraud and a war profiteer.

Both Xavier and Serena had paid terrible, ultimate costs with full knowledge of what they were doing. *I cannot dispute the decisions of my friends,* Vor thought, feeling a universe of sadness on his shoulders.

And he realized that his own burden must be to *let them do what they intended.* He had to resist the impulse to change what Xavier and Serena had done, and to let the untruths stand in order to achieve a long-term result. In accepting their fates and accomplishing what they had hoped, Serena and Xavier had left Vor to carry on in their behalf, and to bear an unseen banner of honor for all three of them.

*Not an easy task, but that was my sacrifice.*

"We are approaching the target planet, Primero," called his navigator.

On the flagship's screens, he saw the unremarkable planet—wispy clouds, blue oceans, brown and green land masses. And a bristling force of weirdly beautiful machine warships converging to form a defensive line. Even from a distance, the angular robotic battle vessels flickered with bursts of fire as they launched machine-guided projectiles in a hailstorm toward the League fleet.

"Engage our Holtzman shields." Vor rose from his chair and smiled confidently to the officers on the bridge with him. "Summon the Ginaz mercenaries into ground teams, ready to shuttle down as soon as we break the orbital defenses." He spoke automatically, confidently.

Decades ago, Serena had started this Jihad to avenge the murder of her baby. Xavier had fought beside Vor, crushing many machine foes. Now Vor, without his friends, intended to see this impossible war through to its end. It was the only way he could be sure the martyrs had made worthwhile sacrifices.

"Forward!" Vor raised his voice as the first robotic shells impacted against the Holtzman shields. "We have enemies to destroy!"

# ABOUT THE AUTHORS

Author painting by Gregory Manchess

FRANK HERBERT is widely considered to be the greatest of all science-fiction writers. He was born in Tacoma, Washington, and educated at the University of Washington, Seattle. In 1952, Herbert began publishing science fiction, but he was not considered a writer of major stature until the 1965 publication of *Dune*. Then *Dune Messiah*, *Children of Dune*, *God Emperor of Dune*, *Heretics of Dune*, and *Chapterhouse: Dune* followed, expanding the saga that the *Chicago Tribune* would call "one of the monuments of modern science fiction." Herbert is also the author of some twenty other books, including *The Eyes of Heisenberg*, *The Dosadi Experiment*, and *The Green Brain*. Frank Herbert passed away in 1986.

*Photo by Jan Herbert*

BRIAN HERBERT (right), the son of Frank Herbert, is the author of multiple *New York Times* bestsellers. He is the winner of several literary honors and has been nominated for the highest awards in science fiction. In 2003, he published *Dreamer of Dune*, the Hugo Award–nominated biography of his father. Brian's own science-fiction series is forthcoming, beginning with the novel *Timeweb*. His earlier acclaimed novels include *Sidney's Comet; Sudanna, Sudanna; The Race for God;* and *Man of Two Worlds* (written with Frank Herbert).

KEVIN J. ANDERSON has written dozens of national bestsellers and has been nominated for the Nebula Award, the Bram Stoker Award, and the SFX Reader's Choice Award. His many original novels, including *Captain Nemo, Hopscotch,* and The Saga of Seven Suns series, have received praise from critics everywhere. He has set the Guinness-certified world record for the largest single-author book signing.

www.dunenovels.com